Kylie Chan started out as an IT consultant and trainer specialising in business intelligence systems. She worked in Australia and then ran her own consulting business for ten years in Hong Kong. When she returned to Australia in 2002, Kylie made the career change to writing fiction, and produced the bestselling nine-book Dark Heavens series, a fantasy based on Chinese mythology, published by Harper*Voyager* worldwide. She is now a full-time writer, based on Queensland's Gold Coast.

Books by Kylie Chan

DARK HEAVENS
White Tiger (1)
Red Phoenix (2)
Blue Dragon (3)

JOURNEY TO WUDANG
Earth to Hell (1)
Hell to Heaven (2)
Heaven to Wudang (3)

CELESTIAL BATTLE
Dark Serpent (1)
Demon Child (2)
Black Jade (3)

Small Shen

DRAGON EMPIRE
Scales of Empire (1)
Guardian of Empire (2)

KYLIE CHAN

GUARDIAN OF EMPIRE

DRAGON EMPIRE TRILOGY 2

HARPER
Voyager

Harper*Voyager*
An imprint of HarperCollins*Publishers*

First published in Australia in 2019
by HarperCollins*Publishers* Australia Pty Limited
ABN 36 009 913 517
harpercollins.com.au

HarperCollins*Publishers*
Level 13, 201 Elizabeth Street, Sydney NSW 2000, Australia
Unit D1, 63 Apollo Drive, Rosedale, Auckland 0632, New Zealand
A 53, Sector 57, Noida, UP, India
1 London Bridge Street, London SE1 9GF, United Kingdom
Bay Adelaide Centre, East Tower, 22 Adelaide Street West, 41st floor, Toronto,
Ontario M5H 4E3, Canada
195 Broadway, New York NY 10007, USA

A catalogue record for this book is available from the National Library of Australia

ISBN 978 1 4607 5327 9 (paperback)
ISBN 978 1 4607 0791 3 (ebook)
ISBN 978 1 4607 9999 4 (audio book)

Cover design by Design by Committee, based on original cover design by Darren Holt,
HarperCollins Design Studio
Front cover images by shutterstock.com
Author photograph by Bradkay Photographix
Typeset in Sabon LT Std 11/14.5 by Kirby Jones
Printed and bound in Australia by McPherson's Printing Group
The papers used by HarperCollins in the manufacture of this book
are a natural, recyclable product made from wood grown in sustainable
plantation forests. The fibre source and manufacturing processes meet
recognised international environmental standards, and carry certification.

1

Night had fallen, and the warm breeze was soft against my skin. The white sand shimmered beneath the phosphorescent sea, splashing where my dog, Endicott, raced around in it. The cat invasion fleet was clearly visible above the horizon; sixty-four thousand ships, in a formation like a many-legged starfish, glowed against the sky. In a few months they'd be close enough to the dragon homeworld to drop out of warp and attack it. They hovered in the sky as if they were taunting us. No communication except for light could go in or out while they were in warp, and they were ignoring all our attempts to talk to them. We had to be ready to defend ourselves when they dropped into normal space and tried to destroy the Imperial Capital the way they'd destroyed so many of the Empire's member planets.

Only humans could use chilli as a chemical weapon to incapacitate the cats. Rogue cat ships regularly attacked Empire planets, and we humans worked together with the dragons to knock them out with chilli and return them to their own sector of space. The fleet massed in the sky was the largest the cats had ever sent, and once we'd dropped them home it would take them three thousand years to return. Hopefully the distance would discourage them from trying again. We had to stop them before they destroyed the Imperial Capital then moved on to attack every other inhabited planet in the Dragon Empire.

Endicott ran to me, her tongue flapping from her huge grin, then raced back to splash in the shallows, snapping at the small breakers.

'My dragonspouse, Noriko, didn't want me to go to Nillitas, but I went anyway,' Snapclick said. Its three pink, mantis-like bodies, each a metre and a half tall, squatted at the edge of the paving next to the sand. Grey dragon scales gleamed on the sides of its three heads; the clicks were reproductively colonised by the dragons a thousand years ago. 'Noriko called me in to intervene when everything went bad. When she arrived in their system – the first alien the Nillitas people had ever seen – it brought their long-standing conflict to a head. It was a close thing. I arrived just as they were about to detonate their mutual destruction devices.'

'And you talked them down?' I said. 'After ten thousand years of war, you actually did it?'

'I did,' Snapclick said, and rubbed its front pincers together with pride. 'Saved them all.'

'But at the cost of transforming all of them to dragonscales,' I said grimly.

'Now that humanity has made the new pact with the dragons, this will no longer happen, dear Jian,' Snapclick said, its voice softening in the translator. 'At least they are alive. You should come visit them; they are very beautiful. Like your birds.'

'I can't visit anywhere, I'm stuck here.' I gestured towards the cat fleet glowing in the sky. 'No rest for me as long as that is there. I live my life from attack to attack, never knowing when I'll be called to fight.'

'Your mum's documentary is up,' Marque said from a sphere above us. 'Do you want to watch it here?'

'No,' I said. 'Snapclick's eyes can't see it here; let's watch it in my theatre. Want to see, Snapclick?'

'I would love to. I adore your mother, she's so badass,' Snapclick said.

I called Endicott and she raced back to me, bouncing between me and Snapclick and showering both of us in sand. Snapclick affectionately rubbed her ears, then we headed back to my residence, one of several strung along the beach. The peaks of the snow-capped skiing mountains fifty kilometres away were visible behind them. Each residence was the size of a mansion back on Earth, fitted with every luxury that we could imagine, personally tailored for each of us – but they were still the barracks for the dragons' army.

We walked along the path through the tropical gardens, full of flowers, and through the gate into my yard. The pool shimmered blue, lit by internal lights. Artificial candles and torches illuminated the terrace around the pool.

Endicott jumped into the shallow end of the pool and swam from one side to the other, then came out and shook herself, spraying water everywhere from her long golden fur. Marque kept us dry, then dried the dog.

'I will never understand your preoccupation with swimming,' Snapclick said. 'Even your dog's obsessed.'

'Perhaps because you sink to the bottom in a bunch of green bubbles,' I said, and gestured for it to enter the house. 'Golden retrievers are a water breed.'

'Animal eugenics as a hobby!' Snapclick said with disbelief.

We went inside through the living and dining room to my personal theatre. Outside the theatre, Marque used energy to bend light to produce images, but inside this theatre it produced tiny floating dots that glowed to form a physical image that Snapclick could see. I sat in one of the chairs, and Endicott flopped to lie next to my feet. Snapclick sat its three bodies on the floor, and Marque put the documentary up on the central three-dimensional stage.

A young woman came into view next to a dragon, standing in the middle of her potato farm. As usual, it took me a moment to recognise my mother – she'd transferred her soulstone to a new cloned body on her eightieth birthday the previous year, and she now appeared about twenty-five. Her name – 'Connie Choumali' – appeared next to her, and the dragon's name in their own tongue appeared next to the dragon. The dragon's name quickly reassembled itself to the dragon's designated Earth name, 'Yuki'.

Endicott whuffed at my mother's image and thumped her tail on the floor. Mum was brown-skinned from working in the sun, but she looked well-fed and healthy, a reassuring change from the thin and worn-looking woman she'd been before the dragons' aborted invasion of Earth twelve years ago. The red soulstone glittered on her forehead as she raised a straw basket containing potatoes.

'You hand-grow all of them yourself?' Yuki said.

'Yes,' Mum said. 'Marque doesn't have any input into the process. I hand-nurture my potatoes from seed to harvest.'

'Original Earth potatoes, grown by hand,' the dragon said, her voice hushed with wonder. 'What's the process? Is it time-consuming?'

The scene shifted to earlier in the day, and Mum was digging with an old-fashioned hoe.

'Not even the ground-breaking is motorised,' she said. She dug out the tubers, shook the dirt from them, and held them up. 'The plant can stay in the ground, it's very hardy. All I have to do is dig up some of the roots—'

'Skip this bit where she demonstrates how they're grown, everybody's seen that multiple times,' I said. 'No, wait. Do you want to see that, Snapclick?'

'No, I've seen it before when I visited her. She gave me three hats and made me dig! I looked completely ridiculous; a hat on an exoskeleton is a crime against fashion. I can't believe people *pay* her to do that. By all means, skip it.'

'Did she ask you to find me a mate while you were there?' I said.

The playback of my mother froze.

'Of course she did, she pesters me constantly about it.' Snapclick rubbed its wing cases together with a high-pitched rasp, its equivalent of laughing. 'She said that your species is more psychologically stable in a pair-bonded relationship. She wants what is best for you; you've been "single" for a long time.'

'Did Mum teach you that term?' I said.

Its rasp intensified.

'I won't start anything as long as I'm on standby,' I said. 'But as soon as the cats are dealt with, I'm leaving the military for good, and you can damn well pass that on. I'll travel the Empire and meet all these wonderful people that you describe, and then I'll find a partner, settle down and have a family. I'm done with living like this, never knowing when I'll be called in to drop bombs on the cats. I can't make any long-term plans, I can't be too far from my armour and bombs – I can't even go visit my kids for any length of time, and every time they come here to see me, I'm called away. I am so damn tired of living on standby!' I realised that I was breathing heavily and tried to calm myself. 'Three more months and they drop out of warp and we finish this. Then my life will change.'

'I agree with you,' Snapclick said. 'I wasn't going to mention it, but you brought it up.'

'Thank you.' I nodded towards the ceiling. 'We're done with the drama, Marque. You can turn the interview with Mum back on.'

The hologram scene shifted to later in the day, and Mum stood holding one of the potatoes she'd just harvested. 'This one is a Welsh Gold, a local specialty. It's sweet, with a stronger flavour than the white potatoes.' She broke it open to reveal the interior, and Yuki made a soft sound that could be delight or pain. 'They're good roasted in their skins; the flesh becomes soft and flavourful. I have some up at the house, would you like to try?'

'Yes, please,' Yuki said.

They headed back along the rows of green potato plants towards my mother's house. The early prefab box had been replaced by more luxurious accommodation for her: a tall and narrow three-storey residence on stilts with storage for her farm equipment at ground level. She'd converted as much of the land as she could to growing the valuable crop.

'And your daughter is in the army, stationed on planet Barracks and preparing to defend Dragonhome from the cat invasion fleet?' Yuki said.

'That's right,' Mum said, striding through the soft soil. 'She was one of the first to use the pepper spray on the cats, and she's ...' Her smile turned warm. 'A leader in the defensive operation. I'm very proud of her.'

'Oh, Mum,' I said.

'So am I,' Snapclick said.

'Thanks,' I said.

'All the hopes of the Empire are with her,' Yuki said.

Marque lifted them to the first-floor entrance of Mum's house, and they went in.

'That smells wonderful,' Yuki said as they passed through the ultrasonic cleanser in the entry hall and the farm's dirt was whisked from them.

'I'm roasting them over a wood fire,' Mum said. 'It's a fragrant timber from Earth that enhances the flavour of the potatoes. Real wood, not replicated.'

Yuki stopped in the middle of Mum's narrow living room. 'Real wood? From *dead Earth trees*?'

Mum nodded and put the basket of potatoes on her kitchen bench. 'Our farmers' co-operative has a restaurant where we serve our potatoes in this style.' She turned and smiled indulgently at Yuki. 'But you'll need to book at least forty-five Earth years in advance, and the meal costs a whole dragonscale.'

'Worth it,' Yuki said, breathless.

Mum gestured to Yuki and led her out onto the deck overlooking the fields. The other farmers' residences were spread over the flat land that had once been under water. She opened the wood-fired oven on the deck and checked the foil-wrapped potatoes inside. 'They look ready; take a seat.'

Yuki reclined on a mat next to the table, her eyes wide with anticipation.

Mum pulled the potatoes out of the oven with tongs, placed them onto a platter, and carried them to the table. She opened the foil and the room around me filled with the rich smell of roasted sweet potato.

'I just used an untranslatable word suggesting excellence in flavour,' Snapclick said.

I looked up. 'Untranslatable? Really, Marque?'

'Marque doesn't translate the expression; other species find it disturbing,' Snapclick said. 'It references my species' reproductive process.'

'Oh.'

Mum carefully sliced the potatoes and placed them onto two

plates decorated with the motif of a potato plant sprouting from the globe of the Earth. She filled her glass with red wine, Yuki's with tea, and sat across from Yuki.

'What's that in your glass?' Yuki said. 'Can I try some?'

'Fermented Earth grape juice; the alcohol in it relaxes humans and makes us feel warm and pleasant. You can have a sip, but they're like the potatoes – have too much and you'll be sick. Take care.'

'Deadly poison to more than ninety-three per cent of species in the Empire and you drink it as a recreational substance,' Snapclick said. 'You people are so weird.'

'You wouldn't have the chilli without us,' I said.

Yuki picked up a dragon-sized fork, scooped some of the potato up, and put it into her mouth. She raised her snout and closed her eyes.

'That is ... wow,' she said. 'I've had the synthesised replica, and I've had the ones that are grown on some of your colonies, but this is ...' She shook her head. 'Words fail me.'

'Cooking it over real Earth wood makes it even better,' Mum said, smiling over her own fork. 'And my potatoes are some of the best on the planet.'

'So how much is this many potatoes worth?' Yuki asked, taking another bite and moaning with bliss.

'What we have here is probably enough to buy one-tenth of an oxygen-water planet,' Mum said. 'Half a dragon scale.'

'Worth every bit of it,' Yuki said. 'I wish I had a spare scale to give you.'

'You can take some home with you,' Mum said.

Yuki choked with delight. 'Thank you! Earth has brought us so much. These potatoes, and hope that we can prevent the cats' destructive ways. You've given us the chance to live in a future where we no longer have to run from the terror of the cats and our children don't need to fear them.'

'I'm sure Jian can do it,' Mum said. 'She's been training for years, she's ready. They're all ready.'

'I think I'm in love,' Yuki said, and smiled a dragon smile that Mum returned.

My son David entered Mum's kitchen in faded grey fleecy pyjamas. He'd recently turned thirty, and was tall and lean like his father, Victor, with dark skin and hair from his other mother, Dianne. Having his long hair clipped military-short highlighted his wide, dark eyes and chiselled cheekbones.

'You finished doing this yet?' he said, and sighed with dismay. 'Not potatoes *again*.'

'Oh! Lieutenant Baxter,' Yuki said with pleasure. 'Come and say hello to everybody. You've just graduated from the officers' academy, correct? You'll be joining your mother in preparation for fighting the cats?'

'No!' David yelled, and ran out.

'He's sensitive about being "put on display" because my daughter Jian is famous on Earth.' My mother smiled indulgently. 'He passed out from the academy two weeks ago; he'll be deployed soon.'

'He's joining the fight against the cats?'

'I'm so proud of him.'

'Please ask him if we can share his image,' Yuki said. 'It's a great morale-booster. I'd love to interview him.'

'I'll talk to him,' Mum said.

Yuki turned and appeared to speak directly to me. 'I've been to the original source of potatoes, the part of Earth called South America, and I've visited Colonel Choumali's mother and tasted her Welsh Golds. Next time, I'll visit Eastern Euroterre and taste an alcoholic spirit they make from potatoes – vodka. Apparently, the beverage is rich with the potato flavour once the toxins are removed.'

The projection filled with the credits of those who had helped make the documentary, along with their three-dimensional portraits, then blinked out.

I stared at the stage for a moment, transfixed, then looked up at Marque's sensors on the ceiling. 'Did Yuki stay with Mum for a while after the documentary was finished?'

Marque hesitated, then said, 'Yes.'

'Is my mother pregnant?'

'That information is under a privacy seal,' Marque said.

'Oh, fuck,' I said.

'Don't you want a little sister?' Marque said.

'Oh, *fuck*.'

'Why wouldn't you want a little sister?' Snapclick said, shocked.

'That would blow my brain out of my skull. I'm old enough to have grandchildren, and my mother is having a new baby? Mum had the awareness training, she knows about the reproductive responsibilities now that we're effectively immortal. She can't just have a kid with the first dragon that comes past!'

'You know Yuki's not the first to go past, she's had many dragon visitors to her farm,' Marque said. 'But Yuki and your mother did hit it off. Would it really be so bad if they had a child together?'

'What does David think?' I said.

'He doesn't know,' Marque said. 'He was deployed the next day.'

'Geez,' I said.

'Speaking of having kids ...' Snapclick said. 'We all have responsibilities. Creating a family is the noblest goal a sentient can aim for—'

I quickly stood to face it, waking Endicott. 'Oh no you don't. Don't you *dare*—'

It lowered itself on its jointed legs. 'I am sorry, dear one, it is already done.'

I went to it and put my hand out to the edge of the bubble containing the methane that it breathed. 'The cats attack in a few months. Can't it wait?'

'No. It needs to happen now, I'm close to the end of my childbearing ability.'

'What will I do without your advice? You taught me everything about the Empire. I don't know what I'd do without you. You've given me skills in negotiation, wisdom in relationships—'

'I wish there was a way to avoid it,' it said. 'It's a horrible way to die. But we talked about this, and you said that if I chose to do it, you'd accept my decision. I know you'll miss me, but this is about my needs, not yours.'

'I know, I'm sorry. It's just that you're right – it is a horrible way to die.' I flopped to sit on my chair again. 'Are you sure you've exhausted every possible solution to this, Marque? Everybody else in the Empire is effectively immortal, surely—'

'Not everybody, you know that,' Marque said.

'The Council of Clicks approached me,' Snapclick said. 'They said that I can choose to live on without reproducing if I want, they won't force me. But my negotiation skills are legendary, and it's my duty to pass them to future generations.'

'Clone some bodies and transfer your damn soulstone after you're done,' I said.

'My bodies are needed to feed the babies.'

I opened my mouth to protest.

'Alive, Jian. With me in them. They need to spend two of your weeks ingesting material from my living bodies to successfully complete their early growth and genetic structuring. It will take them at least ten days to work their way to all three brains in the centres of my bodies and kill me. The soulstone cannot be removed until the babies have eaten all of me. By then the stone will have lost attunement. There's no avoiding it.'

'Use a clone without a soulstone. Alive but brain-dead,' I said.

Snapclick swiped its claws over its head. 'You know the cloned body only lasts a few hours without an active soulstone.'

'You're a dragonscales. Find a dragon partner and have a dragon child that won't fucking *eat* you!'

'Your own species is responsible for the limitations on dragon reproduction. You made them limit the creation of both dragonscales and new dragons; a new dragon can only be born if one is deceased, and there's a long waiting list. This was a treaty that you, yourself, were part of creating.'

I gestured with frustration. 'I can't believe there isn't a scientific solution for this. This is so wrong!'

'Jian, please remember: I can choose whether to do this or not. I've made my choice.'

I subsided. 'And I respect it. Who will co-parent?'

It raised itself on its legs and spoke with triumph. 'Terrclick!'

'No *way*,' I said. 'The Empress' favourite consort is going to die *too*? She'll be heartbroken.'

'Terrclick's the best of our species. I'm profoundly honoured to be its chosen. The children will be exceptional. Will you help me—'

'Cat attack, Jian,' Marque said.

'Anyone else able to take over for me?' I said.

'Not at your level.'

'Dammit!' I waved my finger in Snapclick's face. 'We are not finished here. How long before the mating party?'

'It's scheduled in twelve of your days. We need to settle our affairs and perform the cleansing ceremonies.'

'We are talking about this as soon as I return.'

'I'll be here,' Snapclick said.

I headed towards the armour bay, a white-walled round platform in the centre of the house. Endicott whined and followed me; she knew what the bay meant. I stepped onto the ceramic-like floor and put my arms out.

'What do we have, Marque?' I said as the armour bay fitted me with my protective equipment. I checked my weapons and chilli micro-bombs, loaded the heads-up display, and confirmed that everything was green. I rubbed Endicott on both sides of her head. 'I'll be back soon, Endie.'

Fumi, my allocated dragon transport, popped into existence in front of me. Her scales were a rich dark brown, and her snake-like body was three metres long with four legs. I put my hand on her shoulder.

'Three cruisers attacking a gas giant in a system at the edge of Empire space,' Marque said into my helmet comms. One of its spheres floated to touch Fumi as well. 'Be ready, it will be bumpy.'

'Wonderful,' I said, and we reappeared in the gallery of Fumi's ship. The top half of the ship was transparent, giving a spectacular view of space around us. Fumi's ship was fifty metres wide and the gallery, the top half of the ship, was fifty metres long.

Fumi disappeared, reappearing with my second-in-command, Lieutenant Naomi Griffith. Griffith, like me, was fully human, and born before the dragon invasion of Earth. She had dark skin from her African heritage, was tall and muscular, and chose to appear in her early forties, slightly older than my own age choice.

'I have a message from Shiumo,' Marque said into my comms.

'Tell her to fuck off,' I said.

'She's still at it?' Griffith said.

'She's being very insistent,' Marque said.

'Tell her for the thousandth time: no. I have an excellent relationship with Fumi, *who I trust*, and Shiumo can go to hell.'

'Heh, trust,' Griffith said. 'All the dragons are as bad as each other.'

'What Shiumo did to Richard is unforgivable.' I checked my bombs. 'Enough about Shiumo, we have cats to fight.'

Fumi reappeared with Leckie, one of the new recruits. He was only twenty-three, and like many humans his age had joined the dragon defence effort as soon as he was old enough. Our ranks were swelling, but we were still short on numbers to face sixty-four thousand ships, each full of thousands of cats. Leckie was still in his original mixed-heritage South American body, engineered like the rest of the human force to be stronger with more endurance, and his soulstone in his forehead was blue to signal his Earth loyalty.

'Marque said gas giant?' Leckie said.

'That's right,' I said. 'What could the cats possibly want on a gas giant? Are there rare elements on it? Lithium? Beryllium?'

Fumi transferred the rest of the squad in one by one, bringing two junior officers and thirty infantry to handle the three cat ships. She shifted onto the nose of the transparent ship.

'Prepare for fold,' Marque said, and we all hesitated with our mouths open to avoid lung damage from the possible pressure difference.

The view of space around the ship shifted to the gas giant, large enough to cover most of the sky. It was an unusual, striking shade of green, with a few narrow rings around it and a number of small satellites. The ship shuddered around us, buffeted by the atmospheric currents and gravity of the enormous planet.

'Whoa, that's nearly as big as a star,' Leckie said, impressed.

Three cat ships were nearby, focusing all of their energy cannons onto the centre of the planet. Another dragon ship with a bright orange metallic skin was parked next to us.

'The native species on this planet have nothing that the cats want,' the other dragon said over comms. 'They're destroying the planet because I'm here.'

'Can they actually destroy a gas giant? They're tiny compared to it,' I said.

'If they can start a fusion reaction in the core of the planet, they can turn it into a brown dwarf star and destroy all life in it,' Marque said.

'They'll do that?' Leckie said.

'They've started doing it in the past three years or so. If they see a dragon ship in orbit, they blow up the planet without even talking to them,' I said. 'Three groups. Alpha team with Lieutenant Imran to the ship at nine o'clock. Bravo team, with me, I'll take the basket, ship in the middle. Lieutenant Griffith, take Charlie team to the ship at three o'clock. Ready to carry us, Fumi?'

'Ready to go,' Fumi said. 'Hands, Alpha team.'

Alpha team put their hands on Fumi and she folded them out. Marque floated from the back of the ship with a basket of synthesised potatoes and dragon scale, and passed it to me. Fumi returned, and my team put our hands on her. She folded us to the cat ship, and we immediately released the chilli bombs.

Cat ships had dark grey interiors, with limited views of the outside, reflecting their mild agoraphobia. The bridge was higher than it was wide, with the cats sitting on platforms containing two-dimensional viewscreens and control panels at various heights, sticking out from the walls.

The cats had no way to communicate over interstellar distances like the dragons did. They were unaware of our chilli weapon, and had no defence against it. The bridge crew went down immediately, falling off their platforms. I put the basket next to their captain's comms panel, then we proceeded through the ship dropping chilli bombs on every cat we found. They were completely incapacitated by it, falling and screaming in agony. The entire crew were down – the chilli powder spread through the ventilation system and no cat could avoid it. We headed back to the bridge, and I stopped next to the captain's head, where I'd placed the potatoes.

'We're taking you back to your home system,' I said to the captain. 'Please stop attacking us. The potatoes are a gift in apology for doing this to you. We wish to negotiate in peace – there's a dragon scale in the basket; just tap on it and we will immediately come to talk terms.'

I pinged Fumi. 'Ready to go.'

'Prepare for fold,' Fumi said, and we were stretched through space as she carried the cat ship back to its home system. She appeared on the bridge. 'Hands.'

We gathered around her and she folded us off the cat ship and onto her own, still floating above the gas giant. The final cat ship was visible next to the gas giant, and had turned upside-down from its original orientation – the galactic standard symbol of surrender.

'They turned turtle!' I said. 'Did they surrender to you?'

'Dunno,' Griffith said from the third ship. 'We dropped the chilli on them before we knew they'd turned the ship over – we were inside and never saw it happen.' Her voice turned wry. 'Sorry, all. Nothing we can do about it – they're completely out of action – we're dropping them home with another scale and hoping that once they're back up to speed, they'll use it to ping us and we can talk.'

'I'm taking them home,' Fumi said, and disappeared.

'If they did it deliberately, it's a huge breakthrough for us,' I said.

'If they did it deliberately, they've been warned about the chilli,' Imran said. 'They're somehow communicating with their homeworld, and sharing information about what we do.'

Fumi reappeared with Charlie team. 'I need to tell my mother about this,' she said. 'I wonder if other cats have done that. If they have, we may finally have a breakthrough towards peace.'

'Excellent,' I said. 'Drop us home, and then head off to talk to her.'

The whole raid – from start to finish – had taken less than an hour. Hopefully we would be this efficient when the time came to take on the fleet.

*

When I arrived home, Snapclick was still there, throwing a ball into the glowing pool for Endicott.

'Now tell me what you'd like for a mating-party gift,' I said, sitting at the outdoor table next to the pool.

Two of its bodies joined me at the table while the third one continued to throw the ball. 'You're okay with me doing this?'

'I said I'd support you, and I will. What can I give you? You were about to ask me something, as well.'

'To be a post-ingestion for my children.'

I stared at it, silenced, for a long time. Eventually I managed to choke out, 'I am so honoured.'

'You have done well with the cat child, Jian; you are an obvious choice.'

'Oliver's the way he is because he is awesome,' I said. 'He has a heart as big as a planet and he's smarter than just about anyone I know short of you.'

'This is why I want you. You will push my children to be the greatest clicks that have ever existed.'

'I'll do my damndest, my friend.'

2

I couldn't leave the Barracks planet for any length of time, so Oliver came to see me and catch up two weeks later. We sat on the poolside deck together, surrounded by the remains of our extremely carnivorous replicated meal. Oliver swivelled the three-dimensional model of Victor's statue so that I could view it from all sides, the black pads on his fingers appearing strange as they pressed against the force field. The statue was a symbol of hope for the Empire; it was my two sons Oliver and David, cat and human, standing as brothers. Endicott crunched a bone under the table – Oliver had been slipping food to her all through the meal and I'd pretended not to notice. He always spoiled her and she adored him.

'It'll be made of grey granite with shining flecks in it, a natural stone,' he said.

'I like how you have your arms around each other,' I said. 'How big will Victor make it?'

'Half life-size. It'll take him *ages*, he doesn't often work in stone and he's refusing Marque's help; he'll do it all himself. He's completely bonkers.'

'I know that,' I said.

He pushed the model aside. 'You ever thought about getting back together with them, Mum? Victor asked me to tell you:

you're welcome any time. They want to come and visit you. You're all alone here; you've been by yourself for too long.'

I sighed and rubbed my face. 'I wish my mother would just *butt out.*'

'We all want you to be happy, Mum.'

'As long as that' – I pointed at the cat fleet hovering above us – 'is there, I can't do anything. When it's dealt with, I'll start to live my life properly. *My* life.'

'My people are causing the whole world – the whole *galaxy* so much grief,' he said, his emotions turning bitter.

I took his hand and buried my fingers in his soft black fur. 'And you aren't. You have friends and family and you are loved.'

He gripped my hand, then released it. 'Speaking of family, have you heard from David? I haven't heard anything from him since he left Nan's farm, and I'm worried about him. Do you know how he is?'

'He's stationed in the Third Battalion. He's second-in-command of a backup squad, and from what I hear he's already done two chilli attacks and represented himself well.'

'Have you seen him?'

'Not personally. He's not in my part of the force. They keep us separate so that we won't be in the same action and compromised by our family ties.'

He nodded. 'That makes sense.'

'I just told him by scale that you're talking about him,' Marque said. 'He's too far away to communicate directly, he's sending a message through to me via scales. Here it is.' He used David's voice. 'Sorry I haven't been in touch. We're doing team-building with micro-bombs. Just a few more months before the cat fleet drops out of warp and this will all be sorted. I'm fine, and I'll send you a longer message soon.'

'I'm glad he's happy and busy,' Oliver said. He hesitated, his emotions conflicted; he'd been holding something back the entire evening and he was about to let it out. 'There's something I need to tell you.'

I sighed with relief. 'About time. What species?'

'What species what?' he said, confused.

'Whoever you want to tell me about.'

'How did you know that was what I was going to say?' he said, incredulous.

'Oliver, I'm your *mother.* So, what species? Do I know them?'

The words rushed out. 'She's a dragon.'

A million thoughts rushed through my head, and he sat, petrified that I would be angry with him.

'No, of course I'm not upset,' I said. I took his hand again. 'I'm happy you've found love. But is it love? You've been in the Empress' household for nearly a year now; this isn't a political thing, is it?'

He shrugged. 'Kind of, yes. It's a good political move. The cats will attack in a few months. Having me pair-bonded with a dragon – hopefully having a child with a dragon—'

'What?' I said, interrupting him. 'A *child*? She's not pregnant already, is she?'

He smiled.

'You are too young to be a father!'

'Cats are mature at nineteen years old, Mum. I'm thirty-two – an old man by cat standards.'

'Is it love?'

He looked me in the eye. 'Yes.'

'Is she pregnant?'

His gaze didn't waver. 'No.'

I relaxed, relieved. 'So which Princess?'

'Runa.'

'I don't think I've met her.'

'She's one of the Empress' youngest. Not much older than I am. Would you like to meet her?'

'Yes. If you love her I'm sure I will too.'

He pulled out a green scale.

'Wait,' I said, and he hesitated. 'I know cats don't see the illusion – what does her two-legged form look like?'

'It is strange, but—' he began, but Marque interrupted him.

'Cat attack, Jian.'

Oliver rolled his eyes. 'I am so sick of this!'

'A few more months and this will be *sorted*,' I said, thumping the table.

'Go, Mum,' Oliver said. 'Endi and I will be fine.'

I went to the armour bay, with Oliver and Endicott following.

I stood in it and held my arms out. 'What do we have?'

'It's New Nippon,' Marque said.

'Holy shit,' Oliver said, then softer, 'Sorry, Mum.'

I waved him down. 'Casualties?'

'None as yet. Princess Masako was there visiting Prince Haruka, and she folded some Japanese soldiers to the cat ships to stop them. It's not working as well as planned, and your backup will be useful.'

'How many cat ships?'

'Four.'

Fumi popped into existence in front of me and I put my hand on her shoulder. Oliver gave me a grinning thumbs-up, showing his long canines, as we disappeared. We reappeared in the gallery of Fumi's ship, then she transferred the rest of the squad in one by one, bringing two junior officers and thirty infantry to handle the four cat ships. She disappeared when we were all loaded, and reappeared above us, sitting on the nose of her transparent ship.

'Marque said New Nippon?' Leckie said.

'That's right,' I said.

'Prepare for fold,' Marque said, and we all hesitated with our mouths open.

Fumi folded us to New Nippon. The Japanese had made tailored alterations to the planet: the entire landmass, bigger than all the combined land of Earth, was in the shape of the original Japanese island group. They'd even had the terrain altered to be identical; the planet's only continent was a giant copy of the original Japan. There'd been some argument about making it earthquake-prone as well, like the original islands, and the dragons had talked them down to having mild earthquakes similar to the controlled ones on Earth. The landmass was sparsely populated for a colony planet; they had very strict rules about who could live there permanently.

The four cat ships were firing on New Nippon, focusing their beams on the capital, Edo, and an orbital Marque sphere, the size of a small moon, was protecting the city with a massive energy shield.

'Let's go before Marque runs out of juice,' I said. 'Alpha team—'

'They respectfully request that you hold off until they've finished their experiment,' Marque said.

'What experiment?' Imran said.

'They're trying wasabi instead of chilli.'

'Is it working?'

'No,' Marque said, sounding amused. 'Good thing they have an orbital instance of me to protect them, otherwise Edo would be toast by now.'

'Let us know if we need to move in and hit the cats,' I said.

'Look,' Leckie said, pointing at the cat ships. They'd stopped attacking Edo and had turned over, the symbol of surrender common to most species in the Empire.

'They surrendered?' I asked Marque.

'They haven't said anything. They just turned over,' Marque said.

We shared a look.

'Even though the wasabi was ineffective?' I said.

'Yes,' Marque said. 'The last two cat attacks did this as well, but they turned over after they'd been boarded and it was too late to negotiate. Are they using the dragons as a taxi service to get them home when they see us coming?'

'That suggests they know that we can incapacitate them. Are they communicating through interstellar distances? I thought they couldn't do that,' I said.

'I'll see if there's something around here that's quantum-entangled,' Marque said. 'They're definitely too far from any other cat ship to be communicating at the speed of light or slower.'

A few spheres whizzed out of Fumi's ship to check the area.

'Let's ask them if they surrender,' I said. 'Open a channel.'

'Done.'

'This is Colonel Choumali of the Dragon-Human Military Alliance—' I began, but they interrupted me.

'Return us to our home system immediately,' the cats said.

'Permission to come aboard and discuss returning you?' I said.

'Agree to take us back to our home system.'

'We agree,' I said. 'May we come aboard?'

The cats didn't reply.

'We need to be physically on your ship if we're going to take you home,' I said.

'Come,' the cats said.

I switched to local comms. 'We're fully loaded with chilli bombs. If they decide that wasn't a peaceful invitation, we can hit them with the chilli and take them home anyway.' I indicated the five most experienced soldiers and we gathered around Fumi. 'Let's go pay them a visit.'

'Before you go, Colonel Choumali,' Marque said.

'Yes?' I said, putting my hand on Fumi's shoulder.

'The leader of the wasabi force was Prince Haruka, and he's still on the largest cat ship. Princess Masako carried him there.'

'Wonderful. Let's go.'

Fumi folded us over.

'By your leave, your Highness,' I said when we arrived on the main cat ship. Prince Haruka and his small team, all in head-to-toe, black, human-fabricated armour, were standing on the bridge facing off with the senior cat crew. Three of the most senior cats had come down from their platforms and stood across from the New Nippon soldiers, who were holding micro-bombs.

Haruka was easily recognisable; as a dragonscales he was taller than average for a human, and his armour indicated his rank. They all wore black nano-fibre suits, but his was enhanced by large golden chrysanthemum motifs surrounded by gold wave-shaped filigree, and he had two Japanese-style swords held in place by a gold silk belt. Their black armour was splashed with the bright green wasabi – powdered Japanese horseradish. A goldenscales dragon stood behind him, her head lowered with submission. She was only a metre and a half long, much smaller than the rest of the dragon population, and her bright yellow scales marked her as a dragon servant.

'Colonel Jian Choumali. Again arriving too late to protect the people of Japan.' Haruka flipped his faceplate up to show his impeccably made-up face. He was furious. 'We did not give you permission to board this ship.'

'The cats did,' I said, and his expression grew darker.

'Where's Masako?' Fumi said. 'She has three times the charisma I do.'

'She is on her way, Highness,' the dragon servant said.

Masako folded onto the ship, and the goldenscales servant hurried to stand behind her, her head still bowed.

'I was transporting the rest of the New Nippon teams off the cat ships,' Masako said. 'Hello, my darling Fumi. Colonel Choumali, good to see you.'

Masako's scales were a dark metallic gunmetal colour, and her eyes were jade-green. Her form was a standard four-legged shape without wings, and she had a lithe, snake-like body. She was the Empress' oldest daughter, and nearly as charismatic as the Empress herself, a skill that grew with age. She was one of the first dragons to be fitted with the – then experimental – soulstone. She would have been an adult when the huge cat fleet left their home system three thousand years before.

'Hello, honoured cats,' she said, and took two-legged form.

One of the human soldiers moaned gently. A dragon's two-legged form appeared to be what every individual found the most attractive, and the body language changed to match the viewer's species. For me, her illusory two-legged form was the most spectacularly beautiful woman I'd ever seen. Her serene, mid-brown face had large, expressive jade-green eyes and her hair, frizzy like my own, floated down to her waist and was a shining cloud around her head. Her human form was similar to the Empress' own: small breasts and long legs, muscular and lithe with very little body fat. She smelled wonderful, of fresh spring breezes and rain on grass.

She spread her hands in welcome, her voice warm and velvety. 'I am the Empress' first-born dragon child. I greet you on behalf of the Dragon Empire. Please, allow me to fold you to my home planet so we can show you our hospitality and peacefully negotiate your return to your home system.'

The cats just stared at her, then a couple pulled weapons and shot at her. Marque blocked the energy beams.

One of the cats stepped forward. Its fur outside the grey cat jumpsuit was slightly longer than most cats', and was patterned in a striking silver and black tabby colour. 'Take dragon form. Your lies do nothing but irritate us.'

Masako changed back into four-legged form and bowed her head. 'I apologise. I just want to communicate with you.'

'We don't want to communicate with you,' the cat said. 'Take us home.'

'How may I address you, honoured sentient?' Masako said.

'Captain,' the cat said. 'Take us back to our home system.'

'Why did you bother attacking the planet if you were planning to immediately surrender?' Masako said.

'Transport us to our homeworld,' the cat said.

'I will be happy to, provided we can speak to you when we get there,' Masako said.

'What? Wait!' Haruka said. 'You can't let them get away with this!' He threw a bomb that exploded with green powder – the horseradish. I didn't feel it, still in my protective gear, and the cat ignored it.

'That wasn't very nice when they're talking terms,' Masako said. 'Back off, my love.'

'Fuck you, dragon,' Haruka said. 'They killed my family!' He drew his sword, and Marque restrained him with an energy barrier.

'Goodness, that is extremely bad manners,' Masako said mildly. She bowed to the head cat. 'I apologise for the human's behaviour, he is young and impulsive. I am Princess Masako, I speak for the Empire. Call off your fleet attacking my homeworld, and we can talk and trade.'

'Speak to our leaders,' the captain said, and leaped gracefully up to its control platform.

'Is that an invitation to parley?' Masako said.

'Take us back to our homeworld,' the cat said. 'Or we will attack this planet again. I do not have rank to speak to you. Speak to our leaders.'

'Finally,' Masako said, and turned to us humans. 'Ready to act as an honour guard? Let's go visit their homeworld.' She nodded to Haruka. 'I suggest that Fumi fold you home to New Nippon before we leave, your Highness. Your royal personage is too important to put in danger.'

'No!' Haruka stomped backwards and forwards inside his energy barrier, still holding the sword. 'You can't do this for them. Let me out of here!' He spun and pointed the sword at the cat captain. 'They killed my *brother*!'

'Please stand down, Highness,' I said, trying to calm him as he radiated raw fury. 'The cats have surrendered.'

'We have not surrendered,' the cat captain said. 'We have what we wanted. Return us to our home system.'

'You only need to ask if you want us to help you,' Masako said. 'We'd be happy to carry you around – if you agree to stop attacking our people.'

'Return us to our homeworld immediately or we will destroy this planet,' the captain said.

'Bomb them with chilli!' Haruka shrieked. 'They need to suffer!'

'Highness ...' one of his team said, his voice mild.

'Remain silent!' the Prince said.

'Take us to our home system and then leave,' the cat said.

'Fumi,' Masako said. 'Take the Prince and his team down to New Nippon and we'll head out. Take Miko with you.'

'I want to stay with you, Highness,' the servant, Miko, said.

'No, little one, go with them so you'll be safe,' Masako said kindly.

Miko bobbed her head. 'Highness.'

The Japanese team put their hands on Fumi's shoulders. She went to Haruka, who backed away from her. Marque held him still while she touched him. Miko put her nose on Fumi's butt.

'New Nippon will not forget this outrage,' Haruka said as they disappeared.

'We will transport you home, then arrange for the creation of a peaceful relationship,' Masako said to the cat captain. 'May we establish a diplomatic post on your planet?'

'What is that?' the cat said suspiciously.

'We post a group of our people on your planet to liaise with your government. We can talk any time and start trade treaties.'

'No. You may not inhabit our homeworld, it is for *us*,' the cat captain said. 'Return us to our home system and then leave.'

'As you wish. We only want peace between our people. We can place an embassy in orbit as well.'

Once again, the cat didn't reply.

Masako went to the nose of the ship and folded it to cat space. She reappeared in the bridge, smiling a dragon smile.

Marque provided me with a heads-up visual of the planet below us with geographic and climate data surrounding it; the cat ships had no displays of external space. The cat planet was larger and warmer than Earth, and mostly desert; they pumped their water from aquifers that filled the sandy soil. The cities on the night side were dimly lit, making sections of it glow faintly. One of the deserts on the day side was covered with a massive black stain that shone in the reflected light of their red dwarf star; it was the size of a continent on Earth and the dragons had speculated that it was a huge solar collector to provide the cat society with energy.

'There,' Masako said. 'I have brought you home. Can we talk now?'

'Carry the rest of the ships then leave us,' the silver tabby said.

'If you like,' Masako said, and she disappeared. She reappeared with each of the cat ships, one by one. It only took a few minutes as we stood uncomfortably with the cat crew. When all the cat ships were in orbit around their planet, Masako returned to the bridge.

'Can we go down to the surface and visit?' Masako asked the cat captain.

The cats on the bridge fired on us, and Marque protected us from the energy weapons.

'Please stop firing, we'd like to talk,' Masako said.

I took out a chilli bomb and hefted it. 'Orders, Highness?'

'No, Colonel, don't attack them when we're so close to peace,' she said.

'You have two minutes until my energy shield goes down,' Marque said. 'I suggest you fold out.'

'Not when we're so close!' Masako said. 'Please stop firing on us; we'll give you anything if you call off your fleet.'

The cats continued to fire on us. The energy shield in front of us became warmer.

'Eighty seconds,' Marque said. 'This is pointless, Masako.'

'Gather around me and prepare for fold, everybody,' Masako said, resigned. 'We'll come back on my ship.'

We put our hands on her and she folded us to her own ship. It was nearly as big as Shiumo's exceptionally large ship; the gallery of Masako's ship was a hundred metres wide and long, with completely invisible walls and ceiling giving us an excellent view of space around it.

'I want to go straight back,' Masako said. 'Are you all prepared to come with me? Have your bombs ready, just in case.'

'We're good, ma'am,' I said.

'All right, let's go,' she said, and folded to the nose of her ship, then took the ship back to the cat planet. We arrived above it, with the four cat ships we'd just transported hovering in the sky next to us, dwarfed by Masako's enormous ship.

'Ask them for permission to visit the planet on their broadcast frequency, Marque,' Masako said.

'Just go down, don't ask their permission,' Leckie said. 'We can gain valuable information.'

'No,' I said. 'The last thing we need now is a symbolic invasion. What do they say, Marque?'

Marque's voice changed to metallic and emotionless. 'This is our homeworld, it is for us. No other species are welcome.'

'We just want to come and talk,' Masako said, her voice high-pitched and sweet, using every scrap of her impressive charisma.

'Leave,' the cats said.

'My son Oliver – no. Marque, say Oliver's name in cat, then "can come to your planet and speak to you".'

'That one is not a cat,' the cat said. 'It is corrupted. Be merciful and destroy it.'

'Any suggestions, Masako?' I said.

'Can we come closer?' she said. 'Would you like some potatoes? We have plenty.'

Marque relayed for the cats. 'Leave immediately or we will destroy your ship.'

'We just want to talk,' Masako said. 'Can we see you?' She lowered her voice. 'Mute me: I could really use a click right now, Marque, are any clicks free?'

'I'm looking,' Marque said.

An enormous beam of energy erupted from the planet and hit us with a blinding flash that caused stars in my vision for the split second before Marque blacked out the skin of the ship. The heat from the blast radiated from the walls around us.

'I can't hold this for long,' Marque said. 'Masako, they just destroyed all of the ships next to us. They wiped out four of their own ships to attack us.'

'Please stop firing, we'd like to talk,' Masako said.

'They can't hear you, they closed the channel,' Marque said. 'You have two minutes until the atmosphere inside your ship is too hot for humans. I suggest you fold out.'

The heat from the skin of the ship became stronger and we humans moved into the centre.

'Eighty seconds,' Marque said. 'This is pointless, Masako; you already gave them potatoes and a dragon scale. Just go.'

'Prepare for fold, everybody,' Masako said. 'I don't want to risk you. This is a breakthrough – let's build from here. Reopen the channel, Marque.'

'They're not listening,' Marque said.

'I'm trying anyway. I am Princess Masako of the Dragon Empire,' Masako said. 'We would like to talk in peace with your people. We don't want to fight. If you are willing to negotiate, use the scale we have provided. We will return with gifts for you.'

We all waited for a reply, and nothing happened.

'Well fuck this, let's go home and I'll report back to my mother,' Masako said, and folded us to orbit around the Imperial Capital without even moving to the nose of the ship. 'What a bunch of assholes. Gather together, dear humans, and I'll take you home.'

'Why does Prince Golden Flower Spring Blossom Haruka hate you so much?' Leckie asked me as Masako took the first of our team back to Barracks. 'What did you do to him? He's not old enough to have been in the Earth-based service with you, is he?'

'No, he was born on New Nippon, his father was an original colonist – apparently they needed a member of the royal family along when they established the colony,' I said. 'His big brother was one of the children that died in the first cat invasion of New

Nippon, nearly thirty years ago. He blames me for the loss, well aware that I had nothing to do with it and needing someone to blame for it anyway.'

'Well that makes a *lot* of sense,' Griffith said.

'Nothing about Haruka makes sense,' I said.

'Is he a dragonscales?' Leckie said. 'He has the scales on his temples – I thought all the dragonscales were women?'

'Yeah, my girlfriend's a dragonscales and she said they're all hermaphroditic females,' Griffith said.

'Haruka's the first dragonscales in the Japanese royal family,' I said. 'His father had a fling with one of the early dragon visitors. The minute Haruka turned five and his soulstone was attuned, he demanded that he be moved to an engineered body that was one hundred per cent male. He made their lives miserable about it.'

'Sounds like he's missing out, if you ask me,' Leckie said.

'Believe me, he is,' Griffith said.

'If he identifies as male then why does he wear make-up and dresses all the time?' MacAuley asked.

We all stopped and stared at him.

'What?'

'You some sort of pre-dragon American or something?' Leckie said. He affected an awful mock-American accent. 'This boy will turn into a ho-mo-sexual if he wears women's clothing.' He changed to his normal voice. 'As if a man can't be femme and pretty now and then.'

'Uh ... yeah.' MacAuley glowered at him. 'I am. I know I look thirty, but I'm eighty-nine years old, and I was born in America. I already had grown kids when the dragons arrived.'

'Whoa, you're ancient,' Leckie said. 'Wait – you've never worn a dress and gone out feeling really pretty?'

'Once or twice?' MacAuley said, obviously equivocating. 'I mean, I've thought about it, but—'

'Dude.' Leckie pushed him. 'We are going shopping and doing a full make-over for you. Dresses and make-up all around. The girls in West Barracks will love you.' He stopped. 'Don't feel forced. Only if you want to. You are single, right?'

'I am, yeah.' MacAuley thought about it, then shrugged. 'If I can do it with you, it should be fun.'

'Excellent.' Leckie turned to Griffith. 'Cathy? Come along. You need to be pretty too. We're all in uniform way too much.'

'I'm in, but only if we do our hair as well,' Griffith said, delighted.

Masako reappeared and I put my hand on her shoulder. 'Let's go home.'

'If I ever wear that much make-up under my armour shoot me,' Imran said, almost to himself. 'All that mascara must wreak bloody havoc with the goggles.'

3

Snapclick's mating ceremony was four weeks later, to give everybody time to prepare. Every click in the Empire wanted to be there, and the Council of Clicks themselves were to preside. We gathered in a large, open-air space with a stone floor that was surrounded by enormous trees on the clicks' home planet. The Empress herself and a small retinue were present, the Empress broadcasting grief at losing one of her favourite consorts.

Snapclick and Terrclick were at the edge of the platform polishing each other's exoskeletons. The upper part of their hard shells had been inlaid with intricate patterns of precious metals that honoured their sacrifice, leaving the soft lower parts free for the babies to eat through. When Snapclick saw me, it came and stopped at the edge of my bubble of higher gravity and oxygen atmosphere.

'Are those what I think they are?' it said, staring at the basket I was carrying.

I pushed the basket through the barrier. 'Welsh Golds from my mother's farm.'

'Thank you!' It took the basket and held it to its nose-analogue behind its front legs. 'They are *divine*, they'll make us delicious. Thank you so much. We'll eat them as soon as the eggs are laid.

The babies will have an exceptional start in life.' It turned to Terrclick and raised the basket, and Terrclick raised a foreclaw.

Snapclick turned back to me. 'I'm so nervous,' it said. 'Both of us feel bad about abandoning our attempt to talk to the cats when we've made no progress. We've been so engrossed in talking to the cats that we haven't done enough practice, and I'm sure I'm going to forget half the dance and the whole thing will be a disaster. I haven't done the dance in *years* and I'm so unprepared—'

'This is a side of you I've never seen.'

It rubbed its rear legs over its wing cases and I felt a blast of its strongest emotion – something I didn't often feel from insect-type aliens. It was terrified.

'I can feel your fear,' I said, wiping my eyes. 'I wish I could give you a hug—'

The Council of Clicks had gathered on the other side of the clearing, and one of them made a few loud clicking sounds.

'That's my cue,' Snapclick said. 'I have to run.'

'I love you dearly, my friend,' I said, but it was already halfway across the clearing, running swiftly on its three sets of eight legs. It placed the basket of potatoes with the other mating-party gifts.

'You'll be able to speak to it more when the dance is done and they're connected,' Marque said. 'Everybody will have a chance to say a proper goodbye and bless their union.'

'It will feel weird speaking to it while it's in the process of mating,' I said.

'Just remember it won't be weird for them.'

I nodded. 'It'll be worth it, even if it is for only a few minutes. I'll be glad to tell it how much I appreciate its help.'

Snapclick and Terrclick went to stand in front of the Council of Clicks. The five senior clicks spoke quietly to them in their own language. Snapclick and Terrclick listened to the council, then turned and went to the centre of the clearing. They moved so that their six bodies were standing in a circle, all facing the centre.

The Council of Clicks proceeded to click their pincers against each other in a slow rhythm. Snapclick and Terrclick lifted their wing cases and released their foremost wings so that they fanned out. The wings were gauzy and transparent, brilliantly pink and purple with gold edges in a vivid display of colour.

Snapclick and Terrclick began the mating dance. They raised their front pincers, then stepped in time to the clicks from the council. The council members sped up their clicks, and added a complicated rhythm. Snapclick and Terrclick danced faster in a circle, raising and lowering their bodies and tapping their front pincers against each other's.

They spread their four hind wings, dark blues and purples splashed with gold. Each click's body now had six wings fanned behind it in a spectacular display. They turned so that their hindquarters nearly touched, then turned back around to face each other, raising and lowering their bodies in time to the clicks. They swung around and joined their back ends together in three pairs. The clicks intensified, and Snapclick and Terrclick rapped their pincers against each other in the circle with their rears joined together. The rhythm became a steady rattle, and the clicks' movements became more frantic.

The clearing went silent, and Snapclick and Terrclick froze. All six of their heads rotated at the same time to see the Council, who hadn't moved. The area filled with the confusion of everybody present.

'Jian, it's happening,' Marque said. 'The cat fleet is dropping out of warp. They're weeks earlier than we predicted. Fumi's on her way.'

All the clicks present spoke at the same time, filling the air with their high-pitched buzz.

'Not *now*,' I said with disbelief. 'I can't bless the union and confirm my role as post-ingestion if I go now! The cats weren't due to attack for six weeks – are you sure?'

'Yes.'

I sighed with feeling as Fumi appeared next to me.

'Tell Snapclick I'm sorry, and that I love it,' I said as I put my hand on her shoulder.

'Snapclick already knows,' Marque said as Fumi folded me home to collect my gear.

*

When I was home, I ran into the armour bay and put my arms out. The bay fitted me and I checked my chilli bombs and the heads-up display on my spacesuit. Fumi folded me onto the main gallery of her ship, where the rest of our battalion were gathering. She disappeared and then popped back with Leckie. The cat fleet filled space around me, still in their glowing warp cocoons.

'Variation in energy,' Marque said, 'I just need to confirm ... give me a moment, synching ...' Its voice became urgent. 'Confirmed! They're dropping out of warp. Calculating. At the rate of energy transfer: you have thirty minutes. I've started the broadcast. ATTENTION CAT REPUBLIC. THIS IS THE DRAGON EMPIRE. DO NOT ATTACK OUR HOMEWORLD, OUR RETALIATION WILL BE SWIFT AND PAINFUL. REPEAT. DO NOT ATTACK—'

'Mute that,' I said, and the announcement stopped running through my helmet.

I led my team to the transfer pod and we entered. The door closed behind us, and we were sealed into a four-by-four-metre room, ready to be transported onto a cat ship. Putting us in modules ready for transfer made it easier for Fumi to carry us across. There were ten pods on Fumi's ship, each with ten human soldiers in them, one pod per cat ship. I hoped we would be onto our cat ship in time to stop them before they were aware of our chilli weapons and could take counter-measures; we were seventh in order to be transferred. My heads-up display showed the scene outside the ship: the energy bubbles around the cat ships were fading.

'Are they replying to your broadcast?' I asked Marque.

'No.'

I checked my bombs again. 'Keep us updated on when we'll be transferred.'

'Cannot wait to have this done and finished and out of the damn way,' Enrik said. 'There's seven galaxies out there for us to explore.'

The time in my display moved excruciatingly slowly as it counted down the thirty minutes until the ships became accessible. The warp bubbles faded out on my display, and the cat ships were in normal space.

I pulled a bomb out and held it ready.

'The ships are completely out of warp. I'm giving Fumi the go-ahead—' Marque said, and my head was split open by an agonised telepathic scream. I bent and put my hands over the top of my head in an attempt to block the pressure. The sound winked off.

'Oh lord,' one of my soldiers said.

I opened my eyes and stared in horror. The cats were accelerating back into warp. The ships gathered the energy bubbles around them as I watched. Fumi had obviously been folding a pod onto one of the ships when it went into warp, and the warp field had pulled her halfway back into normal space. The pod was stuck on the edge of the warp field, stretched like soft plastic, pulled out of shape and squeezed. Fumi was on top and her body was stretched and mutilated. I zoomed the image out, to see that thousands of dragons and their human cargo had been similarly dismembered.

'Get their stones!' I shouted.

'I can't, they're at the edge of the warp field,' Marque said.

'Will the stones still be attuned when they drop out of warp?'

'They aren't in warp. They're at the edge of the field and space is too deformed there. The stones are destroyed.' Its voice softened. 'Fumi's dead. Real Death. They're all dead.'

'Any other casualties?'

'The soldiers who were on the edge of the warp field, and the dragons carrying them, are dead,' Marque said. 'The rest made it through to the cat ships. We just lost over six thousand dragons, and more than sixty thousand humans.'

'How many made it through?'

'Only a hundred and thirty dragons. Thirteen hundred humans.'

Enrik put his helmeted head in his hands and moaned. 'They were ready for us. We've already lost. So many dead.'

I felt weak with despair and flopped to sit on the floor with my back against the wall of the pod. He was right. 'With Fumi gone, we have no-one to fold us onto the cat ship and disable it. If they decide to destroy the dragon homeworld, we can't stop them.'

'We're contacting the dragon sanctuary world to have them send us some more dragons to transport you,' Marque said. 'Word is going out through the Empire. The dragons are rallying. There's a third generation dragon in the gallery of this ship right now: I'm explaining the process to her. The cat ships are still powering up their warp drives; if they decide to attack again, it won't be for at least another of your hours. I suggest you take a break – eat and drink, sit and rest – until the cat ships are capable of leaving warp again.'

I thumped the wall of the pod with my fist. All our plans had come to nothing. Thirteen years of preparation and we'd already been routed.

*

All the officers were gathered in Shiumo's massive ship, more than three thousand of us sitting around tables as the leaders of the Empire decided what to do. The walls of the ship were transparent, and the cat fleet – now fully back in warp, and slowly moving in circles – hovered above us. The dead dragons and the pods they'd been carrying still sat at the edge of the warp field as they'd been for the past two weeks, a testament to our failure.

No dragons were present on Shiumo's ship. The dragons and most senior humans had been called to a meeting on Masako's ship. The rest of us were sharing a meal, spread between the galleries of the largest dragon ships. I was with the hundred most senior officers, sitting around the officers' tables sharing opinions on what was happening next. Shiumo herself was stuck inside the warp field, and we had no idea whether the dragons there were dead or alive.

'We shouldn't leave yet, it's only two weeks,' Major Winters said. 'Two weeks out here is only a couple of days inside the warp field. There are live dragons and humans inside the cat ships. They made it through before the ships went to warp. We should stay on standby. I don't want to leave!'

'You know they've been discussing standing down and moving back to Barracks,' I said. 'If they give the order, we have to do it.'

'More than a hundred ships made it through. They're alive, dammit,' Winters said. 'And the rest of the cat fleet can see our ships waiting for them. The minute we move away, they'll attack the dragon homeworld.'

Our commanding officer, Admiral Blake, appeared in the centre of the gallery with Masako. He was the same Blake who'd taken over from General – now Ambassador – Maxwell; he had been in charge of the original breeding program on Earth and had been recruited by the dragons to lead their defensive force. He was dark-skinned and heavily built, with a square jaw and protruding brows over his sharply intelligent eyes. He accepted our salutes with a nod, then moved to stand where everybody could see him. Masako's expression was restrained.

The room went silent as we waited to hear what he had to say.

'Two days inside the warp field is plenty of time for our soldiers to incapacitate the cats and take them home,' he said. 'We have to assume that they were neutralised and that the cats will now wait until our fleet moves away before dropping out of warp and attacking the dragon homeworld, so we'll do just that.'

The room filled with the sound of the soldiers disagreeing. Nobody wanted to leave our people behind and stand down – it was admitting defeat.

He raised his voice with determination. 'We're not giving up. We're laying a trap. We'll fold most of the ships out of view, but remain in contact through dragon scales. We estimate that it will take them three or four days before they see that we've moved away. They'll think we're standing down, and when they drop out of warp in response, we'll come straight back. The dilation effect will give us plenty of time to be ready for them.'

There was silence for a moment, then the feeling in the room turned positive.

'Your orders are ready, all we have to do is implement them. I just fed them through to your tablets. Finish the meal, rest up, then tomorrow morning we'll run through the plan, do a couple of dry runs, and implement it day after tomorrow.'

The room went silent as everybody checked their tablets. It filled with the buzz of quiet discussion.

'I'm briefing the most senior officers now. If you have any questions, put them to your superior officers,' the Admiral said. 'We can do this. Senior officers, with me, and I'll give you the details.'

We gathered around the dragons, and they folded us to the gallery of Masako's ship. The walls were opaque rather than transparent, and it was fitted with a conference table big enough to accommodate everybody. We gathered around the conference table as Blake addressed us. 'Here's what the plan involves.'

'Stop, Admiral,' Marque said. 'One of the cat ships is dropping out of warp.'

'Put it on the table,' Blake said, and the cat formation appeared as a hologram in the middle.

'Which ship?'

The display zoomed in on a single ship. Its warp glow still appeared bright.

'Are there humans on that ship?' Blake said.

'Yes. Third battalion, Lieutenant Lee's Gamma squad.'

I tried to keep my face emotionless – but that was David's team. David had been missing since the botched attack and he hadn't been on one of the ships that was destroyed on the edge of the field. He could be alive and on that ship.

'Steady, Choumali,' Blake said. 'We'll get them back.' He looked up. 'Double-check – it's really just one ship?'

'Just one, Admiral.'

'Put me through to all personnel.'

'Done,' Marque said.

'Stations, everybody,' Blake said. 'One of the cat ships is dropping out of warp, and there are humans on it. Either the humans on that ship have taken control, or they've been taken hostage. If they're in control, we'll implement the original plan – bomb them with chilli and send the ship back to cat space. If they're hostages, await further orders.' He looked around at the senior officers. 'Any questions?'

'No, sir,' everybody said.

'To your stations, except Choumali to stay with me,' Blake said.

The rest of the officers gathered around their respective dragons and returned to their ships.

I contacted my team. 'Griffith, take the lead,' I said. 'I'm working with the Admiral.'

'Ma'am,' Griffith said.

My comms filled with voices as everybody moved into position on their dragon ships and confirmation went up and down the line.

'Delta squad in place,' Singh said.

'Confirmation: it's only one ship coming out of warp,' Blake's assistant said.

'Stand by, be ready for transfer,' Blake said.

Comms went quiet as everybody took position. The display on the table showed the single cat ship dropping slowly out of warp – the rest of the fleet was still in the glowing warp field. They'd stopped moving, but remained behind an impenetrable field of distorted space.

Masako appeared with a click that I hadn't met before. Its exoskeleton was dark blue and polished to a high sheen.

'Greetings, Admiral, I'm Rapclick,' the click said. 'The Council sent me to help you.'

'We appreciate it,' Blake said. 'The ship's nearly out of warp.'

'Colonel Choumali?' Rapclick said.

'Honoured Click?'

'We need information.' The click studied me, its twelve faceted eyes – four on each body – gleaming. 'Can we sneak your cat son onto that ship to find out what their goal is? There are thousands of cats on the ship; he could lose himself easily among them.'

'Much as he'd like to help his brother, it wouldn't work,' I said. 'We tried using him as an infiltration agent before, and it failed spectacularly. They know who he is immediately. His body language is all wrong. He smells wrong. His fur is worn down in the wrong places from wearing non-cat standard clothing. He's instantly recognisable as a spy, and they can see through the glamour of any dragon who transports him.'

'Very well,' Rapclick said. 'Stay with us, you know more about the cats than anyone; you're mother to one of them. Let's see if we can't talk this out.'

'The ship's fully out of warp,' Marque said. 'They're sending a message.'

'Put it on the table,' Blake said.

A small two-dimensional video appeared above the table, and I moved so that I could see it, then recoiled in shock. A cat held my son David restrained in front of it; David's arms were lifted high behind his back and his face was twisted with pain. There was a dent in the middle of his forehead and I realised with a jolt of dismay that they'd removed his soulstone.

Another cat stepped in front of the camera. This one was taller than the one holding David, and had black fur. 'Return all of our ships to our home system or your human soldiers will die,' it said. 'We have removed their soulstones and crushed them. Agree with our demands or your people will die the Real Death.'

'We agree to your terms. We will return your ships to their home systems,' Blake said.

'We are holding thousands of your people – and the evil dragons – hostage,' the cat said. 'Agree to take our ships back to our home system, or they will all die.'

'We agree to take you back to your system,' Blake said, frustrated. 'Listen to me! We will be happy to transport you around space if you stop attacking – and destroying – the Empire's planets.'

'The rest of the fleet will come out of warp now,' the cat said. 'A dragon may enter each ship and our leader will tell the dragon where to take the ship. Make one wrong move and we will kill eight hundred of your people.'

Rapclick stepped up. 'Many of the hostages have families with young children. Please return those ones, so they can be reunited with their babies.'

'If they cared for their children they would keep them on their ships, the way we do,' the cat said. 'If they are willing to abandon their children, they deserve everything they receive.'

'You're completely correct and we'll stop sending new parents to war if your people agree to a peaceful settlement—' Rapclick began.

The cat interrupted it. 'Do not blame us for your poor parenting! The hostages all stay with us. Don't attempt to get them back or we will kill them. We cannot trust you. Dragons have been lying to their colonised species for centuries. As a gesture of goodwill, when the warp field is down, you may remove the bodies of the soldiers who died when they foolishly attacked us. Then you will carry our ships back to our home system and leave us.'

'What about our people?'

'When we are out of warp, we cannot stop the dragons from leaving. The humans ...' It leaned into the camera and sneered, displaying its sharp canines. 'Stay here with us until we are satisfied that you won't attack us with your cowardly and immoral chemical weapon. Attempt to board our ships, attack us, or fold the humans out with dragons, and thousands of your precious human soldiers will die.'

'That's what we wanted to do in the first place!' Blake said frustrated, but the transmission blinked off.

'How did they know about the chilli? They were locked inside the warp field,' I said.

'I wish I knew. They appear to be communicating over interstellar distances,' Marque said. 'I can't see anything when I search space around them – no entangled nanobots, nothing. The only thing that can get in or out is light – but that's not nearly fast enough to communicate from their homeworld to here.'

'Maybe when we've established peace with them and won them over we'll find out how they're doing it,' Masako said.

'We have our work cut out for us, dear one,' Rapclick said.

'The rest of the cat fleet is dropping out of warp,' Marque said. 'Ready, Masako?'

'Help me co-ordinate the transfer schedule with the scales communication centre,' Masako said.

'I'm there,' Marque said.

'Put me on broadcast to all personnel,' Blake said.

'Done,' Marque said.

'The entire cat fleet is going to drop out of warp,' Blake said. 'We've agreed to take them home without chilli bombing them. The dragons are organising a schedule and will contact their sisters on the ships to help transport them. When the ships are transferred, we can reclaim our dead that are stuck at the edge of the field. As for the people trapped on the ships ...' His voice became grim. 'The cats won't stop the dragons from leaving, but they're holding the humans as surety. They're hostages. We'll negotiate their return when the transfer is complete. I repeat. This is a peaceful transfer. Be ready to use the chilli, but only use it if the order comes through.' He nodded to Marque. 'Inform me the *second* any of those bastards charges up their warp cannons.'

'We're arranging the transport schedule,' Masako said. 'If the dragons on their ships are unharmed, they can help.'

'The cat ships are out of the warp field, and they're not powering up their weapons,' Marque said.

Shiumo folded onto our ship, accompanied by her human team leader, Nadine. Both of them had lost their soulstones, and I'd never seen a dragon with such severe injuries – her back legs had been cut off, her front legs were lacerated, and she bled blue, green and red blood, mixing on the floor into an ugly brown puddle. Nadine had nasty burn wounds from cat energy weapons over most of her torso, and her throat appeared to be half gone. She was probably dead. We raced to help them, and Masako folded them to the ship's medlevel. We followed them down in the internal lift.

Marque laid Shiumo on the table and prepared to lower her into the liquid. Nadine was gone.

'No, wait,' Shiumo said. 'Nadine! Is she dead?'

'Yes,' Marque said. 'There's nothing I can do. Her soulstone is gone. I've put her into cold storage in the hold. Go into the table—'

'Not yet! I need to tell you what happened.' She raised her head slightly. 'The humans bombed them with chilli, and they were incapacitated. But they'd already gone into warp, so we were stuck in warp with them for two days – nobody could fold out.' She panted a few times, her voice hoarse. 'The chilli wore off after a while, and they attacked us with energy weapons. We had to surrender before they broke through our Marque shield and killed us all.'

'That's why they waited,' Blake said. 'They delayed until the chilli wore off, then attacked us. The dragons couldn't fold from inside the warp field.'

'We couldn't run, we couldn't hide, and Marque's energy field ran out ... we had to surrender,' Shiumo said. 'They've removed everybody's soulstones. They restrained me and cut my legs off. As soon as they dropped out of warp I tried to bring my humans—' she choked with emotion. 'And they shot the humans as they touched me.' She dropped her head onto the table. 'Some pain relief would be appreciated, Marque.'

'I'll put you under the minute you're in the table,' Marque said. 'You've lost a lot of blood, you need to go in now.'

'One last question,' Blake said. 'What's their plan?'

'I don't know,' she said, her voice weak. 'All I know is that they wanted our humans.'

'More dragons are folding out of the cat ships,' Marque said. 'The cats are shooting at them as they leave, focusing on any humans that attempt to leave with them. They're holding the humans hostage.'

'Tell them not to bring their human companions,' Blake said.

'I am,' Marque said.

'This is a disaster,' Shiumo said. 'I only hope our friends the clicks can talk to them and stop them from killing ...' She dropped her head onto the table without finishing her sentence, and Marque lowered her into the white liquid.

'Will she be okay?' I said.

'I'll let you know in twenty-four hours,' Marque said, its voice grim.

*

Masako followed the first transfer group to the cat system and parked her ship in orbit around the cat planet.

The black cat leader appeared on the table display. 'Leave now or we will kill sixty-four humans. Stay out of our system, transport our ships and then leave.'

'My ship is a staging point for the dragons transporting your ships,' Masako said. 'I'm needed here to relay communication so that we can safely move your people.'

'You're lying. You can communicate without a ship.' The cat gestured with one hand and the smaller guard cat dragged in a young woman who was either unconscious or dead and threw her to the floor out of view. It moved offscreen and returned with

David, alive and conscious, and still bound. His face was covered in bruising and one eye was swollen shut.

'If you continue to lie to us, this one will die slowly,' the black cat said. It grinned at the camera. 'We have special plans for it. It is from the corrupt family that murdered one of our explorers and took her beloved child to be indoctrinated against his own people.'

She's not dead, David mouthed, and the cats didn't see it. *They've killed a few of us—* The cat dragged him away again.

'You need to tell us where to take your ships!' Masako said, desperate. 'There isn't enough room in this system for all of them. You must co-ordinate with us.'

The cat transmission blinked out.

'Warn us if they charge up their warp cannons, Marque,' Blake said.

'I will. I think they're arguing about whether our ship can stay, but I can't listen in on them without being detected and locked out.'

'Can you create some nanos of yourself to infiltrate them?' Masako said.

'It doesn't matter how small I go, the cats still see me and shoot me out of the air,' Marque said. 'They're masters of nanotechnology and it may be how they're communicating. Incoming message. They're allowing one ship to stay. They've provided me with a map of star systems near to their homeworld and indicated which of their ships is to go where. I'll pass it on.'

'How did they communicate with you?' I said.

'Standard radio frequency.' Marque hesitated, then its voice became urgent. 'Masako, fold home and quickly bring a clean sphere here; I'm self-destructing all my instances in the surrounding light cone. A nanobot entered one of my sentry spheres and hacked into me while they sent their map.'

The sphere disintegrated into black dust.

'Their nanotech has come a long way in the last ten years,' Masako said. 'I'll be right back with a clean Marque instance.' She disappeared.

'Is it possible that they've just hidden their capabilities from us?' Blake said as Masako reappeared with a Marque sphere next to her.

'Entirely possible,' the Marque sphere said. 'It may be what's been happening to me when my spheres disappeared in the past. I'll stay as one instance and keep close to you, Masako. If I start acting weird, the self-destruct word is ...' It said something in dragon.

'Got it,' Masako said. 'Bring the cat leader onto the screen, and let's arrange for these ships to be returned to their home space.'

The cat leader appeared on the table again.

'Stop attacking our AI,' Masako said.

'We are not attacking anything. You are the ones that drop chemical weapons on us,' the cat said. 'Carry our ships back here and then leave.'

'We are,' Marque said. 'I'm putting the co-ordinates of the destination worlds through to each dragon ship.'

'And the other ships?' the cat leader said.

The transmission froze.

'I muted it so we can talk,' Marque said. 'He's sent me the locations of over a hundred thousand additional cat ships scattered throughout the seven galaxies – and some in intergalactic space that's well outside the Empire. Some of these ships have been travelling for a very long time.'

'That sounds like all the ships in the cat fleet,' the Admiral said.

'I think it is,' Marque said. 'They want us to bring every single one of their ships home.'

'Do they even have space for that many cats in their home system?' Rapclick said. 'They will fill even their nearby systems and most of their colonies. They'll be overpopulated.'

'Do we care?' Masako said.

'They've also given me the co-ordinates of some systems in cat space as destinations,' Marque said.

'Put him back on the screen,' the Admiral said.

The cat leader appeared again, looking more irritated.

'Why are you asking us to bring in every cat ship?' Blake said.

'Bringing them here is the only way we can quickly communicate with them,' the cat leader said. 'We do not have your four-dimensional capabilities. We will tell them to stop attacking you. Do as we require, and we will return your people.'

'We'll do it anyway,' Masako said.

The cat bared its teeth. 'We have learned through experience not to trust you.'

'Fair enough,' Masako said. 'Can you allocate someone full-time to help us schedule all the transfers? This will take a while, even with every dragon on the project.'

'You will work with me,' the leader said. 'We want as few of our people to have contact with you as possible. You are deceptive in every way, and I am immune to your lies.'

'All right, I get it,' Masako said with resignation. 'Let's do this.'

'Can we have some of our people back as a gesture of goodwill?' Rapclick said as Masako buried herself in a flurry of scales taps to communicate with the other dragons. 'You have so many. Show that you are serious about—'

'No,' the cat leader said. 'We will return your people when our ships are all accounted for. Not before.'

'What about the ones who are injured?' Rapclick said. 'They're a drain on your resources, we can care for them—'

'They've closed the channel. Dammit!' Marque said. 'Now they're yelling over all wavelengths at me.'

'Just block it,' Masako said.

'I am, but it's really ... annoying. They're flooding all the wavelengths with the code, especially the wavelengths I use to communicate with my on-ship backup storage. My signal is encrypted, but they're not trying to break it, they're trying to override it. It's like someone constantly shouting over me ... I can't do this.'

'You have to!' Masako said. 'Block them.'

'I can't. It's overwhelming for just one sphere, and I can't risk creating more; they'll hack into my code again. I'm leaving a dumb terminal for you to communicate with them, and I'm heading back to Dragonhome. It's a similar interface to what you used when you were back on Earth, Colonel, you should be able to use it.'

A featureless white table coalesced out of the air, then a holographic display appeared above it. Controls appeared on it – the type of controls that I hadn't seen in more than ten years. It appeared to be a pre-invasion human communications panel.

'Let me use your scales, Masako,' Marque said. 'I'll send a message back to myself – communication by scales is so low-tech that not even they can hack into it. All right, the terminal's ready to go. I'm removing myself from the area. If you need me, contact me through scales. I am so sorry, honoured click.' The sphere disintegrated.

The bubble of methane around Rapclick popped, and methane burst from its exoskeleton with a horrible scream. It collapsed in a heap as its legs snapped under the higher gravity. Masako ran to it and folded it out.

They'd probably have to restore the click from its soulstone, as its body was dead. I moved to the terminal and worked through the interface. The terminal had basic communication functions and did everything we needed.

'Can you open a channel to the cats?' Blake said.

'Yes,' I said. 'Channel's open.' The cat leader appeared as a two-dimensional image above the table.

'Now let's start moving your people back to your home system,' Blake said.

'Start with the fleet near the dragon homeworld,' the cat leader said.

'Very well,' Blake said. 'You can send our injured up to us to care for—'

'Mention the hostages again and sixty-four of them will die,' the cat leader said. 'You will have them back when the ships are returned.'

4

'That's the last one?' Admiral Blake said. His eyes were bloodshot and his face unshaven; we'd been co-ordinating the transfer of the cat ships for four days straight with minimal sleep. He blinked at the display of the dumb terminal.

'That's all of them. Wait.' Masako listened to her scales. 'Yes. We're done.'

'Choumali,' he said.

I nodded. 'Channel's open to the cat leader.'

'We've done what you asked. We're sending dragons down to collect our people,' Blake said.

'No,' the cat leader said. 'If we see a dragon on our planet, sixty-four of your people will die.'

'I understand. No dragons,' Blake said. 'So how do we collect our people?'

'Wait,' the cat said.

'We need a time frame—' Blake said, but the cat interrupted him.

'You will have your people back when we are satisfied that you will not attack us,' the leader said.

'How long?' Admiral Blake said.

'As long as necessary,' the leader said.

'As *necessary*?' Blake said, but the leader interrupted him.

'We have two dragon scales. We will contact you when we are ready to transfer the humans. Leave this system and cat space.'

'Some of the hostages are injured. Hand them over to us, and we can care for them without straining your resources.'

'No,' the cat said.

'Then we would like to give you some potatoes as a thank you gift,' Blake said.

The cat bared its teeth. 'Stop trying to open negotiations. This is not negotiable. Leave. If you are not out of this system immediately, we will kill humans.'

'You removed their soulstones,' I said, trying to buy time with the first ridiculous reason I could think of. 'Allow us to provide our people with new ones.'

The cat leader hesitated, looked away, then turned back to the screen. 'That may be acceptable.'

Both of us were silenced for a moment at the unexpected response, then Blake quickly recovered.

'We can provide as many soulstones as you want,' he said. 'You can fit them on yourselves as well—'

The cat hissed and flattened its ears.

'Or not,' he said.

'We will permit you to provide new stones for the humans,' it said, its ears still flat.

'We'll have to bring some people down to implant them ...'

It waved us away. 'We can do that. We understand the process. You may provide the stones, but a dragon is not to bring them.' Its ears flicked forward again. 'Choumali is to bring them.'

'That is not possible,' Blake said.

'Then the stones will not be fitted to your people, and any who die will be dead for good.'

'I'll bring them,' I said.

'You personally,' the cat said to me.

I nodded. 'I will.'

'Alone and unarmed.'

'Choumali ...' Blake said.

'Let's build some goodwill, sir,' I said. *I know more about the cats than any human,* I added telepathically. *Let's put this knowledge to good use.*

'Guarantee her safety. You threatened her earlier,' Blake said to the cat.

'She will not be harmed,' the cat said. 'You may bring stones, then return to the ship and leave this system. We will tell you when you can return and collect your people.'

'They gave us surface co-ordinates,' I said. 'I assume that means we can land.'

'Wonderful. No dragons, no Marque, no backup,' he said, and turned to Masako. 'We need something to carry her down. Do we have an alternate method for travelling short distances like this? Small craft?'

'I'll arrange for one to be manufactured and sent through with enough soulstones for everybody,' Masako said.

Blake lowered his voice. 'They'd better keep their word about not hurting you, Jian, or we will drop more than chilli on them.'

*

Two hours later Masako fetched a small craft – a box with an anti-grav drive on the bottom. She nosed the shuttle towards us, then folded next to us on the gallery of her ship.

'Here's your transport,' she said. 'I'll put you on it, and it will carry you down to the surface.'

'Good luck, Colonel,' Blake said, and saluted me.

I put my hand on Masako and she folded me into the shuttle. The interior was a single empty space, with one row of basic seats and the cases full of soulstones stacked inside. Enough soulstones for over a thousand people almost completely filled the shuttle.

I looked around. 'There's no helm?'

'No need,' she said. 'It knows the co-ordinates and it will take you there, and bring you back up when you tell it to. Take a seat and strap in; this isn't the most comfortable way to travel. Good luck, dear Jian, let's bring your people home.' She disappeared.

I deliberately didn't think about what was waiting for me as I strapped myself into the seat nearest the hatch. My stomach fell out as the ship moved. We had to get our people back, and David was down there.

I grew increasingly nervous about the whole stupid idea for the next hour of noisy shuddering as the shuttle descended. I had no view outside the shuttle, no weapons, and no idea what was waiting for me when I landed. I tried to relax and clear my mind, and was jolted out of my trance when the shuttle landed with a perceptible bump. I unhooked myself as the door opened and a blast of hot, dry air, full of grit, blew into the cabin. I went to the opening, feeling slightly higher gravity than I was accustomed to, and looked out.

The little ship was on a uniformly wide, flat platform that looked like textured white glass. The sun was setting and the lilac sky was reflected in its surface. The shuttle had landed close to the edge of the pad, and a magnificently blue lake to the left stretched to the horizon. The tan-coloured sand at the edge of the lake was damp where the water had evaporated and salt rimmed the periphery. The cat city filled the rest of the view from the edge of the lake to the horizon on the right. Most of the buildings were small, the human equivalent of five storeys or less, with uniformly ochre-coloured walls, polished to a metallic sheen that made the city appear to be constructed from a single lump of gold. The buildings were cylindrical, with dome-shaped tops, as wide as they were tall. Large, smooth, transparent stones, like black glass, ranging in size from twenty centimetres to more than three metres across were embedded in the walls. There were no windows, only the stones, and sections of complex decorative grillwork punched out of the burnished clay walls that probably guided and cooled the breeze through the buildings.

The cat leader and a small entourage were waiting for me and walked stiffly across the landing pad to the shuttle. They went past me into the shuttle, ignoring me, and I followed the leader as it opened one of the cases full of soulstones, pulled a stone out and held it up to the light.

'They're the real thing,' I said.

'I know they are,' the leader said. It gestured and said something in their own language, making me painfully aware of my reliance on Marque's translation ability. I'd been so accustomed to Marque's constant presence that I hadn't even made the effort to learn any alien languages. The rest of the cats came into the shuttle, collected some of the soulstone boxes, and took them out. The cat leader gestured for me to sit on one of the shuttle's chairs.

I didn't move, still standing near the hatch.

'Can I take our people now?' I said.

'No.'

'Even the injured ones? How about the youngest—'

'No.'

'Can I see my son?'

The other cats re-entered the shuttle and collected more stones.

The cat leader sat sprawling over the chairs, but its emotions didn't match the casual body language; it was full of aggression towards me. It spoke in flawless Euro, with a cultured accent. 'Sit, Colonel Choumali. Let's discuss terms.'

I sat in one of the other chairs. 'We transported all your ships. You don't need to hold our people any more.'

'On the contrary, we can't trust you,' the cat said. 'The dragons have been invading other species for centuries. You say that they've stopped—'

'They have!' I said, interrupting.

One of the cats carrying the soulstones stopped and stared at me, then lowered its head and carried the box out. That was the last of them, and the shuttle was empty.

'Do not interrupt me,' the cat leader said.

I raised my hand. 'I understand.'

'We will implant the soulstones into your people, and then they will be our guests while the stones become attuned. We would like to observe the process, so we will hold—'

'That's five years!' I said.

Its ears went flat. 'I had not finished speaking.'

I raised my hand again. 'I apologise.'

'They will stay with us while the stones are attuned. They will be our insurance against dragon aggression – although the dragons are so destructive, it may not be enough. We will study how the stones work, and your people will learn our ways. At the end of the attunement process, they will be free to leave here and return to the Dragon Empire.'

'Why do you want to see how attunement works?'

'To prove to our people that it doesn't work,' he said.

I knew he was wrong, because I'd sensed the nature of the entity that inhabited the body when the stone was attached – even when the body was different, the soul was the same. But arguing with the cat was a waste of time.

Instead I said, 'Five years is a very long time.'

It waved one hand. 'Not when you're effectively immortal.'

I didn't have much bargaining power, so I followed my diplomatic training – agree to their terms and hope that they could be negotiated down later. The diplomatic training didn't cover one painful aspect of the situation.

'Can I see my son before I leave?' I said.

It stretched its arms across the back of the seat. 'I don't know, can I see mine?'

It did have the same colour fur and eyes as Oliver – the resemblance was uncanny, and I kicked myself for not seeing it sooner. He was Oliver's father.

'He's your son? I didn't know. He's well and happy ...'

'Ever since you killed his mother and took my son, I've been making extensive study of your language and customs. I am the most human-aware cat anywhere.'

'I appreciate that,' I said. 'Your grasp of our language is masterful.'

He stopped and stared at me. 'You're not deliberately insulting me, are you? It's all by accident.'

'No, of course not,' I said, bewildered. 'I want to work with you as equals and hopefully one day friends.'

'There it is again. Maybe you should stay with us and learn our ways, so that nobody shoots you for the insult you give.'

'Maybe I should,' I said ruefully.

'Our first-born are living copies of ourselves,' he said. 'They are biologically identical to the parent.'

'What we call clones?' I said.

'Yes.' He leaned towards me and spoke with quiet vehemence. 'When we die, we move to the body of the copy – the child. By taking my son, you have effectively sentenced me to what you so coyly call the Real Death.'

'How do you move to the body of the child?' I said suspiciously.

'I tell him the stories of my past lives as he lives beside me.'

'That's *it*?' I said with disbelief. 'You talk to him, and then you die, and everybody treats him as if he is *you*?'

'Precisely.'

'That's not very scientific.'

'Nothing scientific about it. We are the sum of our memories. As long as he has my memories and my biological structure, I will live on.'

'Soulstones—'

He gestured dismissively towards the stone in my forehead as he interrupted me – obviously the rule about interruption only worked one way. 'Those things don't work. They're a ... what's the word? Scam. The dragons just write the memory in a different body, and then treat it as if it is the same person. Our way is better – the body and the memories live on.' He bared his teeth in a flash, then his face became mild again. 'I want my life back. Return my immortality to me – return my son.'

'Give us back our people, and I'll talk to Oliver about it.'

'No. How about ...' He stopped moving and studied me. 'Your son for mine?'

'They're both my sons,' I said.

'Then they are brothers and he will have no problem taking David's place,' the cat said. 'He's been trying to spy on us for years. This is his opportunity to infiltrate us.'

'Let me talk to Oliver,' I said. 'There's a good chance he'll agree, he wants to learn about your culture.'

'Do not refer to him as Oliver! You should refer to him as ...' He bared his teeth again, and this time amusement radiated from him. 'Your flat mouth can't say it, can you?'

'No. Giving him a name in my language is honouring him.'

'No, it isn't,' he snapped. He rose. 'Go now. You know how to communicate with us.' He walked out of the shuttle, then stopped and turned on the landing ramp. 'You are the only non-cat who is permitted on this planet. If any other alien species attempt to land, or if a dragon attempts to fold here, humans will die. I want my son returned within two of your days. As soon as the exchange has taken place, I want that dragon ship out of our space, and all of you gone.' He walked away.

*

The shuttle took me back up to Masako's ship, where Oliver was already waiting with his new dragon partner, Runa, talking to Blake and Masako.

'The shuttle relayed everything you said,' Oliver said. 'I'm ready to go down.'

'I don't think that's a good idea,' I said.

'Of course it's a good idea!' he said. 'We can't miss this opportunity. My father will give me a complete oral history of every generation since the first time they cloned themselves. The information is invaluable.' He turned to Admiral Blake. 'Tell her!'

'I can't force either of you to do anything,' Blake said. 'This is a decision only the two of you can make.'

'Please let him,' Masako said. 'We need our people back.'

'I'm going down to spend time with that black cat,' Oliver said.

'That black cat is your father—' I said.

'So he won't hurt me,' Oliver said. 'He'll care for me exceptionally well, because he thinks I'm *him*. I'll get the rest of the hostages out ... including *David ...*'

I winced. Both of us would do anything to get David out.

'And move them home safely, and at the same time I'll learn more about the cats than we have at any time in the past. We don't know anything about their nanotechnology, or how they're disabling Marque.' He approached me and put his hand on my arm. 'What if he's a leader on their planet, Mum? What if he's the *king* or something? When he dies, I inherit everything he has, including his identity. We could shut down their bullshit once and for all.'

'What if they brainwash you against us?'

He looked into my eyes, his own bright green ones the same as the cat leader's. 'Do you really think that's possible? You raised me better than that, Mum.'

I sighed and looked away. 'He wants to hold the hostages for five years, until their stones are re-attuned. He wants to study the soulstone attunement process.'

'That makes sense,' he said. He tapped his forehead. 'If they give our people back, I'll let them study mine.'

'Oliver ...' I was running out of objections, and I didn't want to lose my son. My second son.

'Let him go, Colonel,' Runa said. 'I can fold in and contact him telepathically. I will fold into orbit above the planet, talk to him, relay for him, and fold out again without the cats knowing. This is the chance we've been looking for.'

'What do the dragon higher-ups say?'

'I'm speaking to my mother right now,' Masako said. 'We both agree with him. Having someone on the ground to provide us with intelligence would be invaluable.'

I made a gesture of helplessness. 'Five years is a long time to be apart. I'll miss you so much!'

'He said you're the only one allowed on the planet, and I'll make sure you can visit,' Oliver said. He pulled me into a fierce hug. 'I love you, Mum, and I'll be back in no time.' He turned to Runa, and she took two-legged form. He went to her and put his hand on her face. 'I love you. I'll come back for you.'

'I know you will,' she said.

They rubbed cheeks, then she folded him onto the shuttle.

I flopped to sit on a sofa in the gallery. I'd just lost my second son to the cats.

'You'd better be safe down there,' I said to the shuttle as it drifted down towards the surface.

'Don't worry, he's very capable,' Masako said, studying the shuttle as it descended towards the surface. Runa folded back and stood with us.

It seemed an eternity and I was pacing up and down the gallery of Masako's ship with impatience when Runa spoke.

'The shuttle's on its way back up.'

I went to the window and watched as the shuttle – a tiny, fragile box – grew from a dot and approached the ship. It came next to Masako's ship and stopped.

Runa disappeared, and reappeared with David. I ran to him as she placed him gently on the floor. His face was a mass of bruises, one eye swollen shut, and his soulstone was gone. The air filled with the horrible smell of charred flesh – they'd cut his legs off, and cauterised the stumps.

He didn't attempt to communicate. He seemed to be unconscious.

'The cats are firing up a surface-based cannon,' Marque said. 'I suggest we leave.'

'Has Oliver tapped his scale?' I said.

'He sent a human symbol – a check mark. I assume that means he's okay,' Runa said as Masako folded to the outside of the ship and took us back to dragon space.

*

I paced in the gallery of Masako's ship as Marque worked on David. We were parked over the temporary dragon sanctuary world that had been used as a residence when the dragon homeworld had been evacuated. Now that the threat of the cat fleet was gone, dragon ships were folding in and out as residents returned to their homes. Masako had folded Admiral Blake to a meeting with the Empress to update her on the situation.

'You put the soulstone in?' I asked Marque. 'It's in?'

'It's in.'

I sighed with relief and rubbed my forehead where my own soulstone sat. 'What about brain damage?'

'None that I can detect, but psychological damage is a definite possibility. He was new to military action, and this experience will have severely affected him. I think they cut off his legs without anaesthetic.'

My stomach roiled with nausea. 'Can you remove the memory of them cutting off his legs?'

'Not until I can move him into a new body – and I can't do that until his soulstone is attuned.'

'So he'll be suffering psychologically for five years. Can you give him new legs?'

'I've already started growing replacements for him.'

'That will take six weeks. What will we do in the meantime?'

'I'll work something out.'

Runa folded onto the ship with Dianne and Victor, and I ran to them, enveloping them in huge hugs. Victor had taken advantage of dragon biotechnology to make himself more muscular with better skin; his chronic acne was no longer a nuisance. Dianne had kept her soft, round and slightly overweight body shape, much to my delight. She was gorgeous just the way she was, and I was glad she'd made the choice to keep her body birth-natural. Many humans had rushed to make themselves supermodel-attractive when we'd been accepted into the Empire; Victor and Dianne had chosen to be younger, like my mother, but hadn't gone that far.

'Where is he?' Dianne said as they pulled back from the hugs.

'Marque has him in the medlevel. He's in the table, unconscious.'

'If I bring him out of it he'll be in a lot of pain, so I'm keeping him under until I have the nerve damage under control,' Marque said.

'Can we see him anyway?' Victor said.

'This way,' Marque said, and we followed a sphere to the centre of the deck, then descended to the med room. The table was opaque, so Marque made it translucent. Dianne and Victor leaned over it, studying David where he lay in the liquid, his face serene.

'We'll stay with him,' Dianne said.

Marque provided them with chairs, and they sat next to the table.

'How's Shiumo?' Dianne asked me without looking away from David. 'I heard she was injured.'

'In a coma,' I said. 'The blood loss damaged both her brains.'

'Can't Marque fix it?' Victor said.

'It's quite severe, I don't know if she's still in there,' Marque said. 'I've put a soulstone on her, and I'm keeping her in a table on life-support. We'll know in five years, when I move the stone to a new body.'

'That's awful,' Dianne said.

'Take me back up to the gallery,' I said. 'I need to speak to Admiral Blake.'

Dianne and Victor didn't seem to notice when I left the room. All their attention was on David.

'The Admiral is too far away for a hologram,' Marque said when I was back on the gallery. 'Is over comms enough?'

'Yes.'

'Let me see if I can connect with him for you – there.'

'I just had an update on Baxter; I hope he'll be okay,' Blake said through Marque. 'Have we heard anything more from Oliver?'

'No. He just sent that "check mark" symbol and hasn't touched the scale since.' My throat thickened. 'I hope he's all right.'

'I'm sure he will be: he's one of them. Come in, and we'll work out the plan from here.'

'Permission to speak, Admiral,' I said.

'Colonel?'

'I resign my commission with immediate effect,' I said. 'We're taking my son to his other parents' home, and we'll all help him heal.'

Blake hesitated, then said, 'Good luck, Jian. Your resignation is accepted, and if you ever want to rejoin the forces I'll personally accept you. We'll still need a full report on your final interaction with the cats to supplement the shuttle's recordings. Can you work on that while you help your son?'

'Of course, sir, that information's vital,' I said. 'I'll vacate my house on Barracks as soon as my son is settled and we have his pain managed.'

'With the losses we just suffered, there's really no need,' he said. 'It's unlikely there'll be anyone to replace you. Stay as long as you want. You know resources are close to unlimited in the Empire – and if your son Oliver is successful in his mission, the cat attacks will stop. We will finally have peace.'

'Thank you, sir.'

'Damn fine off—' he said before the communication stopped.

'Can you hang around and help us take him back to Victor and Dianne's house?' I asked Runa. 'My mother will probably want to help as well.'

'Of course,' Runa said. 'He's Oliver's brother. Where do you want me to take him?'

'Marque will show you, but before you do that – Marque, I need to contact Richard Alto.'

'A moment,' Marque said. 'He's too far away: he and Echi are touring one of the outer galaxies. You'll have to send a message by scales.'

'Please outline David's injuries to him, tell him the situation with Oliver ...' I hesitated. 'Is that classified?'

'Yes,' Marque said. 'There's been no announcement. The whole situation is classified, and the dragons and human officers are working together on a press release.'

'Tell him the situation with Oliver anyway, eyes only, and ask him if he can meet us at Victor and Dianne's place. We're going to need his assistance to help David through this.'

'He's on his way.'

I turned to Runa. 'Any word from Oliver?'

'No.'

My heart fell. 'Let me know the *second* he taps that scale.'

5

It may have been fifteen years since Earth had joined the Dragon Empire, but New Birmingham hadn't changed much. The original city, perched on the hills, appeared the same, the buildings drab and aged. Shiny new buildings had been erected with Marque's help where the water had receded: spacious white and pale blue residences with well-tended gardens, and clusters of office towers surrounded by parkland. The roads in the city were gradually changing to gardens as everybody used Marque as a transport method. Cars were no longer necessary.

Dianne and Victor were still in the same townhouse that they'd lived in while she was doing postdoctoral research. The road in front of it had already been converted to gardens. Runa folded us directly into David's bedroom, and I was hit with the smell of the place, which filled me with so many memories – like most older houses in Britain, it smelled faintly of damp, with an underlying vague sense of cabbage.

Marque placed David into a specially-constructed medical table in the centre of the bedroom and we stood around it, breathless, as we waited for Marque to stabilise him completely and bring him out of it.

'Let me know if you need me, I'm going to wait at the edge of cat space for Oliver to contact me,' Runa said, and disappeared.

The white liquid on the table receded, and it changed to a hospital bed. David was still unconscious, his legs just stumps, but at least now they appeared pink and healthy instead of burnt. Marque covered him with a blanket and he opened his eyes.

'What happened?' His dark brows creased. 'Did we win?'

Dianne threw herself at him and hugged him fiercely. He looked around at us, and appeared even more confused. He tried to move, and the room filled with his panic. 'Who took my legs?' He thrashed his stumps as he tried to lift himself.

Victor and I held him in place, one arm each.

'I'll restrain him,' Marque said.

'No!' we all said in unison.

'Stay still, David,' I said. 'You were injured. You lost your legs. The cats ...'

David screamed and threw himself back. The scream petered out to gasping sobs. He cried for a while, sobbing uncontrollably, and we held him.

'Why did they do that? How could they do that?' he shouted. 'They're *animals*!' He looked around at us. 'Mum? Both my mums. Dad. Nanna?' He gasped and looked over my shoulder behind me. 'And Marque.'

I turned to see that Marque had taken its nanny android form, a portly woman in her mid-fifties, that it had used when it was caring for David as a child.

'You're all here.' David rubbed his hands over his short hair. 'Okay. I have it. Sorry.'

'Nothing to be sorry about,' I said.

'That was awful,' he said. 'I've never been so scared. And then they—' He choked. 'It was like being in a nightmare where you know something terrible is about to happen, and then they come up to you with a red-hot knife and—' His voice petered out again. 'I want those memories *gone*.'

'Next body transfer,' Marque said from the nanny. 'We need to reattune your stone.'

'What about my legs?' David said.

'Six weeks and I'll have new ones for you.'

'I know that,' David said. 'What about in the meantime?' He looked up at me. 'Prosthetics like Richard's?'

'Richard's on his way. He knows more about what happened to you than any of us.'

David took my hand and squeezed it. 'Good idea. He will understand.' He looked around. 'Where's Ollie?' He saw my face. 'No. He's dead? No.' His expression filled with understanding. 'He swapped himself for me, didn't he? The black cat that did this ...' He waved his hand over the stumps. 'Said that Oliver is his son. Is that true? That *bastard* is our darling Ollie's biological dad?'

'Afraid so,' I said.

'Ollie's going to kill him when he finds out what his father did to me,' David said with grim pleasure. 'Wish I could be there.'

'Richard's at the front door with his dragonscales daughter,' Marque said.

'Go, let him in,' David said. He appeared to be cheering up and working his way out of the initial panic – the reassurance of having us all there was working. 'I haven't seen Echilarghian in forever.'

'That's her name?' Victor said. 'Is that Welsh?'

'Dragon,' Richard said as he came in. He shook everybody's hands and hugged me. He hugged David as well, then pulled back. 'You'll be fine, David. We can talk.'

Richard's daughter entered the room behind him, accompanied by a red dragon. All of us in the little townhouse's bedroom was a crush. Echilarghian was typical of the human dragonscales hybrids; taller than an average human, breathtakingly attractive in an androgynous manner with red scales on her temples that indicated her half-dragon heritage shining against her dark skin. She was only fifteen, but already appeared twenty-five. Her red scales were the same colour as the dragon's next to her.

'This is Eri,' Richard said, indicating the dragon. 'She's Echi's half-sister. Shiumo is dragonfather to both of them.'

'I'm sorry for your loss,' I said.

'Shiumo's dead too?' David said.

'She's in a coma,' I said. 'We won't know for a while if she'll be okay.'

'Everybody out now,' Marque said from the nanny body. 'He needs to rest. I'm going to mildly sedate him for a few hours then you can come back and talk to him. You can sit with him in shifts if you like, but only one at a time. Too many of you is stressing him out and he needs a calm, quiet environment to recover.' She shooed us with both hands. 'Out.'

'I'll take first shift,' Victor said, and sat next to David.

'I'll be next,' Dianne said, and kissed him on the forehead.

David reclined and his eyes closed, his face relaxing into sleep.

'Out,' Marque said, and the nanny body disintegrated.

We all trundled downstairs to the living room and sat on the couches. Dianne and I went into the kitchen and made tea for everybody. I took the tea into the living room and poured. Dianne didn't have a dragon-sized cup for Eri, so we gave her a soup bowl.

Richard sipped his tea and closed his eyes. 'Why is it always better on Earth? Is it the water?' He opened his eyes. 'I saw what happened to Shiumo, it was awful.'

'We had so many losses that we're only just catching up with them all,' I said. 'I had an excellent relationship with Fumi, my assigned transport, and now she's ...' I wiped my eyes as the words wouldn't come.

'A high price for peace,' Echi said. 'Dragonfathers are usually forever. You never think you'll lose a dragon parent. And so many are gone. We're lucky that Shiumo has hope for recovery.'

'The funerals are next week,' Eri said. 'We'll hold the ceremony on Dragonhome. The folding nexus above the planet is queued back for days as people return. We haven't lost this many dragons in centuries. Normally a dragon's Real Death is by choice; they end their days surrounded by loved ones, and the clan succession is known by all. Some of the dragons – Shiumo included – didn't believe that they could really be killed in this conflict. We need to work out the succession ourselves.' She lowered her head, and Echi patted her shoulder. 'The first time in history more than two clans need new leaders – fifty-three of them lost their heads. I'm glad the cats have agreed to a ceasefire until the stones are attuned; it's chaos on Dragonhome.' She raised her head as if she was looking at David in his bedroom above us. 'I just hope the rest of the hostages haven't been treated the same way as dear David.'

My mother came in with the kettle and refilled the tea pot, then sat with her cup.

'I believe congratulations are in order, Connie,' Richard said to her. 'When are you due?'

She stared at him for a long moment, broadcasting a mix of outrage and amusement. She glanced at me, then at Dianne, then back at Richard. 'What the hell are you talking about?'

'Well Marque told me you were in a relationship with a dragon, and that you're ... on privacy,' he said.

She scowled. 'I'm on privacy because it's none of anyone's damn business.' She put the cup on the coffee table. 'No, I'm not pregnant, and I'm not planning to be any time soon.'

I felt a weird combination of relief and disappointment – I'd thought I really had a little sister coming.

'I'm far too busy on a private project,' she said. 'I put Marque on privacy because I didn't want anyone to know about it, but I suppose I can share with you if you don't tell anyone else.'

'What secret project?' Richard said, fascinated.

'You know our restaurant charges exorbitant amounts for our artisanal potatoes,' Mum said. 'We've made a fortune.' She looked up. 'Put an image above the teapot, Marque.'

A floating three-dimensional image of the Earth – as it had been before the climate went to hell – appeared above the coffee table.

'That's not the Earth,' Mum said. 'We're building a whole planetary system identical to the Earth system, with a planet Earth as it would be if people had never appeared. A testament to how beautiful it was before we wrecked it.'

'What, all the animals, the ecosystem ...' My voice trailed off. 'If it's going to work you'll have to go down to bacteria.'

'That's right,' she said, nodding. 'The planet's built and we've introduced single-cell organisms and simple marine species into the oceans. We're ready to start putting plants onto the landmasses.'

'Some of the marine animals were extinct, and I had to genetically engineer recreations based on what you had left,' Marque said. 'Working backwards from the description of the lifeform to the fabrication of the DNA took a massive amount of processing power. Now that the cat fleet is gone, I can dedicate more time to the project, and maybe even replace the planet's moon with an instance of myself to monitor it more closely. I've never done anything like this before.' It lowered its voice. 'It's very rewarding.'

'You are an inspiration, Connie,' Richard said with awe.

'Have you been helping, Dianne?' I said.

'I never knew anything about it,' Dianne said. 'Why keep it such a secret?'

'Because people are people and we don't want them camping out on our pristine hard work,' Mum said. 'I don't think anyone could resist the urge to see an extinct animal, so we've hidden the location and the knowledge is under privacy seal.'

'Can I help now that I know about it?' Dianne asked.

'You definitely have skills that fit the requirements.' Mum looked up. 'Marque?'

'That would be a great help,' Marque said with enthusiasm. 'Your knowledge will be extremely useful. It would be great to have an academic to answer questions rather than searching your databases all the time.'

'I may be able to have some of my colleagues answer your questions without them knowing what the project is,' Dianne said. 'This is a wonderful thing you're doing, Connie.'

'You never cease to amaze me, Mum,' I said. I grinned. 'Any chance I could see it?'

'No, and nobody else will, either,' she said. 'It's strictly human-hands-off, that's the point.'

'We've toured some of the most spectacular places in the Empire, but I think this one will be the most beautiful,' Richard said.

'So life's treating you well?' I asked him.

He smiled. 'When I travelled with Shiumo, I only saw what she wanted me to see. Now that I'm travelling with Echi and Eri, I'm seeing much more of the Empire – the seven galaxies have wonders that you wouldn't believe.'

'Eri's introducing us to the best oxygen-water locations,' Echi said. 'As well as some others that are inhospitable but gorgeous.'

'We've been ribbon-skating and fluoro-diving and toured the iridium-rich gas giant that everybody talks about. It's like floating in a work of art.'

'Now that the cat attack's been stopped, you can do that too, Colonel,' Eri said. 'We're free from their menace, and we finally have peace.'

I stopped at that; in all the rush it hadn't dawned on me – the cats were back in their home system, and it would take them years to approach the Dragon Empire again.

'We're not completely free from their menace,' I said. 'We still need to rescue the human hostages ... and Oliver.'

'As soon as Oliver gives the word, we can find our humans, bring them home, and never have to worry again,' Eri said. 'I hope he contacts Runa soon.'

'I sincerely hope so.'

*

The funerals for the dead dragons and humans were held in one big ceremony, dragon-style, on Dragonhome. The entire Imperial complex, the square, Parliament and Palace buildings, had been changed from white to brown. Brown banners hung from the buildings and even the leaves on the trees were brown. Brown was the colour of mourning among dragons; it was the colour formed when the blood from their three circulatory systems – red, green and blue – mixed. Some of us humans chose to wear black or white in memory of our own who had died, but most of the other species wore either brown clothing or, if they didn't wear clothing, draped themselves in brown ribbons and banners.

A procession wended its way through the entire length of Sky City, all ten kilometres of it. The Empress herself led the procession, accompanied by her fifteen current spouses and several goldenscales servants, all decked out in brown. The bodies of the fallen humans had already been interred on Earth, and dragons and humans carried symbolic banners, each with the abstract motif of the face of their dead on it.

I didn't join the procession; it was for senior representatives of member planets, and those who had lost close family members. I was one of the lucky ones. I joined the crowd and watched it from the side of the square between Parliament and the Imperial Palace where Marque had constructed an enormous holographic stage to transmit proceedings.

Silence fell over the square as the Empress entered. Her head was covered in a brown cloth, secured with rough twine under her chin. She was accompanied by the human ambassador, Charles Maxwell, who wore a black pantsuit. The procession went through the middle of the square and the hologram blinked out when the Empress reached it. They walked up to the Palace and Marque lifted them onto a podium attached to the veranda surrounding the Palace complex. The Ambassador and Empress stood at the front, with the other dignitaries seated behind them. The Empress' spouses arrayed themselves behind them and the goldenscales servants took position at the back with their heads bowed. The Imperial Guard in their blue and silver livery stationed themselves around the podium to watch the crowd.

We had to move to the edge of the square so that everyone holding a banner had room to fit. Marque recreated the holographic image of the Empress above our heads.

'Dearest loved ones,' she said. 'We have lost so much. It has been centuries since so many have died the Real Death in one place. Normally the Real Death is a conscious, loving choice; surrounded by family and those close to our hearts, we depart this world in peace. This was a violent destruction of so many lives, particularly the humans, who have only begun to share the benefits of Empire membership.'

The entire square was completely silent. Nobody moved.

Ambassador Maxwell stepped forward to be next to the Empress. 'Humans and dragons worked together to defend the Empire, and both sides have lost many loved ones. Humanity mourns its loss and acknowledges the courage of our soldiers who fought so bravely.' She seemed to focus on me from across the square. 'We will find a way to bring the rest of them home.'

'Go now and mourn your dead,' the Empress said. 'Each of us has our own way to treasure the memories of those we have lost. I grieve with you, dear subjects, and sincerely hope that we can retrieve our beloved human citizens from the cats – and have peace finally reign in the Galaxies.'

She bowed her head and stepped back. Everybody holding a banner rolled it up and stood quietly.

Marque filled the square with a single crystalline chime that reverberated through the air for a long time. When it finally faded to nothing, people started to move around, some hugging each other and weeping.

'Jian,' Marque said above me.

'Yes?'

'The Empress would like to speak with you. Do you mind going up?'

'What? Me?' I stuttered. 'Why me?'

'Because of Oliver, and the cats, and you being the one that knows the most about them,' Marque said. 'It may also be something to do with you being the only one they'll let on their planet. A few things that make you uniquely qualified.'

'I resigned,' I said.

'From the Empire altogether?' Marque said.

I studied the crowd between me and the Empress' Palace. 'It will take me forty-five minutes to get there.'

'I'll carry you.'

I made a soft sound of exasperation as Marque lifted me above the crowd.

'At least make me invisible so I'm not a spectacle,' I said.

'You are,' Marque said.

I sailed over the heads of the crowd. Other humans enjoyed being carried by Marque, feeling as if they were flying. I hated it, I was too high up and there was nothing under my feet. Oliver said it was because I was old. He was probably right.

Marque dropped me on the podium; Ambassador Maxwell had just left, and the dragons were preparing to return to the Palace.

'Thank you for coming, Jian,' the Empress said, and I bowed to her. 'Come into my salon. I have something to ask you.'

I followed her inside her Palace to the entry hall. The ceiling was four metres above us, and one wall was made up of windows overlooking the square, letting the brilliant blue-white sunshine into the hall. Her assistants and spouses dispersed, leaving us with one goldenscales servant and a couple of Imperial Guards who escorted us through the main hall towards her private apartments.

We rounded a corner to find Princess Masako in her two-legged form, pinning Prince Haruka with his back against the wall. They were passionately kissing, their hands roaming each other. He was wearing a striking black and brown kimono of many floating layers in feminine style with a wide obi – a hot trend among the fashionable young men of New Nippon. He'd even had his long hair dyed brown to match, the first time I'd seen it a natural-looking colour – he usually wore it green to highlight his green dragon scales. They broke apart when they heard us approaching.

'Completely inappropriate on a day of mourning,' the Empress said crisply. 'Take it somewhere else, you two.'

Haruka and Masako bowed to her, obviously mortified, and hurried out through one of the side doors.

The Empress took me into her private office. It was three times normal human size, with a mat for her to recline on behind her massive white and silver desk. Marque was a floating column in one corner, four metres high and a metre wide, a tube of swirling liquid in silver and white to match the decor. A couple of the Imperial Guards stood on either side of the door and I nodded to the captain, Shudo. He nodded back.

'Tea, Kana,' she said, and her goldenscales servant scurried away to make it for her.

She moved behind the desk and sat on her hind legs, then shifted some papers around.

'The Imperial Guard are a democratic order. They choose their own members, inviting prospective guards themselves,' she said. 'The current Captain of the Guard has just had the equivalent of grandchildren, and it is his duty to care for them. He's leaving the guard and they need to choose a new leader.'

'This is why I'm here?' I said, incredulous. 'You want me to join your guard to fill the empty space when someone moves up to replace him?'

She eyed me over the desk, her bright blue eyes piercing. She pulled off the brown cloth that was draped over her head and tossed it onto the desk. 'No. *My guard* want you to join my guard.'

'Why ...' I said, then waved it away. 'Cats. Obviously.'

'Loyalty and bravery under fire are part of it, Jian,' Captain Shudo said from his station next to the door.

I turned to speak to him. 'You are a little pink bastard. Congratulations. How many babies?'

'They'll be born in six weeks or so, I'm already producing milk,' he said, grinning to reveal three sharp rows of purple teeth. 'It's a really big litter, nine of the little pink bastards according to the scans. Come and visit when they're born.'

'I will. I'll miss our drinking sessions; you're about the only one I know who can take alcohol with me.'

'Save it for when the babies are weaned, we'll toast our lost comrades in arms,' he said.

'It's a date.' I turned to the Empress. 'So who's the new captain?'

'The guard themselves vote to decide the new captain,' the Empress said, sounding exasperated. 'I have no say in it.'

'They voted for you,' the captain said. 'I didn't even put them up to it. They've seen that cat son of yours around the Palace for a year, and you've done such magic with him that they want you at the Empress' back in case the cats attack again – and at her back anyway if there's peace. You know the cats' psyche inside-out.'

'Please say you'll do it, ma'am,' said the other guard – a squat scaled reptile on eight legs inside a bubble of higher gravity.

'I just resigned from the military to spend time with my son. My broken son,' I said.

'You have six weeks before I leave,' Captain Shudo said. 'Plenty of time to learn what's involved. It's really not difficult; it's mostly looking angry and stomping around.'

'I believe you are an expert at that,' the Empress said mildly, studying the papers on her desk.

'Are you sure there isn't someone more qualified who's already a member of the guard?'

'Plenty of them are at least as qualified as you,' the captain said. 'But they're all a bunch of lazy bastards who won't do paperwork to save their lives. We need to keep a journal of any security incidents among the royal family. For these guys,' he grinned over his shoulder at the other guard, 'it's too much damn work.'

'Well it is,' the other guard said.

'You are a stickler for paperwork, Ms Choumali,' the Empress said, still studying the papers. She pushed aside a couple of documents that appeared to be written in blood on the tanned skins of rats, and lifted an orange leaf with glyphs burned into it. 'Record-keeping is absolutely vital in preparing strategies for the future, particularly with the cats' ability to disable Marque.' She glanced up at me, still holding the leaf. 'I think they're right, and you're the best one for the job.'

'Go and think about it for six weeks,' Captain Shudo said. 'And when you've decided, come and join us.'

'We really need you, Jian Choumali,' the other guard said.

'I'll think about it; ask me again in a year or so,' I said, determined not to let them talk me into it. 'By your leave, Majesty.'

'No need for formality, Jian,' the Empress said. She waved one claw over the desk. 'Now go and see Charlie Maxwell. She wants to debrief you about your poor son.'

I bowed again. 'Majesty.' I turned and walked out, doubly determined not to let them talk me into this. As a citizen of the Empire my needs would be met regardless of whether I wanted to engage in formal employment or not. I had a son to look after and, when he'd recovered, another son to rescue.

6

I walked the hundred metres from the Empress' Palace through the gardens and wide thoroughfares of the Embassy district. The Earth Embassy was a stately neo-Grecian styled mansion, sitting in a decorative garden of Earth plants that was surrounded by a high wall. The building and the wall around it changed from brown to white as I watched, the garden also changing from brown to Earth-natural green. A couple of human guards in blue and green livery were stationed at the compound's entrance gate, and nodded to me when I arrived.

'I was here three weeks ago, and the Embassy was a Japanese-style multi-storey castle,' I said.

'We shifted from Asia to Euroterre last month,' the guard said.

'Does the interior stay the same?'

He grinned. 'No, everything inside moves around as well. America is a sprawling single-storey compound, a royal pain in the ass to secure.' He opened the gate for me. 'Come on in, Colonel – I mean Ms – Choumali.'

He took me into the marble-floored entry hall, decorated in lavish European style with gilt trimming, and guided me up the grand staircase. We went through a couple of reception halls to a smaller office with an imposing desk and a wall covered by book cases holding paper books with leather covers, some of them obviously extremely old. An antique globe of the Earth – at least a metre across – sat in a special cradle in the middle of the room, surrounded by a holographic display of the different types of Earth's potatoes.

'Jian. So good to see you.' The Ambassador shook my hand, then gestured to one side. 'Through here. Ronnie wants to say hello.' She hadn't changed at all; dragon rejuvenation techniques meant that she could choose to appear any age, and she chose to remain in her mid-fifties with short greying blonde hair.

'I'd love to see Veronica again,' I said as I followed the Ambassador into her private apartments. The rooms here were smaller and more modern, comfortably furnished and not nearly as imposing. We entered the living room where Ambassador Maxwell's dragonscales granddaughter, Veronica, was sitting on a rug with a very small baby dragon – barely a metre long – with bright blue scales. Both of them were surrounded by a collection of toys that would suit a five-year-old child.

'Hi, Ronnie,' I said with pleasure.

Veronica rose and came to me, giving me a hug. 'Jian. So good to see you.' She pulled back to study my face. 'It's awful, isn't it? Mummy's one of them.'

'We'll get her back, Ronnie,' the Ambassador said gruffly.

'Linda was in the attack?' I said.

The Ambassador nodded. 'She's one of the hostage humans.'

'I'm sorry, I didn't know,' I said.

'She didn't have a banner with her face on it. She's alive.'

'Is this Jian?' the dragon said.

'Yes, it is, Margie,' Veronica said. She smiled at me. 'This is my daughter, Margaret.'

The dragon bobbed her head. 'Pleased to meet you, Ms Choumali. Mummy says a lot about you, and I'm glad to finally meet you.'

'Remember when I hijacked you into starting this breeding program twenty-five years ago?' the Ambassador said. 'We succeeded. Not that it makes any difference now, but here's our success. Scales of a dragon, heart of a human, and ready to transport Earth's ships for us.'

'Inside, I feel human,' Margaret said. 'I want to find a way to clothe myself and spend most of my time on two legs so that I'm human on the outside too. I want to return to Earth – that is my real home.'

'I'm delighted to meet you as well, Margaret,' I said. 'I think I recognise those blue scales – is Narumi your dragonfather?'

'Yes, she is,' Margaret said, and lowered her head. 'Was.'

'Come into my private office, Ms Choumali,' the Ambassador said.

Her private office was full of clutter – high-security hardcopy papers and books, hand-written journals and holographic storage flats. She sat me on a couch to one side and pulled her chair out from behind the desk to sit across from me.

'Did the Empress offer you the position of Captain of the Imperial Guard?' she said.

'She did,' I said, not really surprised that she knew.

'Good. Please take it.'

'You want me to spy on her?'

'Oh, there's no need for that,' she said. 'She's quite open about who her agents are, and we are in return. Having a human as captain of her Guard will cement humanity's place as the principal defenders of the dragon administration. It's an extremely prestigious position, and whenever a captain steps down there's a squabble among species as to who will have the honour of replacing them.'

'I need to care for my human son and be ready to welcome my cat son home.'

'I understand completely. My own family is torn apart by loss – Narumi's dead, Linda's a hostage, and Shiumo's in a coma. We all need time to recover. But please consider the role when the grief is less raw.'

'I'll think about it.'

'Excellent. Stay for tea?'

'I'd prefer to head back to my family, ma'am.'

She nodded and her voice softened with compassion. 'Perfectly understandable. Give them my best wishes.'

*

I didn't delay the move from the Barracks planet to the empty townhouse next to Victor and Dianne. Most of the houses in their street were empty, the owners having moved to the new, larger, Marque-built housing on the reclaimed land. Victor and Dianne hadn't moved because Victor was in the middle of the David-and-Oliver sculpture in the back shed, but they planned to acquire a new, larger house on reclaimed land when it was complete.

It took me a few days to unpack, and the final step was the photo collection. I turned on the projector booth and stepped back to admire it as it scrolled through holograms of my time in the military. I was overcome with a strange feeling of nostalgia as the faces of my many colleagues-in-arms flicked through; I had no regrets on leaving the military, but it had been my whole life for many years, first on Earth and then in the Dragon Empire. I'd come a long way since helping Sar-Major Shirani take new recruits through basic back on Earth. I'd never thought back then that I'd have the looks and health of a thirty-year-old when I was more than sixty, have two children, one of them a freaking *alien* I loved as my own, and I'd be living in an intergalactic society.

I turned away from the projection. No regrets on leaving the military. The camaraderie had been special, though. I wondered if the Imperial Guard had something similar, living in the Empress' own palace and travelling with her as she met up with her ridiculously large number of spouses—

Marque spoke from the ceiling. 'Runa just contacted me. She's received a scales message from Oliver – he's free to talk.'

I nearly collapsed with relief.

'She's about to fold close enough to the cat planet to speak to him telepathically – do you want to hear it here or next door?'

'Next door with everybody,' I said.

I raced out of my townhouse and into Dianne and Victor's to find David laughing like a maniac – but he had a brittle edge to his laughter. He lunged around in his wheelchair, trying to pin Dianne against the wall, and she laughed as she ran from him.

'Good!' Dianne shouted. 'Your other mum is here. Annoy her while I bring your dad in.'

David stopped the chair and grinned at me, panting from laughing so much. 'Marque said the scales network is going silent while Runa reports through. Everybody wants to hear what Oliver has to say, and there'll be no competition for bandwidth.'

'Good,' I said. 'Tea?'

'Coffee, but let Marque make it,' David said. 'My personal blend, Marque.'

'Which one?' Marque said. 'Front-ass or double-butt?'

I choked with horror at hearing the nasty slurs some aliens had labelled humans with: we were unique in our females having two permanently engorged breasts on our upper torsos, something no other species exhibited. Most mammal types had four or six nipples, and the breasts of the few that only had two were never permanently enlarged like ours were. The aliens had decided that we looked like we had an ass on both front and back, thus leading to the unpleasant nicknames.

'Sorry, Mum,' David said. 'It was a private joke. I'll rename them.'

'I should hope you will,' I said.

Dianne came in with Victor, who was wearing a mechanic's coverall dusted with stone from the sculpture he was working on. 'Has she said anything?'

'Ten minutes,' Marque said. 'She's ready to fold into cat space.'

Victor patted the couch next to him. 'Jian.'

I sat next to him and waited with my breath held. The past ten days had been a nightmare of worrying about his safety, particularly after David's description of the ways the cats had tortured him.

'Runa's put her ship at the edge of cat space, and she's preparing to fold herself above the planet and into telepathic range,' Marque said. 'I'll stay on the ship and relay through the scales network.'

'This is so dangerous,' David said.

'She folded out,' Marque said. 'She's in cat space. I'm relaying her message.'

It continued in Runa's voice, speaking slightly jerkily as it translated the scales taps.

'I'm in position,' Marque said in Runa's voice. 'I'm calling him telepathically.' She was silent for a while. 'He responded! He says he's fine, the culture is very interesting.'

We all sighed with relief and relaxed.

Marque continued with Runa's voice. 'He's arranged for the humans to be looked after. His father is something like a region, or guild, leader. He says it's really complicated. He says, "Don't worry about me, I'm fine, I'm doing well." Now he has a private message just for me ... what is this? What's happening? Marque, I'm coming back out. What in the seven galaxies ... oh no, what? Help, Marque!'

I was standing without realising that I'd moved. 'Marque?'

'She folded back to her ship. She's severely injured. Just a second, I need to re-route some processing power because she brought some of those *fucking* ... excuse me ... cat nanobots with her. They attacked her in orbit, they surround the planet. The damn things were eating her alive. I need to quarantine everything around her to stop them from hacking into me.' It went quiet again.

'Will they take Marque over?' David said. 'Marque was compromised by them before – and Runa just took some of those bots with her.'

'We can only hope that Marque was ready for them,' I said.

'Of course I was ready for them,' Marque said from the ceiling. 'Runa's ship was in quarantine, and I was only communicating by scales. I've studied their nature, but I want to be absolutely sure I'm not compromised, so I destroyed the nanos, then self-destructed everything within communication distance.'

'What about Runa?' I said. 'What about her soulstone? Could you save it?'

'They killed her, but I have her soulstone,' Marque said. 'I put it in an energy bubble before I self-destructed. It was a close thing: they'd already taken her legs, wings, tail, and most of her scales off. The bots were eating her alive. Fortunately she folded out before they ate her soulstone.'

'Bloody hell,' Victor said.

'Now someone needs to fold to the ship's location and retrieve the stone,' Marque said. 'Give me some time while I arrange it.

I need to ensure that the stone doesn't have any nanobots clinging to it.'

'This is some nasty shit,' Dianne said.

'Message from the cats through the scales we left them,' Marque said. 'No dragons are permitted within cat space. Only Jianchou – Jian Choumali – may enter. If you wish to check on ... Oliver's name in cat ... you may visit. No dragons.'

'Me,' I said, flat with dismay. 'Only me. Why the hell do they always want me?'

'Go and make sure he's all right,' David said.

'The Empress is calling you,' Marque said.

'The *Empress*?' David said.

'Are we close enough to do it holographically or does it have to be through scales?' I said.

'The delay will be weeks if we do it holographically, so scales,' Marque said. It changed to the Empress' voice. 'Jian Choumali.'

Everybody stared at me. 'Majesty,' I said. I scowled at them. 'Stop looking at me like that. She's just a dragon.'

'She's the *Queen* of seven galaxies,' David said softly.

'Jian, the cats will only talk to you,' Marque said in the Empress' voice. 'Please come in so I can appoint you as Ambassador to the Cat Republic.'

'What?' Dianne said.

I sat stunned and gasping for a while, then I said, 'I can't do that.'

'Marque says you're freaking out,' the Empress said. 'I'm sending Masako to carry you; please attend me.'

Masako appeared in front of me and I didn't move.

'I can't do it,' I said. 'We don't know how long they'll hold me there. I'll be stuck there with no way off.'

'That's not the point,' the Empress said. 'You're the only one they'll take. Come to Masako's ship and I'll brief you.'

Masako approached me and I backed away. 'What if I don't want to be Ambassador?'

'Marque, hold her so Masako can bring her in,' the Empress said.

Marque held me in an energy field so that Masako could fold me.

'I did not consent to this!' I shouted.

Masako folded me onto her ship. The Empress was already there, towering over the conference table and nearly touching the ceiling.

'You're the only one they'll take and we need you on the ground,' she said. 'You're a projecting telepath. You can get information out without them knowing – obviously they've been watching Oliver so he hasn't been able to use his scale.'

'I can't be Ambassador, I'm not qualified.'

'You won't be Ambassador, you'll be a spy,' she said. 'Find the human hostages and contact us telepathically with their location so we can fold them out.'

That stopped me. 'Oh.'

'Find out where the humans are, contact Masako telepathically, and we'll send a thousand dragons to get everybody out in one go.'

'I'll fold close enough to hear you once every short time period – a human hour? – then fold out again,' Masako said. 'Broadcast the location to me, and we'll fold all the humans out.'

'I'll have to do it quickly, because I won't be able to stay more than three months there,' I said.

'What?' Masako said. 'You're dragonstruck?'

I nodded.

'When did this happen?' the Empress said. 'We were so careful with the troops!'

'I don't know; it happened during the first five years of my deployment in your army, while I still wasn't aware of the true nature of the process. Shiumo told us it was caused by love instead of proximity, and nobody told us otherwise. After five years of being constantly on call, I broke down from the stress. I went to Mok for flying therapy. I did the pre-flight training for a few weeks, and when I jumped off the cliff for my first solo flight, I passed out in mid-air. They caught me, checked me over, and there it was.'

'But we were so careful,' Masako said. 'Oliver isn't dragonstruck; we made sure he wasn't with us every minute of the day. How could it happen to you?'

'That's beside the point,' I said. 'It's three months for humans. Three months away from one of you and I'll die. Shiumo's lies could have killed me.'

'I'll get you out before you can succumb,' Masako said. 'I promise.'

'What about the nanos?' Marque said. 'They could very well kill any dragons outright – the Real Death. If you fold into orbit – or fold onto the planet – the nanos will eat you alive.'

'What if we remove our soulstones before we fold there?' Masako said. 'Sacrifice our bodies to extract the humans?'

'That would work.'

'Will they kill us before we can get the humans out?'

Marque hesitated, then said, 'No. You should have time to fold them out before the nanos kill you.'

'Go to the cat planet, Jian, find out where the humans are, and we'll get them out. Even if it kills us,' Masako said.

'At least a hundred of my own children are willing to do this for you,' the Empress said. 'We owe you our lives.'

I looked away. So many dragons were willing to be eaten alive to get the humans out. 'I guess if I'm the only one they'll take ...'

'You are,' the Empress said. 'You can communicate completely securely. Please, Jian. I will be forever in your debt. The whole Empire will.'

'Come down to my ship's medlevel,' Masako said. 'I've arranged one of our cat experts to give you a telepathically implanted crash course of everything we know about them, their language, and intergalactic diplomatic protocols.'

I winced. Having a language implanted was one thing, but this much information directly slotted into my brain was going to hurt.

7

A small group of cats were waiting for me on the landing pad when my little shuttle arrived on their planet. The black leader was there, next to Oliver and another cat in a white jumpsuit. Oliver broadcast distress, looking as if he wanted to run to me as he shifted from foot to foot.

It's okay, we can get the formalities out of the way then talk, I said to him telepathically, and he shook his head and frowned. *I understand*, I added. His anxiety didn't ease.

The leader stepped up to me and spoke in Euro. 'Ambassador Choumali. You are the first foreigner we have permitted on our world. You are honoured.'

I leaned into him and sniffed loudly in the cat greeting and he returned it. He smelled vaguely unpleasant, like he'd wet himself, but it wasn't anything I hadn't experienced before. Hell, some Empire species existed solely on a diet of the equivalent of our *e. coli.*

'Thank you for your welcome,' I said in cat, using extremely formal and polite language. 'I am honoured to be the first foreigner.'

He broadcast satisfaction at that, and replied in cat, 'You will stay with me; follow.'

The cat in white had its hands behind its back and its head bowed, broadcasting submissiveness. The cat leader gestured for me to walk beside him and we proceeded away from the landing pad towards a black, egg-shaped vehicle that floated above the ground, big enough for all of us. It had open sides and four slender pillars that held up the rounded roof. There weren't seats, we all sat on the floor and the egg lifted slightly and headed away without making a sound.

The cats sat with their knees bent so they were under their chins, with their arms wrapped around their knees. I knelt Japanese-style.

'Before we arrive at my residence, if you are asked about your status, make sure that you tell everyone that you have had a child,' the leader said. 'If you have not yet had a child, your status will be different.'

'I understand the difference between females who have children and those who have not, but in my species it makes no difference,' I said.

'You are not with your species.'

'May I ask your honoured name?' I said.

The cat in white hissed under its breath, and the cat leader released its knees with one hand to wave the white one down. 'We do not share our names. Address us ...' It appeared confused for a moment.

'You call them by their—' Oliver began, and froze when the floor of the vehicle rose like a liquid barrier around him. His ears went back and he broadcast fear as the walls reached his shoulder level. He bobbed his head to his father.

The floor went flat again, but Oliver didn't relax. He eyed it warily.

'As I said, if you are asked, say you have borne a child,' the cat leader said. 'Defer to me in all things. I suggest you do not speak to any other cat until you have learned the basic courtesies.'

'I understand,' I said.

'To show deference, my title is "sir".'

'As Ambassador, so is mine,' I said.

The vehicle stopped and transformed – like liquid – from a vehicle to a platform. I followed the cat leader as he stood and stepped off. We were in a narrow street, with the gold-clay houses around us. The street's surface was a uniformly black, ceramic-like material. A couple of cats who were walking at the far end of the street abruptly turned and walked away when they saw us.

The vehicle had stopped in front of a tower that had black oval gems, ranging from twenty centimetres to a metre across, embedded in its walls. The vehicle disintegrated into black dust that flew up onto one of the jewels and added to its size. Night was falling, and the stars emerged in the sky above us. Lights flicked on throughout the city around us, but they were so dim that they didn't affect the brilliance of the stars above.

Oliver's father took us inside. The tower was hollow up to the domed roof, and wall platforms extended from its interior all the way to the top, twenty metres above us. The tower's base was joined to a rectangular building with textured grey carpet on the floor, but no furniture. The building was as wide as the tower with a ceiling roughly half the tower's height that stretched for twenty metres in front of us. The walls were the same golden polished clay. A far wall had two openings on it, leading to rooms that were difficult to distinguish. A number of cats – all of them naked – lounged on the carpet around what appeared to be three-dimensional displays. Circular lights sat in the ceiling, but again the light produced was much dimmer than human normal.

The cat leader gestured and his jumpsuit disintegrated, together with the clothing that the other cats, including Oliver, were wearing. I was familiar with Oliver's form so it didn't surprise me to learn that the black cat leader was male – his four testicles were enormous below his two penises in their small shared sheath. The other cat with them appeared to be female, with no external genitalia visible in her fur. Her fur was longer than the males', with deep brown tabby stripes over steel grey.

The cat leader gestured for me to follow him and guided me into the rectangular room.

'Neowra,' he said, and sat me in front of one of the holographic displays. Oliver sat as well, cat-style, and the female hurried through one of the far doors. The holographic display was a collection of glowing nanobots so tiny that they were dots floating in the air, a formation that created a moving, life-like image of the cat planet as seen from orbit.

'We do not have long before we have to leave again,' the cat leader said. 'I have an important duty to perform. We will talk more when it is complete.'

The female cat returned holding a tray containing a milky green hot beverage in ceramic tubular cups.

'Neowra,' she said, leaning over the central holographic displays to serve the cups.

Now we were in an enclosed area, I realised that the unpleasant odour that I'd noticed outside was coming from her. It wasn't heavy, more a vague nastiness that emanated when she moved. I tried to place its mixture of burning acid and sharp ammonia. I'd smelled it before, a long time ago, and I realised with a start that she smelled exactly like Oliver's urine when he'd had small accidents as a child. She was marked by scent as a virginal female in Oliver's possession.

'Normally I'd ask my AI if this is safe ...' I began, holding up the cup.

'It is safe for you to drink,' the cat leader said. 'We have checked all the food and drinks we will serve you against your biology. Your safety will not be compromised, you are too important to us.'

I glanced at Oliver, and he nodded. I sipped the drink and it was a delicious mix of savoury flavours, vaguely reminiscent of rich fish or chicken stock. I opened my mouth to compliment it and the implanted knowledge kicked in: telling the cat leader that it was delicious would make me look weak to them.

'When can I see my people?' I said. 'That's the reason I'm here. All I want is to take them home.'

'After this duty is complete,' the cat leader said. 'It will take ...' He hesitated for a moment, then nodded. 'A couple of hours your time. Then we will tour the facility where your people are being held. They have been constantly complaining that their conditions are unacceptable and I want them to stop.'

'Unacceptable how?' I said.

'They whine about "bathing" as if it is important. They behave like animals and the females are soiling themselves. I've studied human culture but I wasn't prepared for them to be so demanding.'

'I'll talk to them; their needs should be relatively simple,' I said.

'Good. Their facilities are acceptable by our standards.' He glanced at the screen. 'It is time to go.'

'May I ...' I searched for the correct words in the cat language. The implanted information didn't cover this topic, it may even be taboo. Wonderful. 'I wish no offence, but I need to expel body waste,' I said lamely.

'Of course.' The cat leader rose, and I did as well. He gestured for Oliver to stay put with the female and guided me through one of the doors at the end of the room. It contained shelves made of the black nano material, and a collection of red clay bowls, each about fifty centimetres across. He selected one from the shelf.

'As you can smell, this one is unused. It is yours.' He held it out to me and I took it.

'Uh ... where do I go to use it, and where do I empty it?' I said.

'We use them anywhere we have need, but I understand that humans are different. You require to do it where no-one else can see you, correct?'

My face heated. I really didn't want to be having this discussion. 'Yes.'

'Use it here, I will leave. Put it back on the shelf when you are done; that one is for you to use.'

'What about emptying it?' I said.

'That will be handled.'

'I will need to clean myself after using it.'

'That will also be handled.' He turned and left the room, and the nanos sealed the door behind him like black sand falling between two sheets of glass.

'Whatever,' I said under my breath, and set the bowl on the floor. I hadn't been in a while and I was desperate. When I was done, I pulled my clothes back on and turned – to see that the bowl was empty. He was right; the nanos handled everything. They'd cleaned the bowl completely, and probably freshened me up as well.

I put the bowl back on its shelf and made a mental note of its location – I wouldn't be able to distinguish it by scent, the way they obviously did. 'I'm done.'

The door opened again.

'Good,' he said. 'Follow me.'

Oliver, the female and I followed him back out of the building. A cloud of nanos flew from one of the jewels on the side of the building and formed the black vehicle again. We boarded it, the sides rose to half its height, and it took off directly upwards. I planted my hand against the low wall, fighting the feeling of being flung into space.

When we were higher than the tops of the towers, we moved forward towards a space elevator at the edge of the landing pad near the lake. The elevator was lit from below, showing that it was a hollow tube constructed of black shiny material in a complicated series of open hexagons – it was probably made of the nano material as well. The breeze whistled through the open vehicle as we surged towards the elevator above the dimly-lit streets.

I ran through the protocol information as we moved, trying to find a way around the social niceties so that I could ask him about the elevator without causing insult. Asking questions and appearing impressed by their nanotechnology – even complimenting the cat leader on it – would be a social faux pas. The cats placed a great deal of emphasis on appearing cool and disinterested at all times, and excitement and curiosity were seen as weakness. This wasn't their natural state – Oliver had been a bright, curious and inquisitive child but the social pressure to appear casually uncaring about everything had stunted his emotional growth before he came to me, and made his only strong emotion anger. He'd even used unpleasant sexual predatory behaviour as an outlet, when what he really needed was physical affection. It had taken me years to work him out of it with the help of human therapists and AI experts. A whole society like this had to be truly broken.

The space elevator loomed over us and I decided to hell with it – I needed to know.

'I'm curious about your nanotechnology,' I said. 'It's very impressive; we have nothing like this in the Empire. How are you controlling them? It is you that controls them?'

'It is me,' he said with genuine pride, and I relaxed. Obviously stroking his ego would work. 'The method I use to control them is not for sharing, but I am the only one in this entire region that can do it.' He gestured towards the buildings. 'All my nanos are black; the colour shows that I am the controller.'

The entire city below us had black jewels on every building, except for a couple with a lighter shade of grey and one with a washed-out blue.

'You control every nano in the city?' I said with wonder.

'Here we are,' he said, and the vehicle dropped almost vertically towards the base. I clutched Oliver's hand as we plummeted towards the planet and he held it. The floor didn't move to surround him; obviously the cat leader didn't object to Oliver assisting me this way.

We landed at the base of the shining black network of hexagons that formed a tube twenty metres across that disappeared into the sky. A sphere rose through the tube like a liquid drop – forming from the sides as it went up. The cat leader walked towards the tube and an opening appeared to form a doorway. We went in, and the tube surrounded us. The nanos moved like liquid to form another sphere around us, and we shot into the air again.

'Will I have a chance to talk to ...' I gestured towards Oliver, and his whiskers spread in interest. 'I have cared for him for a long time, and I am very close to him. I'd like to spend some time with him.'

'He does not speak,' the cat leader said, a throaty growl. 'He listens. He learns. He is here to take my place, not to make his own.'

Oliver ducked his head and nodded. I wished I could send compassion to him – it must be so hard for him to be without a voice.

As soon as we have our people back, I am getting you out of here, don't worry, I said to him telepathically, and he didn't respond. *You do want to leave, don't you?* I asked, and he shot me a blast of pure desperation without showing any emotion at all on his face.

The elevator stopped and opened onto a black platform spread before us, a circle of a hundred metres across, made from the same nano material. We were still within the atmosphere, but a shimmering grey dome over the platform suggested that the nanos were boosting the oxygen in the air. The sky beyond the dome showed the sun setting over the slight curve of the cat planet on the horizon.

A group of twenty aliens stood on the other side of the platform, with cat warp ships floating in the sky just off the edge. There were four different species, and what appeared to be family groups – larger and smaller aliens together – in each species. One of the species had bowls placed around the perimeter of their group, releasing pale blue smoke. Another group were all decked in greenery and flowers, and a third group had brightly-coloured ribbons through their long fur ... and when I saw them, I realised that not only were they a family of Eh-Ay-Oyau, but the central Eh-Ay was my foster child, Georgina. She was Oliver's toy when I encountered them and killed Oliver's mother, and she'd never forgiven me for taking away her 'destiny' to be paid handsomely to be a plaything for a cat. She was an adult now, and a smaller Eh-Ay stood next to her, decked out in light silky ribbons that floated in the breeze.

I charged towards Georgina, horrified at what she was about to do.

'Ee-yi-oh-ue,' I shouted, using her own species name. 'Please tell me you aren't about to sell—'

I was cut off by the nanos gathering like insects to block my mouth. I tore at them, but as I removed them they replaced themselves. It was like trying to remove an intelligent sticky liquid from my face. The nanos beneath my feet picked me up by grabbing the lower parts of my legs, moved me back behind the cat group, and held me fast. I was immobilised and unable to speak and the cat's precision control of the nanos meant that I had no difficulty breathing despite the fact that I was effectively gagged.

I watched in distress as each family group in turn honoured the child they were selling to the cats. Georgina hugged her daughter, and said, 'We know it will be hard, but remember how many of your family are free. Ninety-three of us won't have to die in the mines. You're doing a great thing.'

'Stay alive, dear one,' another Eh-Ay said. 'Reach adulthood and return to us, so that we can make the rest of your life as rich and comfortable as you deserve.'

'I will do my best,' the child said. 'Honour me if I die for you.'

'We will always speak your name, whether you live or die,' Georgina said. She smiled. 'You are wonderful, Uo, and I'm so glad to be your mother. You'll be magnificent.'

I wanted to shout at Georgina that this was wrong, but no words would come out. I could make random grunting noises, but the nanos grabbed my mouth from both the inside and outside and clamped it shut – with the horrible liquid feeling of them climbing back up my throat if I swallowed any of them. I closed my eyes and fought the nausea from the sensation of them moving through me.

This is wrong! I shouted telepathically at Georgina. *If you return to the Dragon Empire, none of you need to work in the mine and your child will be safe!*

Georgina turned her back to me. 'We are all dragonscales. Not a single pure-blood Eh-Ay remains. The dragons destroyed us, seeding themselves across our planet. We will never forgive them, and we will never return to the Empire.' She glared at Oliver's father. 'Silence the human, she's a telepath.'

Oliver's father waved one hand at me, and the nano liquid swelled to fill my throat. It choked me, and I struggled to breathe, my chest heaving against the blockage. I tore at my face as black spots appeared in front of my eyes.

The nanos retreated and I hunched over my foot bindings and wheezed to get enough air in. It took a while before the black spots disappeared.

The Eh-Ays had finished speaking to the child and had made an honour guard for her. Judging by her size, she couldn't be more than three years old, and Eh-Ays weren't mature until they were twelve. She walked beneath a tunnel of ribbons held by her family, then bowed deeply on her forelegs to the cat leader, who returned the gesture. He placed his hand on her head and guided her to a cat family that was waiting on the other side. He then raised his hand and a clump of nanos coalesced onto her back. She cowered under his hand as the ownership chip was implanted.

The cat family that had bought Georgina's daughter spread their arms, hands held low, towards the Eh-Ay family, and a bulge emerged from the surface of the platform. It flowed across the floor to Georgina's family, and opened to reveal a large black box, at least a metre to a side. Georgina gestured, and a couple of the Eh-Ay took the box into the warp ship. She bowed on all four feet again, then they departed into the warp ship behind them.

Oliver had stood silently with his ears flat against his head throughout the whole transaction, radiating overwhelming grief.

The cat child lunged at the long-furred alien and proceeded to tear the ribbons from the child's fur. It ripped clumps of fur out, and the Eh-Ay yelped with pain.

'Why aren't you running?' the cat parent said to the Eh-Ay. 'We bought you to run.'

The Eh-Ay ran away from them, trailing the ribbons as she tore across the platform towards her family's ship. The cat child followed her faster than she could move and caught her halfway across the platform. It tackled her and took her down, tearing at the ribbons, and kicking at her abdomen with its back claws – one of Oliver's favourite play moves and devastatingly damaging when his claws were sharp.

The Eh-Ay screamed as the cat held her with its claws and rabbit-kicked her as it chewed on her ear.

The little cat's parents strode over to them and knocked the little cat flat, then cuffed it repeatedly over the head.

'You *worthless female*! Don't kill your toy five minutes after we paid so much for it!' the parent shouted, slapping the cat child. 'It's here for you to chase, not kill!' The parent turned and kicked the Eh-Ay a couple of times for good measure. 'I said run, not fall. You are worthless!'

It dragged them both back to the rest of the family, leaving a trail of blood from the injured Eh-Ay. My foster daughter's child.

Oliver made a horrible noise of pain deep in his throat, and I turned to see that he was restrained as well – the nanos were wrapped around his legs and held him in place, and his lower face was covered. The female stood next to him with her head bowed and her hands hidden inside her robe's sleeves, radiating deep humiliation.

The cat family who'd bought Georgina's child went to the space elevator, the bear-like alien still bleeding, and went down to the surface.

Something happened to Oliver – I sensed his pain. He threw his head back and made an awful choking sound at the back of his throat. The nanos released his feet and he collapsed, falling backwards onto his butt and rubbing his ankles. His father had nearly crushed them. I wanted to run to him, but I was still gagged and restrained. Tears sprung from my eyes and the nanos collected them, running over my face in an awful liquid mass.

Oliver's father walked stiffly to stand where both of us could see him.

'You shame me,' he said to Oliver. He turned to me. 'You shame yourself. Control yourself, Ambassador, and I will take you to see your people.'

I raised my hands and furiously gesticulated at him as I tried to speak through the nanos.

'I think it would be best if you remained silent,' he said. 'But I am willing to give you another chance. Are you able to control yourself? No more speaking – either verbal or telepathic?'

I wanted to tear his throat out. Instead I nodded, and the nanos released my feet and face. I fell forward, then picked myself up and went to Oliver, but a wall of nanos sprung up so that I couldn't see him.

'Leave him,' the cat leader said. 'He also needs to learn restraint. If you can remain silent, I will take you to see your people now.'

I just nodded.

'Good,' he said, and gestured towards the elevator.

I threw a despairing look back towards Oliver as I followed his father away.

*

Back on the surface, the cat leader again summoned a black vehicle of nanobots and transported me for more than an hour across the dry terrain. The houses petered out, and the surrounding landscape was limited to smaller clay buildings and some larger, more utilitarian structures that looked like power plants or warehouses, made out of black metal and without any distinguishing features on the outside. Eventually they finished as well and we hit the edge of a black plain. The entire landscape was covered in the black nano material. These were the black blots visible from space – the cats' solar collector – and the view from space didn't do it justice. It stretched across the horizon, glossy and featureless.

The vehicle lifted us, and we travelled over the solar collector for ten minutes. The heat rippled over the nano surface, making it appear that we were floating over a sea of stars from the reflected night sky. A group of lights appeared on the horizon, reflected in the heat haze. As we approached, I realised that it was the prisoner of war camp. The humans were being held in what was effectively a shed over the nano surface; it was two storeys high with a roof and no walls, and the thousand captives sat under the shelter in small groups.

Someone shouted when they saw us, and they all moved to the end of the building as far away from us as they could. A smaller group formed and stood closer, waiting for us to arrive. I was relieved to see that they were standing as I'd been hoping that the cats hadn't cut everyone's legs off to stop them from running – then I saw that all their legs were black. They were standing on legs made of nanos.

The cat leader stopped the vehicle, and we stepped out. The humans saw me and the mood quickly turned jubilant. They knew I was there to get them out.

'Talk to them about their needs; I want them to stop complaining,' the cat leader said. 'I will return in an hour.' He went back to his vehicle and drove away.

I attempted to contact Masako. *I have the location of the humans.*

She didn't reply, so I kept up the transmission, hoping that she could fold into orbit long enough for me to tell her where they were.

The captives mobbed me when I approached and all embraced me, patting me on the back and talking at once.

'Jian.' General Oshala, the most senior officer, had been a respected Indian academic before joining the battle against the cats. 'It's so damn good to see you! How long before you can get us out?'

'I'm working on it,' I said. *If I'm distracted, it's because I'm trying to contact them. We have someone standing by to fold you out.*

He looked down at his legs. 'Mind what you say.'

I nodded, understanding. The nanos were relaying everything we said back to the cat.

'We tried to escape, but we can't ...' He took a deep breath, holding the distress down. 'We can't leave the roofed structure. Our legs only work inside it, and if we try to crawl further a wall grows out of the ground.'

'Don't apologise,' I said. 'I understand how the nano material works. I just hope you're all safe and ... not in too much distress.'

'That was awful,' one of the other officers said. He put his hand over his eyes and turned away. 'My legs still hurt.'

'We just need to get you home and fix you up,' I said. 'Remember, you have your soulstones back, so stay safe and concentrate on reattuning them.'

'Where did they come from?' Oshala said. 'Are they the real thing?' He touched the green stone in his forehead. 'They attached themselves to our foreheads correctly, and they have the weird energy, but it seems ... muted.'

'I brought them myself, and we know the cats can't duplicate them. If you think they've been tampered with, then we can replace them when you're home.'

'Probably my imagination,' he said, dropping his hand. 'Or something to do with this location.'

'Are you comfortable? The cat leader said you were unhappy.' I looked around. 'No furniture, no beds, no nothing?'

'They sleep during the day,' Oshala said. 'They're nocturnal. During the day the floor makes us some sleeping pads. It's not uncomfortable, the nanos cool the air under the roof so we're not too hot. Oh god, Jian.' He hugged me again, and a few of the humans voiced sympathy. 'Thank you so much for coming.'

'Are you here to take us home?' one of the other humans said. 'Please. Get us out of here! Do you know how my family is? What happened? The cat leader told us they had a great victory and killed many of us ... Is this true?'

A few people voiced agreement.

'My wife was on one of the other ships!' a man shouted. 'We have two kids back on Earth.'

'Marque has the full list,' I said.

'Marque didn't come with you?' Oshala said.

I gestured towards the floor. 'The nanos attack Marque and infiltrate its code. It can't come within comms distance of the planet.'

'The dragons?'

'They're murdered by nanos if they approach as well. I'm the only one allowed here.'

'So how are you going to get us out?' Oshala said, desperate. 'Do we have any hope at all?'

'I'm working on it,' I said. 'We're moving slowly through diplomatic channels.'

'Slowly?' one of the humans shouted. 'How long is slowly?'

I am broadcasting your location to the dragons, I said telepathically. *Be ready to be transported out at any moment.*

This caused a frisson of delight through them.

Masako isn't answering, but we will have someone here soon to transport you.

They visibly cheered up at that, and their desperation eased. They'd been close to panic at the thought of being stuck there.

'Is there anything you need right now?' I said. 'They are providing you with food and water and sanitary facilities? I can talk to the leader about improving your housing.'

Oshala guided me to the side of the structure, walking clumsily on the nano legs. A black lean-to stood in one corner of the building. We went inside and he showed me a bin full of small brown pellets.

'This is the food,' he said. 'It's effectively kibble, but it seems to have everything in it that we need, even though it tastes awful.

There's a device here,' he pointed at a black box, as tall as a human, with a spigot sticking out from the side. 'That's an infinite water distillery – it seems to extract fresh water from the air.' He held his hands under the spigot and water came out. 'We pissed the cats off on the first day by using the toilet bowls as water bowls. They were horrified and now they're convinced that we're barbarians.'

'No bathroom facilities?' I said. 'The cat leader said you'd asked about bathing.'

'We tried to explain bathing but they're having difficulty understanding the concept. They don't bathe, so they haven't provided us with any way to do it. At the moment we're using our clothing as damp pads to wash ourselves with.'

'A few of us are birth-natural,' one of the women said. 'They don't believe us about menstruation: they think it's from sexual activity and told us to show some restraint instead of helping us with sanitation.'

'Cats bleed after sex,' one of the men said, incredulous. 'It's normal!'

'Adding to the perception that we're barbarians, rampantly having sex with each other all the time,' Oshala said wryly. 'Even though ...' He gestured around. 'There's no walls so no privacy for us.'

'What if it rains?' I said. 'Does the building grow walls if there's a storm?'

'It hasn't rained yet and I honestly don't think it will,' he said.

I half-listened to him as I tried to contact Masako.

He became concerned at my inattention. 'Jian?'

'I am listening to you,' I said, distracted. *Still no answer,* I added, now becoming concerned. 'Tell me if there's anything I can do to add to your comfort. I'll try to get you facilities for bathing, better food, and hopefully some chairs to sit on. Are the sleeping pads soft enough?'

'They'll do,' Oshala said. 'Bathing is the big one right now.'

'Me!' one of the other people shouted at the back.

'Oh, sorry, Mick,' Oshala said. 'Mick's mentally ill and needs medication.'

'I'm bipolar,' Mick said. 'I won't be a danger to anyone but I may self-harm. My meds are on record – please. Soon.'

'I'll get them for you,' I said.

'We all stink,' one of the others said. 'If I had legs I'd give one of them for a bar of soap.'

'You'll get your legs back when we take you home.'

'We know,' Oshala said. He hesitated. 'Any news?'

I shook my head.

He looked around at his fellow humans. 'If there's a chance that we'll be here for more than a few days ...' He wiped his eyes, then squared his shoulders. 'Okay. I can do this. We need to look after ourselves. Once we get the basics taken care of, it would be great to move up to some higher-level needs. Mental stimulation; some way of recording and sharing our experiences. Even pen and paper. We're using oral interaction to keep our spirits up ...'

'We gather and share our different areas of expertise,' one of the others said. 'Impromptu university. But it's hard without any writing implements.'

'Any conflict?' I said, still broadcasting to the dragons and becoming really concerned. I'd been with the humans for more than half an hour now – where the hell was Masako?

'We haven't really had time to build cliques or have a power struggle. Everybody's breathless waiting for it to happen – for someone to break and become violent. It's only a matter of time. We've established some basic behavioural rules, but we all knew that if we didn't hear from someone back home soon, everything would start to break down.'

'Are there more sociologists than you?' I asked wryly.

'Hey, you know us military are trained in the basics,' one of the men said. 'At least half of us are military.'

'And by the time Oshala's finished with us we'll all have doctorates in sociology,' one of the women said. 'He identifies what's happening, helps us to short-circuit any conflict, and generally keeps our spirits up.'

'Boredom is sapping morale. If we had paper and markers, we could make some board games to keep ourselves entertained,' Oshala said. 'After the soap, I think that's the biggest thing.'

'I'll see what I can do,' I said.

'Now that we've talked about us and our needs, tell us what happened after we were stranded on the warp ships,' Oshala said. 'We're not even sure how long we've been here; the cat days seem to be longer than Earth's ones.' He turned and spoke to the group. 'Sit around us and if you can't hear up the back, say so.'

I'll broadcast what I say telepathically as well, so that you can hear me, I said.

'Do they know about that aspect of your abilities?' Oshala said as we sat on the black floor.

'I'm afraid they do,' I said. 'I'll have to be careful.'

'Damn,' he said under his breath.

'What about our families?' one of them said.

I spoke telepathically to Oshala. *I still have the dragon army enhancements, and one of them is perfect recollection. I know the names of every single human and dragon lost. Should I tell them?*

If I didn't tell these people, they would be in a crisis of anxiety about their loved ones. If I did tell them, they would have grieving on top of the stress of being incarcerated with their legs chopped off – but for some of them it would be good news.

'Tell us,' he said.

I took a deep breath. 'I know the names of every human and dragon that was lost,' I said. 'Sit with me, and I'll tell you the list.'

Masako still hadn't responded when I finished telling them.

8

After I'd sat with my colleagues for another hour, sharing stories and making a list of requirements for their captors, the humans' legs all disappeared into clouds of black nanos.

'He's coming back,' Oshala said. 'No word?'

I've been broadcasting continuously, I said. *I will continue to broadcast.*

'Stay strong, everyone,' I said out loud. 'My first priority is to get you home. I'll remain on the cat planet until we have a way of getting you out; I'm officially Ambassador. We'll establish a mission and work to get you more comfortable.'

'Thanks, Jian,' Oshala said.

The floor moved; one side lifted, forcing us all down to the other side.

'This is to prevent us from attacking him,' Oshala said. 'Just move with it.'

Some of them walked on their stumps as the floor lifted. Others, like Oshala, went down on all fours to crawl – the stumps were too painful to carry their weight. When we were crammed into a corner of the building, with me towering over the other humans on their severed legs, the floor lifted around me until I was enclosed in a black bubble. A platform emerged under my feet, lifting me, and the bubble rolled around me with the platform remaining unmoving in the centre. The bubble opened to show the cat leader, standing next to his vehicle.

I didn't speak, not wanting to piss him off again. I merely bowed with my arms spread in the cat body language of thanks.

'One of them is mentally ill?' he said.

'Yes. He requires medication to control it,' I said.

'You talk about it as if it were normal,' he said.

'It is normal,' I said. 'He just needs his medication, and he'll be fine. He's not delusional or anything, he just has ...' I tried to use the cat language to describe being bipolar. 'Emotional swings from deep depression to high energy, caused by a chemical imbalance in his brain. He's chosen not to have it permanently fixed, as he's decided to remain birth-natural. It's fully managed with his medication anyway.'

'And the other humans are living with him without fear?' the cat said, still incredulous.

'Yes of course they are,' I said, as bewildered as he was. 'What's the problem?'

'I'll arrange for him to be separated and locked up,' the cat leader said. 'He's a danger to himself and others.'

'No, he isn't. Even off his meds, he's no danger to anyone,' I said.

He flattened his ears. 'He said he will harm himself. I will not endanger our guests.'

'You cut their legs off!'

'For their own safety.'

'You don't need to—' I began.

He interrupted me. 'The discussion about him is closed. We will now talk about their needs. They have been annoying me about this for a while, and I need clarification.' He sat on the floor of the vehicle, and it lifted to carry us back to the city.

He gestured for me to sit as well, and I did.

'The word "bathing" seems to have two meanings: one is "exercise by swimming in a large body of water". The other is "washing in a small amount of water with a surfactant." Which one are they referring to when they demand this?'

I gave up on Mick's mental health needs for the moment, to focus on the greater good. 'They mean a small amount of water with a surfactant. Usually a pleasantly-fragranced one that we call soap. We have sprays of warm water that we use to cover ourselves with water and soap, and it removes the oils from our skin.'

'That sounds extremely unhealthy.'

'We smell bad otherwise.'

'No, you don't. I can't believe you dislike your own smell. That's ridiculous.'

'Put it that way, you're right,' I admitted.

'The women regularly *bleed*? And this is *normal*?'

'Yes. There are a few species in the Empire that do it. We require absorbent bandages to manage it. Bathing also helps – it is messy when it happens.'

'Does that happen to you?' he said, looking me up and down as if I was about to spontaneously explode in a blood-soaked horror show.

'No. I've had it turned off, because I don't want children right now.'

His ears went up. 'I see. It's part of the reproductive process. That makes sense. We have something similar.'

'Your females bleed after sexual contact?'

'We do not discuss that,' he said stiffly. 'Your people asked for writing material. I have shown them how to use the nanos to record their thoughts.'

'When did you do that?'

'I'm doing it now. A model has appeared in their residence with instructions on how to record memories onto nanos.'

'This is fascinating,' I said. 'How do you do it?'

A copy of him emerged from the floor of the vehicle. It was shiny black, made from the nanos, and about one-third his size.

The model pushed its hand into the surface of the car and pulled out a handful of the thick liquid nano material. It moulded the material between its hands until it was a rough flat ovoid, then ran its hand down the sides to make them straight. After thirty seconds of deft manipulation of the nanos, the model was holding a square tablet fifteen centimetres to a side and half a centimetre thick.

The model put the tablet in one hand and ran the other hand over it. The nanos turned from black to dark grey. It continued to run its hand backwards and forwards over it, until the tablet was pale grey.

'I'm so impressed at their flexibility and usefulness,' I said.

'You haven't even seen the beginning of their usefulness,' the cat leader said.

The model buried its hand into the nano surface again, and pulled out a smaller handful. It placed the pale grey tablet on the floor and rolled the new piece of nanos until it was a rough tube. It pulled one end into a point and squished the other end flat, and used it as a stylus to mark on the tablet. It wrote the first few lines of a famous cat poem onto the tablet in a flowing hand in the cat script.

I will return for you
I will fulfil my duty
I will return for you
And live as I please
My child will be treasured
And I will be free
And when all my duty is done
I will return to you.

I'd talked with the clicks about possible meanings of the poem in the past, and they'd focused on the different preposition used in the repeating line – return *for* you, then return *to* you. We'd speculated for ages and hadn't worked out why the obviously significant difference was made by the poet. I was sure it was something meaningful about their culture and had no idea what it was.

'Can you store the writing?'

'Everything is stored,' the cat said.

The model turned the tablet over and pressed it onto the floor. The image was transferred, and a hyper-thin slice of the floor floated up and into its hand. It had effectively created a piece of paper with writing on it; it wasn't even mirror-reversed.

The model wrote the next stanza of the poem, pressed the tablet to the floor, and produced another sheet of poetry. It touched the two sheets along one side, and they glued together. It had the beginnings of an old-fashioned book.

'Once it is more than a few pages, or requires longer storage, it is easier to record it within the nano matrix itself,' the cat leader said. 'But your people are not familiar with the data retrieval methods that we use, so a hard copy is probably their best option.'

'Thank you for showing them this,' I said. 'It will make their captivity much easier.'

'I do not want them to suffer while we study their soulstones,' he said.

The model and the book it had created sank and disappeared into the floor.

'You are welcome to send some cats to our planet to study the stones, instead of holding my people captive,' I said. 'There's no need to hold them prisoner; we want to live in peace with you. Please release them and send them home.'

'This is our destination,' he said.

We'd arrived outside a two-storey-high tower made of nano material that was ten metres across. It was at the edge of the black solar array, and no other buildings were within view. I followed him off the vehicle without asking what was up, not wanting to piss him off while he was being so forthcoming.

'Through there,' he said, opening the front door.

'Oh,' I said, realising that this was my residence. I wasn't staying with him. There was a human-furnished room, with a toilet bowl room, a kibble room and a water dispenser. A thick-glassed window looked out to the sandy desert beyond. I turned back to the cat leader. 'Thank you, this is very comfortable.'

'It will do,' he said. He went out and closed the door.

'Oh shit no!' I shouted. I tried the door, and of course it was locked. I thumped on it. 'You don't need to lock me up, I won't go anywhere! I *can't* go anywhere!'

There was no reply. I checked the floor; a sleeping mat was placed on it, and the floor was made of the black nanos.

The floor tilted and I reeled back. Loud metallic clangs rocked the building, and I was nearly knocked off my feet. There were three deafening clicks that sounded hard enough to make the ceramic walls crack, then silence.

I banged on the door again. 'This is a breach of diplomatic protocol. You cannot keep me prisoner!'

Masako, help, I added telepathically, but she didn't reply.

The room filled with a metallic whine and I stepped back from the door, worried that it might be electrified. I tried to place the whine – it rose in pitch and volume until I thought that something would explode.

There was a rush of air, then silence.

I sat on the floor and wiped my face. I knew that sound. I was inside a warp field.

*

I woke and stared at the ceiling. I'd dreamt that I was back on Barracks, playing with Oliver and Endicott. I rolled onto my side and curled up at the thought of my boys, my mother ... my family. I wondered if they knew whether I was alive or not.

The tower was connected to a warp ship, and there were a couple of windows looking out into space, made bright and fuzzy by the warp field. Light was the only thing that could enter and leave the field, meaning I could only communicate with visual signals – and there was nobody out there to see my messages. Not even my telepathy would carry through.

I used the little bathroom and scooped some kibble out of the bin. It was spongy and moist, and tasted like a vile mixture of liver and bone marrow. I'd grown to hate it so much that I was losing weight because I was avoiding it. I held the handful of kibble under the water – cats did not use bowls for food, they placed their kibble directly on the table and ate with their hands. The concept of crockery was alien to them, so I didn't have anything except my clay toilet bowl. I scrunched the foul kibble with some of the water in my hand to make a brown slurry, and struggled to eat it. I was so repelled by it that I had difficulty keeping it down. I finished it, rinsed my hand in the bathroom, and drank some of the water.

I didn't have soap, and I wondered if the cat leader had given some to the captives. I hoped so.

I returned to the main room and proceeded with my first daily task. I turned some of the floor nanos white, constructed a stylus, and proceeded to make an exceptionally large sign – the full width of the floor – out of the nano material. I wrote on it in Euro and cat, and it said: *I need dragon medical attention soon or I will die.*

I didn't have anything to measure the passage of time. The ship's lighting was constantly dim, with no distinction between day and night. I marked the wall every time I went to sleep, and I had been on the warp ship for forty-seven sleeps. Adjusting for short naps where I didn't know how long I slept, I had to conclude that I had no idea how long I'd been there. I wouldn't start feeling the effects of being dragonstruck for at least three months, but that didn't stop me from having a galloping heart and difficulty breathing sometimes. Stress. Just stress.

I was running out of things to do. I'd been recording my memories on the nano material and binding them into a nano book. I made the huge sign every time I woke up, and when I went to sleep the sign disappeared. I practised constructing things out of the nano material – it was great for things that required flexibility, but hopeless for more rigid surfaces. I tried to make a chair and failed because the material wouldn't hold the shape.

I wondered how long my sanity would hold up. I went to the window and looked out – the star field was glorious, even through the warp distortion. With the roughly one-to-six time ratio, I'd only been on the ship for about a week to those outside. It was possible that the dragons hadn't even noticed my absence, and the cats may be hiding my location from them.

Had the cat leader known that I was telepathically transmitting to the dragons? The fact I was incarcerated in a warp field suggested that he knew – it was the only way to block telepathic communication. But why didn't he just expel me, instead of holding me captive? Maybe I was another hostage – and the only telepathic one, meaning that I had to be held incommunicado. The whole thing made no sense.

I picked up the stylus and made another sign. *Why are you doing this to me? You are harming my mental health. This isolation is torture and will drive me insane.*

I sat on the floor and rubbed my hands over my face. The tears came by themselves, and I shook with them. I was breaking down more and more often, and I couldn't stand being alone. I was desperate to get out and wanted to get up and run in circles, throwing myself at the walls. I giggled as I wiped my eyes – by the time I died of being dragonstruck, I would probably be too insane to care. I sniffled and wiped my nose on my sleeve, then scowled at how stiff it was. I only had one set of clothes. I washed them in the water, but they were starting to smell anyway. Busy. Busy. I needed to find something to do.

I picked up the deck of playing cards that I'd made out of the nanos. Solitaire would keep me occupied for a while. I dealt the cards, and my mind wandered as I made the moves. Putting me in a warp field was an effective way to stop me from communicating telepathically, so it made a kind of twisted sense. I shivered; at least they hadn't cut my legs off – and why hadn't they done that? I turned the poem over in my head again. What was the significance of the difference in words? How long was I going to be alone here? And where was this warp ship taking me?

I fell over sideways and curled up. What was the point?

I bolted to my feet when the lights dimmed. Silence rang in my ears – the warp drive had stopped. I choked with sobs of joy at the thought of being released. Even if they'd come to kill me it would be better than being stuck here alone.

The door flew open and a young cat – slightly smaller than me, so probably in its mid-teens – charged in, followed by two burly cats who appeared to be guards. Oliver's father followed them with Oliver, broadcasting confusion and distress, bringing up the rear.

'And she's been here how long?' the small cat shouted at Oliver's father.

Oliver's father was meeker and more subservient than I'd ever seen him – he broadcast fear. This young cat must be powerful.

'Four meshkas,' Oliver's father said.

'You kept her for four meshkas. Alone.' The young cat rounded on Oliver's father. 'You kept a virgin female – who you owed Aishishistra to – alone for four meshkas.' It growled low in its throat. 'I cannot believe that you broke Aishishistra!'

Oliver's father stiffened and spoke with dignity. 'Aishishistra is not owed to aliens.'

The young cat let loose a string of words that I didn't understand, and Oliver's ears went back. All the other cats cringed. These terms weren't in the vocabulary that the dragons had given me, so the young cat was probably swearing – but what was *Aishishistra*?

I opened my mouth to ask but Oliver frantically shook his head.

'You really thought we wouldn't find her?' The young cat was furious. 'Stupidity like this is a sign that your data has started to decline. Maybe we should give your nanos to someone else. Aishishistra is owed to the one who finds the child. She found your child. Aishishistra is owed.'

'She is an alien—' Oliver's father began.

The young cat pulled an energy weapon from one of his attendants' holsters and shot Oliver's father in the face. Half his head burned off from his shoulder up, and he fell.

A cloud of black nanos – so thick that they were opaque – coalesced out of the fallen cat's body into the air. They gathered together, and then shot towards Oliver. He ducked and put his hands over his head, and a cloud of pale blue nanos screamed out of the young cat towards the black cloud. The two clouds of nanos swirled around each other, and the young cat turned the weapon on Oliver.

'No!' I shouted, and ran to block it. The energy beam hit me as I reached to cover Oliver. My right arm disintegrated, taking some of my shoulder and side with it, and I fell.

'Whatever Aishishistra is, I think you owe it to me now,' I said as the floor slammed into me.

There was an awful loud wind rushing in my ears and I was lying on my back. I couldn't see properly, and Oliver was shouting at me.

The words coalesced but didn't have much meaning. 'Hang on, Mum, we're getting you help,' he said.

'I love you,' I said. I couldn't see properly, everything was dancing white lights. Oliver was there somewhere. 'I love you so much, Ollie.' The air was too thick to breathe, and I gasped with the effort. 'Tell David I love him, too. Mum, love you, Mum. And if you ever see Geo ... Geor ...' Her name wouldn't form, I didn't have enough air.

'Stop trying to talk,' he said. 'We're arranging a dragon to transport you back to the Empire. Don't worry, even if you die we'll move you to a new body.'

'Keep me alive!' I wheezed. 'I want to keep these memories! Take a copy of them before you shift me across.'

'We'll do our best, Mum,' he said, and the rushing became loud again.

*

I was freezing cold. My fingers were numb and my insides quivered as I shivered. Where was I? Everything was floaty and meaningless, and I was so damn cold.

A warm woman's voice appeared in my head. Her tone was gentle and reassuring. *You are safe. Relax. You are cared for. Don't move, you are receiving important medical treatment.*

I tried to reply to her and nothing came out. I wanted to ask ... What did I want to ask?

The voice returned. *You have had an accident. We are caring for you. You are safe.*

Oh, I'd done this script ... What script?

Don't try to remember where you are. You are heavily sedated; try not to think too much. Relax. Float. Don't think about anything.

Yeah, and I'll try not to think of purple elephants while I'm at it. What happened? I *knew* this script. Whoa, but everything was – as she said – floaty. I hadn't been sedated like this since that time ...

Oh.

Oh.

All right, I knew what to do. Relax into it and try not to use the new brain too much while the neurons settled into their pathways.

Is everyone okay? I broadcast telepathically. I wasn't really sure who I was concerned about, but I was damn sure there were people I cared for who needed to be safe.

The warm voice sounded amused. *Everybody on the ship heard that. Yes, everybody is okay. Nobody is hurt. The people you should not be thinking about are waiting patiently for your return.*

All right, all I had to do now was warm up – damn it was cold! – and let the process take its course. Just this small interaction had been exhausting. Sleep sounded very good.

*

The Empress spoke into my head. *Jian?*

Yes?

How do you feel about coming out? It's a little soon but you're really needed. Oliver has brought another cat with him and I need to know if they can be trusted.

I tried to move and remembered where I was. *If I'm needed, I'm ready, but you can trust him.*

Marque lifted me out of the liquid and I felt the chill. I opened my eyes, and the ceiling came into focus. Marque rotated me so that I was vertical, and placed me in front of a chair, ready for me to fall into it.

I stood without difficulty and looked around for some clothes. They were on the table and I spoke to Marque while I pulled them on. 'Status report.'

'Twenty-four hours have passed since you died. You're on Masako's ship; the Empress herself collected you from the cat ship. Oliver contacted us by scales to come and get you.'

'Is Oliver okay?'

'Yes. He's here, and he told us what happened. The cats haven't communicated directly.'

'What other cat did he bring with him?'

'A female. Oliver said he rescued her.'

'I think I know who she is. What happened to Masako?'

'She was biologically infiltrated by nanos when she folded into orbit. They destroyed the telepathic parts of her brain, then ate her from the inside out.'

'Is she okay, though?'

'She took her stone out before she left, and I've put it in a new body for her, but she saw a recording of herself being eaten and she's very shaken. She doesn't want to be near cat space, so she left her ship here for the Empress to use and went to the scales communication centre to act as communication relay. The Empress is here; she wanted to speak to you personally.'

'Good. I know where the humans are. We can get them out.'

'This way,' Marque said, and I followed a sphere to a point in the floor where I was lifted to the gallery level of the ship. The walls were transparent, giving a view of space in a location I didn't recognise. 'You don't need to rescue the humans. The cats are sending them back to us on a warp ship.'

Oliver and the Empress were waiting for me on the gallery of Masako's ship. Oliver rushed to me and embraced me.

'I'm so glad you're okay,' he said, and squeezed me hard. 'Thank god we're out of there.'

I pulled back to see into his bright green eyes. 'You okay, Ollie? He killed your father ...'

He scowled. 'That place is *so fucked up*,' he said. 'Everything is full of nanos – the air, the water, and their bodies. Fortunately when you're far enough away from the cat homeworld, the nanos have no power source, so they run out of juice and die. The damn things were everywhere.' He gestured for me to sit on a couch that Marque had provided for us on the deck. 'The nanos saturated my father's biology. They kept track of the state of his brain – and when he died, they tried to overwrite mine.'

'That's how they deal with mortality?' the Empress said, incredulous. 'We tried that, before we found out about the nature of souls. We grew clones, and Marque wrote the memories onto the clone brains for us – but the result was just a copy, and very often the personality of the inhabiting soul would conflict with the past experiences. It was just a copy, and creating a copy of yourself doesn't solve the mortality problem when the original ends up just as dead. And overwriting the memories doesn't work; without an active soulstone the result is your soul with his memories ...' She went silent.

'Yeah. That would be weird,' Oliver said.

'Not weird. Toxic,' she said. 'If your father wrote over your brain, your soul would be incompatible with his past actions. If you do that ... the result is mental illness. It breaks your soul.'

'That explains some of the quirks of their society,' he said.

'Quirks. That's one word for it,' she said.

'He said you would just witness his life!' I said. 'Not destroy your memories and replace them with his own.'

'Yeah, that's a lie,' he said with a sad smile. 'It's not commonly known, even among the cats themselves – I managed to find out with careful snooping. Only males in the ruling class can do it. My father's nanos tried to overwrite me on his death, but the other cat stopped them and tried to kill me to avoid him being resurrected in my body. Your obvious attempt to save me, under the rules of Aishishistra, means that he has to let me live, but I'm *surplus to requirements*, so they're happy to see the back of me.' He shook his head. 'We knew they were fucked up, but this is beyond belief. If my father hadn't made the mistake of locking you up and breaking Aishishistra, we would still be down there.'

'What the hell is Aishishistra anyway?' I said.

'Sometimes the mothers find out that their child's brain is going to be overwritten and they make a break for it, taking the kid with them.' He shrugged. 'That's what my mother did with me. Stole a ship and ran. It doesn't happen often – most of them are caught before they get too far – but it does happen. I'm the first one for two generations.'

'Your mother ran away to save you – and I killed her,' I said with remorse.

'Oh, no,' he said. 'She would not have hesitated to kidnap a hundred of Earth's children to sell and then blow up the planet. You did the right thing. Aishishistra is the debt that society owes to anyone who returns the clone. That person will receive anything they ask for, for the rest of their life. The ruling class want to be very sure that no female ever attempts to escape with their first-born.'

I filled with understanding. 'And I returned you, so they owed me. Even though I did it without realising.'

'You set a precedent by returning me to my father. You were the first non-cat to be owed. There was a big argument happening in the background while you were there, and the Senate decided that Aishishistra is owed to anyone, regardless of species. That was why he silenced you inside the warp field – you have a unique status among the cats and they have to do anything you ask of them while you're there. I don't think they'll let you back, and they may try to kill you by "accident" to avoid the debt.'

I shook my head. 'I sat there for *weeks* trying to work out why they did that to me.'

'They did it because of internal politics that make no sense,' he said. 'And just so you know: I brought my wife with me.'

'Marque said you brought a female cat, I thought that might be her. You didn't bring her against her will?'

'No. She wasn't pregnant, but she was "contaminated" by being with me. She hadn't fulfilled her duty of providing the clone for my father to move into when I was too old, so she was expected to commit suicide. I'm delighted that she wants to live – there's a really smart, capable young woman in there when you get past the brain washing.'

'Would she like to come up here to the gallery?' the Empress said. She waved one claw at the glittering stars around us. 'We can blank the walls if it will make her more comfortable.'

He studied his feet. 'Right now she's hiding in her quarters, and Marque says it would be best to leave her alone. It will take her a while to adjust.' He looked up into my eyes. 'It's very hard when you can never go home again. Everything is alien to her. She's homesick already.'

'We'll look after her,' I said.

'We will. She has a lot to unlearn, she's heavily brainwashed. The whole society is so messed up. Females are indentured servants until they have their first child; they've been engineered to produce a clone of the father for the first child. Our reproduction seems to be like Earth cats; our women can produce children from multiple fathers in the same litter. They have litters of two or three. The males didn't like the uncertainty, so altering the females was the first thing they did when they discovered genetic engineering.' He shook his head. 'Their reproduction – my reproduction – is as messed up as everything else. When we have some private time, I *really* need to unpack all of this with you, Mum. Being with a cat is completely different to being with a dragon.'

'I'm here,' I said.

'So they produce small litters? What about the clone business? That's the first child?' the Empress said.

'That's right. The first one, the clone, is born alone. This makes virginity highly prized, and virgins are bartered between families to produce the clones. They're held by the family until they produce that goddamn child, then they're free to live a life of their own. Everybody seems to think that this is so fucking *noble* of them it makes me sick.' He gestured towards the back of the ship where the quarters were. 'She was considered especially martyred because I'm such a barbarian. She was being celebrated as the one who would save my father's line at great cost to herself, and she gained as much self-pitying mileage out of it as she could.'

'Damn,' I said. 'You're right about it being fucked up.'

'That's just the start,' he said. 'Ee-yi-oh-ue had bought in to the whole "saving my family from the mines" thing so hard – but there are families who go there all the time to sell their children. Once again, the children are celebrated as martyrs. This whole society is built on celebrating people who willingly let others hurt them. It is *messed up*. Fucking child slavery, and nobody seems to think there's anything wrong with it.'

'They don't hurt the children, though? They're just little playmates?' the Empress said.

'The alien kids are maimed and killed *all the time*. And again: celebrated. "This exceptional child gave his life and happiness for the safety and comfort of his family. What a hero".'

'Our humans are here,' the Empress said. 'The cats sent them in a warp ship on the express agreement that we stay out of each other's space and never speak to each other again.'

'I don't think that will be a problem,' Oliver said.

'Marque will self-destruct to avoid the nanos, then I'll dock with the cat ship and we'll bring them physically across.' The Empress turned to me, her bright blue eyes full of approval. 'Well done, you two. You freed the humans, and gave us extremely valuable insight into cat culture. Your courage is unparalleled.' She turned back to the cat ship, which was losing its glow as it returned to normal space. 'Please reconsider my offer, Jian. I think my guard are right.' She disappeared, then reappeared on the ship's nose to guide it to dock with the cat ship.

'Right about what? What offer?' Oliver said.

'Ugh. They voted me Captain of the Imperial Guard, and they want me to lead them.'

'Don't you dare.'

'I know.'

Masako's ship shuddered as it connected to the cat ship. There was a loud clang and the ship shuddered again.

The Empress appeared next to us. 'Without Marque here we'll have to open the hatch manually. Hands on me and we'll go down to the docking level.'

The Empress carried Oliver and me to the belly of the ship, where Marque had constructed a round, physical docking airlock.

'This is so hard without Marque,' she said. 'We take it for granted. I'll pop outside and shift us into position.' She disappeared.

'Without Marque there aren't even inertial compensators,' Oliver said. 'They really are reliant on it.' His ears twitched. 'How do dragons move short distances through space anyway? I've always wondered. They look like they're swimming through the vacuum.'

I smiled. 'You don't know?'

'Another gap in my education because I'm a cat. I suppose action and reaction, so they must be expelling something. Pooping or farting or pissing through space.'

I nodded.

He turned to me, incredulous.

'Farting,' I said. 'They have their own manoeuvring jets. They wiggle their bodies, like they're swimming, to produce the gas.'

He grinned. 'That is an awesome party trick.'

'No, it isn't; if they do it inside it stinks. Worse than Endicott.'

'Ew.'

The ship shifted and there was a loud clang as we connected to the cat ship. I went to the airlock controls and pressed the button that Marque had labelled, 'This one first to engage the clamps'.

More clangs made the ship shudder as the clamps engaged.

A green light went on, under a label that said, 'You can press the second button to open the inside door now'.

I pressed the second button and there was a loud hiss of escaping air.

'That doesn't sound good,' Oliver said.

A sign appeared that said, 'If you can hear hissing, move your asses. You have two days before the ship loses all its air.'

'Marque really adores its drama,' Oliver said, as the airlock hatch opened to reveal the pale, traumatised faces of twenty human captives on the floor of the airlock.

Oliver and I helped them out – physically carrying many of them – and placed them on the floor of the belly of the ship. The escaping air was on the far connection, so it produced a stiff breeze around us.

'I think we should just open the far side without doing any hygiene,' Oliver said. 'We're losing air anyway; may as well hurry it up.'

I studied the buttons. 'Marque didn't leave us that option.'

'Well damn,' he said. He checked the airlock. 'Clear.'

'I'll go inside and help them,' I said.

'No,' he said, and pressed the button that said 'Close and cycle the airlock when everything is working.' The door closed and the breeze stopped. 'There's a small chance that you'll be stuck in there if the mechanism jams – and it's leaking. I won't risk you.'

'What he said!' one of the captives shouted.

I rounded on them. 'Proceed further into the hold, please, to make room for the next batch.'

'Ma'am,' the captive said, and Oliver busied himself helping them to move.

The light went green above the airlock door and I opened it again.

9

Runa dropped me onto the click homeworld, and Rapclick was waiting for me under the enormous trees.

I clapped my hands at Rapclick. 'May your shell be shiny. I came as soon as I could.'

It clicked its front pincers at me. 'May your bones be solid.' It lowered its pincers. 'You didn't need to rush, dear one, the babies are growing well and they won't moult and separate for at least a couple of your years. I'm sure the Empress has you busy with important work in the aftermath of what the cats did to your people.'

'Not really. The hostages are recovering with their families and receiving therapy. If the cats try to attack us again, it will be years before they reach the edge of their space and we have to worry about them. The Empress started harassing me to be Captain of the Guard again, so I left.' I looked around. 'Where are they?'

'This way; they're in a growth cell protected from predators.'

I followed Rapclick through the enormous trees. The knee-high moss was too soft to walk on top of, and I ploughed through it, glad for the oxygen bubble around me that protected me from the liquid methane. The click moved swiftly on its jointed legs over the mossy brush and stopped to let me catch up. We were on the edge of the growth cell; a round hole a hundred metres across stretched before us.

'Down here,' it said, and scuttled down a ramp that curved away as it fell, matching the interior wall of the cell. Twenty metres down there was a viewing gallery of packed earth with windows overlooking the mossy interior of the cell.

Snapclick and Terrclick's five young were still in their proto stage; juvenile, of low intelligence, and not yet sentient. They'd already had soulstones fitted, but it would take four more years before the stones were attuned. The babies were half the size of the adults, and their colours were a soft mix of Snapclick's pink and Terrclick's violet. The three bodies that would separate when they reached adulthood were connected at the head, making the resulting creatures look like Earth spiders with three bodies and far too many legs.

The juvenile clicks seemed to manage their weird connected state without difficulty; they moved slowly over the surface as they grazed on the moss.

'They ingested their parents successfully,' Rapclick said. Several simple baskets made of woven click-spit sat along the bottom of the window, and it reached into one to pass me a shining pink piece of shell. 'Even though you could not serve as post-ingestion for these outstanding young ones, we wish to honour you.'

I held the piece of Snapclick's shell between my hands and lowered my head over it. It still had some of the delicate silver filigree that the clicks had etched onto it to honour Snap and Terr when they performed their dance. My throat was thick as I nodded to Rapclick. 'Thank you. This means a great deal to me.'

A grey cube, five centimetres to a side, rolled down the stairs and stopped next to us. Another followed, and I watched incredulously as a third appeared.

'You were not invited,' Rapclick said, its voice full of irritation that I had never heard in a click before.

'We observe,' one of the cubes said, and it expanded to a spacesuit that appeared to be four legs without a visible body or head, with the join of the legs at the height of my waist.

An energy creature that looked like a blue-white spark emerged from the lights above and hung down over our heads, roiling with energy. 'What the fuck are you assholes doing here?' the spark said. 'I cannot believe how rude you are. This is a private, invitation-only viewing for close family friends.'

The other two cubes expanded to suits that were the same size as the first, and all three approached the window.

'We observe,' the first suit said again.

'Intensify their social filter, Marque,' I said. 'They sound like psychopaths.'

'They are psychopaths,' the spark said.

'That's the best I can do,' Marque said. 'They're not really psychopaths, they're just radically different from you. I don't have much to work with when it comes to communication between your species.'

The spark hung below the light. 'Please don't for a moment think that their behaviour is typical of us energy types, honoured sentients. These guys are the essence of bad manners.' It retracted back into the ceiling.

'I don't believe we've met,' I said to the spark. 'I'm Jian Choumali. I used to be in the Earth forces.'

'Six Eighty Four Hertz,' the spark said. 'I was good friends with Terrclick on the dragon homeworld, where we were joint spouses of Silver. I miss Terrclick, we had some good times.' The spark flared brighter. 'Don't worry, if these suited fuckers decide to try something, I'll stop them.'

'Can you handle all three?' I said.

'With a hundred volts tied behind my back, to use an expression your Earth soldiers taught me,' Six Eighty Four said. 'I love you humans, you're so small and so squishy and you have a great sense of humour.' It swung down from the light fitting again. 'What are you observing, *lightning strikes*?'

The suits went smaller at the insult, then grew again. 'We observe. Small things.'

'I can see you're watching the babies, but why?' Six Eighty Four said.

'Speculate. Cut. Mature. Quick,' the suits said.

The click scuttled to stand between the suits and the window. 'Touch these babies and I will ensure that you are expelled from the Dragon Empire.'

The suits stood in front of the window, swaying in the air, then all three of them folded up into cubes and shot back up the stairway so fast that they left a methane breeze that lifted the mossy leaves in their wake.

'Marque,' I said. 'What the hell was all that about? Did they want to cut up the babies to make them mature more quickly?'

'They thought it would help,' Marque said.

'Are they really that stupid?' Six Eighty Four said. 'You keep telling us that they're intelligent and sensitive. What they just did is neither. Hell, I'm just as much an energy being as they are, and I would never consider performing surgery on a physical-manifest *child* without the parent's permission.'

'If I cut you into three pieces would it hurt you?' Marque said.

'Well, no,' Six said. 'But I know damn well what it would do to one of my pet breks.'

'They don't have physical pets,' Marque said. 'They don't even know what physical-manifest is; they can't see their home stars' planets. They have trouble processing the existence of physical beings because the nature of matter is outside their realm of understanding.'

'And a dragon had sex with that,' I said, incredulous.

Six went a darker shade of blue. 'When the dragons take energy form, they look so ...'

'I know,' I said wryly. 'They do it to us, too.'

There was a thump above our heads and I peered up through the window. The cubes had attempted to enter the cell and Marque had blocked them. One of the creatures oozed out of its suit onto the energy barrier above the cell. Six Eighty Four was a brilliant blue-white light; the creatures without their suits were a deep orange-red flickering spark.

'Tell them again,' Rapclick said. 'If they enter the cell they are banned from the Empire.'

'To be honest, I wouldn't mind if they were,' Marque said, sounding exasperated. 'I've tried to explain the properties of matter to them, and they refuse to understand. It's like trying to explain the dragons' four-dimensional manipulation to three-dimensional people. Impossible.'

The other two creatures exited their suits and the three of them sat on Marque's barrier.

'Six ...' Marque said.

'I'm on it,' Six said, and retracted into the light fitting.

The energy creatures oozed through Marque's barrier as if it was a minor hindrance, then dropped onto the floor of the cell and disappeared.

'Six won't let them near the babies,' Marque said.

'You sure Six wasn't overestimating its abilities?' the click said. 'Three against one?'

Marque was silent, then said, 'I'm putting an alert out on the network. There has to be another energy citizen within light-travel range; there are a few of their preferred habitat stars around here.'

'I can't see anything,' I said. 'Their frequency is outside my range of vision.'

The interior of the cell glowed and the energy creatures became visible. Six was still blue-white, and had stretched itself like a curtain in front of the click babies. The three red creatures were floating on the other side of the cell in the shape of flexible cylinders that were joined at their middles into a single star-like cluster.

'I think they're discussing how to make it through Six to get to the babies,' Marque said.

'Call a dragon to evacuate the babies,' Rapclick said. 'We must save them!'

I ran back up the stairs and stood on the edge of the hole. 'Neutralise my higher gravity,' I said.

'You can't do anything to stop them: they'll carve straight through you like you aren't there,' Rapclick shouted from below.

'I can give them a demonstration,' I said. 'Stay there and wait for backup, Rapclick.' The gravity around me lessened and I jumped into the cell. One of the babies, spooked by the presence of the suits, scuttled into my landing zone and Marque shifted me sideways so I wouldn't hit it.

I moved to stand next to Six Eighty Four. 'If you cut up a physical creature, it will be harmed.'

'I don't think they understand the concept of harm,' Six Eighty Four said. 'We can't be hurt in any meaningful way: we're either alive or dead, nothing in between.'

'Then tell them that the babies will be killed. Did they kill their dragonspouse when she first arrived?'

The suits separated and hovered in front of me.

'Yes, they did,' Marque said. 'She went straight back to them, so they didn't see it as death. She was fascinated; they were the first energy creatures she'd encountered, and she'd heard how good the sex was with them.'

'You killed a dragon,' I said to the suits.

'What is "killed"?' the suits said.

'You destroyed your dragonspouse.'

'We will not destroy dragons,' the suits said.

'I'm coming in as well,' Rapclick said from the other side of the glass.

'No, stay out there, you may need to provide medical attention if things go sideways,' I said. I turned back to the suits, who hadn't moved. 'And I'm more disposable for a demonstration.' I spread my arms in front of the suits. 'Do to me what you are planning to do to the babies. You will see how much physical people are destroyed by being separated.'

'I will see,' one of the suits said, then rushed straight through Six Eighty Four, and sliced my torso horizontally in half with an energy extension. I was still in shock at the speed of the attack when I hit the moss face-first, the bubble around me broken and methane burning my skin.

The air filled with high-pitched screams that sounded like a sports whistle, and my face was full of burning moss.

'Destroyed,' all the suits said at the same time.

'The same thing will happen to the babies if you do this to them!' Six Eighty Four said.

I wanted to loudly agree with it but breathing the methane was killing me. I was too busy screaming anyway.

*

Marque lifted me out of the medical table in my new body to be greeted by the sight of an enormous opalescent spider with way too many legs and a blue and silver kerchief tied around its hairy abdomen. I hopped off the table and walked up and down, making sure all the bits were working again, as it towered over me, nearly touching the three-metre ceiling.

'Hello, Captain Graf,' I said. 'Did we save the babies?'

'You were remarkable,' Graf said. 'The entire Empire watched you throw yourself in front of them and die a painful death – just to demonstrate what death is.'

I glared at it. '*Did we save them?*'

'Oh.' It lowered itself on its legs with shame. 'Yes, you did.'

'I take it you're here because the Empress wants to see me,' I said.

'Yes. You're in her Palace right now. The Senate attempted to censure the suits about their behaviour and tell them that they're risking expulsion from the Empire, but failed to break through the communication barrier,' Graf said. 'The suits rarely interact with matter, and they have trouble understanding it, so the Senate has delegated the task to the Empress herself. She requests your presence for the hearing.'

'Let's go, then,' I said.

Graf escorted me from the medical centre to the Empress' hearing room. The room was a secure hall within the complex, three storeys high, with an arched roof plated with silver and walls painted sky-blue. Rapclick and Six Eighty Four were already present in front of the Empress, and four of the suits were standing as far as they could from the click.

'Good, here you are, Jian,' the Empress said. 'Have you recovered?'

'Thank you, Majesty, I have,' I said.

'We are about to replay the incident,' she said. 'Would you prefer not to watch?'

I waved it away. 'I'm fine. Go ahead.'

'Marque.'

Despite my casual dismissal, the recording was unpleasant to watch. The suit effectively disembowelled me when it sliced me in two, and I lay screaming on the moss, bleeding out and turning livid purple. Eventually I made some horrible choking sounds and expired. On the image, Six Eighty Four moved in front of the babies, and said, 'If you separate the babies this will happen to them.'

The suits in the recording approached my corpse as Marque lifted my soulstone from my forehead.

'Destroyed,' one of the suits said in the recording.

'Nova,' another said.

'Yes,' Six Eighty Four said, latching onto the common experience. 'She was in a star that went nova. She is destroyed.'

'We contemplate,' the suits said, and disappeared from the recording.

The image blinked out and everyone in the room focused on the suits.

'Not destroyed,' one of the suits said.

'The dragons moved her to a new star,' Rapclick said.

The suits shrank with shock. Before they met the dragons, moving to a new star was a rare achievement for their kind. When their home star went nova, they frantically mated to produce some space-wandering larvae, then attempted the traumatic, dangerous journey to a new star. The attempt usually ended in their destruction as they travelled too far from the stellar winds and died of starvation. This had stopped happening since they'd met the dragons, who carried them to a new star when the sex was done.

'Do you enjoy the company of dragons?' the Empress asked the suits.

'Enjoy,' one of the suits said. 'Nova star, company of dragon, exceptional. Transport, new star, valuable.'

'Yeah, we think the sex is pretty amazing as well,' she said wryly. 'Your sharing with dragons will go nova and be destroyed if you harm another citizen of the Empire.'

'Clarify exactly what we did to avoid repeat,' the suit said.

Rapclick gestured for Six Eighty Four to move closer to them. 'Six Eighty Four is energy. Six lives in a star.'

'We live in stars,' the suits said.

'The rest of the citizens here live on matter,' Rapclick said. 'They are physical. Do not separate them – they must stay in one piece.'

'Matter. Physical. One. Piece.' The red-gold energy creatures left their suits and joined at the middle to discuss the concept. 'What is "one"?' they said in unison.

'Do not touch physical citizens,' Rapclick said.

'Dragons are physical? Can touch dragons.'

Six Eighty Four flared with frustration. 'Don't repeat what you did to poor Colonel Choumali!'

'Which is Colonelchoumali?'

'I am Colonel Choumali,' I said. 'You separated me into pieces and I was destroyed.'

The energy creatures writhed above the floor, still talking to each other.

'Assistance, Marque,' they said.

Marque formed an energy iteration of itself and joined the four energy creatures. They writhed around each other, shifting in colour from deep red through bright orange to yellow.

Marque broke away from them. 'They'll try. They're not really sure what they did wrong, but they'll ask in future. I'll keep an eye on them, Silver.'

'Let me make this abundantly clear,' the Empress said, enunciating carefully. 'If any of you – and I know you are more like a single joint consciousness than individuals – harm another physical-manifest citizen of the Empire, you will be expelled and no dragon will share an exploding sun with you ever again.'

'Marque help. Avoid. More dragons,' the suits said.

'I will make sure you don't make the mistake again.'

'We like the Empire,' the creatures said. They re-entered their suits and left in a hurry.

'Do you think they'll keep their word?' the Empress asked Six Eighty Four.

'They'll make a mistake,' the blue energy creature said with certainty. 'Help them out, Marque. I'd hate to see what happened to Colonel Choumali happen to anyone else.'

'Just Jian, please,' I said. 'I'm not a Colonel any more.'

'Sure, Jian. I think we're done here, thank you all for your attendance,' the Empress said. 'I'm glad the click babies are safe, and I must come to see them, I'm sure they're adorable. Colonel Choumali, you have my highest esteem for throwing yourself in front of those babies. You gave your life to save them – you really are exceptional.'

I tapped my soulstone. 'I didn't really give my life, I'm still right here.'

'That looked extremely painful,' she said, studying me.

I looked her in the eye. 'I'm glad I don't remember it.'

'Dismissed, everybody, thank you,' the Empress said. 'Colonel Choumali, would you like to come up to my apartment and visit with me? Tea and company?'

I gave up with the Colonel business. It looked like everybody had decided that my first name was Colonel, and it was a waste of time correcting them, so I just used the formal words of polite refusal. 'Thank you for the kind offer, Majesty, but I respectfully decline.'

She nodded, unfazed, and delivered the courteous acknowledgement. 'I respect your wishes and treasure our friendship.'

'As do I. Now, if there's nothing else, I'd like to go home to my family.'

'Six Eighty Four?' the Empress said. 'How about you?'

'Let me arrange for someone to feed my breks, and I'll be right with you,' Six Eighty Four said.

'Show the guests out, Graf,' the Empress said.

'Majesty,' Graf said, and indicated the way with its three front legs. The door opened onto a towering hallway that went through the middle of the Palace, and Rapclick and I followed it out towards the square.

'Do you require dragon transport? I can arrange it,' Graf said.

'Yes please,' I said.

'Not for me, I have some dragons to visit,' Rapclick said. It stopped and clicked its front pincers together. 'Colonel Choumali. Thank you for your sacrifice. You are always welcome on the click home planet, and will be celebrated and honoured whenever you visit. May your bones be strong.'

I clapped my hands in reply. 'Thanks, Rapclick. I'm glad I could save the babies. May your shell be shiny.'

'This way,' Graf said, and led me towards the square. 'We have a transport waiting for you in the folding nexus; I'll escort you to the private elevator. The Empress' own elevator car will take you up.'

'Thank you.'

'Colonel, while you are here, please reconsider the Empress' offer for you to take the position as Captain of the Imperial Guard,' Graf said as Marque lifted us through the atmosphere and onto the private space elevator platform. Designed for the exclusive use of parliamentary staff and the royal family, the platform was circular, three hundred metres across, and shining white. Wedge-shaped cars sat around its edge, each on their own elevator ribbon leading up to the folding nexus. 'What you did on the click planet demonstrated courage and sacrifice that would be a real asset to the Empress' household.' We stopped at the Empress' own elevator car, sky-blue with silver scale-shaped decorations over it. 'And I'm terrible at it!'

'You're doing fine,' I said as the door opened. I entered the wedge-shaped space, littered with cushions and rugs dragon-style, and with a small kitchen and separate bedroom. I turned and faced Graf where it stood on the other side of the door. 'The cats are back on their homeworld, the humans are safe, and I'm planning to enjoy every experience the Empire has to offer. Prince Haruka has invited me to view the cherry blossoms on New Nippon.'

'Of course he did; you saved the humans,' Graf said. 'I think a lot of people will want to honour you.'

'Just as long as I have a chance to enjoy myself at the same time,' I said. I smiled at the thought of travelling and meeting new people. 'Thanks for the offer, Graf, but I think I will be having far too much fun to even think about it.'

'Just keep the offer in mind,' it said.

'I will.' I raised my hands to it, then went further into the car and sat on the rugs.

It raised its front legs in return and the door closed.

I reclined on the cushions and closed my eyes. Time to have some fun.

10

The pink petals were a blizzard over the grass of the Imperial gardens on New Nippon. This closed event was only for the citizens of New Nippon who'd been rescued from the cat planet, as a celebration of their freedom and the new peace. The captives and their families had spread picnic blankets on the grass and were enjoying tea and snacks from a row of stalls nearby. A few people greeted us as we walked along the path, but they didn't approach.

Haruka was his usual grumpy self, strolling through the gardens with his hands behind his back. In the spirit of the traditional festival, he wore a dark green, masculine-fashioned kimono under a traditional haori jacket that highlighted his green hair and the scales on his temples. The jacket was embossed with the gold chrysanthemums that indicated his rank. He was flanked by two bodyguards who were as tall as he was.

'Nobody's coming up to say hello,' Masako said, sounding disappointed.

'They were told to stay away from us,' he said. 'The last thing we need is to be mobbed.'

A small child ran up behind me and grabbed me around the legs, nearly knocking me over. 'Choumali! Choumali!' she yelled.

'Sorry,' a woman said, and I turned to see.

'You brought my mother home!' the little girl shouted. She appeared about four years old and was wearing a tiny pink silk jacket and pants, with her hair in cute buns. She released my legs and jumped in circles. 'Thank you thank you thank you!'

The woman picked up the child and put her on her hip. She was obviously one of the captive humans, but I didn't know her. 'Sorry, Ms Choumali, Highnesses, I couldn't stop her.'

'She'd still be there and hurt if it weren't for you.' The little girl reached out to me. 'Thank you.'

I touched her hand. 'You are most welcome. Your mother was very brave.'

'My mother's the bravest!' she said, and the woman laughed.

'I wouldn't say that,' she said. 'I still have nightmares.' She squeezed the little girl. 'But I'm home now, and you and Daddy are looking after me.' She turned back to me. 'I appreciate all you've done, and I'll leave you to enjoy the festival.' She nodded around. 'Apologies.'

'I'm not sorry because Colonel Choumali is the best!' the little girl said as the woman carried her away.

'Come this way, where we've set up a table and chairs to watch the fireworks display,' Haruka said. 'Hopefully no more interruptions.' His face softened. 'No matter how cute they are.'

'Do you have children, Highness?' I said as we sat. Masako's personal goldenscales servant, Miko, was waiting for us and served us with sake and a selection of small dishes that were meticulously prepared to look like the cherry blossoms on the trees around us.

'Masako and I have a monogamous relationship,' he said, nodding to the dragon. 'Any children we have will be dragons, so we must wait for permission from the Empress.'

'You're monogamous, Masako?' I said. 'That's ...' I didn't say 'unheard of'. '... Unusual. What about your other spouses? Surely you had some before you met him?'

'I have never met anyone like Haruka before,' she said. 'I had only two other spouses that I shared with other dragons, and I still see them – but it's not the same.'

'She spends time with her children,' Haruka said. 'I make sure she fulfils her parental responsibilities.' His face went wry. 'Having children with me is another matter.'

'Do you want to have children together?'

They shared a look that said it all.

'Don't look like that, Jian,' Masako said. 'It's not a difficult restriction. It's quite likely we'll be given permission with so many dragons lost during the cat action. It's for the best.'

Haruka glowered at the table but didn't say anything.

'I still feel responsible,' I said. 'If you want to have children, I'm the reason you can't.'

'Ambassador Maxwell's the reason,' Masako said. She bunted Haruka with her head. 'We dragons deserved it. You humans were correct – what we did was wrong.' She grinned up at him. 'We will have a child one day. And he needs to have some human children as well. I cannot wait to see them.'

'As the Emperor's nephew it is my duty to have a backup heir to the throne,' Haruka said. 'Only the current Emperor, me, and one other are direct descendants of previous Emperors, and we are required to have children to continue the line. The children can be at most dragonscales – a dragon can't inherit – but regardless.' He looked into Masako's eyes. 'She is my only one.'

'And you are mine,' she said. 'But you still need to have some human children, my love.'

He sighed loudly and looked away.

A small, round Japanese woman in traditional attire – hair ornaments in a complicated setting, paper parasol, heavy make-up, the whole works – approached us and bowed to Haruka and Masako, then to me. 'Choumali-Sama. I am delighted to finally meet you.'

She wore a delightful blue kimono with a green obi that had plum blossoms embroidered on it, but something about the glint in her eye – and her aura of maturity – made me look twice. She lacked scales on her temples, so she was fully human, and I stared at her hair, trying to work out whether it was a wig or her own thick black hair.

'This is Akiko, my second cousin?' Haruka said. 'She is visiting from Earth.'

'Great-Aunt,' she said as she folded the parasol and sat at the table. She smiled, revealing enchanting dimples in her cheeks. 'I hear that you're planning to travel and experience things like the ice-ribbon skating of Aerna and the fluorocarbon diving of Sillon.'

'Absolutely. Before the cats attacked, I'd finished the flight training on Mon but never did my first solo,' I said. 'I'd like to go back and finish it now that things are resolved between the cats and the Empire.'

'I want to do all those things so much ...' She sighed. 'But I always seem to be stuck wearing restrictive clothing doing ceremonial bullshit—'

'Akiko!' Haruka said.

She ignored him. '... and being introduced to men that I have no interest in. I told the Imperial Household staff about my preferences, and they completely ignored me. They see me as a brood mare.'

'If you fulfilled your reproductive duty to the family, it would not be an issue,' Haruka snapped. 'Only three of us remain, and we *must* continue the line.'

Both Masako and Akiko stared at him, then burst out laughing.

Akiko controlled her mirth to speak to me. 'My mother was the previous Emperor's sister. Haruka's father was the current Emperor's brother,' she said. 'I'm trying to find a place for myself, and I thought New Nippon might be it.' She smiled again. 'I know a spot on the hill where you can see the fireworks over the city; would you like to see?'

I was totally enchanted by those dimples. 'I'd love to.'

'This way,' she said, rising and gesturing with the folded parasol. She bowed to Haruka and Masako. 'Nephew. Princess.'

They nodded to her, then Masako took two-legged form and sat closer to Haruka. It was definitely time to move.

'Do you know how old I am, Princess?' I asked Akiko as she led me away.

'About the same age as me, Jian, early sixties, right?' she said, and stopped. 'May I call you Jian?'

'Of course.'

'Call me Akiko, don't stand on ceremony,' she said, switching to perfect Euro with a slight American accent. 'The reason I'm on New Nippon is to get away from that stifling ceremonial bullshit in the Imperial Household. It doesn't seem to be working, though. How *dare* he scold me about reproductive duty.' She looked around and took my arm. 'This way. Quickly.' She guided me to a stand of cherry trees, then led me through them until we weren't visible from the rest of the group. 'Here, take this,' she said, and handed me the parasol. She ripped off the wig to reveal her hair in a black buzzcut, and suddenly looked completely different. She bent and rubbed her hands over her head. 'Thank god for that, it was driving me *nuts*. So itchy!' She tossed the wig into the air. 'Take it back to the Palace, Marque.'

'I'll take the parasol too,' Marque said, and it lifted from my hands.

'Can I have something to wipe the gunk off?' she said, and a damp cloth appeared in her hand. She wiped the make-up from her face, and a completely different person emerged. She had a squarish, intelligent face under the short hair and her smile was delightful, the dimples becoming even cuter.

She turned the obi around on herself so that the bow was at the front and undid that and the complicated under-ties. The kimono fell open to reveal ripped black pants and a black shirt with thick black boots.

'Do you like punk rock, Jian?' she said. 'Are you into traditional music?'

'I'm British!' I said.

'I'll take that as a yes.' She raised the kimono and Marque took it. 'The Rooster Stews are playing at a basement in town. Once in a lifetime chance to hear them live and acoustic, and they didn't even publicise it. Care to join me?'

I linked my arm in hers. 'Lead the way, Princess.'

'First beer's on me,' she said, and we shared a smile.

*

Rhythm-of-Slaps looked like a blue stingray, except it had two rigid bone projections on its belly that acted as skates. It tapped the ice with its wings to speak as it gave me the final run through.

Marque translated for it. 'This will be much harder without the energy barriers. Remember, if you feel you're going too fast, tell Marque—'

'I know, tell Marque and we can start again.'

'Nobody finishes the course the first time they do it without barriers.'

'I think Jian can,' Akiko said from the other side of the launch platform. She was wearing a black jumpsuit to keep her warm as she waited for her skating window.

I turned and faced the flat ribbon of ice in front of me. It hung suspended from slender ice pillars from the ceiling of the cavern, something only possible in the low gravity of Aerna. The ceiling was transparent, pale blue ice that let in enough sunlight that I could see the first few hundred metres of the path before it disappeared into the expansive space. I blew on my hands to warm them, pulled my gloves on, and readied myself.

Akiko wasn't at this stage yet; she was still skating the ribbons with energy barriers on the sides.

'Come on, Jian, you can do it,' she said from the other side of the platform. It was twenty metres wide and the flat ice ribbon passed through the middle, coming in steeply from the more difficult parts of the run.

A few Aernians were on a platform ten metres above us, supervising the gap between skaters. 'Three minutes,' one of them shouted.

A marine creature in a full enviro-suit skated down the ribbon and through the platform on its skate-equipped fins. It emitted a high-pitched whistle as it passed us.

'Go, Bubbles!' I shouted as it went through. It was so fast that it was gone in a flash of bright pink bioluminescence visible through the transparent suit.

'Show me how it's done, Jian,' Akiko said. I glanced over at her and she smiled, the dimples appearing on her cheeks. She was so gorgeous, so courageous, incredibly educated and successful, and I once again couldn't believe my luck to have her in my life. She saw my face. 'We can celebrate when you succeed. For now, concentrate.'

I turned back to the ribbon. She was right.

'Clear to go, follow me,' Rhythm-of-Slaps said, and launched itself onto the ice ribbon, flapping its wings to propel itself across the sheet. The ice was only a couple of metres wide, and after weeks of practice with Akiko I was finally skating it without Marque's energy barriers on either side.

I pushed myself off and slid down the ribbon as it descended towards the cavern floor. I couldn't see the spectators, but ribbon-skating wasn't much of a spectator sport anyway; it was a jump-in-and-give-it-a-try sport. I hit the first turn; the ice wasn't terribly sloping there, and I had to work hard to stay on the ribbon and make the turn. I made it successfully and skated up a small rise and then around the next turn, following Rhythm's graceful lead.

My breath fogged in front of me as I rounded the turn. Shafts of light from holes in the cavern ceiling made the ice glow, and I felt that I was sliding through a blue-white fairyland. I went down for a hundred metres of exhilarating freefall, then hit the hardest turn. The ribbons were a natural formation, not artificial, and the path narrowed precipitously and did a sharp left turn twenty metres from the wall of the cavern.

I dug the edge of my skates into the ice, pulled a massive amount of traction, and didn't make it. I slid off the edge of the ice ribbon and hurtled in low-gravity slow motion towards the wall of the cavern. The floor was so far down that it wasn't visible. Marque gathered me up and carried me back to the starting platform for another try.

'I notified Rhythm-of-Slaps,' Marque said. 'It'll be here shortly.'

'Thanks,' I said.

'You did great!' Aki shouted. She came to me and hugged me, jumping to reach my height. 'Just a little too fast on that corner, but I'm sure you'll have it next time!'

'Thanks, love,' I said. I bent to kiss her quickly. 'Your turn next.'

'I have a message from the Empress for you, Jian,' Marque said. 'I thought it best to wait until you're free to pass it through.'

'Tell her to piss off,' I said, and the ice rays around me sniggered by slapping their wings on the ice.

'You are amazingly rude to her,' Aki said. She shoved me with her shoulder. 'I love it.'

'It's now a full Earth year since you rescued the hostage humans,' Marque said in the Empress' voice. 'You said to wait a year and then ask you. So, are you willing to be the captain of my guard now?'

'Graf is doing the job and it's doing well,' I said. 'You don't need me.'

'Graf sucks,' the Empress said, and the ray slaps went louder and faster behind me. 'And the usual thing is happening when you have a bad team leader: people are resigning. I've lost twenty members in the last six of your months. They said they'd come back if you became captain.'

'Go away,' I said. 'I've met someone and I'm having a great time ribbon-skating. End transmission.'

Rhythm-of-Slaps skated down the ribbon to join us on the platform. 'Marque, quickly,' it said.

'I'm here,' Marque said.

'What are the current odds? I want to put another couple of hundredths on "No".'

'Current odds are fourteen to one against Jian being Captain of the Guard in the next five Earth years,' Marque said. 'Odds are shorter for a longer time frame, and I won't take bets past ten years.'

'Put another three hundredths of a scale on her not being captain,' Rhythm-of-Slaps said.

'You and everybody else,' Marque said. 'Odds just went in to ten to one.'

'Put a full scale on me becoming captain in the next year,' I said, grinning with mischief at Rhythm-of-Slaps. 'And tell everyone I did it.'

'Wait, what? A whole scale?' Aki said. 'We talked about this, what are you doing?'

I'm just yanking his fins, I said, and she scowled. She didn't believe me.

'Whoa, odds on her not being captain just went out to thirty-three to one,' Marque said.

'You're not serious,' Rhythm-of-Slaps said. 'I have a lot of scales on this!'

'No, I'm not serious. But when you win you'll win a lot more,' I said.

'But you'll lose!' Rhythm-of-Slaps said. 'A whole scale?'

I shrugged. 'The Empress gives me a scale every few months when she asks me to be captain. This is a much better use for them than just destroying them.'

'You destroy *Empress'* scales?' Rhythm-of-Slaps and Aki said in unison.

I chuckled. 'I might as well; they're in storage in my apartment.'

'Two more to pass through, then it's your turn, Princess Akiko,' Rhythm-of-Slaps said. 'How do the Earth authorities feel about you turning down this prestigious position, Miss Jian?'

I scowled. 'The Ambassador and the Empress are both pestering me to captain the guard.'

'So prestigious,' Rhythm-of-Slaps cooed.

'Jian was on call to defend the Empire for more than ten Earth years,' Aki said. 'She deserves some well-earned rest and recreation.'

Aki's supervisor slid down from the viewing platform. 'Princess Akiko, be ready, please. Your window is after the next skater.'

'Please, just Akiko without the Princess bullshit,' she said.

An enormous tentacled mollusc with a black conical shell skated through, squealing like a child. Its aura of pure joy lifted my own emotions.

Akiko grinned and readied herself. 'Energy barriers on, please, Marque.'

'You're nearly ready to try with them off,' Rhythm-of-Slaps said. 'Beat Jian to a clear circuit without them.'

'It's not a competition,' Aki said. 'And I'm quite enjoying doing it without the stress of staying on.'

'Go, Akiko,' her supervisor said, and slid down the ribbon.

Aki flashed me a grin and took off after it, her small round frame moving gracefully over the ice.

'My mother is pestering me to have a child with Akiko, as well,' I said, watching her with delight as she joyfully slid over the ribbons and through the drifting sunshine.

'Oh, that's wonderful!' Rhythm-of-Slaps said.

'Both of us are having far too much fun to worry about having kids right now,' I said. 'I just want to enjoy life, like she said.'

'You deserve it. Five more through, and then it's your turn.'

A legless reptile, like a snake except shorter and rounder, slid past on its belly, hissing like a steam engine.

'I'm going to do it this time,' I said, and stretched.

*

Oliver, David and Runa joined me and Aki on Sillon to try fluorocarbon diving. The tutor was offshore, too big to come close, and she guided us with a human-shaped hologram. Marque passed the breathers around, and we studied them carefully. Each one was a mouthpiece attached to a horizontal tube that held the liquid circulators.

'While I'm teaching you, I'll call the liquid water because it's easier for you,' Basks-in-Sunshine's holographic surrogate said. 'It's slightly less dense than water, so be ready to float more than you're accustomed to. Don't worry about changes in the breather's sound; it will manage your oxygen level and adjust the circulation accordingly.'

I checked the breather; it had a switch on the side to turn it on.

'It will feel like you're drowning,' Basks said. 'You'll find your serious survival reflexes get hit every time your lungs fill with the liquid. It takes a while to get used to it, but no rush. So: time to check your breathers. Turn them on.'

The air filled with the gentle hum of the rotators.

'Step carefully, and follow me,' Basks said, leading us down the ramp into the fluorocarbon sea. She turned and walked backwards, watching us as we descended the ramp. 'When you're up to your shoulders, stop.'

We did as we were told, standing along the ramp.

'Okay, your buoyancy looks neutral. If you have issues, raise your hand and Marque will lift you out of the water to reset your buoyancy. Ready?'

We all nodded. I wasn't worried at the idea of filling my lungs with the liquid; I'd died too many times already for death to be a concern. I just didn't want to embarrass myself by panicking when it happened.

'Right,' Basks said. 'Step down the ramp until the breather is under water. You may find it easier to deal with the feeling of drowning if your head is entirely under water, but this next part is all you. Ready to drown?'

We nodded again and sidled down the ramp until the breathers hit the water. My breather's noise changed from a hum to a vibration as it submerged, and the liquid gushed down my throat. My throat closed up, my lungs filled with liquid, and I panicked at the drowning feeling. I charged up the ramp to wrench out the breather and cough up the transparent fluid. When I could breathe again, I straightened to find everybody else next to me doing exactly the same thing.

Runa didn't need a breather, and she floated patiently in the liquid, waiting for Oliver to gain the skill.

I heard hissing and looked up. Oliver's wife, who still hadn't shared her name with us, had declined to join us but was watching from a viewing platform near the ramp. She covered her mouth and turned away.

Oliver studied her. 'That is the best noise I've heard in a while.'

'It's a big breakthrough,' I said. 'Let's leave her to think about it without any pressure. Marque, if her body language shows that she's relaxing and enjoying herself, ask her gently again if she'd like to join us.'

'I will,' Marque said.

David coughed again and wiped his mouth. 'How the hell do you do that?' he said. 'That's awful!'

'It's just practice,' Basks said. 'You'll be floating around by the end of the day.'

'I'll be doing it before David,' Oliver said. He fitted his breather back in and strode with determination down the ramp again.

'Take it slowly, don't rush or you'll hurt yourself,' I said. 'This isn't a race.'

'Don't be silly, Mum, we're brothers,' David said. 'It's always a race.' He fitted his own breather and followed Oliver. He stopped and removed his breather halfway down the ramp. 'And your fur looks ridiculous when it's wet, big brother.'

Oliver pulled his breather out. 'Less ridiculous than your naked hairlessness, simian boy,' he said, then turned and went into the liquid.

Oliver's wife hissed again and nobody paid any attention to her, but we all shared a smile. The Oliver-and-David show was always entertaining.

I honestly thought Oliver had it, but he charged back up, ripped out the breather, and coughed the liquid up.

'I can do it,' David said, strode into the liquid, and failed as well.

'This is going to take time,' I said, and added sternly, 'and it is *not* a race.'

Oliver's wife cackled with laughter on the platform above us. David hesitated, thinking, then glanced at me, turned, and went up the ramp to the platform that she was sitting on. He sat next to her and leaned in to speak to her, and I couldn't hear what he said. Her body language seemed receptive; she didn't move away from him, and she appeared to be listening carefully to him. She answered him, speaking softly, and I felt a bolt of pride and happiness.

'Leave them to it, Mum,' Oliver said. He lowered his voice. 'I think they really like each other, but neither of them has said anything about it.'

'Another local is here,' Runa said from where she floated at the end of the ramp. Her voice went higher in pitch. 'Goodness! I'd heard that they're big ... but ...'

'This is a small one,' Marque said.

We removed our breathers and made sounds of wonder as a massive bulk edged its way towards us. One of the liquid-breathing locals had come to visit in her own body, without a surrogate. She was transparent blue-green, almost see-through, and fifty metres across, with two-metre-long fins all around her circular edge. She dwarfed us, lying in the water just deep enough to avoid being beached.

'Hello, Deep-Dives,' Basks said. 'This is my third-level reproductive partner, Deep-Dives-Through-Undersea-Caves. She wants to join us when you have the skill.'

Marque translated for her. 'You people are so slow! Hurry up, I want to give you a ride – the red eggs are hatching and the sea is full of them. They glow! Come on, get those breathers going so I can show you.'

'Oh we need to go see that,' Basks said. 'It's glorious.' Her body further out in the water made a sound of pleasure that was a bass rumble so loud that I felt it through my chest. 'And delicious.'

'Deal,' Oliver said. He put his breather back in and went into the water.

'How long will the reds be spawning?' I asked Deep-Dives.

'They just started, so really you guys have ages, I'm just being impatient,' she said. 'I have to be too careful not to knock you over this close to shore, so I'll move away a bit.'

'Do you want a surrogate to talk to them?' Marque said.

'No, no need, Basks is better at training than I am. I'll wait for you in deeper water.' She blinked at us with six crystalline eyes set over the top of her dome-shaped body. 'I want to show you all the pretty things! Hurry them up, Basks-in-Sunshine.'

'We want to see them,' I said, and walked down the ramp again. 'Aki, you are amazing.' Aki was floating in the liquid, breathing it like a pro and blinking in the sunshine. She said something unintelligible in the breather, then switched to throat-speak through the attached microphone. 'Come on, Jian, it's all right once your lungs are full. It's just the transition that's awful.'

Twenty minutes later, everybody else had it and was floating at the end of the ramp. David and the female cat had left to talk in privacy and I hadn't even seen them go. I couldn't work the breather; I couldn't master the feeling of panic and still hadn't managed to control it.

'It's because she's fought for her life too many times,' Marque said. 'It's a survival reflex.'

'You guys go with Basks and Deep-Dives,' I said, disappointed.

'Deep-Dives can take them, I'll stay here and help,' Basks said. 'I've never failed a tourist, and I don't want a war hero to be my first.'

'Are you sure?' Oliver said.

'She'll catch up,' Basks said. 'We will do it!'

'Catch up soon, Jian,' Akiko said, and the rest of the group swam out to Deep-Dives. She opened her purple sphincter-shaped mouth, and they went inside so that she could carry them into deeper water.

'Now that they're gone, we have an option that may work for you,' Basks said. 'It's not pretty to watch, but I think you can handle it.'

'You're going to hold me under water and stop me from running out?' I said.

'Precisely.'

'That's what I was planning to ask you. You can do that?'

'Only with your permission. You won't be harmed, but it may be very stressful for you.'

'How do you hold me?'

'Marque will do it with an energy barrier.'

I put my breather in and spoke through the throat mic. 'Go right ahead.'

'Confirm your permission,' Marque said.

'I confirm. If I die I absolve you of responsibility.'

'You don't need to say that; you won't die,' Marque said. 'Okay, walk down the ramp. I won't warn you, it will be sudden. It might be a good idea to close your eyes and try to relax into it. Ready?'

I nodded and walked deeper into the liquid. I'd been at it long enough now that the feeling of panic began to overwhelm me even before the breather hit the surface.

Marque grabbed me with an energy field, pushed me down the ramp, and held me down. Even though I was expecting it, the liquid poured down my throat and filled my lungs. I was dying. I couldn't breathe. I struggled to get enough air in, and it didn't happen. My intelligence took a back seat to the wild animal panic of the certainty that I was dying, and I thrashed and screamed. Marque held the breather in my mouth and spoke softly in my ear.

'Relax. You're fine,' it said. 'You aren't drowning. Breathe. Breathe.'

I panted against the breather, and my awareness slowly returned to me. I opened my eyes. Breathing the liquid was more difficult than air, but that was because I was trying too hard. I didn't need to breathe, the mechanism did it for me.

I closed my eyes, made an effort to relax, and stopped trying to breathe altogether. My body would still breathe by reflex, and the effort of breathing the liquid would make my chest muscles hurt after a while, but as long as I stayed in control I would be all right. The breather circulated the liquid through me, and I became aware of a floral taste to it – like Earth roses.

I spread my arms and floated. The liquid moved through my lungs, and I wasn't drowning any more. I yelled with triumph into the throat mic.

'Let her go, Marque,' Basks said.

Marque released me and I was free to move through the liquid under my own power. Marque fitted me with some fins and I swam towards Basks' body – it felt like flying; even more than the real winged flying on Mon.

'Open your mouth and we'll catch up,' I said. 'Sorry to hold you back.'

'No need,' Basks said. 'Deep-Dives is just behind my body waiting for us with your family. Let's go.'

Marque guided me towards Deep-Dives' body, over a stunning formation of fluoro-coral in deep purple and black, with bright green highlights.

'The corals are darker here near the shore where there's more oxygen,' Basks said. 'The colours become more blue and paler the deeper we go. Here's Deep-Dives. Hop in and join your family, and we'll go see the reds.'

'Thanks, Basks,' I said.

Deep-Dives opened her mouth and I went in. She closed it, and I was surrounded by my family floating in the liquid. Deep-Dives' mouth was as circular as the rest of her, with orange serrated teeth in two circles around the entrance to her digestive system. She could easily eat all of us alive. Her body was transparent enough to see out through her sides.

She rotated so that her eyes were towards the front and her ring of fins at the back to propel her. Then she took off through the water, and we felt the movement even with the liquid surrounding us.

Akiko floated to me and wrapped her arms around me. 'I am so glad we can share this,' she said. 'I wish I could kiss you. We could take the breathers out ...'

I touched her cheek as I smiled down at her. 'Don't risk your life for a kiss, when the future is ours and we can have all the kisses in the world together.'

She put her head on my chest and I held her, basking in the feeling of being together with someone who brought me so much joy, and with my family who were safe.

11

'What are the tourists behind us saying?' I asked Marque as we walked through the warm, Earth-biology gardens. The ground was paved with silvery tiles, and the planters between the walkways were rich with the scent of the damp loam from the recent rain. The clouds were bright and fluffy, similar to those on Earth, but the sky was a pale watery blue-white. 'I can catch about one word in three – they're speaking a combination of dragon and something else – and they're talking about scales and planets.'

'They're speculating on the cost of keeping the gravity so high and an atmosphere on such a small planetoid, and whether it's tasteful to have a unique twin planet like this so removed from its natural state.'

'We can afford the cost so they can shut up.' Aki tossed her head. 'The Moon is the humans' twin planet and what we choose to do with it is none of their business.'

'You could gently explain to them why we have the barrier and want to protect the site, as well,' I said.

We approached the invisible barrier separating the expensive higher gravity and atmosphere from the enclosed bubble of original Moon landscape. We stopped at the edge and both went silent at the sight of the tiny moon lander – barely more than three metres tall – that appeared to be cobbled together from a mass of spare parts in no particular order or symmetry. The astronauts' footprints were visible in the dust, the path they trod so long ago still there in the vacuum. Dragon footprints skirted the area where a visiting dragon had trodden perilously close to the site, then jumped quickly away when she was warned by her accompanying human spouse. There was a loud ping, and holograms of the astronauts appeared, walking over the footsteps and demonstrating what they had done. The capsule appeared as a hologram on top of the lander, and the whole thing looked far too small to house the astronauts for three days. Holographic information appeared around the astronauts, providing details about the Apollo missions.

'Their little transport vehicle is over there,' Marque said, indicating with an arrow on the surface of the dome.

We followed the edge of the dome until we reached the moon buggy; there were fewer tourists here viewing the historical site. I felt a movement next to me and turned, then my stomach fell out.

Aki was down on one knee, and holding a small ring case out to me. Oh no. I should have seen this coming; it was an anniversary of sorts ...

'Darling Jian,' she said, her smile still causing dimples that made me feel so lucky to have her.

But commitment ... did I want commitment? Could I *face* commitment? I should have known this was coming and been ready for it. Did my expression show my ambivalence? Don't hurt her feelings, Jian, she's the goddamn Princess of your dreams ...

'Two and a half years ago, we met for the first time on New Nippon. It was the six-month anniversary of the release of the humans by the cats. Now it's two and a half years later, and the humans have been free for three years. You did this. I am so lucky to have you ...' She choked up and wiped her eyes with the back of her shaking hand, still holding the ring case. 'You have brought me so much, you are so ...' Her voice squeaked with the effort. 'Wonderful! Please marry me, Jian, and be my Princess.'

I looked into her eyes. I loved her dearly, but the rest of my life? I wanted to run, but I couldn't do that to her. I wouldn't hurt her feelings. The adoration was pouring off her, and I adored her in return. I gathered all the courage I could and did what I had to do.

'I am so honoured, Princess, yes, I will marry you,' I said, loudly enough for all the gawking tourists around us, and they cheered.

Aki burst into tears as she placed the ring on my finger – it was a massive pearl from the beds on New Nippon, surrounded by faceted stones in my favourite shade of green. She threw her arms around my neck and reached up to kiss me, and I lifted her from the ground and spun her around, to the cheers of the crowd. We pulled back and smiled at each other, then kissed again.

I was so glad she wasn't an empath like me. She couldn't know that there was a cold stone full of terror in my gut, sure that this was a huge mistake. I kicked myself. The last two and a half years with her had been nothing but love, light and happiness. Whenever she was called to royal duties without me I was miserable, and she always knew what to say when words failed me. She was an accomplished diplomat, respected scholar, and goddamn royalty. Cruising the seven galaxies with her was non-stop delight, and she threw herself into every experience with courage and fierce enthusiasm.

The stone in my stomach was freezing cold, and I would *not* let this fantastic woman have any idea that I felt this way. I hadn't shared my fear of commitment with her, thinking that it wouldn't have any effect on our relationship. And now this had happened ...

'I'll have to get a ring made for you,' I said into her smiling face.

'I'd love that,' she said.

'A pearl with purple stones around it,' I said. 'Your favourite colour.'

She turned and leaned into me. 'You are the best thing that ever happened to me.'

'And you for me,' I said, giving her a squeeze.

The stone in my gut was still ice-cold, and I was determined to ignore it. Maybe I should seek therapy about this fear of commitment and stop goddamn ignoring it and hoping it would go away. I loved this woman with all my heart and I couldn't imagine life without her.

'Are you sure you want to give up your place in the royal family for me?' I said as we studied the moon buggy together.

'I've been wanting to get out of that stifling atmosphere for ages,' she said, and nudged me. 'You are the perfect pretext. Thanks for getting me out – you're my hero.'

*

It was a spectacularly clear and bright Welsh day, and I suspected that Marque had manipulated the weather for our wedding as we shared our vows in a small family ceremony on my mother's deck.

'Jian, do you take Aki to be your lawfully wedded wife?' Marque said.

I gazed down at her, and she smiled, making the dimples appear. I didn't hesitate. I'd worked through my issues with commitment, and wanted to be with Aki forever.

'I do,' I said, and her smile deepened.

'And do you, Aki, take Jian to be your lawfully wedded wife?' Marque said.

'I do,' Aki said, her eyes glistening with tears.

'Then I pronounce you married in the eyes of the law of the Dragon Empire as it is interpreted on planet Earth, and all human territories.'

My family applauded as we kissed, then laughed when I lifted Aki off her feet and twirled her around.

'*Now* do we eat the potatoes?' Oliver said loudly, and the laughing intensified.

We held each other's hands and walked to the table Mum had set up on the deck, decorated with Welsh dragons and Japanese paper cranes. She and Marque had outdone themselves – the table was loaded with roasted Welsh Golds, a platter of fatty tuna sashimi for Aki, and the cake in the centre was two layers – one chocolate for the humans, and one with a more toned-down sweetness for the hyper-sensitive alien tastebuds.

'So you're not a Princess any more?' Mum asked Aki as she served her dragon partner Yuki some potatoes. 'How does that work?'

'Tradition rules everything,' Aki said. 'Only men can take the throne, and the Emperor has to be human and born naturally. The last time Japan had an Empress, they had sixteen years of drought and the Kyoto Palace blew down in a storm, so it's considered against the will of the gods. There's so much angst about women contesting the throne that when a female member of the family marries outside it, she loses her royal status.' She nudged me with her shoulder. 'Not that this is a problem for us.'

'Born *naturally*?' Diane said, horrified. 'But that's so dangerous! Even with modern medicine, pregnancy and childbirth aren't one hundred per cent safe. That's insane.'

Aki nodded. 'It's one of the reasons why I refused to provide them with the male heir they're so desperate for. And now that I'm married to Jian, I don't need to worry.'

'There's a ferocious team of bureaucrats who run the Imperial Household,' I said. 'They still chase her to "fulfil her duty". The current Emperor lost his wife before they had children, and he's completely heartbroken. He's not mentally strong enough to handle having kids, he needs time to heal. Haruka is a dragonscales, not birth-natural, and won't allow his soulstone to be put on a fully human body to sire eligible children for them. Aki's the only other royal who's capable of bearing a suitable heir.'

'They make my life miserable,' Aki said. 'Hopefully now that Jian and I are legal, they'll stop suggesting that I marry Duke this or Count that and provide them with a couple of heirs because it's my *duty*.'

'Right after we're done here, she has to rush back to New Nippon to preside over the Cherry Blossom festival there,' I said, stealing some of Aki's fatty tuna and dunking it in the sashimi sauce. 'Haruka's gone missing again, and if Aki doesn't show, anything that goes wrong will be her fault.'

'Haruka's gone missing?' Dianne said.

'If there's a ceremony that he doesn't want to attend, he and Masako piss off for the duration, then pop back up when there's no danger he'll have to do it,' Aki said. 'Asshole was supposed to be here, too,' she added under her breath.

'He's avoiding the Household staff, and making sure that Aki regularly meets them so they can pressure her to do *his* job and have kids for them,' I said.

Aki wiped her eyes. 'Let's not think about that now, eh? Let's just celebrate. Now that the certificate is signed, I don't have to worry about them any more and it's all Haruka's job. They can nail him down, put him in a human body, and he can do it for them.'

'We have many more places in the seven galaxies to explore together,' I said, raising my glass of champagne.

'Life is so good!' Aki said, and leaned into me.

*

The take-off platform on Mon was high above the dense jungle of tall, spindly trees in the low gravity. I stood with my wings ready to launch and turned back to check on Aki. She was still in virtual conference with her student, sitting across a holographic table from him.

'No, listen,' she said for the fourth time, her patience starting to wear thin. 'Ivo did the original excavation, but her findings were inconclusive. McNamara went back over the dig, and discovered that things became radically different after the dragons arrived on Ex!ion. Their society was completely changed by the dragons' colonisation.'

'But McNamara's work was later disproved by the Enigmatic Collective.'

'The Collective's results aren't scholarly enough—' she repeated patiently.

'But they are!' he said, protesting. 'I read through them – they're extremely thorough.'

She sighed with exasperation. 'Privacy, Marque.'

'Done.'

Aki lowered her voice. 'I've been trying to hint at this and you haven't been seeing it – but the Collective fudged the results because they didn't want to piss off the dragons. The Collective is so socialised to avoid offence that it will change its reporting of reality – okay, lie – to avoid it. Nobody uses the Collective's findings, they're never unbiased.'

The student from New Edo University, a man who appeared to be in his mid-twenties, stopped with his mouth open. 'That actually happens?'

'Damn straight. Back to public, Marque. The Collective's results are not rigidly scholarly enough to use, so McNamara's results still stand.'

'I see,' the student said, still stunned.

'Now, if you don't mind,' Aki said, smiling at me through the student's transparent head, 'I have places I need to be. Is there anything else you need?'

'Uh, no. Thank you, Professor.'

Aki nodded to him and the hologram blinked out. She rose and came to me. 'What a waste of good dragonscale communication resources. The nature of the Collective's scholarly work is in the basic information kit we give to all archaeology first-years. I'm surprised he made it to post-grad level without knowing.' She touched my right wing. 'Thank you for waiting for me; you are a saint. Ready?'

I took a deep breath and nodded. 'I don't know which is harder. Drowning, or launching myself off a cliff.'

'You can do it!' she said with enthusiasm.

'Princess Akiko, the Grand Steward is on the line,' Marque said. 'He says it's urgent, you're needed back on Earth immediately.'

We shared a look.

'What pretext this time?' she said. 'They have to be running out of excuses.'

Marque changed to the steward's voice, something I'd grown to loathe in the three years we'd been together.

'My Princess,' he said with deference that didn't match his real attitude. 'As you know, there are insufficient members of the royal family able to fulfil all of the ceremonial commitments—'

'Skip to the fucking chase,' Aki snapped.

The steward ignored her. 'And Prince Haruka has been called away to an important diplomatic event on the dragon homeworld, a guest of the Empress herself—'

'He ran off with Masako again and you can't find him,' she said with scorn. 'I can't believe you used *one of my own students* to locate me.'

'A member of the family of at least second rank is required for the full moon ceremony on New Nippon, and you are the only other family member who fulfils that condition.'

'I married Jian and I'm not a member of the family at all,' she said grimly. 'Jian and I are legally married in fifteen jurisdictions, Tokugawa, I'm already outside the royal family.'

'Not until you wear the junihitoe, have the ceremony in the Palace, and the Emperor seals the paperwork,' the steward said, his impatience coming through his voice. He changed to perfectly mild and in control again. 'All we need is for you to have some royal children, Princess, and the pressure will be off you.'

'All right, I'll do it, but I'm still married to Jian,' she said.

'Excellent. Come to New Nippon, we have a husband with *impeccable* Imperial bloodlines lined up for you—'

'No, I meant I'll do the ceremony!' she barked. 'I will not be unfaithful to my Jian!'

'Oh. Well, then, thank you for this small concession, Princess, and please reconsider your attitude. This is not productive for any of us, and with a little flexibility, you can have everything you want. Tokugawa out.'

'Marque,' she said, her voice still full of irritation. 'Block them. I don't want to hear a single thing from either Earth or New Nippon for the rest of our trip to Mon. Let them know that I'll return in time to do the full moon ceremony – but to leave me the hell alone until then.'

'What level of emergency should I let through?' Marque said.

'Nothing less than the Imperial Palace burning to the ground. No, forget that, I won't even go if that happens. Only if something happens to a member of the family, otherwise I don't want to hear anything at all from either place.'

'Done.'

Aki touched my face. 'If a member of the family doesn't perform the ceremony, it's awful bad luck. I'll be blamed for everything bad that happens for the next twelve months.'

'I know. Maybe when we're home, you should talk to them about having kids—'

'Go jump off a cliff,' she said, and gave me a push. 'Go. I'll talk to them and explain to them for the millionth time that we're married, and they're wasting their time.'

'We seem to be at an impasse with them,' I said. 'Maybe you should just marry Kenji or someone, have a couple of kids, get it out of the way, and then come back for ... Oh.'

'Oh?'

'Much as I'm enjoying this drama, you need to take off in the next two minutes or you will lose your window,' Marque said. 'A queue is forming behind you.'

'It's the cat poem,' I said. 'Do your duty, and come back for me. It's about forbidden love, which is probably tragic in a society where reproductive responsibility is everything ...'

'Ninety seconds, Jian.'

'Go. We'll talk about it when you've landed,' she said.

I turned, took some deep breaths, and launched myself off the cliff. The updraft lifted me and the bio-sensors on my wings passed the exhilarating feeling through to me. I pulled higher with a few strong wing beats – I could feel every artificial feather – and I lost myself in the freedom as the jungle passed beneath me, then a wide white sandy beach, and the translucent, turquoise shallow water of the bay. I banked to turn back towards the cliff, a buttress of shining white against the green of the jungle full of spindly low-gravity trees, and surrounded by the glittering wingspans of other aliens who were sharing the experience of flight. I refused to let the inevitability of Aki's situation get to me, but we both knew the truth. The Imperial Household wouldn't let her go – or us be together – until she'd fulfilled her duty to them. There weren't enough members of the royal family to go around, particularly when New Nippon was looking to expand onto two more planets with large amounts of water that would nurture their tuna farms. She had to marry within the royal clan, and she had to produce some kids for them before they would leave her alone.

*

Runa and Oliver dropped us at our apartment in Tokyo and Marque turned the lights on for us.

'Thanks, guys,' I said to them as Aki wandered into the bedroom to check the messages. 'Stay for food?'

'Since we're on Earth we might go visit Nan,' Oliver said. 'I haven't had any of her potatoes in a while, and I think David and Cat are visiting her. We'll bring Endicott back to you when we're done.'

'Sure,' I said. 'Tell Mum I'll come visit after we're settled back in, and Aki's dealt with the Imperial Household. I'm sure there's a million messages for her—'

Aki made a loud sound in the other room that sounded like a cross between a gasp and a small scream, and we all went in. She was watching the holo messages, and her eyes were wide. She looked at me, then back at the screen.

'I cannot believe they did this,' she said, her voice weak. She fell to sit on the bed. 'I don't believe it.'

'What did they do?' Oliver said, and moved so that he could see the messages more clearly. 'Oh, that's cute? Messages from schools ... so many messages from junior and middle schools ...' He swiped his hand in the air to bring up more messages. There were thousands of them. 'Uh ...'

'A petition,' she said, and her emotions were shattered. '*Millions* of people signed it.'

I read it out loud. 'We, the people of New and Old Nippon know that Princess Akiko loves her nation and its rich history. The vital legacy of the Imperial family is at risk. We humbly request that Princess Akiko save the Imperial line ... Oh, no way.'

'This is emotional blackmail,' Runa said. 'You don't have to do it, Aki.'

Aki waved one hand at the screen and it scrolled over hundreds more messages from well-wishers. 'A million of my own people are concerned that they're going to lose their Imperial family. I cannot—'

'The Chief Steward of the Imperial Household is downstairs, with a relative who doesn't want to be named,' Marque said.

'Damn Haruka to hell.' I sat next to Aki and put my arm around her shoulders. 'We could pull a Haruka on the man himself, and disappear again.'

'I'll take you,' Runa said.

'Bring them up, Marque.' Aki stood and straightened her favourite leather jacket. 'I can do this.'

I turned to Oliver and Runa. 'Go visit your grandmother, Oliver. Ask Marque when you can come back.'

'Don't do it, Aki,' Runa said, and they disappeared.

Four men rose on the elevator platform into our apartment. The Grand Steward and two Japanese Imperial Household Guards accompanied the Emperor himself. The Emperor had a strong family resemblance to Aki in height and solid body type. The guards stayed at the platform as the Emperor strode to us with a wide smile, pulled us up from our bows, and shook both our hands. 'So good to have you back, Aunty. Miss Jian. May I talk to you? Only for five minutes, I won't take much of your time.'

Aki didn't smile. She was fond of her nephew, but we both knew why he was at our home.

'On the terrace,' she said, and the full-height glass doors opened onto our private rooftop garden. We had the entire top floor of the large building, and the apartment occupied half. The other half of the roof was a Japanese garden that Aki had designed herself – it had a small stream running through it, over stones that she had painstakingly collected during our travels. She'd even named the koi carp that resided in the pond at the end.

Aki led the Emperor and Household steward out to the garden, and we walked along the path that meandered through it. The view over the city was spectacular – Japan had limited the use of three-dimensional advertising, so signs were restricted to two dimensions, but with the advent of dragon technology they were sharper, clearer and not limited in size. The city glowed, with some brilliant moving billboards covering the entire sides of skyscrapers.

A couple of buildings were lit up with images of Aki, with 'Welcome Princess, saviour of the Imperial legacy' written beneath them.

'Have you seen the news, Princess? I'm surprised you didn't return sooner,' the Emperor said.

'I'm horrified,' she said.

'I am so sorry that this happened,' he said. He stopped and bowed to her. 'It is unforgivable that the people are asking so much from you, when this is my duty.'

'It is, isn't it?' she said without stopping.

He seemed flustered for a moment, then followed her. 'And I am failing in this duty, so they have turned to you. No single person suggested it – it went viral on the social network, a royal-watcher designed the petition, and everybody signed it. Schools added to the petition, and then sent you their own messages.'

'We tried, but we could not control it,' the steward added.

'Of course you couldn't,' she said without looking at them. She stopped and sat on a bench overlooking the pond, and I stood behind her with my hand on her shoulder. They stood in front of her, straight and determined.

'The people adore you, Princess,' the Emperor said. 'They love you far more than Prince Haruka, and want you to be the mother of the next Emperor. But we support you in your decision not to suffer this temporary inconvenience. If you choose not to produce an heir for the good of the nation, we cannot force you.'

The steward gave her a moment, then twisted the knife. 'We think it would be best if you made a formal announcement to tell them that you are rejecting their very reasonable request, and putting your own happiness before the needs of our nation.'

The Emperor bowed again. 'I am sincerely sorry that we must ask this of you.'

'Please go away,' she said, as if from a million miles away. 'I need to talk to my wife.'

The steward filled with triumph that was completely unnoticeable from his demeanour.

'I understand,' he said. 'We will return tomorrow with a crew to make the announcement.'

The Emperor was filled with sadness so deep and crushing that I wanted to weep for him. He bowed to Aki again, and they walked out without another word.

'Temporary inconvenience,' I said, loud enough for them to hear as they went down on the elevator platform.

'I'm so fucking tired of running from them, Jian,' she said.

I sat next to her and held her hand. 'It's your choice. They'll let you do what you like if you give them the goddamn kids. We're effectively immortal, we could have the rest of our long lives together, without them chasing you.'

She gazed into my eyes. 'What's the point of being immortal if I can't be with the one I love?'

She put her head on my shoulder and I held her.

*

A black limousine picked me up from our apartment and took me to Senso-Ji Temple in Asakusa. The area had been cleared, the bazaar next to the temple empty, as I walked under the enormous main gate with its huge lantern. Aki and Kenjiro were standing beside a table with half-a-dozen Imperial Household stewards behind them. Grand Steward Tokugawa was in the middle, standing quietly in a perfectly tailored old-fashioned morning suit, the expression on his thin face cool and detached.

Tokugawa gestured for me to sit at the table, which had a folder and a pen on it and nothing else. I ignored him and studied Aki. The Household had taken her a week before and she looked strained. She was miserable at being forced to do this, but determined to survive. Her fiancé Kenjiro stood next to her, broadcasting awkwardness. He was similar in build to her – much shorter than me, and slightly overweight with a squarish face. He was a distant cousin through the complicated Imperial bloodlines, and a complete sweetheart that both Aki and I considered a friend. He was deeply distressed to be doing this to both of us, and I didn't have the emotional strength to tell him that I would survive – because I wouldn't.

Tokugawa opened the folder and held the pen out to me. I felt like this wasn't real as I approached the table and saw that Aki had already signed the divorce papers and sealed them with her personal chop.

'I'm sorry, Jian,' she said as I took the pen from the steward.

'Not your fault. We'll make it,' I said as I signed the paper. I smiled sadly at the irony. 'I had so much therapy to overcome my issues with commitment – and here we are.'

Tokugawa broadcast triumph as he snatched the pen from my hand and closed the folder with a snap. He turned to Aki. 'We will now proceed with the blessing of the marriage.'

Aki and Kenji went up to the wishing slots, where a couple of the resident monks were waiting for them with charms and coins. Aki tossed a coin into the slot, then clapped her hands to make the wish.

She turned and spoke over her shoulder. 'Come and make a wish, Jian.'

I looked to the faces of the other people present; Tokugawa looked furious but didn't stop me. Kenji nodded. 'It's all right. Go make a wish.'

'You too, Kenji,' Aki said.

I went up to the slots. The monk smiled at me and handed me a coin. 'We appreciate your sacrifice, Choumali-san. Hopefully one day you and the Princess will be together again.'

'We will,' I said as I took the coin. I tossed it into the slots and clapped my hands as well.

Kenjiro touched my arm. 'I'll look after her, Jian, and hopefully you two will be able to visit—'

'That will not be possible,' Tokugawa said stiffly behind us. 'There will be no more time alone unless it is the Duke and the Princess.'

Aki lowered her head over the slots. 'I'll be buried alive.'

'We'll arrange something,' Kenji whispered.

'No, you won't,' Tokugawa said. 'This marriage is important for the *nation*. For *both* nations – old and new. When the children have reached adulthood we can discuss the future. In the meantime, this is a traditional marriage between a Princess and a Duke and nobody else. Consider yourselves lucky that we have permitted you to say goodbye.' He lowered his voice. 'I know it's a long time, but Haruka refuses to do his duty and won't have a child unless it's with Masako. Your sacrifice – all three of you – is honoured; you do this for your country. You will be honoured throughout history, and your first-born son could very well be Emperor of all Japans if the current Emperor doesn't recover from the loss of his wife.'

Aki glowered at him.

'We're effectively immortal, Aki. Just take very special care of yourself and come back to me,' I said.

'Same to you, my love,' she said with tears in her eyes. 'Haruka *owes* me. I will miss you.'

I took her hands but didn't put on a more public display of affection in the temple grounds – particularly when she was going off to marry someone else. 'I love you,' I whispered.

'I love you too,' she said.

'We'll work something out,' Kenji said.

'No, you won't,' Tokugawa said. 'I have a car waiting for you, Princess Akiko and Duke Kenjiro; if you will come with me, we have a wedding to prepare for.'

Aki gave me a last despairing glance as the bodyguards closed in around them and guided them to the car at the front of the temple.

'I'll be here,' I shouted.

She nodded to me and disappeared into the car.

*

I sat next to the koi pond on our rooftop terrace, not really feeling the warm breeze. Endicott, sensing my melancholy, had put her head in my lap and I stroked it absently. The hologram in front of me didn't look like Aki at all; she stood unsmiling wearing an exquisite multilayered junihitoe kimono with a small crown adorning her wig. Kenji stood next to her holding a sceptre indicating his rank. Both their sets of robes were flawlessly arranged around them, and they looked more like a pair of dolls than real people. The image had been released six weeks ago, and there'd been nothing on the news since.

'You should eat something, Jian,' Marque said. 'You've been sitting there doing nothing for hours.'

'I don't feel like doing anything,' I said. 'Leave me alone.'

'What if I told you that Akiko had a message for you?'

I shot upright, startling Endicott. 'What? Show me!'

'Only if you eat something.'

'You are not my mother!'

Marque's voice became sly. 'Do you want me to arrange for your mother to come supervise you?'

'All right,' I said. 'But not something that I ate with Aki. The memories hurt too much.'

A small table appeared in front of me holding a bowl of something hot with a spoon. I tried it; it was a Western stew of meat and vegetables, warm and filling, and entirely unlike any of the food that Aki and I had shared. 'Thank you. Now where's my message? It's been weeks! Is she okay?'

Aki appeared in holographic form above the small lawn and I gasped. She was wearing a horribly old-fashioned women's skirt suit in pale pink, and she'd grown her hair out, tied into a bun at the nape of her neck. She looked a million years old, and she'd lost weight.

'I don't have long,' she said, wringing her hands. 'Kenji is a saint smuggling this holo out for me. Okay: I'm all right, it's tedious and repetitive and I never have any *fucking* privacy but I'm alive. This was way more important than they let on. The Emperor is severely depressed – suicidally depressed – from a combination of grief and the torturous bullshit they put us through in here. The stewards won't let Marque change his brain chemistry to alleviate the depression, because he has to be birth-natural to be Emperor. Anti-depressants are the only thing keeping him alive. The stress of having a child right now would probably tip him over the edge.'

I glanced up at a floating Marque sphere and it froze the recording.

'If I could shrug I would,' Marque said. 'The internal workings of the Imperial Household are under privacy seal. She'll be in trouble if you share this information, that's why they won't let her talk to you.'

'I see,' I said. 'Resume it. I won't tell anyone.'

'Jail would be a *holiday* compared to this – at least I'd have some privacy and be left alone occasionally!' Aki raised her hands to rub her eyes, then lowered them and smiled sadly. 'Can't ruin the make-up.' She took a deep breath. 'What I'm doing here is more important than we realised. Haruka's too proud to share the truth, even with Masako, but dragonscales can't inherit at all. The Emperor must be fully-human, and as a dragonscales Haruka is ineligible to continue the line. If he moved into a fully-human body, it wouldn't be birth-natural. Please don't share this with anyone, he's deeply humiliated by what he sees as his failure, and runs away to avoid difficult questions.' She choked with emotion. 'I am the *only one* that is capable of having a suitable, fully human heir right now. I wish I could fast-forward through this on a warp ship or something, but I have to do it.'

'They're coming, Aki,' Kenji said to one side.

'I love you, darling Jian. Kenji got your message to me – Marque tells me that you're just as depressed as the Emperor, that you're sitting around at home being miserable. Go find something to do, please? To keep yourself busy? Accept the Empress' offer and be her guard captain. Do it for me, because I worry about you, and if you did that at least I'd be able to see you on the news when they report on the things she does.' She lowered her head. 'We're trying to get me pregnant, so that this is over with as quickly as possible—'

She blinked out. Kenji appeared.

'The stewards arrived and we had to stop. We're alive. Please wait for her.' He disappeared.

'So Haruka's lying to everybody – even Masako?' I said. 'His whole life is a lie?'

'You've been living with dragons for more than fifty years, I thought you'd be accustomed to lies by now,' Marque said.

'Not from humans.'

'He's half-dragon. And it would ruin him if you were to share this information.'

'Don't worry, I won't.'

'You have visitors.'

'I don't want to talk to anybody right now,' I said, looking around for something to wipe my face with. 'You shouldn't have told them.'

Oliver, Runa, David and Cat appeared in the living room, then came out to the terrace. Female cats didn't have names, they were just labelled as possessions of their males, and she'd taken the human name of Cat as an alternative that still respected her heritage.

'Hi, kids,' I said. 'Tea?'

'It's been six weeks, Mum,' David said. 'Marque told us what you're doing. You need therapy. Or a distraction. Something.'

'It's breaking our hearts to see you like this, gentlewoman,' Runa said.

'You're the one who told *me* that staying busy would help with the homesickness,' Cat said, and she and David shared a smile. Their love for each other was what had really helped with her homesickness.

'I appreciate you all coming. I love you dearly, kids.'

'Aww, Mum,' Oliver said, and hugged me. David joined him and they wrapped themselves around me.

'Now we need to find something to pull you out of this funk,' Oliver said. 'It's making us just as miserable.'

'Don't guilt-trip her!' Cat said, horrified.

'There is something,' I said. 'Aki just asked me to accept the Empress' offer to be Captain of the Imperial Guard. What do you think?'

All their faces lit up.

12

I stepped out of Dragonhome's space elevator onto the platform and headed towards the edge.

'Captain Jian!' someone shouted to one side, and I turned. Five Imperial Guards, in their blue and silver uniforms, were waiting for me. Two were small mammals, one was an aquatic in a liquid bubble, and one was a metre-long slug. Graf itself towered over all of them at the back.

I went to them and they each placed a limb over various parts of their bodies. I put my hand over my heart in return.

'Thank the thousand-legged hellspawn you're here,' Graf said. 'Welcome, Captain. Come with us.'

I followed the group towards a transparent floating disk, and we all stepped up onto it. The disk lifted and carried us over the edge of the platform then headed down towards the Imperial Palace. I'd travelled this way enough times that I didn't panic at the lack of walls. Flying over the Palace precinct wasn't encouraged, to preserve an uncluttered vista, and when people did fly on transparent disks, the preferred travel method was to have the passengers made invisible by Marque.

'Captain Shudo can't make it; the babies are still too small,' Graf said. 'So unfortunately you're stuck with me to show you how everything works.' It raised its three front hairy legs, which reflected the light in pearlescent rainbows. 'I am so sorry.'

'Marque can help,' I said. 'I'm sure you did fine.'

'Yeah, that's not the case,' Graf said.

'Graf tried, ma'am,' the aquatic said. 'It did its best.'

'That's the part that hurts the most,' Graf said. 'It's terrible when your best isn't good enough.'

We arrived onto the square next to the Empress' Palace.

'I've moved out of the captain's quarters, and the habitat's been erased,' Graf said. 'Come this way.' It turned on all thirteen legs to face the other guards. 'Leave us to it and come back tomorrow.'

'Captain?' one of them said, and they all focused on me.

'Uh, dismissed?' I said. They appeared satisfied with that and left.

'Good,' Graf said. 'Excellent start.' It gathered itself, rising and dipping on its legs. 'The Empress sleeps in a floating dome above the Palace – it's not physically connected to the rest of the building; she's carried by Marque into her bedroom. We occupy the top of the building beneath her; anyone else who wants to see her outside audience hours has to go through us.' The disk lifted again and carried us through the floor of the mushroom-shaped tower in the centre of the Palace. We arrived at a round room that was twenty metres across, decorated in blue and silver, and obviously their common room. There were tables, chairs, mats and holographic entertainment areas.

'Ready to see your quarters?' Graf said. 'You should start there; you have to tailor them.'

'Yes.'

It guided me through the door – ducking so that its eyes didn't hit the top of the frame – into a curving corridor with more doors opening off it. It led me along the corridor for a few doors, and we arrived at a door that was the full height of the corridor, nearly three metres, with a blue and silver chevron embossed into it. Graf led me through to an area that was obviously a section of the circular tower. Each long side was thirty metres, and the curved part was a similar size, with huge windows overlooking the Imperial Square. The room was a massive triangular space thirty metres to a side, and the short wall with the door was ten metres across. The gravity was so low that I grabbed the door frame to avoid slinging myself into the room. The oxygen was too high, the humidity was saturating, and it was raining gently.

'Sorry, I left it on Graf's specs,' Marque said, and the weather stopped. The air dried to Earth-normal bio parameters and the gravity became close to Earth-normal.

'How long do you need to work with Marque to set it up for you?' Graf said. 'Let me know and I'll have everyone gather in the common room to meet you when you're done.'

I walked up to the windows; the room was up so high that nearly the entire square was visible, with many citizens of the Empire strolling among the exhibition domes displaying the current featured planet's wildlife. The blue-white sun was setting, throwing pale blue shadows across the white tiles of the square.

'I want to see my office first,' I said. 'I take it there's a workspace with a private meeting area and room for the records close to the Empress' own? That's more important than my living space.' I looked around. 'Marque, put together something like I had on Shiumo's ship to start off with – bedroom, bathroom, living room – and I'll tweak it later. Create a small garden-type area for Endicott, and ask a dragon to bring her.' I turned to Graf. 'I want to see the workspace, catch up with the protocols, and speak to the Empress. I'll talk to the rest of the team after that – there's no point in giving them a huge lecture about what I'll do in the job if I have no idea about the internal culture.'

'This way, ma'am,' Graf said, broadcasting awe.

'How many members in the guard at the moment?' I asked Graf as Marque took us down to the administrative centre.

Graf's mouthparts moved uncomfortably. 'We lost many, ma'am, because of my incompetence. I'm very intelligent with numbers and records, but hopeless with species that aren't similar to my own. Eating your young is just so *normal* for me, and in other people's eyes it makes me a monster. I keep forgetting not to joke about it.'

'You must have a blast comparing social cues with the clicks,' I said.

'I have asked a click to give me tips on negotiating and dealing with—' Graf began, then stopped. 'By the many-legged. That was a *joke*. I adore you and want to hold you down and force you to have sexual relations *right now*.' It made a low rumble deep in its abdomen. 'We have twenty-seven members remaining from the allocation of forty-six. Eight are on rotation at any one time, but this does not give us sufficient numbers to handle sudden time off in emergencies. The Empress is not sufficiently guarded by living subjects.'

'I am deeply offended,' Marque said.

'She's only guarded by a worthless AI that would rather see drama than safety,' Graf said with emphasis.

Graf showed me to the captain's office: the area was still configured for its own species, who kept records in their webs. There was a central open space with a scaffold for Graf to sit on, surrounded by a dense tangle of scarlet webs that were its records.

'Marque hasn't reconfigured it yet,' Graf said. 'You need to tell it what you want.' It stood in the middle of the room under the scaffold and fidgeted with its front palps.

'Did you cross-index the records? How did you organise them?' I said, looking up at the maze of threads. The ceiling was twenty metres above, in a cone shape, and the webs covered every surface.

'Yes!' Graf said, and raised all three front legs with enthusiasm. 'The records were totally disorganised when I came – Shudo relied completely on Marque and cared more about morale than efficiency.' It lowered its legs. 'Probably why we lost so many staff. I've reindexed them, cross-indexing on date, officer involved, and type of incident. Some interesting trends have appeared – I think you need to talk to one or two of the officers about their relations with particular species types.' It crouched with shame. 'I didn't want to bring it up with them, after doing such a poor job.'

'I understand.' I hesitated, then ploughed on. Graf was hopeless with social cues, and Marque wasn't helping. 'I'm going to move everything in the office around, and you don't need to stay and watch. You've done a great job, and I'll convert this to something more suitable for myself. If you want to go out while I mess up your hard work, I would understand.'

Graf stood looking at me with all ten of its eyes. 'You will be a wonderful captain,' it said, turned and went out, closing the door behind it.

'Marque, you *fucker*!' I shouted at the ceiling. 'You complete *bastard*. You do that to *any* of my fucking staff *ever again* and I will fucking banish you from *every* family meeting that I have for the next ten years and you will hear no more Choumali drama for a *long time. Do you understand?*'

'What did I do?' Marque said, sounding bewildered.

'How fucking *dare* you,' I grumbled, still pissed. 'You'll put up a strong socialisation filter for the clicks because they're useful, but poor Graf gets its words translated directly. You know damn well that Graf's compliment was an offensive threat of violence to humans, you fucker.' I waved at the webs. 'Turn this into a written searchable database in Euro on a standard holodesk.'

'Oh,' Marque said, and the room reorganised itself. The webs disappeared, revealing white walls, and the desk grew from the floor, with the display above it showing all the incidents in a complex network of connections.

'Meeting table for six, with space big enough for aliens of Graf's size,' I said, moving behind the desk to see the database. I pulled one of Graf's marked connections closer and inspected it. 'Make an area for Endicott behind my desk, with a dog bed for her. Heh. Graf's right, it looks like Five-Shriek really hates aquatics.' I looked around for another door, and none were visible. 'Does this room connect to the Empress' office?'

'Yes. There's a portal in the ceiling that comes out through the floor, next to my decorative tube at the back of her office.'

'Move this office next to hers and give me a connecting door that I can use. Confirm with her as to whether she wants a privacy atrium between the two areas.' I swung the display around. 'Bring up the roster.'

The names, species and designations appeared on the desk, and I sat to go through them. I checked the local time; it was near to the end of the working day. 'Tell the guard I'll meet with them first thing tomorrow, and let me know when Endicott arrives.' I glanced up and said, 'You'd better look after my dog.'

'I will, ma'am,' it said, sounding sheepish.

Many hours later I yawned and stretched; it was nearly two a.m. my time and I should really get some sleep, even though the incident records were fascinating. I rose to head towards my quarters, and realised that I'd been so engrossed in the job that I hadn't been thinking of Aki at all. The knowledge that she'd be glad to see me like this pierced my heart.

*

My investiture was a major ceremony held in the middle of Sky City square. A raised circular dais stood in the middle of the square, three metres higher than the surface. Marque carried the Empress and me over a surprisingly large crowd of spectators – there must have been more than a thousand, human and alien, but many of them were probably there for the obligatory post-ceremony party. Marque dropped us onto the dais, where the rest of the Imperial Guard were arrayed in ranks waiting for us, with Graf at the front. A couple of smaller dragons that I didn't recognise were there as well, and a goldenscales servant dragon.

Even though the blue-white sun had set, artificial light wasn't needed. The dragon homeworld had no moons, and its location close to the centre of the Milky Way Galaxy made the sky a haze of bright, colourful stars. A blue and purple nebula was close enough to fill half the sky in Sky City; the city's location was chosen to give the maximum benefit of its beauty, and the dragons occasionally moved the floating city when the view became stale. The folding nexus of linked satellites with their space elevators connecting to the ground glittered like a web over the brilliant surface of the sky.

The Empress stepped forward, and Marque created a projection of her above our heads. The crowd went quiet.

The Empress turned to face the guard. 'Captain Graf.'

'My Empress.' Graf raised its three front legs and stood quietly in front of her.

'You are discharged from your position,' she said. 'I accept your resignation. You have served me faithfully and well.' She turned to the spectators. 'We recognise the exemplary service of Captain Graf and wish it well in the future.'

'I pass my commission to my successor, Jian Choumali,' Graf said. It stepped back and gestured with one of its palps for me to come forward.

I stepped up and stood in front of the Empress next to Graf.

'Do you promise to protect the Empress, even to the loss of your own life?' Graf said.

'I do,' I said.

'Do you promise to obey her orders without question?' Graf said.

'Oh, hell no,' I said. 'I'll question her orders if I think she's being unwise.'

Graf turned to face the Empress. 'I recommend you accept Jian Choumali's service as Captain of the Guard. She'll protect your life, and intelligently advise you in matters of household security.'

'Jian Choumali,' the Empress said, and the crowd went silent. 'Do you place your soul in my hands?'

I reached up and levered my fingertips around the edge of the soulstone in my forehead. There wasn't any adhesive holding it in; it was more like a magnet, clinging to the soul within my body. I prised one edge away and the entire stone popped out of my head. It was three centimetres across, and faceted red in acknowledgement of Shiumo, the first dragon to visit Earth and begin our reproductive conquest. I knelt and held the stone out to the Empress.

It seemed that everybody present was holding their breath. The Empress took my stone and nodded to me. She raised it to the crowd. It was highly unlikely that a drop from a couple of metres could damage a soulstone, but there was still a chance of it happening, and it truly felt as if she were holding my life in her hand.

'I accept Jian Choumali as Captain of the Guard,' she said. 'Obey her as you would me.' She gave me the stone back, and I popped it back into my forehead with relief. It really did feel like a magnetic tug, and the weird energy from the stone pulsed through my head. It wasn't painful, more like a rush of pins and needles as it attuned itself to my soul frequency.

'Tomoyo,' the Empress said, and a pale grey dragon, almost white, with deep brown eyes stepped forward. She had four legs and a pair of massive wings that she kept carefully folded at her sides. 'This is your personal dragon transport,' the Empress said. 'Tomoyo is yours to transport you anywhere you wish, any time.'

Tomoyo bowed her dragon head to me. 'I am honoured to work with you.'

'Wait what—' I began, but the Empress didn't let me finish.

'Please join me in celebration for the new Captain of the Guard,' the Empress said. 'We will have a four-sector celebration, with fringe contests of strength, skill, intelligence and battle. Enjoy!'

Transparent walls of rainbow-like energy sprang up from the corners of the square to the centre, and four grey symbols appeared above each person's head.

'I don't need a personal dragon transport,' I said to the Empress through the cheering of the crowd.

'It's part of the job. It's as prestigious for her as it is for you.' She glanced down at me. 'Deal with it.'

'What she said, Captain,' Tomoyo said. 'Any time you need me – day or night, on-world or off-world – you can call on me. I'm based on the folding nexus, so I can carry you from the homeworld at any time.' She eyed me appreciatively. 'I'd be delighted to show you my two-legged form later.'

The Empress snorted with amusement, then grew serious. 'Heads up, diplomats incoming.'

A group of ambassadors approached the central area. The Empress graciously introduced me to everybody, and Ambassador Maxwell had brought her husband. He was much taller than her, and had undergone the rejuvenation treatment to make him appear in his thirties, to her fifties. His translucently fair skin glowed under the lights of the party and highlighted his bright red hair – something not often seen since the Great Migrations of the early twenty-third century.

'I'm showing my husband how dragon celebrations work; this is his first time,' the Ambassador said.

'How do you know which section is which?' he asked her.

'Ask Marque for confirmation when you move from one to another,' she said. 'We have preference indicators over our heads; nobody will ask you to have sex with them, don't worry. Tell Marque which sector you want to participate in, and the symbol above your head will glow. It stays grey if you don't.' The Ambassador nodded to me. 'No rest for poor Captain Choumali, though, she has to follow the Empress through all the festivities.'

'It's shapes as well,' I said. 'Squares for food and drink. Circles for music and dance. Triangles for storytelling, and a wobbly rounded shape for the orgy.'

'It's not an orgy,' the Empress said with scorn. 'Reproduction is an important social activity for many species. And I should ask: if you do it in private, how do your young learn to do it right?'

The Ambassador smiled. 'There are ways.'

'And the fringe?' the Ambassador's husband said.

'The fringe contests are fun to watch, if you're interested,' I said. 'Although the contest of battle skills can get a bit ... bloody.'

He made a face. 'Maybe not.' He turned to the Ambassador. 'I'm relying on you to help me out here, Charlie.'

She put her arm around his waist. 'Don't worry. I'll make sure you have fun.'

Shudo staggered up to us, holding a wooden cup full of the fiery alcohol from his homeworld. He barely came up to my waist, and was covered in bright pink fur. But his size was deceptive; he was a master of his species' particularly nasty blend of martial arts that used their poisoned heel-spurs to lethal effect. He grinned at me, revealing his three rows of sharp teeth. 'Jian! Silver! It feels so good to be away from the babies for the night.' He waved his cup around. 'Isn't this party the best?'

'This is a new Shudo for me,' the Empress said. 'I've never seen you drunk.'

'There's other parts of me that you've never seen, either, honoured dragon,' he said. He carefully placed the cup on the ground, then lifted his tunic and turned to bend over, revealing his bright pink furry hindquarters. 'Check out the genital slit – I had a full cleanse and fragrance today, and it is *fresh*.'

The Empress buried her nose in his slit and sniffed loudly. 'Delightful.'

Shudo waved his backside at me. 'Want a sniff, Jian? It's a new blend for the season, based on the scent used by my nation's leader, and everybody's been trying it. Come on, I know you're not into genital freshness but this is special.'

'I can't appreciate it, I have no sense of smell,' I said. 'Go wave it at someone else.'

'Spoilsport,' he said, standing and straightening his tunic. 'Graf tells me you're already doing a fine job.' He lifted his cup and took a deep swig. 'Thank you for taking the position. I'm enjoying being an over-parent and I'm glad the Empress is in good hands. Oh! There's my friend. She has to smell this.' He wandered away.

'Tomorrow morning he will wake up and think – "Did I really ask the Empress to have a good sniff of my slit?",' the Empress said.

'It's not that much of a faux pas,' I said. 'It's how they greet each other, after all.'

'He's never done it before; it was too intimate to be respectful,' she said, studying where he'd gone to wave his slit in a companion's face. 'He even used the close-family-pronoun for me.' She turned her sapphire eyes onto me. 'If that's the case, it looks like he's not planning on returning to the job.'

'He's always welcome,' I said, scanning the crowd. 'The paperwork's a bitch.'

'Is it safe to come back?' the Ambassador said from where she and her husband had quickly retreated. 'No more slit sniffing?'

'Yeah he's gone,' the Empress said. 'To be honest the fragrance was very enticing. Please excuse me, Ambassador.' She nodded to the Maxwells. 'I've been inspired to visit the pleasure quarter. Come on, Captain.'

Maxwell and I shared a wry glance, and I followed the Empress towards the orgy quarter. I looked up to see that all four of the symbols above my head, representing the four social celebrations, were dark grey to show that I wasn't participating.

'You don't need to be grey, you know, you're not officially on duty and can have some fun,' she said, as I followed her through the dazzling rainbow of colours between the food-and-drink and dancing quarters. We were hit by a barrage of sound and I gestured for Marque to lower the volume in my personal space. A few clicks were teaching some other species their mating dance in a large circle that rotated between the dance and the sex quarters, losing a few people to the orgy every time they went through.

The Empress gestured towards the dance. 'Come on, Jian, enjoy yourself.'

It looked like fun, so what the hell. 'Marque, turn on everything except sex,' I said, and the Empress grinned.

She took two-legged form, grabbed my hand, and inserted us into the dancing circle. The clicks had programmed Marque with their mating click-music, and everybody was attempting the moves around the circle – tapping their arms or legs against the people next to them and rotating to wiggle their behinds into the centre of the circle. With so many species present – many who didn't have the right number of appendages – it was chaos, but it was joyful chaos that glowed in my empathic sense like an aurora of shared hilarity. Nobody was doing it right, and nobody cared, and we were all laughing in our different ways. When we followed the circle's trajectory through the rainbow wall to the orgy quarter, the Empress broke off with the slug next to her and they took themselves to a mating platform not too far from the edge. I stayed in the dance, enjoying myself more than I had in a while.

The next time I rotated through the orgy quarter, I was slapped over the head by fifteen tentacles as thick as forearms, covered in dark blue slime, and dragged from the dance. One of the tentacles massaged the top of my head as I pulled the others away from my nose and mouth to breathe.

I turned with difficulty – the tentacles had an iron grip – to see the dark blue cephalopod holding me. It was as tall as me, with tentacles all around its egg-shaped body.

'You are beautiful and the party is beautiful and the Empress is beautiful and I am beautiful and here!' it shouted. It shoved a ball of pale blue goo, the size of my head, into my face, nearly choking me again. I pushed the mass away and scowled at it.

'You are as high as a kite, I have sex greyed out, and I have no idea who you are.'

'That's the best part of the experience and yes! Chemical assistance. I am name that cannot be translated into your perception. Party! Love! Your brown skin is beautiful like delicious food. Give me potatoes now, human. I love you!'

'Marque, sober it up.'

The cephalopod changed from dark blue to white, then a rainbow of colours shifted across its slimy skin. Its tentacles waved, then it realised that it was holding the ball of sex cells in front of my face and quickly hid it.

'Profoundest apologies, honoured sentient,' it said, and turned grey all over. Fluorescent blue symbols marched over its sides as it mirrored the sentiment onto its skin. 'I had a little too much. Please forgive me.' It flashed completely black. 'Oh. You are the new Captain of the Guard. I am extremely remorseful, and personally apologise to you, most honoured sentient.'

'I'll let you off with a warning for now,' I said. 'Moderate your chemical intake. You're on my watch list, and if you try something so flagrantly unacceptable again, you'll suffer the consequences.'

It turned neon pink and hot orange stripes ran over it. 'I understand, Captain. It won't happen again.' It scuttled away so quickly that it became almost flat against the ground.

I sighed and looked around. 'Am I authorised to do that sort of thing? My duties don't mention whether I have jurisdiction outside the Palace. I didn't step on any local law enforcement toes, did I?'

'Since I'm local law enforcement and I don't have toes, I don't think you need to worry. You handled it perfectly. You are well within your authority; anyone who is chemically affected to that degree is a danger to the Empress. You were right to do what you did.'

The Empress and the slug were hard at it and had collected a small, enthusiastic cheer squad. I turned to walk through the dancing section to storytelling where it was more my type of fun. My mother had a rapt audience gathered around her as she told them the graphic story of human natural birthing processes. I changed my mind and headed back to food and drink.

A group of armed aliens stopped me halfway. One stepped forward and waved its shell axe at me. It appeared to be a pile of humanoid-shaped mascles with red ropes of tendons wrapped around them and no visible head or face.

'Come and join us!' it said. 'We've been waiting for you; we haven't started yet.'

'I'm sorry, Soft-Comfort, I can't risk death while I'm Captain of the Guard, my backup bodies are too precious to waste,' I said, and Soft-Comfort's axe drooped. 'Some of you are unable to compete without killing me, so the contests will have to wait until I'm no longer captain.'

The aliens all shared a look – eyes and tentacles waved at each other, then back to me.

'We understand, Captain. We wish you well – and we'll—'

'We'll miss you from the tournament!' they said in not-quite-unison.

'I'll miss you guys as well,' I said. 'You all taught me so much – I appreciate the time we've spent together killing each other.'

'At least come and watch,' Soft-Comfort said. 'You are our honoured guest.' It bent to speak conspiratorially to me. 'Any heads I take are yours to keep.'

'How can I resist a generous offer like that?' I said, and followed them towards the battle arena.

13

The five-year anniversary of the release of the humans was a celebratory time for everyone. The victims' soulstones were attuned and they were once again immortal – and they could move into new bodies if they chose, leaving the memories of the torture they'd suffered under the cats behind.

Tomoyo dropped me off in front of the Dragon Embassy on Earth. The Embassy occupied the original Dragonhome island, a mushroom-shaped facility floating on a long stalk above the Mediterranean. It brought back fond memories; I'd spent many years here, helping the parents of the first generation of dragonscales children with their gifted and passionate daughters – until the children had reached maturity and immediately started the reproductive conquest of the entire planet. The facility was now used as the Dragon Embassy, with the accommodation converted to guest villas and the main hall made into offices and a reception area. The pale pink buildings on the surface of the island were all dragon-standard domes, with Earth greenery in carefully-tended gardens between the shining pink tiles of the square. The sky was a particular clear Mediterranean blue, and I breathed the air of home deeply to appreciate it. Earth air always smelled different no matter how Marque tried to duplicate it off-world. The main building, which had been my administrative centre, had been enlarged and expanded into a white double-storey dome with blue and silver accents.

'Tap my scale when you want me back,' Tomoyo said, and strolled away.

'You're not heading home?' I said.

'I want to have a look around the island.'

I shrugged and went into the Embassy. The lobby was dragon-sized, with a towering twenty-metre roof, and inlaid with the Empress' own livery of blue and silver. A few heads turned to see me, and the human dragonscales receptionist rushed from behind her desk and raced up to me, glowing with smiles. I recognised her; she was one of the original half-dragon girls that I'd helped to raise on the island.

'Captain Choumali. Welcome! Come this way,' she said, and gestured towards the entrance to the administrative section.

'Hello, Ingrid, is all well?' I said.

'It's lovely to see you again,' she said. 'I'm so sorry about what happened with Princess Aki – oh, I felt that.'

'Sorry,' I said, and tried to control the pain of loss. Aki was alive. We would be together eventually.

'Don't be. It's wrong what they're doing to her – to both of you. Anyway, here we are, through here and turn left to the medical centre.' She bowed to me. 'I'll return to my duties, but I'd love to spend time with you when you're done with your son.'

A buzz of conversation followed me through the double doors at the end of the hall. Maybe I shouldn't have worn the captain's uniform; the blue and silver livery was instantly recognisable.

The entire family was gathered around David in the medical centre. He was one of the first to undergo the procedure, and his expression was serene. He was on a standard gurney, and the medical table of white liquid holding his cloned body was next to him, ready to take the stone.

'Are you sure the stone has been in his head long enough to be attuned?' Dianne said.

'If it's not attuned it won't work,' Marque said. 'The new body won't do anything.'

'I'm not sure I'm happy about what will happen to the old body,' I said. 'He'll still be alive and in it. We're killing him.'

'You aren't,' David said. 'My soul transcends any number of bodies that I exist in. This is what I want.'

'I feel the same way, Jian,' Marque said. 'It's unpleasant to do this when the old body isn't dead.'

'I want it!' David said.

Cat rushed in. 'Stop! Don't do it.'

David sat up. 'It's okay, Cat,' he said. 'The memories of what happened to me are ruining my life, and I want them gone. I won't die.'

'Yes you will!' she shouted. 'You have to stop this. This will kill you!'

'The soulstones work,' I said. 'His soul will be transferred. His essence can never be destroyed. It will still be him.'

Her face screwed up. 'It's a fake soulstone!'

That stopped me. 'What?' I turned to Marque. 'You've said that's not possible?'

'It can't be fake, I put it in myself,' Marque said, and David's soulstone lifted from his forehead. 'It looks genuine to me. Cat – what makes you think it's fake?'

'We need to hide, David. We need to hide *now*.' She took David's hand. 'David, I love you, and I'm betraying everything I stand for to save you. I replaced your stone with a fake when you were sleeping, and sent it to my people. But I can save you. Please come with me!'

'What the hell, Cat?' I said. 'This is insane. Hide from what?'

'It is fake,' Marque said. 'A clever duplicate – down to the nano level. Probably created by their nanobots. It doesn't have the unique crystalline structure that our soulstones have deep within them – on the outside it's identical. Not even I could see it was a copy until I examined it at the quantum level. When did you swap it in?' It answered its own question. 'When you two were on privacy together.'

'David, come with me,' she said, gripping his hand. 'They're coming. It's time!'

'Time for what?' I said. 'What the hell is going on, Cat?'

'Something just appeared within Earth's planetary system,' Marque said. 'It's growing. Nanobots? What is this? Matter transmitters? Two of them. Three. Five ...' Its voice went quiet. 'Nanos are building them all over the place. The transporters aren't very big, less than five metres across. I can't see all of them in such a large space. The cats must have seeded them when they were here before. The nanos are gathering material, assembling solar collectors, and building transport portals on the spot. Twenty.'

'But matter transmission is death, the transmission process destroys your body,' I said. 'Your body is rebuilt at the other end, and a different soul inhabits it.'

'Is that what happened to our soulstones?' David said. 'The cats kept them so that they could use matter transmitters?'

'See? You're so clever,' she said. 'They will leave their soulstones behind when they come through; that's why we took them.'

'What's coming through the transporters, Marque?' I said.

'Nothing as yet.'

'Cat.' David held her hand. 'What are they doing? Why are they creating teleporters?'

'I can't tell you, I've told you too much already,' she said. 'Just come with me, and we'll be safe.'

'What about my family?' he said.

She hesitated, then rushed on. 'Nothing can be done for them. We're too strong.'

'Thank you very much,' I said.

David dropped her hand as if it were red-hot. 'You're a *spy* for them?'

'I didn't plan to fall in love with you,' she said. 'This makes things complicated – so we need to run.'

'How can you do this to my family?' David said. 'You'll just let them die and save me? How could you?'

'But I love you,' she said.

'Walkers in powered nano battle armour are coming through the portals,' Marque said.

'Walkers?' I said. 'What are walkers? More info!'

'One of the species that the cats have colonised,' Marque said.

A three-dimensional representation appeared in the air. The walker was an alien that looked like a cross between a two-legged hippopotamus and a meat-eating dinosaur, with the colouring of a killer whale. It was smooth-skinned, with splashes of black and white across its stocky body. It had short arms and long, strong legs, its face was wide, and its mouth was open, revealing sharp, carnivorous teeth.

'How big is that?' Oliver said.

'Each of them is three metres tall and wearing bio-powered nano battle armour. Walkers are very efficient killers – and they take a great deal of pleasure in killing things.' It lowered its voice. 'The cats give them targets, and they go on murder sprees. They're really nasty.'

'Notify the dragons!' I said. 'Tell them we're under attack, and to round up our defensive troops. Spread the word!'

'Come with me, Cat,' David said gently. 'Let's go somewhere safe. Nobody will survive an attack by those – the rest of Earth is doomed.'

'Yes!' she said. 'We only use walkers when we need to completely wipe out a species. There's nothing we can do to save humanity – but I can save you.'

He led her out of the room and glanced meaningfully back at me. I nodded a reply to him. I trusted him to put her somewhere where she couldn't do more damage.

'Any idea what their targets are?' I asked Marque.

'At this stage I have to say Earth. All the portals are within this region of space.'

The walker representation in the air changed to a map of the solar system, with dots popping up indicating the locations of the portals. Three more appeared as I watched, all within Earth's orbital track.

'Wow, we really pissed them off,' Oliver said. 'Time to find some weapons and defend our home.' He turned to David's other parents, and my mother. 'You know where my old room is, at the back of the administration offices? Where I lived when I was a child?'

'I remember,' Dianne said.

'There's a door at the end of the corridor. That's the bunker. Take Nan—' He put his arm around Mum and pushed her towards

Victor. 'Take yourselves into there, and shut the door. Grab anyone you pass and take them with you.'

'Got it,' Dianne said, nodding. She rose, gestured for Victor and Mum to follow her, and they went out and headed back towards the admin offices.

'How many defensive soldiers on Earth right now, Marque?' I said as more and more portals appeared in the display. There were now about twenty of them, still within Earth's orbital track.

'About two hundred thousand soldiers are stationed on Earth right now. Most of the human army is on Barracks or the dragon homeworld, on standby to defend the Empire. We weren't expecting the cats to attack Earth – although it makes sense that they'd want to wipe humanity out. You – and your chilli bombs – are the first line of defence.'

'How many walkers are coming through?'

'I don't know. I can't see all the portals. They start off nano-sized and grow exponentially.'

'How long before the walkers are here?'

'I don't have enough data to extrapolate from!' Marque said, sounding frustrated. 'I'll tell you in half an hour when I've seen how fast they can go.'

'If they're all inside Earth's orbit, then at light speed it will take about five minutes to get here,' I said.

'If they can travel at light speed they don't need armour, because they'll be a bright smear on the surface of space-time.'

'Let me know when you find out how long it'll take. Do we have weapons here in the Embassy? Can you synthesise some similar battle armour for me?'

'Blake's been notified,' Marque said. 'He's establishing a command centre in UN headquarters in Old Geneva, and I'm putting together armour and weapons there. He's asked for you.'

'Let's go,' I said. 'Does Tomoyo know?'

'She's on her way. Meet her in the entrance hall.'

The display blinked out and I headed down the corridor back to the entrance, with Oliver close behind me. Dianne, Victor and Mum were guiding a small group of people towards the bunker. Tomoyo appeared at the end of the corridor and we went to her.

'Tomoyo, Marque, listen,' I said. 'As soon as we're in Old Geneva, the two of you liaise with other dragons to evacuate as many people from Earth as you can.'

'That's a big ask with our population so diminished,' Tomoyo said.

'Marque, keep an eye on where the walkers are. Try to extrapolate their landing sites: they'll probably go for strategic locations. Evacuate children and their mothers first. Got it?' I put my hand on Tomoyo's shoulder. 'Let's go.'

Tomoyo folded us outside the Old Geneva headquarters of the UN. The UN building was a glass tower next to the lake, built after there was enough oxygen in the air to breathe at the top without assistance. We raced into the main entrance hall, which was a large two-storey atrium with an interior first-level balcony and stained-glass light in the ceiling that depicted humans and dragons working together peacefully. Obviously Marque had warned them as people were already running from the building. They weren't screaming; they just ran in terrified silence, the only sound their footfalls on the stone floor and the occasional call as people linked up and went out together.

'This way!' Blake shouted from the balcony surrounding the entrance hall, and we went up the stairs to him.

'Sir,' I said, following him as he rushed through a pair of double doors and down a corridor to a lift.

'Marque is synthesising weapons that will affect the aliens,' Blake said without slowing. 'Evacuation protocol is in effect. We're rounding up the Prime Minister and Cabinet and putting them in the old nuclear bunkers.' We took the lift a long way down and arrived in the protected bunker, which was set up as a conference room full of people talking over scattered paper files and on phones. 'War room.' He leaned on the table. 'Right. We have limited troops here, and Marque tells me that these walker things aren't indestructible. So I'm going to provide you with all the guards assigned to New Geneva, and I want you to lead them to defend the facility against the aliens. Ready?'

'I am, sir,' I said. I looked up. 'Armour, Marque?'

'I don't have the resources to synthesise both armour and weapons,' Marque said. 'I'm producing weapons first, and I'll provide you with an energy shield until I can produce the armour.'

'Can any dragons collect our armour from Barracks?'

'All Barracks troops will bring their armour, but we're really short on dragons, particularly with the evacuation order in effect.'

'Any idea how long we have?' Blake asked Marque.

There was a loud crash that made the entire building tremble. Another crash resounded, and the ground lurched again.

'I think that answers your question,' Marque said. 'But it's only two of them. They came in through the front door, and they've stopped in the entrance hall.'

'Where are these weapons?' I said, looking around.

'Not finished yet,' Marque said. 'I'm spread so thin! Give me a moment.' It went quiet.

'Oliver, with me,' I said. 'Admiral, when I'm out of the room put the firewalls up. Where are the rest of my people?'

'Gathering at the back of the building,' Blake said. 'The utility rooms we used for storage back when we were supervising Dragonhome.'

I nodded. 'I remember.'

Oliver towered over me as he followed me out of the room. The doors closed behind us, and the firewalls clanged as they went up. The room was sealed. We went back up the lift and came out above the expansive entrance hall with the emblem of the UN inlaid in the stone floor. An organic wheezing rattle was coming from below, and I crept forward to see.

The walkers had entered the hall and were shooting anyone remaining in the room. They were nearly the height of the ceiling in their black-and-white battle armour and were spraying the area with red-hot pellets from small, hand-held weapons. They killed indiscriminately, and a high-pitched rattling noise came from their heads within the armour. It took me a minute to realise that they were laughing. They chased down the people trying to escape and killed them with the weapons and their bare hands. A young woman tried to run and one of them moved with devastating swiftness, picked her up by the arm and threw her at the wall. The impact must have killed her.

When the room was clear, the walkers moved to the centre of the hall and each pulled something off their backs. One of them flipped its object open – it appeared to be a set of three metal legs. The walker placed the legs on the floor and the tripod stood a metre and a half tall. The other walker added a spherical black object to the top of the tripod.

'What's that thing they're building?' Oliver said.

'A neutron emitter,' Marque said.

'A neutron bomb?' we said in unison, and shared a look. Neutron devices were outlawed everywhere in the known universe. They destroyed all life, leaving non-organics – buildings and materials – relatively untouched outside the small blast radius.

Marque hesitated, then said, 'I can disable it. They can't set it off.'

I sagged with relief. 'Then we just have to deal with them.' I glanced up at the ceiling. 'Weapons?'

'Head down to the back of the building where the rest of the defence team are gathering. I've synthesised some weapons there for you.'

I turned to Oliver. 'You're not a soldier, Ollie—'

He touched my arm. 'My people are responsible for every death down there. I am making things right.'

'Stop arguing and join up with the team,' Marque said.

I grunted with frustration and crept towards the back of the building.

Tomoyo appeared in front of me. 'Stop, Captain Choumali.'

I checked behind me; the walkers were still in the entrance hall and the area was clear. 'What, Tomoyo? I need to meet up with the other defenders.'

'The Empress requires the Captain of her Guard,' she said. 'She is concerned that the walkers may attack the dragon homeworld as well.'

That stopped me dead. I'd made a vow to protect the Empress above all others, but I hadn't expected it to be this difficult to fulfil.

'I have a message from the Empress,' Tomoyo said. 'She says that Admiral Blake will handle the defence here, Captain. She needs your skills. Return at once.' She lowered her head and her voice became more high-pitched and sweet. 'Please go defend my mother. I don't know what I'd do without her.'

'All right,' I said, putting my hand on her shoulder. 'Take me to the folding nexus, I'll go straight from there to the Palace. Ollie, put your hand on Tomoyo and come with us.'

Earth disappeared from around me and I was on the orbital folding nexus above Dragonhome. The planet gleamed below, half in darkness, the cities glittering next to the shining ocean. I was alone: Oliver hadn't put his hand on the dragon.

'Go back and get Oliver,' I said. 'Marque, can you carry me down in a hurry?'

Tomoyo disappeared.

'Yes.' The transparent wall in front of me vanished and I was looking out into open space, high above the planet, and feeling that I could fall into it.

'Jump,' Marque said, and I did.

I'd never jumped from orbit before. The planet glowed beneath me, and I didn't feel the movement. It was as if I were suspended above it. The network of elevator cables from the surface to the nexus appeared and disappeared as the light hit them and flashed down their silvery lengths. The sky in front of me glowed orange and then red in a curving flame as I hit the atmosphere. Marque protected me from the heat and I felt nothing as the flames danced in front of my eyes.

'Can you hear me, Marque?' I said.

'Yes.'

'Give me a heads-up display of what's happening back on Earth.'

The HUD appeared, showing the two walkers in the entrance of the UN. They were obviously trying to fix whatever Marque had done to the bomb.

'Are they the only walkers that attacked us?' I said.

'No,' Marque said. The scene flicked to New Windsor Castle, where another pair of walkers were constructing a neutron bomb on the main forecourt, surrounded by the corpses of dead Queen's Guards.

'Is Her Majesty in her bunker?' I said.

'She is. The Prince-Consort and their children are there as well.'

'List the other sites where they've appeared,' I said, and groaned when I saw the locations. 'Please tell me Aki's safe.'

'She's in the Japanese Imperial bunker. She'll be fine; even if the bomb goes off, the bunker is sufficiently shielded.'

I huffed out a relieved breath. The flames still danced at the edge of my vision. 'Keep a rolling image of the Earth locations in the corner of the display. Put a list of my staff on the main view, and who is currently on duty.'

The list appeared. The flames began to subside, and I was glad the display blocked the sight of Sky City rushing up to meet me. It was evening, so the Empress wouldn't be holding court.

'Where's the Empress?'

'In her room with a couple of her consorts.'

'All right. Graf is to station itself on the ceiling below her. Put Ak-Ak, Deep Blue-Green, and Three Lost Pinions – all three of my flyers – patrolling around the tower. Six Eighty Four Hertz is to patrol the electrical grid, and I don't want to hear about your privacy concerns. The rest of the guard are to station themselves in the tower below her in their usual posts. Any further suggestions?'

'I think that covers it. Arrival in three minutes.'

'Thanks, Marque. Update? Any teleport stations near Dragonhome?'

'No. They're all near Earth. Looks like your people really pissed the cats off.'

'We knew it was a possibility.'

The heads-up display minimised to the side, and the glowing white expanse of Sky City's main square, with Parliament on one side and the towers of the Imperial Palace on the other, became visible.

'Hover me at one hundred metres above the square. I want a quick scan,' I said.

I slowed as Marque did as I asked, and then I was motionless above the tallest tower of the Palace. Marque scanned through the people in the square, identifying anyone of interest. There wasn't much activity; it was too early for most nocturnals, and diurnals were already asleep.

'Show me who's armed, and any natural or artificial explosives.'

Three of the individuals on the square lit up, two stink-bug types courting with their bioluminescent butts, and a shark-like Murakh floating in its liquid sphere with its ceremonial tooth-dagger.

'Any other energy types riding the grid?'

'No. Six Eighty Four is the only one in Sky City. A blue giant is going nova in one of the peripheral galaxies and there's a massive party happening as they prepare to ride the wave.'

'Okay, take me in and keep me updated on the situation on Earth.'

Marque carried me under the floating top of the Empress' tower and lifted me through a portal into her bedchamber. She was up and viewing the events on Earth in her theatre, and two of her current spouses – brilliant yellow and blue striped lichen-like creatures that were neither plant nor animal but a bit of both – were next to her and watching with interest, their appendages waving above their flattened bodies as they grew and absorbed light-sensing eyes.

'Please escort my darling slime monsters out, Jian,' she said, without looking away from the multiple depictions of the situation on Earth. The screens flicked slowly from image to image, a limitation of Marque communicating through dragon scales. 'And then return and help me co-ordinate the defence.'

'Ma'am,' I said, and ran one hand over each lichen to politely greet them. 'If you'll come this way, honoured sentients.'

'I hope Earth will be okay, Captain Choumali,' one of them said through Marque as we proceeded to the elevator. 'We appreciate all your people have done for us.'

'We're honoured to serve,' I said. They slithered onto the elevator disk and Marque carried them down and out of the tower.

'Scent flush?' Marque said when they were gone.

'Oh god, yes, please,' I said, and the air around me whipped to clear the pungent sulphur smell that the lichens had exuded. I took a deep breath of the cleaner air and walked back to the Empress. 'I don't know how she handles it.'

'They smell lovely to me,' she said.

14

'We should have anticipated this,' the Empress said, studying the different locations where the walkers were attacking. 'Earth is the main source of both chilli and humans, our two major weapons against the cats. Of course they'd attack the source.'

'Can they destroy the entire planet or population with the weapons they've sent?' I said.

'No,' Marque said. 'Without ships, this is the best they can do. I have the impression that they gathered back home and made the joint decision to teleport agents to Earth to attack strategic centres.'

'That won't gain them anything,' I said. 'We'll still be on the dragons' side, particularly after what the cats did to our hostages.'

'Thank you, Jian,' the Empress said, without looking away from the displays. 'The obvious strategy here is to disable the human administration and cause enough chaos that the humans can't defend against whatever's coming through next.'

'Anything other than walkers coming through, Marque?' I said.

'I can't tell. The portals are too damn small for me to identify,' Marque said. 'There aren't enough iterations of me, and comms is limited to tapping dragon scales – I have five dragons next to my orbital instance on Earth, and the entire scales comms centre here working for me.'

One of the displays went white, then black.

'Marque?' I said. 'That was South American Parliament.'

'I wasn't expecting that,' Marque said. 'They detonated the bomb by hand. One of them put the two masses of nuclear material together, and the other one shot into it to start the reaction.'

'They killed themselves?'

Another screen did the same thing.

'It's a suicide mission,' Marque said. 'They know that matter transmission is death.'

'That's why they took our soulstones,' the Empress said. 'And why they waited five years. The walkers must have left their attuned soulstones back on the cat homeworld.'

'I am far too accustomed to your non-violent nature, Silver,' Marque said. 'Our past avoidance of conflict is working against us. I have no previous experience of this sort of ...' It went silent.

'I think the word you're looking for is evil,' I said.

Another screen blinked out.

'You are protecting the targets with energy domes, right?' I said. 'This isn't hurting anyone?'

Marque was silent.

I glared up at its sensors on the ceiling. 'Tell me my people aren't dying while I'm sitting here in safety!'

'I am protecting them with energy domes,' Marque said. 'But ...'

'Spit it out, metalman,' I said. 'Who's died?' My heart leaped. 'Not *Aki*!'

'The bunkers are lead-shielded, they're protected against the neutron blast, but there is a significant shockwave and I'm not sure ...'

'Any signs of a second wave weapon coming through to kill the rest of the population or destroy the entire planet?'

'No.'

The rest of the images blinked out as the walkers shared the strategy for working around Marque's defence – there wasn't much it could do if they pulled the devices apart and detonated them by hand, particularly when it was spread so thin. The last of the screens went off and we were left in a darkened room with no communications. I flopped to sit on the floor next to the Empress. 'Any details on the targets?'

'I can't get close yet. The area around them is heavily irradiated and my drones aren't equipped to handle it. Oh.'

'Oh?'

'Comms stopped altogether. I think something destroyed my orbital instance above Earth, and the dragons I was using to communicate.'

'No sign of matter transporters anywhere else?' the Empress said. 'Our homeworld is clear?'

'I'd definitely see one if it appeared in this part of space,' Marque said. 'I'm spread through this system at the nano level, almost as much as the cat nanobots in their system.'

'What about our colonies?' I said.

'I don't know,' Marque said. 'They're not communicating at all. Wait, the last instance of me is sending a message relayed through scales stations ...'

I fidgeted as the silence surrounded us.

'The walkers are all dead,' Marque said. 'The attack is over, but the damage to Earth facilities is extensive. It will take me some time to bring communications back up, but it's finished.'

'How many dead?' I said.

'At this stage I don't know. There's only one instance of me left on Earth, and the radiation is frying my circuitry ... it's gone.'

*

I didn't sleep at all the rest of the night as we slowly reconnected to Earth's communications. I deployed the guard to defend the Empress and wasn't satisfied until the entire Palace complex was covered. When morning came after the fifteen-hour night of Dragonhome, I was trembling with a combination of grief and exhaustion as I escorted the Empress from her quarters to her office. She settled herself behind her desk and brought up the surveillance; she'd been watching the relief effort from her quarters and hadn't slept at all.

She glanced at me. 'Marque, provide chemical assistance for the Captain. She's about to fall over and I need her at my side when I talk to Parliament.'

'No,' I said.

Energy rushed through me and I stood straighter as my mind cleared and my grief subsided to be replaced by cold intellect.

'Never mind, that was exactly what I needed,' I said. 'Thank you.'

'Trust your sovereign,' the Empress said. 'You probably haven't been paying attention, so here's what's happening in the next two hours. Marque has limited connectivity to Earth, but we know for sure that many neutron devices went off all over the planet and there's a great deal of radiation to clean up. The younga are radiation-eaters who can do that, but they must be paid for their work. I wanted to immediately pay them myself, but it's more than I can personally afford, so Parliament needs to approve the funding. Once that's approved – and don't worry, it will be – I want to tour the disaster area and personally inspect the relief effort. Our humans will be cared for.'

'I've found David and Cat,' Marque said. 'I think Captain Choumali needs to go to Earth now.'

'Are they alive?' I shouted.

'Cat: no. David: yes, but critically injured. Human medical staff are working to save him.'

I sagged against the wall and wiped one hand over my face. 'What about the rest of the family?'

'They're at the bottom of the Mediterranean Sea, and we need the younga to clear the water of radiation before we can search for them.'

I stood again. 'Majesty. Permission to—'

'Go, Jian,' she said. 'Graf can mind me while I address Parliament. Marque, notify Tomoyo to transport her.'

'Go outside and I'll carry you up to the folding nexus,' Marque said.

'Dismissed, Captain,' the Empress said. 'Go.'

*

Tomoyo folded me to the cliff overlooking the site of the Embassy. The pink island was gone, and the water was full of dark mud where the sea had been churned by the collapse. Not even the stalk was present; the island was completely obliterated.

'Hold still and put your arms out, Jian,' Marque said. 'I need to put a proper suit on you – the radiation here is lethal. It will take me *weeks* to clean it up, even with the help of dragons.'

'How much was I exposed to?'

'None. I protected you.'

'What about Tomoyo?' I said.

'I eat it,' she said. 'Radiation doesn't actually harm me until I reach the core of a hot star.'

'Damn you're tough,' I said. I looked around. 'Where are David and Cat?'

'Not far away, and in the care of paramedics. But we have something much more important to worry about. Tomoyo, transport us to these co-ordinates.'

Tomoyo transported us again. I staggered when we arrived; gravity was lower. We were in the centre of a city square, and the buildings around us were collapsing upwards in a vortex of wind.

'This is more important than my son?' I said.

'Yes. The whole planet is in jeopardy.'

A second, brighter, sun was in the sky. I felt lighter, as if it was pulling me upwards. The wind whipped past me into the sky, a visible vortex of matter spiralling into it. It shone brighter than the sun with the energy released from the matter destroyed in it.

'That's a miniature black hole, isn't it?' I said with horror.

'Yes,' Marque said. 'It's only four millimetres across.'

'How long before it devours the planet?'

'The atmosphere will be gone in less than a day. Earth will be completely destroyed within a week.'

I looked around. 'Can you transport it, Tomoyo?' I shook my head. 'Of course you can't – you'll be sucked into it before you get close.' I turned a circle. 'An energy shield will be sucked into it as well. Can we move the Earth away from the black hole?'

'The black hole will travel with the planet. They're locked together.'

'How many people are left on Earth?'

'About nine hundred million.'

'So what do we do? We can't move the black hole. We can't move the planet. Can we move the population in time if we get all the dragons to help?'

'No. But I have an idea,' Marque said. 'I'm talking to people.'

'I hope David's okay,' I said, trying to wipe my eyes and hitting the energy field around my face. Marque had said that he was in a critical condition and I could only hope that the medical team could save him.

The ground shuddered beneath me.

'Tomoyo, move us – the ground's giving way,' Marque said.

The ground lifted, and I leaped to touch Tomoyo. She fell away from me, and I rose gently into the air, sucked up by the great vacuum above. The ground cracked, and two pieces lifted separately, each fifty metres across. I panicked; if I was between them when they rose, I could be crushed, suit or no suit. Tomoyo appeared next to me, flew to me using her large wings, put her snout on my chest, and folded us away.

I landed on my stomach on grass and picked myself up. Tomoyo had moved us a hundred metres from the edge of the hole where the ground had lifted. The wind still howled up into the glowing black hole, and a couple of burst water pipes added to the chaos with water that spiralled straight up.

'The planet's coming apart, Marque,' Tomoyo said. 'What was your solution?'

'Go back to your homeworld and pick up Kana.'

'That is not a solution,' she said. 'It's a death sentence. It will kill her – and we protect our goldenscales.'

'It's the only solution you have. Do it!'

'I won't force her into a suicide mission!'

'So ask her when she gets here. Go get her.'

She stared at Marque for a heartbeat, then folded away.

'I agree with her,' I said. 'Just because she's a servant doesn't mean she's expendable—'

Tomoyo appeared with the goldenscales servant, bright yellow and smaller than her multicoloured sisters. Kana was the

Empress' maid, and helped her out with grooming and household management.

Kana looked up and then at Marque.

'The only way to save this planet and everybody on it, is to gate this little black hole,' Tomoyo said. 'Can you do it?'

'You want me to *gate*?' Kana said. 'I thought I was just here to help carry things!'

'The Empress said it's okay,' Marque said.

Kana stared up at Marque, her golden eyes wide. 'Are you sure? This is a capital offence – the punishment for gating is the Real Death.' She swung her head to see Tomoyo. 'Isn't there another way?'

'No,' Marque said. 'This is the only way to save millions of lives. You must gate the black hole.'

'Can you do it?' I said.

'We are strictly forbidden from doing this,' Kana said. 'If we get it wrong – and it's not hard to get it wrong – we could put the gates inside each other and destroy the universe.'

'I confirm before Marque and the Captain of the Guard that you have permission,' Tomoyo said. 'You'll save millions of lives. Please!'

Kana lowered her head and thought about it, then raised her head. 'It's worth dying for, if it'll save the humans. They worked so hard to defend the Empire.' She straightened and appeared larger in her small frame. 'Captain Choumali, you saw Tomoyo give me permission?'

'I did.'

'All right. I'm willing to take the risk. Just ... please don't let Tomoyo crush my stone.'

'I'll hold it for you,' I said.

She turned to Tomoyo. 'My lady?'

'She can hold it.'

Kana pulled her soulstone out of her forehead and gave it to me.

'Please don't crush it,' she said plaintively to Tomoyo.

'Don't worry, I won't,' Tomoyo said. 'You have my word.' She looked up. 'Can you do it?'

'It should be relatively straightforward,' Kana said. 'I'll put the other end of the gate close to a much larger black hole, and when the small hole is sucked through, I'll close it from this end before it kills me.' She looked up at Marque. 'Quickly confirm my calculations.' She rattled off a series of numbers. 'Other end at—' Another series of numbers. 'What do you think?'

'You know you're better at it than I am,' Marque said. 'But it looks good to me.'

'Please don't tell any other species that we can do this, Captain Choumali,' Kana said. 'We're slightly better at building gates than our coloured sisters, but gating is strictly prohibited – it's too dangerous. We seem to have this knack with the numbers, even though we don't know how we do it.'

The ground beneath us shifted.

'Less talking, more gating, I think,' Kana said. 'Tomoyo, take me to these co-ordinates.'

Tomoyo touched her nose to Kana and they disappeared. Tomoyo reappeared a moment later. 'Marque, please show us her progress.'

A two-dimensional display appeared in front of us, showing Kana near the tiny black hole. She swam against its gravitational pull to stay stationary. The equipment that the walkers had used to construct the black hole stretched to either side of it. They'd used a floating particle accelerator – a long circular tube with a small reactor at one end. The equipment was unrecognisably warped as it entered the hole. The black hole itself wasn't visible; only the lens-shaped distortion of gravity around it.

'That thing is churning out hard radiation on every band,' Marque said. 'I can't get close with any of my instances, it wipes them out. I've heavily filtered what you're seeing, otherwise it would just be white noise.'

The gate appeared. It looked like a shining glass ball, two metres across, with thick walls and a black centre. It glittered in the reflected light of the black hole. Kana moved towards it, then backed away as her front legs were distorted by its proximity.

The miniature black hole rushed into the gate and the gate went brilliantly white as it travelled through, then rotated in shifting colours. The circle of brilliance shrank and blackness grew from the edges of the glass ball towards the centre.

'Kana, quickly, close it,' Tomoyo said to the image. Kana had her head twisted all the way back, but her front legs were twice as long as they should be and were becoming slimmer all the time. She was being sucked into the gate.

The black edges of the gate shrank towards its spherical centre, dragging Kana with it. Her front end went into the gate as it disappeared, and the rest of her looked like spaghetti. Half of her was inside the gate as it closed with a loud rush of air, then silence. What was left of Kana fell out of the sky and hit the ground with a wet thump. It looked like a lump of raw meat, with red, blue and green blood in a puddle around it.

'Damn that was brave of her,' I said.

'It must have hurt like anything,' Tomoyo said. 'And she closed the gate when half of her was already gone. Our goldenscales often outshine us.'

'I hope I have the chance to thank her.'

'You will,' Tomoyo said.

'Earth is still severely damaged,' Marque said. 'I need to build a full-sized instance of myself to return the planet to stable orbit. Let's head back to the homeworld, and I'll start building one.'

I wanted to stand but my legs were like rubber, and I was still shaking from the aftermath. 'Are my family okay? My mother? Oliver? David? Aki?'

'At this stage I don't know,' Marque said. 'There isn't anything left of me apart from this sphere, and all comms are down. You'll need to give me some time to clean up the radiation and sift through the remains. This will take a while.'

'Tomoyo? You went back and collected Oliver, right?' I said.

'He wasn't anywhere when I went back,' she said. 'I looked for him – but moving humans off Earth was a priority. I'm sorry, Jian, I don't know where he is.'

'You did the right thing. You probably saved many.' I put my head in my hands, feeling the energy barrier around me as I tried to touch my own face. My family were in the epicentre of the Embassy blast, and I hoped they'd made it to the blast shelter in the facility. There wasn't much chance that the family had survived, and even their soulstones were probably gone. David's soulstone wasn't even the real thing; if he died, that was it for him. Oliver was probably dead as well, but at least he had a real soulstone and could be salvaged.

'You said David was alive. Where is he?' I said.

'Tomoyo can take you,' Marque said. 'Tomoyo, these co-ordinates.'

'My scales are going nuts,' Tomoyo said. 'All the dragons are rallying to help our human friends.'

'Subjects,' I said. 'Slaves. Conscripts. If we'd never met you, this would not have happened.'

She didn't rise to it. 'We'll work with Marque to clean up the radiation and repair the planet. Now, let's go check on your son. I hope he's okay.'

15

Tomoyo folded me to a stand of trees a few kilometres from the edge of the Mediterranean where the Embassy was located.

'Give me the stone and I'll take it back home to put Kana into a new body,' she said.

I wanted to make sure that the goldenscales would be okay, but my son was nearby and hurt. I glared at her as I handed it over. 'Don't you dare let them crush this stone. That dragon is a hero.'

'I know,' she said, and disappeared.

The trees around me were dead, their leaves all blasted off and covering the ground in a brown blanket. A scorched trail led to the area covered in black goo.

'The black goo is dead nanos, isn't it?' I said as I trudged over the papery leaves to the site.

'Yes,' Marque said. 'I don't know what other nano devices Cat brought with her. She could bring the seeds of the devices, put them in the sun, and then grow just about anything. From the crash marks it looks like it was a spherical, single-passenger nano vehicle, and she overloaded it by putting David in as well.'

'Was the crash caused by it being overloaded, or by the bomb blast?'

'The blast. The cats really have no value for their own kind.'

A corpse, covered with a red sheet, lay in the puddle of dead nanos. Another corpse lay in the centre of the clearing, also covered in a sheet, and surrounded by disposable medical equipment. A group of humans in radiation equipment were packing up their vehicle in preparation for leaving, with no gurney in the vehicle.

'Oh lord,' I said. 'I'm too late.'

I went to the body in the middle of the clearing and lifted the red blanket. It was David. One of the rescue staff approached me.

'I'm sorry for your loss, Captain Choumali,' she said, her voice muffled by the helmet. 'We did everything we could, but we couldn't save him. We didn't find a soulstone in his forehead? I hope you can find it.' She looked back at the vehicle. 'We can't do any more here; we have to move on to where people are alive. We will deal with the dead later.'

'I understand. Go,' I said.

She nodded to me and they entered their vehicle and flew away. I was left alone with the dead trees and my dead child.

David's body still had a neck brace on, and his expression was serene. I lifted his body to hold him. His head flopped against me, filling my nose with the fresh scent of his shampoo. He smelled the same as he always did, but he was ice-cold, limp and pale; a shell of the vibrant young man he used to be. I didn't want to let him go; as long as I held him, he was still with me. I clutched him against me in a suspension of the reality between his being in my life and the acknowledgement of his death.

I wasn't aware of the passage of time, but eventually I rose up out of the grey vacuum of my grief, gently laid him back on the ground, and covered him with the red blanket. I'd never see his lively face again, touch his hair, call his name. He was gone.

'What about the rest of the family?' I said.

'I don't know,' Marque said. 'The Embassy is at the bottom of the Mediterranean.'

'So they were either killed by the explosion or drowned. Either way they're dead and we need to find their soulstones. How badly damaged is the island down there? Is there a chance that the stones are still intact? We only have forty-eight hours before the stones lose attunement.'

'The water is heavily irradiated. I'll be able to investigate the area after the younga have eaten the radiation.'

'Has Parliament agreed to pay them?'

'The younga are volunteering their skills without payment and they've already started to clean up the sites.'

'Any sign of Oliver?'

'I'm sorry, Jian, no. You can stay here at the Embassy site and wait to see if your family are in the water, or go to Tokyo if you like. Aki is probably safe inside the Imperial bunker.'

I nodded to myself as I decided; my family came first. 'Is there a dragon available to take me to the Embassy site? It's too far to walk.'

Tomoyo appeared next to me. She looked from me to the crash site, then back again.

'I am so sorry, Jian,' she said.

'I thought he'd survived the war with the cats,' I said with grim humour. 'In the end one took him out anyway.'

She stared at me.

'It's a soldier thing,' I said.

'She's also pumped full of chemical assistance,' Marque said.

Tomoyo studied me carefully. 'Are you sure you're capable of handling the Embassy site? We don't know what we'll find ...'

'Take me,' I said firmly. 'I need to know. There's a chance their stones weren't destroyed. I ...' I took a deep breath. 'I need to know before I can move forward. Are you sure you haven't seen Oliver?'

'I'm sorry, Jian, I thought he was with you.'

'Let's go then.'

I put my hand on her shoulder and she took me to the cliff next to the remains of the Embassy. A younga floated on the horizon and I shaded my eyes to see it as it approached. Its ten-metre-wide pearlescent dome was full of helium, and the many tentacles that hung suspended from it each carried independent digestive siphons to absorb and convert hard radiation. Younga insisted that each digestive unit was a unique and sentient individual, and what we saw as a single organism was actually a symbiotic colony. It floated to me and raised its closest tentacles in greeting. It had purple dragon scales around the edge of its dome; the dragons had reproductively conquered even this gentle species.

'Captain Choumali,' it said through Marque. 'We attempt to empathise at the loss of close entities. We proceed without payment.'

I nodded to it, well aware that it didn't understand the gesture. 'I am profoundly honoured that you would debase yourselves by proceeding without payment, but that is not necessary.' I reached into the pocket of my new uniform – I'd had the design altered to include pockets, and other guards were mimicking my innovation – and pulled out a handful of dragon scales that I'd collected from my quarters the night before. I held them out to the younga.

'Please accept these as payment for your assistance,' I said. 'They are all from the Empress herself.'

The younga's tentacles went wild, lashing with delight.

'This is acceptable,' it said. It carefully took the scales from me without touching my hand – its tentacles were all covered in irradiated slime – then turned to face the water. 'We will find your soulstones.'

*

I woke some time later and blinked at the dim light. I rolled over on the thin mattress and remembered: Marque had set up a temporary camp for me, with a small tent and adjoining radiation-free bathroom facility, on the edge of the cliff.

'How much time has passed?' I said, still groggy from the drugs wearing off. I remembered David and the grief hit me again. I looked around for tissues to wipe my eyes, even as I pulled on fresh utilitarian clothes that Marque had synthesised for me.

'You're weeping,' it said. 'Do you—'

'No more drugs,' I said, using my sleeve to wipe my face as I gasped through the emotion. 'Give me paper to mop it up. I'll cry on and off for weeks, and there's nothing you can do about it.' I sniffed loudly. 'Have you found Oliver yet?'

'No. Nobody seems to know where he went. You do realise that this means he probably—'

'I'm well aware of that,' I said. 'How's the recovery proceeding for the rest of the family?'

'The younga is eating the radiation and I'm moving the broken pieces of the island so that we can reach the bunker that was at its centre. At this stage I have no idea how much longer the process will take.'

'Thank you.' A towel appeared in my hand and I blew my nose into it. 'I'll need more than one of these.'

A stack of them grew organically next to me, then a large glass of brown-coloured liquid.

I tasted the liquid – it was a chocolate protein shake, one of my favourites. I stared suspiciously at it; it was sweeter than I was accustomed to, even through the obvious flavour of added protein and vitamins.

'Does this have lactose in it? You know I'm intolerant.'

The liquid disintegrated. 'I'm working off limited data here,' Marque said. 'This instance of me has only a small subset of my knowledge. I'm constructing a full-size version of me in orbit, but it will take a while. Assume I don't know anything until we get communications re-established.'

A new shake appeared and I tasted it, then drank it down.

'All right,' I said through the tears that kept running down my face. 'Let me out.'

The energy-based radiation shielding appeared around me, and I popped open the tent and walked out to the edge of the cliff. The area was deserted; the radiation was too extreme for anyone without heavy shielding to approach. The younga was a series of blinking lights in the water far below me.

'Any luck?' I said as I settled myself on the edge of the cliff to wait. I had a horrible thought. 'Oh wait – if I fall you have enough juice to catch me, right?'

'I do. Don't worry,' Marque said. 'The younga is having trouble eating the radiation because it's in liquid that keeps spreading it around, but it's doing its best. The island broke into three pieces when it hit the water, and the younga is sifting through the remains, with a couple of spheres of me close by to lift the heavier pieces of rock.' It hesitated, then said, 'This is taking longer than I anticipated. The island is still in very large pieces that are hard to shift, and the bunker appears to be intact inside.'

'Was it air-tight? Is there a chance they're still alive in there?'

'No. It was definitely flooded and they have definitely drowned.' Its voice became urgent. 'Move, Jian. Move, move back, quickly!'

I rose and stepped back, not knowing what the problem was. Everything appeared fine and there was a vibration through the ground that I assumed was aftershocks from the collapse.

'More,' Marque said. 'Move back at least twenty metres. Oh come on!' It lifted me into the air and my arms and legs dangled as it pulled me away from the cliff edge. Thirty metres from the edge it dropped me and I collapsed onto the dead leaves.

The vibration grew and then a shockwave like an earthquake went through the ground. A wave hit the cliff overlooking the site – nearly a hundred metres high – and the ground shook so hard I was rolled over. The wave surged over the edge of the cliff and charged towards me in a torrent of salt water. Marque put a barrier in front of me as the deluge passed, and I gasped at its ferocity.

When the wave had finished, I was floating in the air above the water, and the cliff was gone. Marque carried me backwards another twenty metres and dropped me on the new edge of the cliff.

'Is the salvage site still workable?' I said.

'I need to transfer the younga's stone to a new body,' Marque said, and the sphere whizzed away.

The cliff top was now clear of all vegetation, which had been washed away. Only bare brown mud remained. My little tent and all its contents had been destroyed as well. I looked around for something to sit on and gave up to plonk my behind in the sucking soft mud. The rescue effort had just been set back at least half a day.

Marque reappeared. 'This sort of thing is happening all over the place. The planet is severely damaged and we're working together to remove the population and try to save it. If there's another vibration like that, run, because waves that big are bouncing through the planet's seas.'

'I understand,' I said. 'Can we save the planet? Would it be easier to build a new one? How about we use my mother's copy?'

'Your mother's project isn't habitable yet. If we stabilise and repair the Earth, we won't need to move your entire population off it – and there's a lot of people living here. I don't want to see your historical artefacts wiped out. Saving the planet is the better choice.'

'Okay,' I said.

Marque fabricated a mat for me to sit on, then set to work making me another small tent.

'I don't need it,' I said. 'The stones in the water only have less than a day left.'

'If you're going to stay here, you need a clean place to rest out of the radiation. Do you want to leave?'

'Absolutely not,' I said, and it continued to build.

*

I was lost in what-ifs, wondering if there was any possible way that I could have saved David. I hadn't been there for him at the end, I'd been messing around with the stupid black hole and contributing nothing to its destruction. I should have been with him and said goodbye. If I hadn't let him join the dragon army – if I'd insisted that he be in one of the follow-up teams rather than the vanguard – if I'd stopped him and not let him go with Cat ...

Marque woke me. 'Jian.'

I shot upright and checked the time display that I'd asked for. I'd been greyed out and lost in my grief for nearly eight hours, and hadn't been aware of the passage of time.

My voice cracked from the crying, and I coughed. 'Have they found Oliver?' I said.

'No, but we found a soulstone in the water, and we're bringing it up.'

It fitted me with the radiation suit and I left the tent to stand on the new cliff edge. More than twenty hours had passed now, and the stones were halfway to losing attunement. There was no news of Oliver, and little chance that he would be found alive if he was found at all. I stomped in a circle as I tried to focus on the possibility that the rest of the family could be salvaged. The morning chill was piercing.

The younga rose majestically from the water, its tentacles waving. I couldn't see what it was holding until it approached; it had a soulstone – a red soulstone – in one of its tentacles. I held my gloved hand out and it gently passed the stone to me.

'We continue,' it said, and floated back off the cliff and down into the water.

I studied the soulstone; it appeared intact. 'Is it all right?'

'It's irradiated, which will be a problem, but the attunement is undamaged.'

'Who—' I began, but Marque answered for me.

'It's Connie.'

I gasped with relief and clutched it to my chest. 'Mum.'

Tomoyo appeared. 'I'll take it back to the homeworld and put her into a new body for you.'

I passed her the stone and she held it in one claw, her large brown eyes wide with delight. 'I'll look after it, Jian, we'll get your mother back.'

'Thank you,' I said, but she'd already disappeared.

'We're in the bunker, so we're just sifting through what's in there to find the stones,' Marque said. 'It's a little difficult with so much silt, but we have high hopes that we'll find the other ones.'

'I hope you can,' I said, settling myself on the edge of the cliff again. I breathed a sigh of relief. 'I can't wait to hug my mum again.'

'Uh ... there is a problem,' Marque said.

I shot upright. 'What? What problem?'

'Not that major. The stone is irradiated. We'll have to put her stone onto a radiation-proof body and then attune a new stone in that body before we can transfer her back to human.'

'Wait. You mean my mother will be a dragon for five years?'

'That's the gist of it, yes. Either that or a younga, and I don't think she'd enjoy that.'

'My entire family will be dragons?' I said, aghast.

'Hopefully more people than that are in the bunker,' Marque said. 'This has never happened before. It will be *extremely* interesting to see how the dragons respond to this development. They've always been very protective of their unique biology, and they've spread it to half-dragons, but they've never allowed another species to inhabit their bodies.'

'That's beside the point,' I said, sitting again. 'The important thing is getting my family back.'

'We found another one,' Marque said. 'The younga's coming up. It's not a member of your family, it's one of the other Embassy staff members that you didn't meet.'

'I'm delighted,' I said, and stood. 'I'm crying again and I need to go into my tent to wipe myself up. Let me know if you find another stone from my family.'

*

'I have news,' Marque said some time later.

I pulled myself out of the greyness and tried to concentrate. 'Have you found Oliver?'

'We think he's in the UN bunker in Geneva.'

I sagged over my knees with relief. I was all cried out; no more tears would come. 'How long before you know for sure?'

'Another twelve hours. We're busy clearing people from dangerous areas before we get to those who are safe in the bunker. There's something else, Jian – it's about Akiko.'

'Tell me she's alive!' I said.

'She is.'

'That is the best news. Oliver, Aki, Mum – you already have Victor – all that's missing now is Dianne's stone.' I smiled as my heart lifted through the misery. 'Thanks so much, Marque.'

'Would you like to see Akiko? I can arrange for someone to take you to her. I'll let you know if we find Dianne's stone – we're still finding them down there.'

I hesitated, then nodded. I couldn't help look for Dianne's stone, but I could grab this moment to be with Aki before protocol closed in around her.

*

When I arrived in Tokyo, the Imperial Palace was gone. The hundred-metre-wide crater centred on where the old Palace building had been, and the small hill was blasted to nothing. The beautiful ancient maple and ginkgo trees that had covered the elegant lawn were destroyed. The bunker inside the hill was exposed by the blast. It hadn't taken the blast well; half of it had collapsed, making the exposed concrete ceiling slope precariously to one side. None of the people in the area were shielded, so the younga must have finished decontaminating the site.

Aki was speaking with Kenji and a couple of people that I didn't recognise. When she saw me she nodded to them, and approached with her hands clasped in front of her.

I didn't grab her and hug her; there were media watching. She seemed smaller than when she'd been with me; collapsed in on herself and meek. The brilliant courageous woman I loved was disappearing and it broke my heart.

'Marque, can we have some privacy for a moment please?' she said.

'Done,' Marque said. 'But I can't break protocol and give you a visual screen. Audio only, I'm afraid.'

'I know that,' she said.

'Are you okay? You didn't catch any radiation?' I said.

'I didn't,' she said. 'We had suits in the bunker.' She lowered her head. 'Jian, Hiro killed himself. When he saw that the ceiling was coming down, he ran under it.'

'Is his stone okay?'

'It's crushed. The Emperor's dead. They're preparing the statement now.'

'Oh, holy shit, no,' I said as horrified realisation filled me. 'They are not ... they won't ... they can't do that to you.'

She looked up into my eyes for the first time. 'I'm the only fully human one left.'

'But most of the Household administration must have been killed by the blast,' I said. 'There's no bureaucracy left to terrorise you! You don't have to do this.'

'It's awful, isn't it? That was my first thought as well – that they're dead and they can't hurt me any more,' she said. 'But I've been having other thoughts while I waited for them to bring us out. Japan needs its Emperor – in my case its Empress. It's a tradition that's been handed down unchanged for thousands of years. We are the longest-lasting unbroken monarchy in the world – one of the longest in the Galactic Empire, actually. I won't be responsible for the destruction of something so valuable. After all my ancestors went through during the Meiji restoration, I can't throw it away. I'll be Empress, and abdicate when Kenji and I have a grown child to take my place.' She took my hands and held them. 'I'm sorry, Jian, I put my country before you.'

Steward Tokugawa came from behind the bunker and saw us. His face went fierce and he charged towards us, but Kenji grabbed him and stopped him, talking furiously into his face. The steward glanced at us again, then gave up trying to free himself from Kenji's grip.

'And, of course, he survived.' I turned back to Aki. 'You are doing the right thing, my love. Just stay alive long enough for us to be together eventually.'

'Are you enjoying the job of captain?' she said, smiling sadly.

I hesitated for a moment, then told her the truth. 'Actually, I am. It's interesting and varied and I'm meeting all sorts of weirdos. The Empress is a complete blast to work with – I never know what dumb shit she's going to pull next.' I lowered my voice. 'It's a bit like being with you.'

'Good. I knew it was the right decision. Now.' She squeezed my hands. 'It'll be at least twenty years before we have a grown kid, so in the meantime, find someone else to make you happy. Don't stay alone. You had a good relationship with Dianne and Victor, and if you find someone, I'll be sure to love them too. Find someone to make you happy, please?' She quickly kissed my hands. 'Promise me.'

'I promise,' I said, not meaning it at all.

'Good. The Empress will have to come to my coronation – we don't really have a crowning as such, and most of the ceremony happens in private, but we'll still have something you guys can attend. I heard about your family, and I'm so sorry about David.' She squeezed my hands again. 'You are strong, and magnificent, and I love you with all my heart. Now go do your Imperial duty while I go do mine, okay?'

'You can change the protocol when you're Empress.'

'You fucking bet I can,' she whispered. 'Just watch me. There are some untouched archaeological sites that only the Empress has access to, and you can be damn sure I'll be accessing them, as well.' She pushed me away. 'Now go make sure the rest of the family is okay. I love them like my own.'

'And they love you.'

'Time's up,' Kenji said, approaching us. 'We have a great deal to rebuild.'

'I know.' Aki quickly embraced me, released me, and walked away with them.

'She's going to stir some shit,' I said.

'Good,' Marque said. 'Juicy drama.'

'Can someone take me back to the Embassy site?'

'Tomoyo is on her way.'

'Thank you.'

16

I sat in the waiting room with a large group of other humans in a similar situation as me: their families had been killed on Earth and the dragons were restoring them from their stones. The four-metre-square windows overlooked the main plaza of Sky City, giving a view of Marque's news sphere a hundred metres across floating in the middle of the square, relaying images of the clean-up and rebuilding on Earth.

The Earth Ambassador, Charles Maxwell, was sitting in one of the chairs and waved to me. I went up to her. 'Ambassador.'

She gestured for me to sit next to her. 'Captain.'

'I didn't know you lost someone on Earth.'

'I didn't. It's five years since we put Shiumo into stasis to reattune her stone, and Marque is restoring her. My daughter and granddaughter are in there with her.'

'Shiumo's all right?'

'We'll know soon enough. The girls ... Veronica has been impatient to see her dragonfather again; she really misses Shiumo.' She quirked a small smile. 'Despite what she did to Earth – and particularly to Mr Alto – Shiumo is still a member of the family, and my granddaughter's dragonfather.'

'I understand. How soon before you know?'

'Marque?' the Ambassador said.

'The procedure is finished. Please come inside and speak to your family, Ambassador.'

'Oh. I see.' The Ambassador rose and nodded to me. 'Captain.'

'General,' I replied, and she smiled sadly. A door opened at the end of the room, and she went through.

'Shiumo's dead, isn't she?' I said. 'If she was alive, she'd be coming out. You sent the Ambassador in to share the news in private.'

'I won't be able to share the result of the procedure until the family are fully notified. What I can say is: you are very perceptive sometimes, Captain Choumali.'

I sorted through my feelings about Shiumo and came up short. Maybe they'd change when I had more time to think about it, but at that moment I didn't feel grief for the dragon that had caused so much pain to my friends. My family came first anyway; I'd already lost my darling son and I still had to hear whether everybody else could be restored. If it didn't work for Shiumo then it was a possibility that the rest of my family were lost as well ...

One of the human medical staff came through the door and approached me. 'I'm Adriana Menendez, the psychologist caring for your family members. They're in their new bodies, Captain Choumali. We've talked to them, and you can see them now.'

I rose, full of relief. 'Are they all right?'

'The procedure worked. We took the radioactive stones, attached them to dragon bodies, and your family are inhabiting the bodies. We took out the radioactive stones and put in new stones that aren't radioactive, and your family will have to be careful while we wait for the new stones to attune. So physically, your family are fine.' I walked beside her as she explained. 'Mentally, the transition will be difficult. Our psyches are built from childhood to be in human bodies. Putting them in dragon bodies causes profound dysmorphia; on top of that, Dianne and Victor have just lost their son. You can talk to them for a while but they're not being very communicative, and it will take time for them to heal. Putting them back in human bodies is the best thing we can do for them; it will be a tough five years.'

'And my mother?'

She opened the door for me and lowered her head. 'She isn't as deeply traumatised as they are, but she's still grieving for David.' We arrived at an administrative section with white walls and floor made from a smooth, ceramic-like material, and soft light coming from no visible source. She pulled up several medical charts, with yellow dragon faces next to their human ones in the floating three-dimensional displays. 'I hope you can assist her more than your spouses, because she won't have anyone to stay by her side as she works it through.'

'She has Yuki ...' My voice trailed off as I realised. 'Dragons never have relationships with other dragons. They'll break it off?'

'Yuki will. Even if your mother wasn't a goldenscales and prohibited from having children, Yuki would still be unable to have a relationship with her. It's a deep psychological barrier for the dragons – I'd love to know why, and how they reproduced before they went interstellar.'

'Have you told Mum this?'

She shook her head. 'She was so devastated when she learned about David that I thought it best to let it wait.'

'I see.' I checked the charts again. 'Oliver? Where's Oliver?'

She smiled. 'He's grieving for his brother, but he's in a cloned cat body and he'll be out of the table soon. I hope you can look after him.'

'I will. Is his partner Runa around? She can help him.'

'She's with him right now, but he's still in the table. I suggest you speak to Dianne, Victor and Connie first – they need you more than he does.'

'Take me.'

Dianne was a two-metre-long goldenscales dragon, sitting in the middle of the padded floor looking bewildered. I stopped at the door and smiled. 'Dianne?'

She saw me. 'Jian. Thank god! You can help me.'

'Sure,' I said. 'What do you need?'

She turned on the spot. 'What do you think? Aren't dragons amazing? They put me into a whole new body, my memories, everything.'

'I'm glad you're okay. We'll get you back to human as soon as we can.'

'I have strict instructions not to try to fold – but goldenscales can't fold anyway. I guess that's why they put me in this particular body.'

Something wasn't right; she seemed entirely too cheerful. 'They did tell you what happened, didn't they?' I said. 'You know about David?'

'Isn't it awful?' she said, reclining on the mat. She lifted her butt and moved her back legs into a more comfortable position, then did the same thing with her tail. 'Do you have any idea how freaking weird it is to have a tail? It feels really wrong.'

Now she really sounded strange. 'We'll have you in a human body as soon as we can.'

'They have clones of our human bodies, right?'

'Yes, of course,' I said.

She moved closer to me. 'And they must have clones of David's body. So they can just activate the clone, fill it with David's memories, and ...' Her eyes went wide with excitement. 'There you are, we have him back!'

'Without a soulstone that won't work, love,' I said, my heart breaking. 'And the soulstone he was wearing was a fake. The cats gave our stones to the walkers.'

'No, listen,' she said, explaining patiently. 'That doesn't matter. If we have the body, and the memories, that's good enough, right? That's our David, back to us. We don't need a soulstone, I just need ...' her voice broke. 'I just need to hug my David again, you see? We can bring him back, and he'll be here again. It's just ... I have this hole inside me, where he was, and I need to fill it. And we have cloned bodies, so why not use one, to fill the hole? We can have him back; isn't dragon technology wonderful ...' She reclined on the mat and closed her eyes. 'We can get him back. Don't let them stop you – you can order it. You're important.'

'Dianne, I can't—' I said, but she didn't respond. She appeared to be asleep.

'Don't sedate her too much, Marque,' I said.

'I ordered it,' the doctor said from the doorway. 'Please be patient, it will take a while for us to work this out with her.'

'Is Victor this bad?' I said.

'It's hard to put into words. He's not very responsive. Having you visit might help.'

'All right.'

Victor was in the next room. A goldenscales dragon lay on the floor with her eyes closed, and I couldn't distinguish it from Dianne. It seemed to be an identical goldenscales body, but all of them looked the same to me anyway – it was hard to tell the servants apart.

'He heard his voice – his female voice – and is very upset,' the doctor said softly to me. 'The dysmorphia is more pronounced in him – we humans are very attached to our gender.'

'Was there no other way?'

'Not with the stones as radioactive as they were. It would have killed their bodies before their souls were connected.' She raised her voice. 'Jian's here to see you, Victor.'

'Hi, Victor,' I said, but he didn't respond.

I went in and sat next to his head. I stroked his shining metallic scales. 'You always were solid gold,' I said.

He sighed softly.

'We can work this out,' I said. 'We will all survive.'

'I don't want to,' he said, and his voice was female. 'Oh fuck this for a game of soldiers. David's dead, and I'm stuck in this awful body for five years. I will never finish that sculpture. Never.'

'Not even as a memorial for a fantastic, courageous young man who gave his life to protect humanity?'

He raised his front claws. 'I can't even write my bloody name with these things.' He fell onto his side. 'When can I see Dianne?'

'She's ... not well,' I said.

'I'm not surprised,' he said, and closed his eyes.

'Victor?'

He didn't respond.

'I'm going to see Oliver and my mum now, and I'll be back, okay?'

He still didn't reply. He appeared to be asleep.

'Marque, please stop sedating my family,' I said.

'I didn't,' Marque said.

Victor was completely unresponsive. I ran my hand over the smooth scales of his head and went out. I looked up and down the corridor, then returned to the admin station.

'Where's Doctor Menendez?' I said.

'With one of the patients,' the staff member said from behind the desk. She had a female voice in Marque's translator, but was two metres tall, solid and hairy with a single faceted eye on the front of her head, and no mouth. 'Oh! You're Captain Choumali. Doctor Menendez is with your mother. Let me show you the way.'

She fell to all fours and I followed her down another corridor to a room containing my mother in another identical goldenscales body. My mother was howling, making a long, inhuman noise of grief and pain. I rushed in and knelt beside her. 'Mum. Mum! I'm here.'

'Jian, oh Jian!' she shouted, and grabbed me.

'Mum, you have claws, loosen up,' I said, pulling her forearms away from me. 'You're digging them into my back.'

'Sorry, honey,' she said, and relaxed her grip. She pulled back to see into my eyes. 'David's dead! Our little one! What are we going to do?'

Her desperation and grief set me off, and we held each other. I wept, and she made loud agonised noises of pain – dragons didn't cry, they keened for their losses.

'Tell Marque when you want me to come back,' the doctor said. She went out and closed the door softly behind her.

Half an hour later I went to find Oliver. He and Runa were sitting in a sunlit ward with a human-style bed and window showing the blue-white sky of the dragon homeworld. Oliver smiled when he saw me, rose and swept me into a huge embrace. He pulled back, his bright green eyes full of concern. 'How is everybody?' He saw my face, obviously swollen from crying with Mum. 'That bad?'

'It will take time,' I said, hearing my voice quiver. 'We'll get there.'

'I learned something new about my cat nature today,' he said, morose. 'I don't grieve. I feel like: okay I lost my brother. That's bad. But I can function.'

'That's not necessarily a bad thing, Ollie.'

'I feel like a psychopath.'

'We do the same thing,' Runa said. 'We keen, but we move on. Species are different in their ways of dealing with loss.'

'How does everybody feel about me? My people did this,' he said.

'We all love you,' I said. 'You're family.'

'See? What did I say?' Runa said.

'It's just ...' He turned and sat on the bed human-style. 'Every time someone sees me on the square, they're going to remember how many people died.' He looked up at me, full of misery. 'Can I move into a human body?'

'Don't you dare,' the Empress said behind me.

I glared at her. 'This is private family business, Silver, what the hell?'

'As Empress I am your family,' she said. She was so large that she had trouble fitting through the door, and it was a squeeze with all of us in there. She towered over Oliver and turned her laser-bright gaze onto him.

'Listen to me, young man. One day I sincerely hope we will have peace with the cats. You are living proof that your people can be sensible – hell, you're smart and wise and a fine citizen of the Empire, and having a whole nation of people like you can only benefit both sides. When the cats finally grow up and come around, we'll need someone to represent us, that they can trust.' She put her claw on his shoulder. 'That's you.'

'I'm an outcast,' he said. 'If I return to the cat homeworld they'll kill me on sight.'

'Like I said, when they grow up,' she said. 'It may take some time. Fortunately time is something we have plenty of.' She turned to me. 'Jian, as soon as you're feeling confident about your family's care, I want to tour Earth and inspect the rebuilding and relief effort so I can be a symbol of the Empire's concern for our human citizens. Let me know when you feel strong enough to do it, because I want you at my side to represent your people in my esteem.'

I was torn. I wanted to stay with my family, but being at the Empress' side while she showed empathy for the plight of Earth would demonstrate a positive message and be a real morale booster.

'I'll talk to them and let them know what I'm doing,' I said. 'Give me a few hours.'

'I understand,' she said. She turned to Oliver. 'Your training has just begun, young cat. Your quarters in the Imperial complex are still here, and if you're willing, I'd like to give you full security clearance, Imperial family status, and unrestricted access to diplomatic training.'

'I'd be honoured, Majesty,' he said, smiling for the first time.

'Good.' She winked at Runa. 'Look after him.'

'I will, Mama,' Runa said.

'Captain.' The Empress nodded to me and went out, squeezing through the door with difficulty. Her goldenscales servant was waiting for her in the hallway, and it wasn't Kana.

'She's very wise,' Oliver said.

'She truly cares for all the people of the Empire,' Runa said. 'Her role may only be symbolic, but she's a powerful symbol.'

Oliver raised his head. 'I hope that I will have the chance to be an intermediary one day. It's a goal to aim for.'

'I am so proud of you,' I said, and embraced him again.

As I exited, I went past my mother again and spoke to her, then checked on Dianne and Victor, who were both unresponsive. I had the unpleasant realisation – they were in Kana's bodies. All three of them were in Kana's spare cloned bodies.

I rushed back to the Palace to find Five-Shriek and Six Eighty Four stationed at the entrance. Five-Shriek looked like a small round feathered crocodile with wings and a long-toothed snout, and Six Eighty Four was a dancing blue flame next to the door.

'You're out of uniform, Six,' I said.

'Apologies, ma'am, it's being repaired,' it replied without missing a beat.

'Is she in her quarters?'

'She's in the audience chamber with a whole bunch of goldenscales and threw us out,' Five-Shriek said.

I went along the corridors to the chamber entrance; the doors were closed.

'Open up,' I said, and Marque didn't respond

I have an urgent message for you from Earth, I broadcast telepathically. *I need to come in immediately, this is extremely important. The fate of the Empire is at risk.*

The doors opened and I stormed in, then the doors slammed shut behind me. The Empress was reclining on the floor at the head of the room next to her throne, with Masako's goldenscales servant Miko next to her. The rest of the hall was packed with at least two hundred goldenscales servants. A yellow soulstone stood on a small plinth in the middle of the room in front of the Empress – Kana's soulstone.

'What's the message?' the Empress said. 'This had better be important, Jian, this is an extremely private ceremony.'

'The message is this,' I said. 'If you execute Kana I will resign on the spot and tell the entire Empire how you mistreat your goldenscales *slaves*.'

There was a ripple of consternation through the goldenscales.

'Thank you!' she said, and raised herself. 'Another reason to spare her life, my children. Let her live!'

One of the goldenscales stepped forward. 'This is our decision to make, not the Empress', Captain.'

'And we were discussing that decision, Saki,' the Empress said. 'Continue, Miko. Your argument is sound.'

'As I was saying, our coloured sisters receive training in folding from an early age,' Miko said. 'If we received similar training in gating, it would be just as safe.'

'If a fold fails, the dragon dies,' Saki said. 'If a gate fails, *everybody* dies.'

'A fold hasn't failed in centuries,' the Empress said. 'Mostly because of the training. If you received the same training, your gates would be just as safe.'

'It's not worth the risk,' Saki said. 'Marque, what's the chances of a gate failing, even after the goldenscales has been trained?'

'Insufficient data to form a conclusion,' Marque said.

'Extrapolate from the results of fold training for the coloureds,' Saki said.

Marque hesitated, then said, 'It's too different, you're too different, and the risk is exponentially higher. As you said, if a fold fails the dragon dies, but if a gate fails *everybody* dies.'

'Coward,' I said.

'Raise your head if you believe Kana's stone should be crushed. Lower it if you believe she should not pay the penalty for gating,' Saki said.

Only the Empress and Miko lowered their heads.

'The vote is cast,' Saki said.

'You can still change your minds,' the Empress said, desperate.

'Don't do this,' Miko wailed.

'Kana knew the consequences of her actions.' Saki nodded to me. 'Dear Captain Choumali, we understand your concern, but the penalty for gating must be enforced. We honour Kana's sacrifice to save the people of Earth, but gating must be a method of last resort, and the price must remain this high.'

'We will honour Kana's sacrifice,' another goldenscales said, and I didn't recognise her. 'We have a hall where we pay respects to our greatest sisters. We'll build a statue of her to contain her crushed stone. She will be venerated for centuries.'

'I can't believe you will murder your own sister,' I said. I strode up to the plinth to grab the stone, but Marque was protecting it in an energy field.

'Back her up,' Saki said, and Marque pushed me backwards and held me.

'I will resign if you do this,' I said.

'You don't work for us,' Saki said. 'Begin the ceremony, Marque.'

'No!' the Empress wailed, and thrashed against a similar barrier. 'Don't do it.'

Marque floated a soft leather pouch to Saki, and she pulled a golden scale out, then passed the pouch to the goldenscales next to her. The dragons passed the pouch around, each taking a golden scale. They skipped Miko, who was behind the barrier with the Empress.

The next goldenscales to take the pouch held up a silver scale – an Empress' scale.

'I can't watch,' the Empress said with her head bowed. 'Why are you helping them, Marque? Why? Stop this now.'

'It must be done,' the goldenscales with the silver scale said. She stepped forward to the plinth, took Kana's stone off it, placed it onto a silver bowl at the base of the plinth, and crushed it with her foot. It felt like my own heart was being crushed, and the Empress wailed softly with grief.

'Why are you helping them commit this atrocity?' I shouted at the ceiling.

'Because I'm sorry, Jian, but they're right,' Marque said. 'When they first started gating they nearly destroyed the entire universe – more than once – and it must not happen again. Any goldenscales that is willing to take the risk is too dangerous to live.'

'My child,' the Empress moaned, and collapsed sideways. Miko curled up next to her, leaned her head on the Empress' shoulder and keened softly.

The Empress raised her head and looked me in the eye. 'Please don't resign. Stay with me, Captain, so that next time – if there is a next time – you can help me hide the soulstone better so that my child will be safe.'

Marque released me and I stood, shaking with fury. Then I turned on my heel and went out of the audience room. As I stormed angrily through the Palace to my office, I decided that I would stay with her, because she was right. The next time this happened, if it happened, I would stop them from taking an innocent – and courageous – dragon's life. I couldn't even tell the rest of the Empire about this atrocity because dear dead Kana had asked me not to tell anyone about their abilities, and I would keep my word to her.

17

We arrived in Tokyo on the grounds of the Imperial Palace, which had been cordoned off for Aki's enthronement. The stewards guided us to a dais separate from the other dignitaries, befitting the Dragon Empress' status, but still slightly lower than the building where the ceremony would take place. The Empress reclined on the tatami mats they'd provided for her, and I stood with my hands behind my back at her shoulder. Two goldenscales servants stood on the other side behind her, ready to assist. My mother, in her goldenscales body, lay on the tatami in front of me – Aki had invited her as well, to honour her relationship with both of us.

The buildings had been reconstructed, and the pavilion stood above us on the hillside – a hundred metres to a side and raised on stilts, elegantly understated in its minimalist grace. The other dignitaries were guided to their seats on a large stand next to us, and an old-fashioned brass band played parade music as they found their places.

The Empress lowered her head, then gestured for me to attend her. I moved closer.

'What are these mats made of? They smell divine,' she said.

'Rice straw,' I said.

'They are the ideal softness for my royal behind. I must order some.'

'I'm sure they'll be delighted to provide them.'

'Make way for the Imperial family!' a steward shouted, and the crowd went quiet.

The band stopped playing, and Haruka appeared at the end of the glass-walled corridor that ran along the side of the building. He was wearing the wide traditional Japanese male formal outfit of pants and jacket, with a hat that had a flange standing up and bending towards the back. He held a sceptre vertically in one hand and walked extremely slowly towards the coronation room at the end of the building.

Goodness, he looks totally ridiculous, the Empress said to me.

Can't tell the difference from how he normally looks, I replied with a straight face, and my mother thumped me on the arm. She wasn't telepathic, but still knew when I was misbehaving.

When Haruka was at the room, he turned and stood to one side in front of the small curtained tent that would hold Aki. The stewards and senior government officials were lined up behind him, wearing pre-nineteenth-century styled Western formal gear. They all stood with their faces carefully composed and without moving. Normally during a coronation, the male and female Household members would enter the room in a procession and stand on either side; in this case Haruka was the only other family member left.

'Make way for the Emperor!' the steward shouted, and everybody gasped.

'What?' I said out loud, feeling a rush of hope. They weren't going to make Aki do this after all?

Another man appeared in traditional male dress, holding the sceptre, his kimono deep bronze in colour. His hat's flange stood straight up for nearly a metre. Then I saw his face – he looked about twenty-five years old, but he was Aki.

The crowd stirred, making soft comments, then someone up the back loudly hushed them and they went still.

She was definitely a woman, right? the Empress said.

Definitely, I said.

Well she's a man now, the Empress said.

Marque spoke into my ear and I heard the echo as he spoke softly to the other dignitaries present. 'Now that you've seen her, the privacy seal is off and I'm allowed to explain. The last time Japan had an Empress, there were sixteen years of major natural disasters, and they've decided that having a woman on the throne is an insult to the spirits of the land. Aki had a fatal "accident", and I "messed up" when I created the cloned body for her, producing the man that they needed.'

'She agreed to this?' I said, incredulous.

'It was her idea. She doesn't want to let her people down.'

'So brave,' the Empress cooed.

'This isn't birth-natural,' I said loud enough for a few heads to turn towards us. I lowered my voice. 'It's a cloned body, not naturally born!'

'I've made no alterations to the body – apart from the sex chromosome thing,' Marque said. 'It's effectively birth-natural. The previous Emperor had leukaemia as a child and moved into a birth-natural cloned body as well, so there's precedent. In light of the alternatives, the stewards have decided that this is the best option for satisfactory continuation of the line.'

'What about Kenji?' I said.

'He also agreed to it – but now that Aki's a man, they need to find an Empress for their new Emperor.'

I felt a bolt of hope. Would she have me again? Would they let me be with her? Could I live in that stifling atmosphere? If it was with Aki, I could—

'It can't be you, Jian, the Empress must be pure-blood Japanese and birth-natural. You could be a concubine, but then you'd have to be completely hidden from the world and never go out at all. You'd effectively be a prisoner. Aki requested that you not even consider it, and if you try to join her, she will reject you.'

'You must love this drama,' I said.

'Delicious,' it said without emotion.

Aki entered the two-metre-wide curtained tent at the back of the room, and the area was silent for at least ten minutes. Two stewards pulled back the curtains to reveal Aki, standing unnaturally still and holding her ... his ... sceptre. It took another painful five minutes for the stewards to carefully fold and secure the curtains, then they moved back. Tokugawa himself stepped up to Aki and bowed to him. Aki nodded back, and Tokugawa handed him an accordion-folded document. Aki opened the document and read the speech from it in stiff ultra-formal Japanese, sounding completely different from the woman I'd known.

Aki was Emperor.

*

A huge reception was held for all the visiting royalty in another pavilion overlooking the grounds of the castle. My mum stayed close beside me, intimidated by the guests.

'I'm half my real size, I'm worried someone will step on me,' she said. 'I keep looking up people's noses. Oh, there's Aki. Doesn't she ... he ... look strange?'

'He looks like my Aki,' I said as he approached, and heard the lie in my voice.

He'd changed into a Western-style suit similar to what the stewards were wearing; an outfit so ancient in its fashion that it looked more like a costume. He had several medals pinned to his chest, a ribbon across the whole lot, and he looked like something out of an archaic photograph.

'I am so sorry about this,' he said, and again his voice was completely different. 'Please come outside onto the veranda with me, and I'll explain.'

I gazed into his eyes, looking for my Aki in this serious young man, and not finding her.

'Of course,' I said.

He gestured over his shoulder at two guards in old-fashioned soldiers' uniforms. 'With us.' He smiled sadly at me. 'I can't be seen in public alone with a woman.'

'Marque,' I said. 'Move Graf to the entrance of the hall, Namazozo next to the Empress, and keep Five-Shriek on the roof.'

'Done.'

'Does it feel strange, being a man?' I asked Aki as I walked beside him onto the veranda. 'I've wondered what it would feel like to change sex, now that the option is open to us.'

'It's awful.' He looked down at himself. 'I feel sorry for your family. It's bad enough being the wrong sex; being a completely different species must be devastating.'

'It's only for five years,' I said.

'Not for me,' he said bitterly.

The generous veranda spanned the width of the building. We went to the edge where it overlooked a Zen garden of raked white sand in ripple patterns around weathered black stones, and surrounded by manicured pine trees.

'I still have the miniature sand garden that you gave me a couple of years ago for our anniversary,' I said. 'It's in my Captain's quarters in the Imperial Palace.'

His smile was deeply sad. 'Jian, I erased the memories of our time together.'

I stood gasping at him like a goldfish. Eventually I struggled out, 'Why?'

'Because being apart from you was breaking my heart. It was affecting my mental health to such a degree that I was contemplating suicide. The doctors were afraid I'd actually do it.' He leaned both arms on the railing and looked out over the garden. 'The memories are in Marque storage, and Haruka has a stored backup. When my duty is done ...' He turned back to me. 'I'll have them restored, move back into my real body, and we can be together again.'

'So you don't love me at all right now?' I said with disbelief.

'I'm fond of you,' he said, in such a restrained burst of mild affection that I nearly screamed at him. 'Don't worry, once my memories are restored, we can go back to what we had.'

'Now I'm terrified that you won't feel the same way when you do restore them,' I said.

'You don't need to worry. Here with you I'm finding myself ... enchanted, and we should probably not spend too much time together before my duty is done.'

'You just have to hurry up and have a couple of kids,' I said. 'Have you selected an Empress yet?'

'Don't even think about trying to get into the Household,' he said. 'If you attempt anything at all they will throw you out. No. The search is ongoing for the right woman.'

'Surely all she needs to be is fertile, royal, and breathing?' I said with more irritation than I intended. I winced. 'Sorry.'

'Yes,' he said. 'That's all that is required, but I'm going to be spending years with her, so I'd prefer a good friend who's intellectually stimulating, stubborn, loyal and gallant to a fault.' He moved to take my hand, and one of the guards coughed loudly. He withdrew his hand from mine. 'So they're looking for a copy of you and we're all aware of the fact that they won't find one. There's the added complication that everybody knows what a shitshow it is in the Imperial Household, and nobody is willing to take the job.'

Some shouts rang out from inside the pavilion and one of the guards approached.

'Captain Choumali, your mother is involved in an ... incident.'

'Oh shit,' Aki and I said in unison, and hurried into the pavilion.

Mum was standing in the middle of a small group of people, her dragon head raised as she yelled at the purple dragon next to her.

'And you will treat me with the respect earned by the mother of a war hero, by the mother of the Captain of the Imperial Guard, and if one more dragon asks me to fetch her a drink, I will practise my non-existent folding skills on them!'

'I am so sorry,' the purple dragon said. She had six legs and no wings, and a short, stubby head with teeth that protruded from her jaws. 'It won't happen again, Ms Choumali, I can't believe I made this mistake.'

'You coloured dragons have been making this mistake since I was put into this damn body,' my mother grumbled. 'I am not a servant!' She saw me. 'Come on, Jian, I want to see this Zen garden my *other* friend – who was treating me with *respect* – was describing.'

She stormed out of the room onto the veranda and I trailed after her. Aki didn't follow us; he was led by one of the stewards into an exceptionally polite and restrained scrum of officials as they discussed how to deal with the incident.

'This has happened before?' I said as we stood at the railing overlooking the garden.

'It happens all the damn time,' she said, impatient. She took a deep breath. 'Jian, sweetie, I didn't want to bring this up with you when it's so soon, but I need your opinion.'

'On what?'

She ran one claw over the railing. 'I'm very vulnerable right now. We all are. It will take five years for these stones to be attuned, and if anything happens to me before then, it's the Real Death.'

'Just keep yourself safe.' I put my hand on her shoulder; her scales were warm and textured with tiny ridges. 'I need you.'

'Are you sure?' She put her claw on my hand and looked up into my eyes. 'Could you do without me for five years?'

I froze. 'What?'

'It's an option. Marque can put me into hibernation, in a coma, in a secure location – a bunker – until the stone is attuned.'

'You'll be unconscious for five years?' I realised what she was saying. 'This is because of the body, isn't it? You want to sleep through attunement because being in this body is a pain in the ass.'

'You always could see through me,' she said wryly. 'It's not just the ... racism from the other dragons. Here we are, in an enlightened interstellar society, and the last thing you'd expect is *racism*.'

'You should see the Imperial Guard records,' I said wryly.

She continued. 'This body isn't *me*. It's wrong. I hate being in it, I hate walking around in it, and waking up every morning in it is driving me crazy. If I allow Marque to store me during the attunement, I can sleep through it and then be myself again. My *real* self.'

'Have you talked to Victor and Dianne?'

'They feel the same way.'

'I'll lose my entire family?' I said, incredulous.

'You'll have your son. Oliver will keep you company. It's only for five years. If you say no, that you really need me, I won't do it, but I'd prefer to sleep through this god-awful body.'

I rubbed her shoulder. 'If it's that bad – of course. Sleep through it. I'll be busy guarding the Imperial Silverbutt.'

'Thank you.' She grinned. 'You'll need to find someone else to mind your dog while you're traipsing around.'

'Oliver can do it. He's moving into the Imperial Palace, he'll be close by.'

'Thank you. One other thing.' She glared at me. 'When I wake up, I want you to be in a happy relationship with someone.'

'But Aki ...'

'Aki will be married to someone else for twenty years. Don't you dare wait for her. Find someone, Jian; twenty years is a long time to be alone. Most relationships don't last that long anyway.' She reached up to take my hand. 'Find someone.'

'Yes, Mother,' I said patiently.

'Just not a dragon,' she said.

'Oh, you can talk!' I said.

Mum's head drooped. 'Another reason to skip five years. Yuki is unable to love me like this.'

'Oh I am so sorry, I forgot about that ...' I took her dragon head in my hands. 'Will she wait for you?'

'She says she will, and that five years is nothing.'

'You won't rush into this, will you? We can spend some time together before you do it?'

'Of course. I need to sort out my crops – and my project – and make sure they're cared for.'

'I'll miss you, Mum.'

'I'll be back before you know it.'

Marque flashed an image into my vision of five armed people – wearing samurai-style outfits and carrying guns, with swords shoved into their belts – charging towards the hall.

'They're modified,' he said. 'Select a plan.'

'Beta,' I said, and ran inside.

The attackers were almost as enhanced as me. The crowd was in slow motion as the attackers operated with flawless teamwork. One threw a concussion grenade into the middle of the room and Namazozo leaped on top of it in an attempt to stop the blast. Namazozo was only the size of a weasel and didn't have much effect on the blast, exploding everywhere in a fountain of blood and flesh. Marque deadened the blast, but it still knocked people and furniture over and deafened me. Everything was thumping bass as I picked myself up off the floor, half-stunned, to protect the Empress, who'd been talking to the Queen of Euroterre.

Another of the attackers used a laser-based weapon to fire a red-hot beam on Marque's sphere, and the sphere was forced to protect itself with an energy barrier. With Marque occupied in self-defence it was on me to defend the Empress. She quickly moved into the corner of the room, away from the other people present. One of the attackers fired a similar energy weapon at the Empress. I shot the attacker's hand off and she missed the Empress, but the wood behind the Empress was scorched and started to burn. I shot the attacker in the chest to finish her off.

'Running out,' Marque said in my ear.

'Gotcha.' Another attacker raced towards the Empress, pulling a sword from his sash. I shot him in the chest before he could reach her, and he fell with a look of confusion on his face. I went up to him and picked up his sword, then turned to face the rest of the attackers. The attacker who had been focusing the beam on Marque turned to run towards the Empress, and I shot her before she could attack the dragon. Another ran to the Empress and I shot him in the chest before he could reach us.

The last attacker shot at the Marque sphere and must have winged it as it was running out of energy; it fell out of the air. With Marque down I was no longer invisible, and the attacker turned the weapon on me and fired, but missed because Graf lifted him from behind and dangled him from Graf's front legs. Graf ripped the gun from him, taking his hand with it, and the attacker screamed with agony as he pulled his blade out with his other hand.

'Don't let him kill himself – he has no stone!' I shouted as the human stabbed himself in the abdomen and ripped the blade up through his lungs and heart.

I staggered to the Empress as someone found a fire extinguisher and put out the blazing wood behind her. 'Are you hurt?'

'I'm fine,' she said. 'You were all magnificent.'

I looked out onto the veranda to check on my mother, and didn't see her. I went to the door and found her cowering as far away as possible.

'Stay there,' I said. 'I think we have all of them.'

She stared at me blankly.

I went back in and spoke to Graf. 'Did we get them all?'

Graf made some random clicks, waving its front pincers.

I switched to dragonspeak. 'Marque must be completely down. That means there could be others around. Five-Shriek,' I shouted at the ceiling.

'I'm checking the perimeter,' the flyer shouted back in dragon. 'I can't see anything.'

'Do a thorough search of the area for any other armed humans.'

'Ma'am.'

Graf stood holding the dead attacker with a look of confusion on its face.

'My dragon is terrible,' it said with a thick mushy accent.

'I can understand you, so good enough,' I said.

People were picking themselves up, but a couple were still prone on the floor, possibly killed by the grenade. Something was wrong with my left side, and when I my put my hand to it, it came away wet with blood – I'd been injured and didn't even know how or when it had happened. I went to the woman lying on the floor closest to me, and saw it was the Queen – she'd been knocked over but seemed to be okay. She was breathing and blinking with confusion at the ceiling. The man next to her was the Prince-Consort, and he must have jumped in front of her to protect her from the blast, because he had a couple of broken bones, and from his racing pulse and cold skin could be either in shock or have internal bleeding. Namazozo was shredded by the blast, and I looked around for her stone. It must be embedded in one of the lumps of her flesh.

Aki came and crouched next to me. 'What can I do?'

'Find medical assistance,' I said. I raised my head and shouted, 'I need a dragon.'

'I'm here,' my mother said behind me.

I turned to see her. 'No, I need a dragon to fold us a new Marque sphere.'

'Masako already went,' Haruka said. He crouched next to the Prince-Consort, raised his eyelids, and felt his pulse. 'Nothing life-threatening, but he should go to the Palace infirmary. Is it functional? Or should they go to a hospital?'

'It's functional,' Aki said. 'It needed to be – to do this—' he gestured towards himself '—to me.'

Masako appeared next to him with a new Marque sphere. 'Are you okay, Mother?'

'I'm fine,' the Empress said from behind me. 'Poor Namazozo. Is her stone anywhere around?'

'We'll find it,' I said.

Five-Shriek spoke to me through comms. 'We found their backup team, ma'am, in a vehicle just outside the secure perimeter. Your orders?'

'I sincerely hope they are scared of spiders, because Graf and I are on our way,' I said. I rosed and brushed at my stained blue and silver uniform, and my hand came away wet with more blood. 'Time to have some fun with the man in the van.' I took a step and the polished floorboards rushed up to meet me, hitting me hard on the head.

*

I rose into wakefulness in a bed full of the scent of miso soup and barley tea, and I was at home with Aki beside me. I opened my eyes and the ceiling was wrong, then looked left and saw the Empress watching me. It all came back to me and I lifted the blanket and pulled up the hospital gown to see a sheet of artificial skin twenty centimetres to a side covering a scar nearly fifteen centimetres long over the left side of my abdomen. I dropped the blanket and turned to the Empress, feeling the twinge as I did.

'What hit me?'

'Namazozo's soulstone. You cushioned its impact with your body, and saved Namazozo's life.'

'Oh.'

'Jian.' She put one claw on the sheet. 'Did you see that they weren't wearing soulstones?'

'After the first one, yes, I did.'

'And you shot them in the chest instead of the head anyway?'

I smiled without humour. 'I couldn't help it. Extensive training with battle hobbyists. We all know that the location of the stone is sacred, even if they take it out beforehand.'

She nodded. 'Excellent. It's good to know that my Captain will take care not to inflict the Real Death, regardless of the circumstances.'

'Did they have stones stored elsewhere? Marque would know,' I said.

'No.'

'So I did inflict the Real Death.'

'Do you feel guilt about that?'

I hesitated, then said, 'No. It was their choice to attack us and I was doing my job.'

'Good.'

Aki came in. 'How are you feeling, Jian?'

'Sore and woozy but I'll be fine,' I said.

Aki turned to the Empress and bowed deeply. 'I take personal responsibility for this outrageous crime. The terrorists are dead—'

'Aki,' the Empress said gently, and Aki stopped. 'This has happened every single time our colonised species realised what we were doing. There'd always be an assassination attempt; in fact, many dragons bet on how long it would take. The attempts always stopped when the reproductive conquest was complete.'

'When you become family,' I said.

'Precisely.' She raised her silver claw. 'In the case of Earth, you negotiated your way out of conquest, and your subjugation will never be complete. Never more than half of your population will be dragonscales. It will be *fascinating* to see if the assassination attempts continue.' She turned her head to me. 'Do you need more staff in the guard?'

'No, we had it under complete control, even with Marque as limited as it was. On a planet with a full-size Marque you would be in no danger at all.'

'Good.' The Empress turned back to Aki. 'This is why I have living guards as well as Marque. It happens all the time.'

'I would still like to pay reparation for the uncouth behaviour of my people,' Aki said stiffly.

'There's no need ...' The Empress' voice trailed off. 'Actually, come to think of it, my royal behind has an extremely good suggestion.'

18

Fifteen years later, Tomoyo folded Bartlett and me onto Mum's deck. Mum was waiting for me holding a basket of potatoes.

'Disappear,' Mum said as she pushed the basket at Tomoyo. 'This is private.'

'With pleasure,' Tomoyo said, and did.

'You're early,' Mum said as I followed her into her living room. Bartlett raced between us, his tail wagging furiously, hoping that I was going on a trip again and leaving him with Mum instead of Oliver.

'You said I could view your project if I turned up a little early,' I said.

'Only if you tell me what the announcement is about,' she said, her smile sly.

I followed her into her little theatre. 'It's about the cat ships that left their homeworld fifteen years ago.'

'They didn't waste any time about heading back after we dropped them home. I heard there'd been skirmishes at the border with them. Are they going to invade the Empire again?'

'That's beside the point, because we have a new way to stop them, and the Empress herself wants to share it with everybody. We don't have to wait for them to drop out of warp and attack us – the second they enter Empire space, we can bundle them up and send them home.'

'About time,' she said. 'This war of attrition has been exhausting.' She gestured towards the theatre's circular projection area. 'Is there anywhere in particular you'd like to see?'

'Can you show me Wales?' I said. 'The Wales we knew – mostly under water – is gone, and it's been so transformed I don't recognise it any more. I'd like to see Wales *before* we wrecked everything.'

A towering forest appeared around us. The ground was thick with leaf litter, and an animal trail meandered between the trees. A stream gurgled nearby, and I could smell the rich, damp soil.

Bartlett ran around the projection, then back to me, disappointed. He knew the difference between projection and reality.

'This is the location on Gaia that matches here,' Marque said.

'Wow,' I said, turning on the spot and watching the sunlight filter through the canopy as birds sang and flitted high above. 'The trees are huge.'

'Humanity does seem to have an issue with trees,' Marque said. 'This part of the world was mostly covered in forest, and you destroyed it all.'

'We're very good at destroying things,' Mum said.

I walked around the small area that Marque projected, relishing the experience. There was a rustle nearby, and a red doe as tall as me walked out of the foliage onto the trail, her nose quivering as she scented the air. A fawn emerged a minute later, awkward on its spindly legs. The doe headed along the trail towards the water with the fawn following her. I walked behind them until I reached the edge of the projection and had to stop.

'If you want to, I can—' Marque began.

'I've said it before, and I'll say it again, no direct neural stimulation,' I said. 'I never want to doubt the reality of my experiences.'

'Suit yourself,' Marque said. 'I should point out that you trust me with your soulstone—'

'Can I see the mountains of China?' I said. 'The location where Mum's family is from.'

The view shifted so that I was standing on a ledge two metres long and a metre wide, close to the top of a steeply vertical mountain. A river meandered through a forest far below, the sunlight reflecting off it to make it appear as a ribbon of light. A cold breeze brushed my face as it rose from the greenery below and swept up the side of the mountain.

'This is nothing like the place I was born,' Mum said. 'Back then, it was a few steep islands sticking out of the water, and they were covered in shanty towns made of mud and shit, pockmarked with damage from the war. Show her North America.'

'How much longer before it's finished?' I said as the view shifted. I was on a great plain of long golden grass, with thousands – millions – of American bison trundling across it and lifting a towering cloud of dust.

'It will take another fifty or so years before it's completely stable,' Mum said. She lowered her voice. 'No idea what I'll do with myself when it's finished.'

'Do the same thing, but with dinosaurs,' I said. 'Not many planets have had what we did – a full ecosystem and major species completely wiped out and replaced. Viewing that one would be very popular.'

'Yeah, I thought about it, but that's a little too much like a theme park.' She shrugged. 'I might just do what Richard and Echi are doing – travel the seven galaxies. There's an awful lot to see.'

I turned to smile at her. 'There is. You'll love it.'

'Aki's press conference is on,' Marque said.

The image of Gaia disappeared, and we sat to watch Aki's announcement. Bartlett reclined next to me and put his head in my lap, and I stroked it. 'I wish you had a chance to meet Aki, Bartlett. Your grandmother adored her.'

'We all did,' Mum said, and saw my face. 'Sorry, honey.'

The projection changed, and it was obvious that the Japanese had gone all-out in an attempt to mimic traditional royal announcements. The antique Japanese television logo appeared in the corner of the display, then a black old-fashioned electric car rolled up to the kerb in a leafy street in Tokyo. Aki and his wife stepped out, and they guided their two children as they emerged. Aki didn't appear nearly forty; he hadn't changed much as the years had passed. His wife was much taller than him, obviously physically fit, and had a striking chiselled face that was full of intelligence and good humour. The older son was ten and their younger daughter was eight. Both children were wearing modernised school uniforms and seemed happy to be attending school after years of private instruction.

An official from the school – probably the principal, Marque didn't bother translating her office – met them at the gate and the usual bows and greetings were exchanged. She took the girl's hand, nodded to the boy, and led them inside.

Aki smiled at his wife, and she returned it. I felt a pang of pain; that smile used to be for me. He stepped up onto an antique podium – complete with microphones – for the press conference. He'd finally caved in to public demand for media access with the children present and was using their first day of school as an opportunity to do it.

'Thank you for your well-wishes on our children's first day of school,' he said. 'We hope that by attending here, the future Emperor will gain valuable insight to the needs of the people.'

'Are you planning to change back to a woman?' one of the press corps shouted.

Aki frowned, and I snorted at the vlogger's audacity. The Emperor usually gave a five-minute speech followed by carefully pre-assigned questions.

'Yes,' Aki said, and there was a gasp of consternation. Aki glanced back at his wife, who nodded. He turned back to the scrum and straightened his shoulders. 'I am in the wrong body. I am a woman in my heart ...' He touched his chest. 'At my core. The Queen of Euroterre has set a precedent for this. As soon as our son is old enough to take the reins, he will become Emperor. I will return to my true, real sex, and become a woman again.'

'And how do you feel about that, Empress Hanamaru?' one of the vloggers shouted.

The Empress stepped up to the podium, and clutched Aki's hand. She nodded to the microphones and dipped her head to speak at their level. 'I love the Emperor with all my heart. He has asked me to stay with him – he will be her, then – after he transitions. I will stay with my love because she will fill me with joy, regardless of whichever body she resides in.' She looked directly at the Marque sphere so that it appeared she was speaking to me. 'I do not love Emperor Haruhito selfishly. I am not possessive. I love her, and love whoever she loves.'

'A message for you,' Marque said.

'Shut up and butt out,' I said.

Aki returned to the microphones. 'The honoured Empress has brought me great joy and two children. My joy will be even greater when our next baby is born, because she is pregnant again, and due in six months.'

The vloggers cheered and applauded, and Hana bowed to them, blushing with genuine delight.

'My family comes first. When our beloved children are old enough to understand, I will return to my true body.' Aki appeared to look right at me as well. 'Even as I am now, I have my loving family, and I am content. I am happy. Truly happy.'

I wiped a tear from my eye.

'I'm sorry,' Mum said. 'That must have been painful to watch. It was a good idea to keep the rest of the family away.'

I chuckled and shook my head. 'Are you kidding? They're genuinely in love and happy together, with two terrific kids and another on the way. I'm thrilled to bits for Aki. I thought I'd be jealous and bitter, but I'm just ... really happy for her. Him.' I shook my head. 'Imagine needing an act of Parliament to define your pronouns!'

'What about the offer for a relationship after she transitions?' Marque said.

I sat back and stroked Bartlett's head. 'I'll think about it.'

'Good, I was worried that you'd rush back to her,' Mum said. 'That Household business sounds awful – it would kill you.'

'It's been a long time, Mum,' I said. 'Others have come and gone for both of us. People change. Aki's happy, and I don't want to ruin that for her. As she said: we're both effectively immortal. We have plenty of time. Probably the kindest thing I can do is to let her enjoy family life without the complication of a polyamorous relationship.'

'Do you have a message for her?' Marque said. 'I could pass it on.'

I stroked Bartlett's head and he licked my hand. 'I suppose ... what I just said. If they want me, I can come visit after Aki transitions. See how we feel about each other.' I felt a pang as I thought of my small, round, fierce and intelligent wife, and lowered my head. 'I do miss her.'

*

The dragon Empress lay on the floor of her quarters as her servant decked her out in jewels. She checked herself in the mirror. 'That's enough, Kiko, the Captain's here. Thank you.'

'Majesty,' the servant said, and set to work collecting the jewellery and putting it away.

The Empress turned to me and nodded. 'Time to head out?'

'A crowd's gathered on the avenue to see you to the elevator.'

'Let's give them a show.'

I straightened my uniform collar. 'Ma'am.'

Four more guards met us as we took the elevator from her quarters to ground level and escorted her through the Palace to the front. A crowd of a few hundred people had gathered in the square to see her off and cheered when she appeared.

She stopped on the veranda, waved to them, and indicated with a flick of her claw that she wished to address them.

'My darling subjects,' she said, and Marque amplified her voice. 'I am about to visit the border with the cats to see Marque's new method for turning them back and preventing them from invading our space. In the past we were forced to follow their ships and attack them with chilli when they dropped out of warp inside the Empire. With this new method we can turn them back at the border and retain full control of Empire space. I'll send back visuals of the process for you when I get there.'

The crowd cheered again, and we stepped from the veranda onto a floating transparent disk. The disk rose and carried us down the broad avenue that surrounded the square, past the Imperial Palace towards its rear and the elevator platform. Scattered small groups of people lined the avenue to catch a glimpse of the Empress, some of them cheering. We reached the platform, a white-paved area fifty metres to a side with a single car in the centre. The door opened and we went inside, then stationed ourselves around the edge as the Empress reclined in the centre. The car took us up to the base station for the space elevator a thousand metres above, and we stepped out onto the massive platform. The main elevator car, as big as a small town, wasn't present, so the centre of the platform just held the shining ribbon that carried it up to the nexus. Private cars sat around the edge of the platform, and the Empress' own car was waiting for us. We went inside to travel up to the folding nexus.

We left the car at the folding nexus and followed the Empress through the specially-enlarged nexus tube to her own ship. The ship itself wasn't one of the larger dragon ships as the Empress didn't travel and collect spouses. I stayed with her while the rest of the guards checked it over and gave us the all clear to depart. She folded onto the nose of the ship and carried us to the blockade at the edge of cat space.

We arrived at the border where a dragon ship was stationed, with more dragon ships on either side and above and below visible as glowing blobs in the distance.

The Empress folded us onto Chiharu's ship, where the dragon and her human crew were waiting for us. Chiharu was a senior daughter of the Empress, and her scales appeared grey to me, their ultra-violet colour outside my visual spectrum. She had six legs, no wings, and a red soulstone.

Admiral Blake was with her and he stepped forward. 'Glad to have you here, Majesty. There's a cat ship within an hour's travel and we're ready for it to cross the border into our space.'

The Empress nodded. 'Have you done this many times before?'

Blake grinned. 'This will be the twelfth time for Chiharu's ship, but nearly the hundredth cat ship overall. The fleet they sent out fifteen years ago is approaching the border, and there's well over a thousand of them. The process has become so routine that we felt it was safe to share how it works with the rest of the Empire.'

'This is excellent,' the Empress said with satisfaction.

'The cat ship is visible,' Marque said, and a glowing circle appeared on the floor of our ship. It was coming from below us; we were parked at ninety degrees to the border.

'Move out,' the Admiral said, and the team of humans went to the back of Chiharu's ship and into a pod. Chiharu folded the pod near to the border, and folded back onto her own ship. The pod gathered a glowing cloud around it as it went into warp.

'I want a better view,' the Empress said, and swung her head to see me. 'Jian, I want to see this from the outside.'

'Me and Six, Marque,' I said, and put my hand on the Empress' shoulder. 'Six?'

'I'm waiting outside the ship, on a wavelength outside your visual range,' Six said through comms.

'You in uniform, Six?'

'Sorry, ma'am, it's at the cleaners.'

The Empress folded us into space below the ship, and Marque surrounded me with a spacesuit and put a gravity platform under my feet to make me feel more secure. The space around me was filled with distant stars, and a brilliantly glowing nebula shone pink and purple below my feet. I'd been in raw space enough times that I didn't panic, and I felt a bolt of satisfaction at my reaction. About time I could handle it. The Empress floated next to me, shining pink in the reflected light of the nebula, and glanced at me.

'You okay, Captain?'

'Just fine,' I said.

She nodded and turned back to the border. The dragon pod in its warp field floated towards the border. The border wasn't marked, but both sides knew exactly where it was. The pod waited on the dragon side of the border and didn't move.

A cat teleport portal grew organically on their side of the border, and Marque showed it to me in the heads-up display. It was less than a metre tall, and a tiny sensory probe, only twenty centimetres in diameter, floated out of it and hovered next to it, watching as well.

'Without Marque's assistance I would never know that teleporter was there,' Six said through comms, its form a vague outline of energy next to me. 'I'm not surprised we never saw them and were wondering how they communicated.'

'I should have realised,' Marque said. 'Everybody has rejected the use of teleporters in the past because they kill the organic life inside them. It never occurred to me to use them to transport *in*organic life like me.'

'Does teleporting damage you?' I said.

Marque hesitated, then said, 'I hate losing instances of myself, so I've never had the courage to try. I have dragons to carry me around, so I don't think I ever will. The cat ship is now officially in Empire space. Here we go.'

The cat ship was one of its smaller exploration ships, fifty metres long and with elegant fins along its length to channel the warp field. The dragon pod – a utilitarian cube containing the team – approached it and their warp fields merged into a single glowing cloud.

'Filters please, Marque,' the Empress said.

The warp glow around the ships faded to give me a clearer view. The pod and cat ship were now locked together inside the warp field, and the cat was unable to fire on the pod without damaging the field and destroying both of them.

The warp field began to fade into nothingness as the Marque instance inside the pod reached into the cat ship and disabled the engine.

'This is the tricky part,' Marque said. 'I have to power down the pod's engine at the same rate as the cat one. I've messed it up a couple of times, and needed the humans to board the cat ship, disable them with chilli, and power down the warp engine from inside.'

The warp field gradually dissipated, and the two ships fell into normal space. Chiharu folded on top of the cat ship, folded it back to the cat homeworld, then reappeared on top of the pod and folded it back onto her ship.

The little cat sensory probe went into its teleport portal, then re-emerged.

'This is an act of war,' it broadcast, then went back into the portal. The portal self-destructed into a cloud of pale grey nanos.

'Not much of a war when you can't even enter our space,' the Empress said. She put her claw on my shoulder and folded me back onto Chiharu's ship. The team were smiling and embracing each other.

'That was magnificent,' the Empress said. 'Thank you for sharing.'

'I'm glad our team is the one demonstrating for the Empire,' Chiharu said. 'People have been asking us for a while what the strategy will be when the cats reach the border and start to attack us again. It will be good to show them that we're ready and we can protect the Empire.'

'Let's head home, and notify the rest of the Empire,' the Empress said. 'I cannot wait to share with everybody. We've all been concerned about the cats returning to our space and attacking us. This is excellent news.'

*

I led Bartlett out of my quarters and into the garden at the base of the Empress' own residential tower. Marque had a capsule waiting for us, and I sat inside. Bartlett whuffed and curled up on the seat next to me. We lifted off, and Bartlett whined, then banged his tail on the seat back. He didn't like the height, but he enjoyed the trip anyway.

We sailed over the Imperial Palace's white spires with their multicoloured banners, and through the buildings of Sky City. The buildings became taller as we moved further from the Palace complex, but they were never permitted to be more than about five storeys tall, in order to maintain Sky City's unique celestial view.

I put my hand on Bartlett's furry head to reassure him as we reached the edge of Sky City and Marque floated us down towards the surface of the planet below. The white sides of the floating city were carved in an enormous depiction of dragons going about their colonising ways, talking to many different species, in a frieze that was more than three hundred metres high. We dipped below the edge and the massive, ancient anti-grav engines that held up the city came into view, glowing blue-white beneath it. Marque had often complained that they were severely out of date and asked the Empress to land the city so they could be replaced with ones that weren't visible, and the Empress always said no because she liked the shinies.

The surface of the planet was covered in blue-green grass and a forest of trees with bright orange leaves. We travelled five kilometres in the capsule out from under the shadow of the massive city to Oliver's rural estate with its two-storey villa constructed cat-style in polished clay that shone gold in the blue-white sun. Oliver was waiting for us in his front garden, a grass-covered area littered with children's toys. His daughter, Annie, was next to him, jumping up and down with excitement.

We landed and Bartlett tested the edge of the capsule with his nose. The wall was gone, so he shot out and bounded to Annie, who squealed and ran in circles with him. They raced off together to find a ball to throw. Annie was five years old now, a cat dragonscales, and already as tall as a twelve-year-old human. Her fur on her little naked form was a mix of Oliver's black with orange patches from a ginger ancestor making her a pretty tortoiseshell colour. She had green scales on her forehead from Runa, her dragonfather.

'Hey, say hello to your grandma!' Oliver shouted at her.

'Hello, Grandma!' Annie squealed, breathless, then ran away again.

I embraced Oliver and we touched cheeks. 'Thanks for looking after him.'

Ollie waved his hand at the delighted child and dog. 'She'll hate it when you come back to take him home. I think I'll have to get her a puppy of her own.' He turned to me, serious. 'Is it really working? The cats are being turned back from the border?'

'It works.'

'A triumph of my ingenuity,' Marque said.

'Good. How soon before you leave?' Oliver said.

'I have time to catch up with my favourite son,' I said, and he led me inside with Annie still squealing with laughter behind us.

'Jian, the Empress needs you back at the Palace,' Marque said.

I raised my head. 'I just got here! How urgent is this?'

'Extremely.'

'What's the problem?'

'Classified.'

'Even from me?' Oliver said. 'I thought I had access to everything.'

'I would be able to tell you if you were in the Palace,' Marque said. 'Down here: no.'

Oliver and I shared a look.

'Leave Bartlett here for a while, and go,' Oliver said.

I embraced my son and rode the capsule back up to the Palace.

'We received signals from one of the scales on the cat homeworld,' the Empress said when I arrived at her office.

'They're not moving the scale again, are they?' I said.

'It's a definite message code,' Marque said. 'It took us nearly half an hour to sort out a communications protocol, and here's the message we received once I'd established it: "We wish to negotiate safe passage through dragon space under terms of peace".'

'Oh, that's excellent!' I said.

'My response was: "We are willing to negotiate treaty terms for long-lasting peace between our two civilisations",' the Empress said. 'That was ten minutes ago, and we're waiting for a reply.'

'They occasionally tap the scale to keep the channel open, but they haven't sent a proper message through ...' Marque said. 'Here it is. "Come to our homeworld and we will begin the discussions".'

'I'd prefer to send our envoy to a neutral area that is in neither empire,' the Empress said. 'Is that acceptable?'

Somewhere where their damn nanos are out of the picture, she said to me, and I nodded.

'A neutral area is acceptable,' the cats said through Marque. 'You may send one ship. We will send our flagship. I am transferring co-ordinates. Are these acceptable?'

'Marque?' the Empress said.

'The location works,' Marque said. 'It's a small orphan planet circling a massive black hole, with nothing else around it for light years. It's a good space, and it will take about six weeks for one of their warp ships to reach it from the edge of their space.'

'Done,' the Empress said. 'May I send my oldest daughter as emissary?'

'Yes. We will send the second to our council,' the cats said. 'The terms are acceptable. The meeting will occur at the time we are sending. Bring one ship only.'

The Empress filled with joyful triumph. 'I am looking forward to moving together towards peace,' she said.

'They've stopped comms. I don't think they heard that last bit,' Marque said.

'They are so rude,' she said. 'I bet they land on planets before they're ready and cause irreparable emotional damage to the populations.' She turned to me. 'I want you leading security to guard Masako. Marque, can you finish the new flagship in the time frame?'

'Yes, it's nearly done,' Marque said. 'Can I make it dragon-shaped for the negotiations? A big silver dragon with blue eyes?'

'Really?' I said. 'Isn't that a little over the top?'

'I want to,' Marque said, sounding like a four-year-old.

'I love you too, Marque,' the Empress said. 'No. Keep it as the standard dragon streamlined shape; let's show some class here. Where is Masako?'

'She and Haruka are supervising the stocking of the tuna on the new human colony.'

'Tell her to get her little brown tail here quick-smart; we have a lot of work to do before this meeting.'

'She just folded into the orbital nexus, and she'll be down in an hour.'

'Where is Oliver?'

'On his estate with his daughter,' I said.

'Let him know what happened and that we may need his advice, but he doesn't need to come up.' She checked her displays. 'Six human weeks isn't nearly enough time to make a plan for universal peace – particularly when I do not trust the cats to negotiate in good faith. I would not be surprised if they have a new secret weapon to use against us.' She looked up. 'I need to speak to parliament about this. Should we make an announcement to the Empire? Let our people know that we finally may have peace? Everybody will be thrilled to bits.'

'I think we should, to ensure a general ceasefire at the border,' Marque said. 'The last thing we need is for someone to attack a cat ship and ruin everything.'

'Agreed.' She swung her head to see me. 'We'll do a small announcement now, and if the ceasefire holds we'll have a big four-sector party to see them off in six weeks. Start the arrangements while I talk to Parliament. Make sure that Masako and that worthless husband of hers are here soon, because those two freeloaders are doing the negotiations, and I don't want them to mess it up.'

'I don't think she should take Haruka at all,' I said. 'He *will* mess it up.'

'I agree. Making Masako agree is another matter.' Her emotions filled with mischief. 'I have an idea that will keep him busy and out of the way.'

19

The double doors opened and I fixed the sleeves of my dress uniform, stood straighter, and strode into the Princess' apartments. I stopped on the grey carpet that covered most of the floor in the huge, high-ceilinged white room, and bowed to the royal couple.

Masako reclined on the cushion-strewn rug and studied herself in a mirror three metres wide and two high as Miko hovered around her, fussing with the jewels that adorned her neck and toes.

'Leave it, Miko,' she said. 'Captain Jian is here.'

Haruka ignored me as he sat at his make-up table in front of the mirror, touching up his eyeliner. He checked himself in the mirror, then rubbed a cloth over his green soulstone until the stone shone. He stood, flicked his long green hair back, then tightened his topknot so that the green scales on his temples were more visible, glowing against his golden skin. He was wearing a magnificent pale pink kimono with wide, sweeping sleeves, and an obi adorned with green bamboo that brought out the colour of his scales, soulstone and hair.

I bowed to him. 'Ambassador Haruka.'

He scowled so quickly it was almost unnoticeable, then composed his face. 'Captain Choumali.'

'The escort is here, Highnesses,' I said. 'The square is full. This will be a send-off to remember.'

'No wonder the dear Captain is grumpy,' Masako said. She turned and walked out the door with Haruka by her side, and I followed them. Miko watched them go with her claws clasped in front of her and an expression of barely contained excitement, tempered with her pride in her mistress.

'The Captain is grumpy? It's hard to tell – she's always so miserable,' Haruka said as we walked down the white stone hallway towards the Palace entry hall.

'Don't tease the dear Captain, Haruka,' Masako said, her voice warm with affection. 'She works so hard to keep us safe.'

'And now that we have peace, she'll have nothing to do,' Haruka said.

'I am right here, you know,' I said as I followed them.

Haruka cocked his head. 'Did you hear something, Masako?'

'Nothing at all, Haruka,' Masako said, her voice full of suppressed laughter.

I sighed loudly as she followed them onto the Palace's front terrace. The Empress was already there.

The blue-white sun was setting over the square and the nebula in the sky lit the white paving with a reflected rainbow of colours. People filled the square below us, producing a loud buzz of conversation. There were a large number of residents of the Empire present – everybody wanted to wish Masako and Haruka well on their peace mission. Marque had erected large screens to give those further away a better view of the Empress, and in the images I was standing behind the dragons, stiff and dour. The Empress' eyes met mine on one of the screens as if she was looking at me in a mirror, and I smiled at her. The image reflected it, and the Empress nodded to me.

'All clear, Marque?' I said silently through comms.

'No ships in the vicinity, no cat ships anywhere near the Empire and the guard are all in place.'

'Give me a heads-up on the crowd.'

My vision filled with an analysis of all the people in the square below us. Marque highlighted the armed people and identified them for me. All were legitimate guards or permitted private citizens. Marque's floating bots pinged on the display, and none of them had sniffed out any traces of dangerous substances.

'This crowd contains a fourteen per cent greater outworlder element than the city's regular population,' Marque said. 'Everybody's in the mood to celebrate.'

I requested a quick wider sweep of the floating city and Marque obliged. Nothing unusual to any of Marque's eyes in the sky, and no munitions anywhere to detect. Marque quickly extended the sweep to ground level below the floating city without being asked.

'All clear, Captain,' Marque said.

'Thank you.'

I relaxed slightly. Maybe nothing would go wrong after all. There was a small but significant chance that the cats had planted non-cat agents in the crowd and would use the announcement to attack us.

The Empress raised one claw and the thousands filling the square in front of the Palace went silent.

'Dearest Imperial subjects of all species, dragonchildren, and dragons, both here on Dragonhome and on other planets listening through the Empire: after six weeks of successful ceasefire, my daughter Princess Masako and her consort, honoured Ambassador from New Nippon Prince Haruka, will travel on the new flagship, the *Silver Lotus*, to the border with cat space and put our name on the treaty with the Cat Republic. Peace will finally reign across the galaxy.'

The Empress let them cheer for a while, then raised her silver claw again, and the crowd went silent.

'In honour of this occasion, it is only fitting that the birth of a new dragon be permitted. We have rebuilt the coloured clans after the last great conflict with the cats, but there is still space for one more dragon in the Empire. I have given permission for Prince Haruka to have a dragon child with Princess Masako.' She swung her head on her long neck to address the Princess and her Ambassador consort next to her. 'We all know the depth of love that you two share, and it's about time we had a new dragon. You may have a child. The resulting dragon will be the head of a new clan: the Clan of Peace.'

There was a stunned silence across the square. Masako lowered her head and gazed down at Haruka, and he looked up at her, his expression full of the love they shared.

The crowd responded with jubilation, and Marque filled the square with glittering, floating dragons made of light. This would be the first new dragon in more than ten years, and every new dragon – and the interstellar transport it represented – was cause for celebration. Triumphant music filled the square, and some of the humans danced together. Haruka and Masako were lost in each other's eyes.

The Empress raised one claw and said, 'Go and celebrate, everybody.' She turned and gestured for Haruka and Masako to follow her into the Palace.

As soon as the doors were closed behind them Masako bowed her head. 'Thank you so much, Mother. I am so honoured. This is a rare privilege.'

'Thank you, my Empress,' Haruka said. 'We will not disappoint.'

'Take Jian with you,' the Empress said. 'Make a party of it. She isn't in a relationship right now; it would do her good.'

I stepped back and tried to control my face. 'Uh ... I had a meeting already arranged.' I quickly recovered. 'Much as I would like to share with them, everyone knows that Haruka and Masako have eyes only for each other.'

Haruka nodded his appreciation in the corner of my eye.

'Nonsense. You could mother a fine dragonscales from Masako, Jian, your talents and intelligence should be passed on to a new generation. I believe there is still room for a couple more human dragonscales on Earth, and you should be first to bear one,' the Empress said. 'How old are you, anyway? It must be close on a hundred, and it's time you had a pure-human child of your own as well. You are neglecting the needs of your species.'

'I'm only ninety-two,' I said. 'Plenty of time for childbearing. And I won't relax until the treaty is signed.'

'Always worried about our safety,' Masako said. Her voice became more brisk. 'Well, Haruka, the Empress has given us a job to do.'

'I don't appreciate everybody knowing about our reproductive activities,' Haruka said. 'This is an invasion of our privacy.'

'We're royal, we have no privacy,' Masako said. 'I'm glad we have Jian to mind the door!'

'Yes,' the Empress said. 'Jian, stand guard outside their door; I'm sure everybody will want to know if I have a new grandchild coming, and their privacy may be breached.'

I nodded. 'Ma'am.'

The Empress nodded and turned away, and I gestured for three of the guards to follow me and the other four to remain with the Empress.

'You really should think about having a child, Jian,' the Empress called back as she headed towards her own wing. 'If not with Masako, then perhaps with me?'

I didn't reply.

Masako lowered her head, and hoisted herself onto her back legs. Her hips and thighs clicked into standing configuration, her two-legged form. She concentrated, and shifted into her human-appearance camouflage. The guards around me made soft sounds of appreciation, but I'd seen dragon two-legged forms enough times that they didn't make me completely spellbound.

To me, Masako's human form was male – a man with black skin similar to my own. He was broad-shouldered and slim-hipped, and wore his hair long and twisted into dreadlocks that were gathered at the nape of his neck and fell down to this waist. He had small eyes, well-defined cheekbones and a strong chin.

I'd seen many artists' impressions of dragon-human forms, all of them different, and none of them looked anything like this. I still found it hard to believe that this was what my brain showed me, when every serious relationship I'd had was with fierce, intelligent, short and round women.

Masako reached to Haruka and he took her hand.

They gazed into each other's eyes as I followed them to Masako's chamber, and they didn't even notice when I closed the door on them. I sighed as I turned to take guard position in front of the door, with the two other guards stationed further down the hall. I did have a meeting arranged, and I hadn't planned on being given door duty. I directed the rest of the Imperial Guard to their strategic positions, then stood at ease outside the Princess' door.

'Please let Admiral Blake know that I can't make our meeting,' I said to Marque through comms.

'The Empress rescinds her order,' Marque said. 'You can put someone else on door duty and go to meet up with him.'

'Sorry, Jian, Marque reminded me that you had a meeting already arranged,' the Empress said through the link. 'I was too caught up in the excitement. Go. Enjoy.' Her voice filled with amusement. 'Stewart Blake is fully human like you, isn't he?'

'He's a close friend and that's all,' I said. 'Childbearing can wait until I find the right person.'

'Don't forget that I am always here if you decide to have a child. You could mother a fine dragonscales Princess for me, my friend.'

'Thank you,' I said. 'Marque, call Green Sunset, will you? Pass on the order.'

'Done, Captain, Green Sunset's on her way.'

I didn't relax until Sunset rolled up the hallway towards me. She was one of the newer members of the Guard, a mobile fungal type that looked like a small moving ball of writhing white threads.

'Captain. Go have fun. I have it covered.'

'Who's minding your children?'

'Marque's set up a funfair with rides for the children on the side of the square, and it's minding them for me. My husband will finish at the gallery, then collect them and take them home.'

'They're having a great time and I don't think they want to go home yet,' Marque said.

I waved my hand over Sunset's sense organs next to her green dragon scales as I departed. 'I've already done the handover to Graf for the next three days while I'm at the border. If you have any queries, take them to Graf.'

'Captain,' Sunset said. She collapsed inwards, then flowed like a liquid along the floor and up the door until she completely covered it.

I strode down the hallway towards the human exit of the Palace – a smaller door on the side of the larger main ones. Marque put the four-sector symbols above my head, and I tapped sex to turn it off, leaving the other three sectors on before heading outside to the festivities.

'Is the Admiral still there, Marque?' I said through comms. 'I assume you told him.'

'Yes, he's waiting for you. He says no rush, he and his new friend are enjoying the light show.'

I slowed my pace slightly, then picked it up again. A new friend? I smiled as I slipped out the door into the street party.

*

I hurried onto the plaza. Marque had lit the sky with twining dragons of light, and the four-sector celebration was in full swing. I walked through the food-and-drink sector looking for Blake. People were sitting at tables and reclining on the ground, eating and drinking and watching the show. Flashing lights to the side of the square marked Marque's funfair for the children, and the occasional delighted scream floated from it.

'Marque, which table is Blake's?' I said through comms.

'Dunno. He's on private.'

That was unusual. I checked the faces of the people at the tables, and saw Griffith, Leckie and MacAuley sharing a table and laughing with a dragonscales and a couple of young human women. They waved to me and I waved back, then saw another uniformed arm frantically waving, attached to a grinning Blake. I eased my way through the tables to Blake and the woman accompanying him.

'Sorry I'm late,' I said.

Blake stood and we shared a quick cheek kiss, human-style.

'The Empress nearly made me into a privacy lock on Masako's door,' I said. 'Marque helped me out.'

Blake slipped his arm around my waist and gestured towards the woman sitting at the table. 'Captain Jian Choumali, this is Merry Pacifica. After I dropped a shipment of embryos to Pacifica on the new flagship, she asked for a ride here to see the dragon homeworld, and I promised we'd show her around.'

I bowed to Merry as much as I could manage with Blake wrapped around me. Merry was an Aquatic; her skin was a translucent pale turquoise and her waist-length hair deeper purple. She wore a long shift of shimmering gold that flattered her enhanced-human shape. I saw past the skin colour and the breathing tube inserted into the side of Merry's throat to the woman beyond, and my appreciation deepened. Merry's golden eyes were bright with intelligence, and full of kindness below the orange soulstone in her forehead. The Aquatic was all curves from the thick layer of fat under her blue skin that provided protection in her home environment. The gold dress was gathered around her rounded body and under her full, soft breasts.

I became aware that I'd been staring, so I returned my gaze to the Aquatic's face, only to see a similar level of appreciation as Merry ran her gaze over my own fit body.

Merry winced and looked up into my eyes, probably realising what she was doing, and we clicked. We smiled knowingly at each other.

Are you telepathic as well? I said to her, mind-to-mind.

'No, Captain, I'm not suffering from that particular affliction,' Merry said.

'By the dragons, you're soul mates?' Blake said incredulously. 'Damn I'm good.'

'Close, but not true,' Merry said.

'Close enough to thank you for bringing us together, dear Stewart,' I said. I kissed him on the cheek and sat at the table. I loosened the collar of my dress uniform by one button for off-duty and smiled at Merry. 'I'm Jian, Captain of the Imperial Guard.' I put my hand out to the Aquatic. 'I am very pleased to meet you.'

Blake was grinning like he'd just won first prize in a high-level competition. Merry shook my hand, and the Aquatic's skin felt cool and rubbery, like a wetsuit, but completely dry.

'I know exactly who you are, and I'm delighted to meet you,' she said. She looked from me to Blake. 'I'm meeting so many famous people today!'

'I wouldn't call us famous,' I said, leaning my elbows on the table to smile at her. I spoke to Marque silently through comms. 'Please put me on liaison privacy settings.'

'Already done,' Marque said. 'But before I go, I suggest that you ask Madam Merry about the sexual practices on her homeworld. They're fascinating and you'll definitely want to visit next time you're on leave.'

'Butt out,' I said, and switched comms to emergency only.

Merry's eyes widened. 'Your Marque just said that if we're going to make this a private party, it would like to join us in an android body of any gender we please. It says that Jian and Stewart are brown, I'm blue, and it would like to bring another blue body along to make a set. Our Marque isn't nearly as forward!'

'Marque, butt *out*,' Blake and I said in unison.

'It's been trying to get into my pants for nearly a hundred years,' Blake said.

'Leave poor Stewart alone, Marque,' I said. 'Go calculate some prime numbers and bring me a beer.'

'It's a long-standing joke between Marque and myself,' Blake said. 'Ever since I refused it when we first met on Earth, it's been pursuing me, and I've been rejecting it. It says that I have self-esteem issues, and I need to be appreciated.'

'And do you?' Merry asked him.

'Marque says if I tell it to stop, it will,' Blake said. 'And I haven't – so probably.'

'Admiral of the Fleet with self-esteem issues,' I said as a tray floated to the table with my beer on it.

Blake picked up his own drink and we tapped our glasses together. I nodded appreciation to him for finding this extraordinary – and exquisite – new friend for us, then turned back to Merry. 'Tell me about your interests, Merry. What is your favourite occupation?'

Merry sipped her own drink and her smile deepened as she answered the unasked question. 'I'm twenty-nine years old, first generation Aquatic. One of the first to breed true after the manipulation, and a triumph of Pacifican genetic engineering, if I do say so myself.'

'You're a genetic engineer?' I said with interest.

'I am trained in genetic engineering, but when the second generation were born I spent some time with the children confirming the sequencing, and enjoyed working with them so much that I decided to stay,' Merry said. 'I'm now chief education officer for Pacifica. We have so many new children that we are in the process of creating family names for them.'

I stared with awe, then gathered myself. 'You honour us with your presence, Lady.' I shared another sly glance with Blake, who looked even more pleased with himself.

She waved me down. 'I'm here on Dragonhome to research the ancient stories of dragonkind, to share with the little ones. I may write a book about it for them.' She leaned over the table. 'Do you think you could arrange an audience with the Empress for me?'

'Absolutely, the Empress loves telling stories from long ago, particularly to honoured educators,' I said. 'You are more than welcome. Please do anything you can to stop her from boring us to death with them. Princess Masako will have some for you as well.'

'Would you like to come with us to the treaty signing?' Blake said. 'You can take the story of the peace treaty back to the children.'

'If I do, can I return to Dragonhome when the treaty's done, and ask the Empress about the past?' Merry asked.

'Yes, of course,' Blake said. 'As soon as the treaty's signed, I'm planning to bring a good part of the defensive fleet back to Dragonhome for maintenance. We're looking forward to spending our time and resources assisting the Empire's citizens instead of constantly slapping the cats back inside their borders.'

'What an opportunity to add to the archives.' Merry looked from Blake to me, delighted. 'I would love to.'

'Is she clear?' I asked Marque through comms.

'Blake just asked me the same question. The response just came back from the Pacifican Marque: yes she is. Pacifica has requested that she receive full Ambassadorial treatment, and I've checked her history: she's clear. Very high-level clearance, actually, she's done some classified work for dragonkind in the past. Loyal Imperial citizen.'

'Come in the flagship,' Blake said. 'The Ambassador's cabin is spacious and comfortable, and there's nobody assigned to it for the treaty signing. You are most welcome.'

'Will Jian be on the flagship?' Merry said.

'Of course, I'll be guarding our royal passengers,' I said.

'Then I would like nothing more.' She smiled at me. 'Nothing in the world.'

'I cannot wait to show you lovely ladies the other lady that has stolen my heart forever,' Blake said.

'He means his ship, doesn't he?' Merry asked me.

'He talks to it sometimes,' I said. 'Not Marque – the ship itself. It's not sentient, but one day I swear I will install a sentient AI control system onto it with the most cranky personality ever.'

'You two must have known each other for a long time,' she said.

'Since the attempted invasion of Earth,' Blake said. 'Jian could be higher-ranked than Captain of the Imperial Guard, but she needs to be around the dragons all the time.'

'I like being Captain,' I said.

'Aren't you worried about becoming ... dragonstruck?' Merry said.

I nodded to Merry. 'I apologise, Lady. I didn't tell you how old I am—'

'Unbelievably rude,' Blake said under his breath.

'I know how old you are,' Merry said. 'You're famous.'

'Well, to fulfil polite protocol and shut Stewart up I'll tell you now that I'm ninety-two years old, and I was on Earth during the original dragon invasion. I joined the forces facing the cat fleet, but what isn't common knowledge is that I became dragonstruck some time during those fifteen years of waiting.' I shrugged. 'Of course, it's beside the point now, but I'll always be dragonstruck.'

Merry's eyes were wide with fascinated horror. 'So if you're not in the company of dragons all the time ...'

I enjoyed her rapt attention. The subject didn't enter conversation much; most residents of the dragon homeworld spared the feelings of the dragonstruck, even though I didn't really care one way or the other. 'If I'm separated from dragonkind for more than about six weeks, I start to fade. I think three months away from dragons is the longest one of us has survived.'

'And when your body dies and you are brought back, you're still struck?' Merry said.

'Still struck. It seems independent of the soulstone; it's something to do with my soul itself.'

'That's awful,' Merry said. 'Surely Marque, the physicians ...'

'No cure,' Blake said. 'But Jian isn't affected much otherwise, so it's beside the point.'

'But they control your will!' Merry protested.

'No, they don't,' I said. 'I can tell them "no" just as much as the next human. What I can't do is hurt them, and if they're in danger I will protect them to my last breath, but as Captain of the Imperial Guard I'd do that anyway.'

Blake finished his drink and raised his glass. 'The evening's still young and you're visiting the floating city for the first time. What would you like to do, Merry? We could show you around if you like.'

'Uh ...' Merry looked from Blake to me.

I sipped my beer, waiting for Merry to make her choice. Anything she chose would be good.

'Captain Jian, can you tell me what it was like when the dragons first invaded Earth? You were there!' Merry said with delight.

I groaned and dropped my head back. 'Anything but that.'

'Don't be impolite,' Blake said. 'Merry already asked for my story and I said yes.'

'Sorry.' I raised my head and smiled at Merry. 'I'd be honoured. But there must be something in Sky City that you'd like to see.'

'Yes, tell me later. For now, the *Heroines* is on show at the Baxter Gallery, the first time it's been toured off-Earth, and I'd love to see it. Is the gallery open?'

'Marque?' I said.

'You told me to butt out,' Marque said from the air next to us.

'Don't be disrespectful to our guest,' Blake said. 'And tell us if the gallery is open.'

'Yes it is,' Marque said. 'It will be open for two more hours. Plenty of time to see the installation.'

'Is there anything else you'd like to see?' Blake said.

'Is there food particular to Dragonhome? I'd love to try something different.'

'Not unless you like char-grilled mutton with the skin still on it,' Blake said.

'Do the two of you have unique cuisines from your parts of Earth?' Merry said. 'I love tasting different flavours.'

'I can ask Marque to synthesise you some Welsh dishes, but Blake's the one you should ask. His mother is a famous chef back on Earth,' I said.

'We can have dinner at my quarters after the gallery; I'll make you some Egyptian specialities,' Blake said.

'If you're in the landside quarters, they're very small ...' I began.

'No, I'm in the Imperial capsule,' Blake said. 'Plenty of room for all of us.'

I finished my beer. 'In that case, lead on to the gallery, Admiral, and if the meal is good I may find it in my heart to tell our beautiful blue guest some of my war stories after all.'

'Frankly, I'm more interested in hearing your side of the invasion story than I am of hearing the dragons' side of it,' Merry said. 'What an experience!'

'Not what I was thinking at the time,' I said dryly.

'How old were you when it happened?' Merry said, linking her arm in mine as we followed Blake to a floating disk.

'Twenty-four.' I shook my head. 'I was a child, and already fully trained and a corporal in the Earth forces. Admiral Blake is the one who was making the decisions; you should hear this story from him.'

'You and Richard Alto were Shiumo's first human contacts,' Blake said. 'You have a unique perspective.'

'I suppose I do.'

20

Merry watched the city pass, rapt, as we made our way to the gallery. Blake enjoyed showing her the sights: the Imperial Palace, the Parliament building, the administration complex, and the lights of the folding nexus glittering in the sky.

The gallery building was a transparent-walled sphere two hundred metres tall, with two smaller spheres, each fifty metres in diameter, orbiting it on paths that looked like they would collide at any time. We waited while Merry watched the revolving spheres, entranced.

I gestured to one of the smaller spheres, which had a large banner slung across it. '*Heroines* is in that one,' I said. 'It docks every fifteen minutes.'

'Wonderful,' Merry breathed.

We escorted her into the main gallery sphere and through to the gravlift in the centre. Merry floated up in the lift making swimming motions with her large feet.

She stopped swimming, embarrassed. 'My feet are ridiculous on land.'

'What, has someone actually said that?' I said with disbelief.

'No, but unmodified children stare,' Merry said as we stepped out of the lift. 'I understand that there's a comedic element to them – there's an ancient comical performance with large feet.'

'I like your feet just fine,' I said.

We stepped out onto the floor where the smaller gallery docked and Merry stopped to turn on the spot.

'So many bright colours,' she said. She pointed at *Brothers*. 'I recognise that one. They're members of your family, aren't they?'

'Those are my sons,' I said. 'The cat is a dragonspouse with a dragonscales child and spends a lot of time in the Imperial Palace aiding the Empress. The human died when the cats attacked Earth with a black hole.'

'I remember that,' she said. 'I was in middle school.'

'I feel old now.'

'You're only as old as your soulstone,' Blake said.

I studied the sculpture; I had a smaller copy in my quarters in the Palace. 'Now that the cats have called a ceasefire, the aspiration that this sculpture represents might actually come true.'

'I sincerely hope so. I'm so honoured to be part of the history being made.' Merry smiled at me. 'Maybe the cats will accept a copy of *Brothers* as a gift.'

'That's a good idea,' Blake said.

Merry walked to a painting hung on the wall, an ancient depiction of brightly-coloured flowers.

'That's an extremely solid projection,' she said, and moved closer. 'Oh heavens, it's real?'

'All of the art on show here is real,' I said. '*Brothers* is carved from natural stone. The pigment was applied to that cloth a long time before all of us were born.'

'It's wonderful,' Merry said, studying it. 'It isn't until I'm out of my environment that I realise what I'm missing. Under the water, everything is tinged blue by our blue-white star, and pure warm colours don't exist. And then, of course, our sight is limited when we descend further than the light of our star.'

'How much of your time do you spend in darkness?' I said, fascinated. 'I thought you'd live close to the surface where you can see.'

'We can see well enough in total darkness, and we bring our own lights. How long before the gallery docks, Marque?'

'It would be best to walk over there now; you can stop and admire a couple of works on the way but you have three minutes for fifty metres.'

'Plenty of time,' Blake said. 'So you carry lights everywhere you go? That must be cumbersome.'

'Not really,' Merry said. 'Show them, Marque.'

'Gentlemen and gentlewomen, I am about to dim the lights for a short time,' Marque announced to all the gallery visitors present. 'I will raise them again when the gallery displaying the *Heroines* docks.'

The lights dimmed, and Merry softly glowed. It was subtle at first, but as our eyes adjusted to the darkness, Merry's shine became more obvious. Merry had shifting bioluminescence on her skin, particularly strong on her forehead around her soulstone. She radiated shades of blue and green, rippling across her skin in waves of brilliant colour.

A few people nearby made sounds of wonder.

'I didn't know,' Blake said. 'That is wonderful. You are as much a work of art as any installation here.'

Marque raised the lights and Merry's glow disappeared.

'The gallery's here; let's go view the *Heroines*!' Merry said.

*

Merry and I laughed together, arm-in-arm, as we walked out of the installation and back into the main sphere.

'I just can't imagine doing it,' Merry said. 'The idea is terrifying. And they considered it normal! The *courage* of those people, risking death for the next generation.'

'The clicks have it much worse.' I said. 'The part about the clicks was hard to watch. I lost some good friends to their reproductive needs.'

'Watching the urushai part was the hardest for me,' Blake said. 'What they go through is awful. Humans had it comparatively easy.'

'Many of us still died,' Merry said. 'I'm so glad we have better ways now; that was barbaric.'

'Jian and I were alive when it was still an option,' Blake said. 'It wasn't common, but it still happened.'

'Actually, I was a result of a natural birth,' I said.

Merry put her hand on her generous chest with shock. 'You were *born*?'

I shrugged. 'Safer birthing options were only for the wealthy back then. There were still a good number of children, like me, born the old-fashioned way.'

'And your mother chose to go through that? What about the danger?'

'As it shows in the installation, the risk was worth the reward.' I made a soft sound of amusement. 'My mother didn't have a choice. This was a long time ago, and things that would deeply shock us today were considered normal back then.'

'You have to tell me more about this,' Merry said with enthusiasm.

'For you,' I said, smiling at Merry, 'I will. I'll ask my mother to tell you all about it.'

Merry took my arm again and held it close. 'I'd love to meet her.'

'Let's all go to the capsule and eat,' Blake said. 'I don't know about you, but I'm starving.'

'Lead on, Admiral,' Merry said, without looking away from me.

*

We rode a disk to the elevator behind the Imperial Palace and entered the Empress' personal capsule to go up to the space elevator platform.

'I can't see out,' Merry said, disappointed. 'Can you make a window, Marque?'

'I can make the walls transparent if you like,' Marque said.

Merry looked from Blake to me. 'Do you mind?'

'Not at all; it's a great ride,' Blake said, and I nodded agreement.

Marque made the walls of the elevator transparent, and Merry watched, delighted, as the floating city fell away from us. She made a loud sound of astonishment when the surface of the planet, lit by the houses of those who chose to live downside, came into view below the edge of the city.

'How tall is this elevator?' she said. 'How high up is the space elevator platform?'

'The space elevator platform is six kilometres from the surface of the planet,' I said. 'It's one kilometre above the surface of Sky City.'

'Sky City is lovely,' Merry said. 'I'm looking forward to returning after the treaty signing to explore.' She smiled at me, her eyes shining in the reflected lights from below. 'Now we're at peace, I hope you can spare some time to show me.'

I smiled and leaned on the wall of the car. 'I'd love to.'

The Marque sphere came into view, four kilometres wide and hovering in the sky above the planet. Text scrolled across its surface: 'Dragonhome welcomes honoured Ambassador Merry from Pacifica', and was followed by images of Pacifica's subaquatic cityscape and varied sealife.

'Please, Marque, don't embarrass me,' Merry said, and the images changed to Marque's usual updates on Imperial happenings, mostly about the upcoming peace treaty and images of the new flagship.

The car decelerated. We were in free fall for a moment, then gravity reasserted itself.

The doors opened and we exited onto the circular platform, gleaming white, high in the evening sky. The platform was three hundred metres across and anchored the bottom of the elevator ribbons in a circle around its perimeter. The central cable ribbon for the main elevator car was twenty metres wide, but the car wasn't present.

Merry looked up at the stars, clearly visible in the thin atmosphere on the other side of the protective dome. 'Lovely.' Her face went strange. 'Why are they moving?'

'They aren't,' Blake said. 'The platform is. The orbital nexus at the top of the ribbons shifts, and the platform tilts to compensate. You don't feel it because of the anti-grav.'

'I see. We don't have a nexus on Pacifica, just a geostationary station. This is much more advanced.' She gestured towards the central ribbon. 'The space for the public car seems impossibly big.'

'I didn't realise it was a car the first time I went on it,' I said. 'I thought it was a space station – part of the nexus.'

'It's very impressive.'

'It will arrive in five minutes if you want to watch it dock,' Marque said.

Merry lit up. 'Do you mind waiting?'

'Pfft, five minutes?' I said. 'To make you happy?'

Her smile widened.

'It's coming into view above the dome,' Marque said.

We looked up. The base of the capsule wasn't lit, so it was just an absence of stars, a hole in the starscape that grew as we watched. It quickly widened, and Merry stepped back and grabbed my arm, broadcasting discomfort. I held her, and she clutched me.

'You're safe,' I said softly.

'I know, I know,' she replied in the same low tones.

Blake smiled but didn't look away from the capsule.

After a couple of minutes, the sunlight hit the capsule and Marque quickly shaded the dome to stop it from blinding us. The capsule's flat bottom was rimmed by sunlight, and the ribbon disappeared into it. The light moved across it as it approached us, and it grew so enormous that it appeared to be bigger than the platform. There was no sound, and no pressure wave; the enormous capsule, as big as a small town, approached us swiftly and silently.

'My hind brain is telling me that I'm definitely going to die,' Merry said.

'Look away if you want,' I said.

'No way!'

The base of the capsule came through Marque's energy dome, and a pressure wave washed over us before Marque stabilised the air and encased us in an energy field to protect us from it. The capsule's outside was a plain white cylinder shape at least two hundred and fifty metres wide. It slowed as it neared the floor of the station, producing a low-pitched thrumming on the elevator ribbon. It touched down onto the platform and a visible puff of vaporised air was expelled from around it. The door opened on the side, and people exited to head down onto Sky City below.

'That was worth the wait to see,' Merry said.

'Let's go inside; the rocking stars make me seasick,' I said.

'As my friend wishes.' Blake guided us across the platform to the Imperial elevator car, and the door opened.

'You have your own elevator car?' Merry said with wonder.

'This is the royal car,' the Admiral said. 'In case the Empress needs to board her ship in a hurry without risking a fold so close to the planet.' He guided us into the car, designed like a small apartment. The living room was ten metres across with observation windows on the sides and a couple of round portals in the bottom. The airlock doors closed behind us.

The car was comfortably furnished with sofas and a large, soft carpet for dragonkind to recline on. A hallway led to the bedrooms and a bathroom. A viewscreen showed a feed of the celebrations in the square, and Blake guided us to sit on the sofas.

'The *Silver Lotus* is at the folding nexus, but I'm staying here overnight and going up in the morning with Princess Masako and Ambassador Haruka,' he said. 'You ladies are welcome to stay the night here and ride up to the flagship in the morning.'

Merry smiled at me. 'Thank you, I'd love to. Jian?'

Blake and Merry both looked at me, waiting for my decision. I studied the gorgeous woman standing next to my dear friend and there wasn't much decision to make. 'I've already handed over my duties, so I'd be delighted.'

'Excellent.' Blake went into the kitchenette and opened the cupboards, checking around. 'Do you have any dietary limitations, Merry? Allergies? Restrictions? You're all right to eat out of the water, aren't you?'

'Yes, I can eat out of or in the water. I have no allergies that I know of. I won't eat animal flesh. Vat flesh is fine.'

'Good. Marque?'

'Admiral?'

'Ingredients for my spiced gellonworm recipe for three, jasmine rice, whatever leafy vegetable's in season right now, pickled kenari, toro. Is there anything we do that they don't have on Pacifica?'

'They don't have toro; tuna haven't been introduced,' Marque said.

'Shocking,' I said.

'I know,' Marque said. 'As soon as the treaty is signed and some ships are freed up, the *Silver Lotus* is carrying a full load of embryos to Pacifica.'

'Tuna?' Merry said. 'I've heard of it.'

'Ingredients are here, Admiral.'

'Excellent.' Blake removed his jacket and rolled up his shirtsleeves. He opened the refrigerator to reveal the ingredients Marque had provided. 'Give me about twenty minutes, and then you can tell us about food on your home planet. I'd love to learn some new recipes.'

'In that case, move over,' Merry said, and joined him in the kitchen. 'Marque: moldweed, vat novafish, grungefruit and some sandberry sauce. Let me show you one of our signature dishes.' She studied the burners. 'I'll have to modify it to cook it in air.' She nodded. 'Should be doable.'

Blake took his ingredients to the side. 'I'll let you go first.'

'Tell us your story while we make dinner, Jian,' Merry said. 'Do you mind if we record it?'

'No, go ahead and record it, Marque. I was twenty-three and a corporal in the Euroterre army. It was just after the end of the war between East Asia and Western Europe, and the nation of Euroterre – New Great Britain – was only twenty-five years old.'

'That was the war started by the attempted assassination of Queen Victoria III?' Merry said, fascinated. 'Richard Alto saved the Queen by jumping on the bomb?'

'That's the one. Queen Victoria was King Charles VII back then.'

'It seems so long ago.'

'It seems long ago, and at the same time only yesterday, for me. Anyway, the war had just ended, but the climate was going to hell, and in a hundred years Earth would no longer be habitable ...'

*

'Food's ready,' Blake said twenty minutes later. 'Come and eat, and tell us the rest.'

'Not much more,' I said as I found plates and cutlery for everybody. 'The dragons negotiated for our assistance to protect the Empire against the cats in return for reproductive restraint and a halt to reproductive conquest. The Empire stayed static and stopped expanding, and the Cat Wars began.'

'And they end tomorrow,' Blake said with satisfaction. 'For the first time in a very long time, the Empire will be at peace.'

Merry tasted the gellonworm, and grimaced. 'Too sweet.'

I tried the fish with grungeweed, and choked on it. 'Way too bitter.'

Blake grinned and ate some toro. 'Lucky for me, I like everything.'

21

'Wake up, little friends.' Marque's voice emerged from the screen at the side of the room. 'Time to move; the royals are on their way.'

I woke and grunted. I was sandwiched between Merry and Blake and Blake had his arm protectively over both of us. All three of us stirred.

'How long do we have?' Blake said.

'Haruka and Masako will be here in forty-five minutes. I've laid out a new uniform for you in the bathroom, Stewart. I suggest you go first so both you and Jian look the part when the royals arrive.'

Blake raised himself on one elbow and smiled down at us. 'Thank you, dear ladies, for a generous time of mutual joy and pleasure.' He took each of our hands and kissed them, then threw the covers off. 'I'd better run.' He sprinted to the bathroom.

Merry pulled me closer and kissed the short hair on the back of my head. 'I don't want to use the formal words of appreciation with you, Jian. I feel more than that, but I must return to Pacifica, so I suppose I can only give you my heartfelt thanks and hope that we will keep in touch.'

I turned and wrapped myself around her. 'I feel the same way, dear Merry; my position here on the homeworld is important to me. Let's make the most of our time together while you're here.'

Merry smiled sadly. 'Come to Pacifica and visit me.'

'Oh, I will, particularly after what you told me about your home.' I raised my head. 'Tell Admiral Blake to move his butt, Marque, I have places to be, and Ambassador Merry still needs to make herself presentable for the royals.'

Merry sat up and pulled the surgical tape off the sides of her throat. She checked the oxygenation pump clipped to her waist. 'That was wonderful. I am so glad I met you and Stewart.'

'You didn't need the tape after all,' I said.

'Oh, yes I did; a couple of times there I definitely lost control and without the tape you would have a soaked bed and an air-drowned Aquatic.'

'Do you need to recharge the water in your gills? You've been circulating that water for a long time.'

'The filtration system is adequate, but a fresh supply of the correct saline formula would be good,' Merry said.

'It's outside,' Marque said.

Blake came out of the bathroom fully dressed and holding his uniform jacket. 'Jian's next. Marque has a gift for Merry outside the windows.'

'What?' Merry pulled herself out of bed and walked to the window, her soft blue flesh jiggling in the light of the morning sun. 'Oh. Is that seawater?'

I went to stand next to Merry and smiled. Marque had pulled a fifty-metre-wide sphere of seawater from the planet below and was holding it suspended two metres above the platform in front of the capsule.

Merry took two big strides towards the door and then looked ruefully down at herself. 'I need clothing.'

'There's a Pacifican bodysuit for you in the closet,' Marque said. 'Jian, you'd better move, they'll be here soon.'

I quickly kissed Merry, said the formal words of appreciation to Blake, and ran to the bathroom. I stopped and turned back at the door. 'And I think your feet are *fabulous*, Merry, don't feel self-conscious about them. They're wonderful.'

'Go!' Merry said with a huge smile.

I stepped under the cleansing shower. 'Report, Marque. Any incidents overnight?'

'Nothing worth reporting. Nobody tried to disturb them. They've slept well and both of them are in a good mood.'

'Haruka doesn't *have* a good mood.' I stepped out of the shower and stood still while Marque air-dried me. 'How long do I have?'

'Put your uniform on; they'll be here in ten minutes. Do you need a hand?'

'No, I'm fine.'

'I'll leave you to it.'

I pulled my clean uniform on, ran my hands over my short-cropped hair, and nodded. Acceptable. I strode into the living room. 'Stewart?'

'I'm on the platform,' he said through comms. 'Wait until you see this – Marque's a genius sometimes.'

I went out onto the transit platform. Marque had put a polarising film on the energy dome to reduce the sun's radiation, but had left a shaft of light on Merry's waterball. Merry was within the sphere of water, wearing the wetsuit-like Pacifican bodysuit. She moved with the joy and grace of a sealion, and her oversized, paddle-like feet looked completely natural when she was in her element.

I stood, breathless, watching Merry swoop and roll within the sphere. The Aquatic's purple hair flew behind her, glittering in the sun's rays.

'Thank you, Marque,' I breathed.

'My pleasure. If you two would like to see more of each other—'

'No need to set us up. One: it's only been one night, and two: we both have extremely rewarding positions on our respective worlds.'

'But you two are so good together—'

'For now we'll leave it long-distance casual.'

'Did you ask Merry what she wants?'

'That's why I'm telling you.'

A frowning emoji flashed over Marque's surface where it hovered nearby and was quickly replaced by a transmission of Merry swimming in the sphere.

Merry was experimenting; she went to the bottom of the sphere, swam quickly to the top, and launched herself out of the water. She breached and splashed back into the water, her face alight with joy.

'Marque's made the gravity lower,' she said to me through comms. 'It's easy to leap out. It feels like flying!'

'Watching you lifts my heart,' I said.

Merry smiled at me through the water. She swam down to the bottom of the sphere, turned, and launched herself to the top. When she reached the surface of the water she leaped out, curving through the air in the sunshine. The sight took my breath away.

Merry splashed back into the water, but hit it awkwardly and slid down the outside of the sphere. She tried to kick out, but it only caused her to leave the sphere completely. She flew through the air, heading for a hard landing. I took two fast steps towards her, painfully aware that I wouldn't be in time to catch her.

Marque caught Merry in an energy field and gently lowered her onto the smooth white surface of the platform. Merry nodded, speaking to it, and laughed. She walked to me, her broad hips swaying gracefully, and smiled. 'Misjudged it.'

'Incoming,' Blake said through comms.

I straightened. 'Masako and Haruka are here.'

Merry lifted her soaked hair from where it clung to her neck and re-inserted her breathing tube. 'Exciting! I'll meet the Princess. Marque, can you dry me off so I don't drip on her?'

'My pleasure, Ambassador,' Marque said, and surrounded Merry in a whirlwind of warm air. Her purple hair was a tangled mess, so Marque smoothed it for her as well. The sphere of water floated to the side of the platform, and disappeared over its edge.

We joined Blake at the entrance to the private surface elevator. The elevator doors opened and Masako and Haruka stepped out, accompanied by Masako's goldenscales servant, Miko. Blake and I saluted them, and Merry bowed.

Marque had tidied the space elevator car and it was immaculate when we returned to it with Masako and Haruka. We went inside and the dragon reclined on the floor. Haruka sat on one of the couches, and Miko took Masako's box containing hard copies of the documentation into the bedroom.

'Marque tells me you're an educator, Ambassador Merry,' Haruko said, indicating for her to sit next to him on one of the sofas. He was wearing a deep green kimono with a dark blue obi, the colours highlighting the green in his hair.

'I am, Highness,' she said. 'Thank you for allowing me to come along for this.'

'Not my decision to make,' he said, gesturing towards Masako. 'She's the boss.'

'Happy to have you,' Masako said. 'Marque, I haven't seen the new flagship in person yet. Can you give us a better view as we go up?'

'I can't make the walls of this pod transparent; it needs to be solid to deal with the stress of the elvator. We'll be at the top in a couple of hours, you'll have to wait until then.'

'Can you arrange a viewing platform for the humans?' she said.

'I'll make one, but the new ship is so big that you need to be about ten kilometres away to see all of it properly.'

'How big is it compared to Shiumo's ship?' I said. I saw Merry's questioning face. 'Shiumo's ship was the largest in the dragon fleet; she had spouses from the lost people of Nimestas that were well over two hundred metres long and they travelled with her.'

'It was enormous,' Blake said. 'And the *Silver Lotus* will be twice its size.'

'What, twelve kilometres long?' I said, aghast.

'Fifteen. It has modular living quarters capable of carrying more than a million human-sized citizens if required. There's space to accommodate a thousand Sillon-sized citizens. It will contain what used to be Shiumo's ship as a lighter in its aft hold. Once the treaty's signed, the main role for the ship will be as a freighter. We'll carry people through the stars on sight-seeing tours, and transport large numbers of items or people that would have been folded individually otherwise. If things don't work out, we can use it to evacuate whole planets.'

'What *used* to be Shiumo's ship?' Merry said.

'Shiumo died in the cat conflict,' I said.

'Call it a war – it's what it was,' Blake said.

I shrugged. 'When I think of war I think of guns and armies, not torture and hostages.'

'Conflict is conflict,' Blake said. 'Show us a model of the *Silver Lotus*, Marque.'

A three-dimensional, metre-long projection of the silver ship appeared in the middle of the room. It was the standard bird-in-space shape but much wider than usual for a dragon ship.

'That doesn't give an accurate idea of exactly how big this ship is,' Blake said, and his voice was full of pride.

'And Marque built it in six weeks?' Merry said.

'I'm that good,' Marque said.

'Liar,' Blake said. 'We started construction shortly after Earth was attacked with the black holes. We never wanted a situation like that to occur again – where there was no way to evacuate a large number of people safely.'

*

'We'll be at the nexus in ten minutes,' Marque said a couple of hours later. 'Would you like to view the *Silver Lotus*?'

'How far away is it?' Merry said.

'It's on the other side of the planet,' Blake said. 'Docked at a part of the nexus with lower traffic.'

'If Masako folds you to co-ordinates I give her, I can put you into an energy bubble so you can see it,' Marque said.

Merry's eyes widened and her breath gurgled through her gills. 'Raw space?'

'You've never been in raw space before?' Blake said.

Merry shook her head.

'It's like swimming, you'll be fine,' I said.

'I will be if I'm with you.'

Masako pulled herself to her feet and approached us. 'I want to see. Put your hand on me if you'd like to come.' She turned back to her dragonspouse. 'Haruka?'

He waved us away. 'We should be heading to the negotiations, not sight-seeing. I'll stay here with Miko.'

'Suit yourself,' Masako said, and looked around. 'Stewart, Jian, Merry?'

Merry nodded, still holding my arm, and we put our hands on Masako's shoulders. She folded us to a location higher above the planet than the flagship, so the ship and the nexus had the planet as a backdrop behind them. The ship was so enormous that only its bow touched the nexus, and its stern was towards us. Marque moved us along the length of the ship and more of it came into view.

Merry gurgled again, and put her hand over her breathing tube. Blake and I put our arms around her waist to reassure her. Marque didn't give us gravity; we floated in a bubble of air.

Merry released the tube and put her arms around us in return, her discomfort turning to awe.

The ship shone in the light of the blue-white star, clearly visible next to the planet, a misty sphere below.

'How far from the ship are we?' Masako said. 'It looks normal size to me.'

'We're ten kilometres away,' Marque said.

'Oh.'

The ship did appear to be normal-sized. Marque shifted us, moving us over its massive bulk, and the view of the ship slowly changed to give us an idea of its true size.

'Goodness it's huge,' Merry said.

The folding nexus on the nose of the ship came into view. On a normal-sized ship the nexus would span the width of the ship, with a two-metre-wide entrance at the bow. The *Silver Lotus* had half-a-dozen nexus points on its bow, and they were so small in the distance that they were almost invisible. The light flashed over the ship as we moved across it, and grooves appeared on its surface.

'Is something etched onto the hull?' I said.

'I wondered if you'd be able to see it from this distance,' Marque said.

'We definitely can't,' Blake said. 'Move us closer so we can see better.'

We zoomed towards the ship and the sun shifted behind it so that we were in shadow. It was like approaching the planet itself. We moved up along its side, the shadow moving with us, and

Merry made a loud sound of astonishment when the light hit the side of the ship again. There were etchings on its silver skin; an abstract embellishment of curling organic grooves.

'That's gorgeous,' I said. 'Who designed it? The ship looks like a work of art.'

'We did,' Masako said. 'The best dragon artists put their heads together and designed it with help from Oliver Choumali Runaspouse.'

'I knew he was involved in the design, but he didn't tell me exactly how,' I said. 'I'm so proud of him.'

'You should be,' Merry said. She lowered her voice. 'I'd love to meet him. I'd like to meet your whole family.'

'I'd like that too. My family will adore you.'

She pulled me tighter and shivered with delight.

'We originally intended the design to be something like the frieze on the side of Sky City,' Masako said, 'with dragons approaching other species in peace and friendship, but Oliver advised us that cats don't like depictions of themselves. Instead we did a stylised message to the cats in their own language that says the same thing.'

'The frieze will change after we've signed the treaty,' Marque said. 'We've installed a set of designs into my storage on the ship, and I'll regularly change the etching on the ship to honour different species.'

'The goal is to have a message in every Imperial language, so that when we approach a planet the ship will tell them that we honour all citizens,' Blake said.

'You're planning to continuously remodel the surface of a ship this big?' I said.

'It's just moving the surface around,' Marque said. 'It would be boring otherwise.' Its voice became more brisk. 'The treaty signing is in three hours. I think we should move the ship into position.'

Merry glanced at Masako. 'You can fold it? It's the size of a small planet.'

'Our folding ability is unlimited when it's a single unbroken piece of inorganic matter,' Masako said. 'If you look at it dimensionally, I'm just punching a simple shape and all its contents through four dimensions. Organics are much harder – the edges are so *fuzzy!*'

'I'm glad,' Merry said. 'I'd hate to see any damage to this shining work of art.'

Masako looked around. 'Hands, dear humans, let's take a look inside.'

Masako folded us onto the main gallery of the *Silver Lotus*, a vast space with its black shiny floor. It wasn't furnished and had no features; it was empty. The matte grey wall, more than two hundred metres high, stretched away on our left, but the other walls weren't visible. It was like being on the surface of a planet with the blazing night sky above us, and a town wall stretching away on either side of us to the left.

A batallion of humans – at least a thousand of them – were lined up and waiting for us in dragon-army uniforms. I recognised some of them; these were soldiers who'd fought in the original cat battles.

Good to see you, Jian! Miranda Twofeathers said telepathically. She was North American First Nations, tall and heavily built, and I knew her from the original psi training academy on Earth.

I nodded to her. *You too, Miranda. It's good to see some familiar faces.*

My old second-in-command, Griffith, stepped forward wearing a colonel's uniform and saluted us, smiling at me. 'Admiral Blake.'

'Are we ready to depart?'

'Sir.'

'Stations, everyone,' he said.

A massive door, ten metres tall and wide, swung silently open on the towering wall, and they went through.

'I'll get Haruka and Miko,' Masako said, and disappeared.

Merry looked around. 'It's hard to judge how big it is when you can't see the walls.'

'This deck is seven thousand metres long, three thousand metres wide at its widest, and two hundred metres high,' Blake said. He pointed down. 'There's a system of transport tubes under the floor, so Marque can carry you from place to place. The freight hold is under this deck, a similar size but twenty-eight hundred metres tall, big enough to carry a full-size Marque orbital sphere. The aft half of the ship is modular quarters of different sizes to suit different species, and Shiumo's ship is at the bottom.'

Merry looked up. 'Does this space develop its own weather?'

'I could if you wanted,' Marque said. 'But that's not the purpose here; this space is for meetings, residences or storage.'

'Every space within the ship has a purpose,' Blake said. 'I can host the entire army in this area in either offices or residences to share information directly. It can contain a small city with enough space for the entire defence force. During the cat conflict we had to divide the army into different dragon ships during briefings, and share information across them. It wasn't ideal.'

'I remember,' I said.

'Did you say a *city*?' Merry said.

Blake smiled at the space. 'I can fit the entire population of Barracks in the aft quarters, and half that number of civilians in this space.' His smile softened. 'I hope I will never need to, and that this treaty means we have peace.' He turned to us. 'Speaking of quarters, the command suite and VIP quarters are here in the nose of the ship, closest to the nexus entrance points.' He gestured formally towards the huge door. 'If you'll follow me, we'll go through to the bridge.'

He guided us through and the doors swung shut behind us. We were in another gallery with invisible walls and roof. The floor was grey and textured like carpet, and the shape of the area matched the nose of the ship. There were a number of comms panels in rows facing the bow, and at the rear of the room a silver desk – a duplicate of the Empress' desk in her office – stood next to a Marque ornamental tube. Some of the humans stood at the comms panels, and I watched with interest as they brought up displays of the surrounding space and the planet below. The nose of the ship was facing the planet, and we were looking directly down into it.

'You're only occupying this small part of the ship?' I said as Blake moved forward between the stations.

'More isn't necessary,' he said. 'Marque can mind the rest of it. If we're attacked and Marque is disabled, we can fly the *Lotus* independently from here. The ship has its own anti-grav engine controlled by these panels, and a few caches of scales to communicate with the homeworld. If the very worst happens, we can jettison the rest of the ship and use the nose as an escape pod.'

'Stewart and I spent quite a lot of time studying the nanos and developing a risk management strategy,' Marque said. 'The cat nanos are capable of disabling me, so I want to be sure that if it happens, the passengers on the *Lotus* are safe.'

'We have safeguards installed to protect the ship if nanos attack,' Blake said.

'Will the cats have nanos in space around the planetoid we're going to?'

'No, there are no stars nearby to feed the nanos, but the cats will have them in their bodies. They have a symbiotic relationship with their nanos. The nanos normally feed off solar energy, but can use the cats' metabolism as a backup. They're programmed to self-destruct if they become so hungry that they cause damage to the host cat.'

'Will they eat us instead?'

'No. Cats only.'

I nodded. 'Good. Where are our quarters?'

'Bring up a floorplan, Marque,' Blake said.

A three-dimensional display appeared between us. It showed the entire ship, with its space divided into huge sections, then zoomed in onto the front two hundred metres where we were standing. The top half was the comms centre, and the lower half of the bow was divided into residential quarters, the med centre, and a Marque storage unit.

'We don't know how long we'll be there negotiating, so your quarters are prepared,' Marque said. 'Knowing the cats, this could take weeks.'

Masako appeared with Haruka and Miko. 'I'm very impressed.'

'Thank you, Princess,' Blake said. He turned to the crew. 'Are we ready to get underway, Colonel?'

'Whenever the Princess wants to fold us, Admiral,' Griffith said.

Masako disappeared to reappear on the bow of the ship above us. The planet disappeared and we were in the treaty location. The skin of the ship flared brilliantly white, then faded as Marque filtered out the energy spewing from the nearby black hole. It sat in the sky above us with rods of incandescent destruction spreading for light years on either side of it.

The cat ship was in front of us, on the other side of a dark planetoid that shaded its warp field. The cat ship was still in warp, its white aura bending the light of the stars around it.

'That's their flagship,' Blake said. 'The *Sandbox*.'

'The what?' I said with disbelief.

Blake shrugged. 'We don't know what its name is so we called it that.'

'Why call it—' Merry began, then stopped as Marque updated her through comms. 'Oh!' She choked off a laugh. 'Don't call it that in front of them.'

'They wouldn't understand anyway; they use those bowl things,' I said.

'How big is it?' Haruka said.

'Ten kilometres long,' Marque said.

Blake looked smug. 'Ours is bigger.'

'That is extremely petty, Stewart,' Haruka said.

'For some species being bigger is inferior,' Masako said.

'Cats?' Blake said.

'... No.'

'That's the planetoid where we'll be doing the negotiations,' Blake said, and pointed. Marque zoomed in on the planetoid so it was visible in front of us. It was a small, dark, and pockmarked potato-shaped object.

'How big is it?' I said.

'A hundred and forty-one kilometres across,' Marque said.

'They've prepared a flat area to sign the treaty,' Blake said.

'If we can get them to sign a treaty.' Marque zoomed in on the planetoid even more, and a glassy platform became visible on its side. 'That's it. No nanos anywhere around.'

We waited as the cat ship dropped out of warp and hovered on the other side of the planetoid. Marque zoomed in on our view of the ship as half-a-dozen bipedal figures left the ship and jetted towards the planetoid. They rotated so that they had their feet towards the glassy platform and landed on it to wait for us.

'Suit them up, Marque,' Masako said, and my vision filled with the heads-up display. 'Hands and let's go.'

Blake and Haruka stood next to Masako and put their hands on her shoulders. I stood behind her and put my hand on her butt. Miko held the box containing the documents in one claw and put the other claw on the end of Masako's tail.

The ship disappeared, and we were at ninety degrees to the surface of the planetoid, with the platform next to us. Marque rotated us and provided us with a gravity platform so we could stand across from the cats. There were three cats in physical spacesuits, and five walkers behind them in their black-and-white battle armour.

The lead cat stepped forward and I saw its face in the helmet.

I spoke through comms. 'I think this is the young cat that killed Oliver's father.'

'A rising political star,' Masako said through comms. She stepped forward, bowed her dragon head, and spoke telepathically to everybody. *Greetings, honoured Ambassadors.*

One of the cats raised its hand and spoke, but its words were muffled by the spacesuit.

'Just a minute,' Marque said, and created an energy dome over the platform. It filled the dome with air. 'There, it's breathable for all species present.'

The cats checked their wrist sensors, but didn't move to take off their helmets. Marque removed the spacesuits from me, Haruka and Blake, and when the cats saw it happen they waved at the walkers.

The central walker undid the clasps on the neck-ring of its helmet and lifted the helmet off with a hiss of escaping air. It took a few deep breaths and waved one chunky hand.

The walker's face was conical and massive with small eyes and a breathing hole at the top of its head. Its skin was the same black-and-white pattern as its armour, and smooth like an orca's.

The cats and the other walkers removed their helmets and stepped forward to a metre-high black stone plinth in the centre of the platform.

'Definitely the same cat that killed Ollie's dad,' I said through comms. 'He's an adult now, but it's him.'

'Are you Princess Masako, the Empress' oldest child?' the lead cat said.

'I am, honoured sentient,' Masako said. She nodded to Haruka. 'This is my partner, consort, and love, Prince Haruka. Captain Jian Choumali you know. The other human is the head of our navy, Admiral Stewart Blake.'

'Is this your child?' the cat said, indicating Miko with one hand.

Miko's eyes widened and she stepped back.

'Courage, dear one,' Masako said to her. She turned back to the cats. 'She's my sister, handmaid, and confidante.'

'Perfect,' the cat said. 'Do it.'

'Nanos—' Marque said, and then my head filled with a piercing scream that broke my brain in two.

22

'She's waking up. Get her some water.'

'Yes, Prince Haruka.'

I shot upright with a gasp. I was on the floor ... I looked around. Prince Haruka approached me, almost unrecognisable without his usual make-up and adornment, his kimono torn and his long green hair loose and tangled. Miko was pouring some water from a jug on a table behind him.

The low-ceilinged cabin had a rough textured floor and a sleeping platform bolted to the wall, so we were on the cat ship. My head pounded with pain and I rubbed my forehead, to find my soulstone missing. 'What happened?'

'I don't know,' Haruka said. His soulstone was gone as well. 'They used something that knocked everybody out except for Miko.'

'It didn't affect me,' Miko said. Her voice filled with pain. 'I thought you were all dead! I wanted to go with Masako, but they separated us and put me with you.'

I bent with pain. 'It hurts like hell!'

He reached to me and touched me on the side of the head, and the pain eased.

'Thank you,' I said. 'I didn't know you could do that.'

'It's a rare skill, and one I'd prefer nobody knew about – it can be misused to cause euphoria.' He sat on the floor next to me. 'People think I'm one of the dragonscales who inherited no psychic ability, and I'd rather it stayed that way. When did you do your last backup?'

'Last night before we left, if this is the same day. How long was I out?'

'Miko?' Haruka said, turning to speak to the dragon.

'It's been more than twelve hours, my Prince,' she said, bringing the human-sized cup of water to me. Her soulstone was gone too.

I drank the water quickly – I was very thirsty – and gave the cup back to Miko. 'Try to contact one of the other dragons through your scales,' I said to her. 'If we can find even one dragon that can fold, we're all out of here.'

'Uh ...' Miko dropped her head and gazed at me with her huge golden eyes. 'My scales aren't quantum-entangled with anyone. We goldenscales never have spouses, and we're always in the company of our coloured sisters who do the communicating.'

'Wonderful,' Haruka said.

I checked my pockets, and they were empty. 'Does anyone else have a scale?' I said.

'Masako's the only one with any scales, and I have no idea where she is,' Haruka said. 'This ship has warped. We could be anywhere. Have a look around, Jian, see if you can locate our people.'

'I need the bathroom first.'

Miko and Haruka shared a look, and I groaned. 'Oh no. Cats don't use bathrooms. Where are the bowls?'

Haruka gestured towards the other side of the cell. A single bowl sat on a shelf bolted to the wall. 'There's a ... drain thing under the bowl when you use it, as they have no nanos to clean it up.' He winced. 'Effectively a toilet. We'll look the other way. Go.'

He and Miko turned the other way and I did what I had to do as quickly as silently as possible. I was still deeply dehydrated. I moved to the other side of the room, took another cup of water from Miko and sat with them. I closed my eyes and reached out, looking for our people, and found them in the belly of the ship. We were in the nose section of the cat battleship that had approached us when we were waiting for the treaty negotiations to begin. Masako was a hundred metres away, also in the nose, and I tried to contact her.

Masako? I said, and she didn't reply. I tried the Admiral. *Admiral Blake, are you there?*

Captain! Sergeant Twofeathers sounded thrilled. *I'll relay for the Admiral. Are you all right?*

Yes, I said to Twofeathers. *I have Prince Haruka and Miko here. Masako isn't responding.*

She isn't responding to me either. I have a message from the Admiral. Welcome to the nightmare, Jian. Captured by cats without a fight.

Status of our people otherwise? I said. *Any killed by this new weapon?*

All alive, we were taken without resistance, Twofeathers said. *Whatever they used on us disabled us completely; the more sensitive the mind, the longer the disability. I'm not surprised you only just came around; I took nearly as long.*

Hypothesis on what disabled us?

No idea, Captain. Has the Prince contacted home? They took all our dragon scales.

Damn. They took Haruka's scales as well. We don't have any. Do you or the Admiral have any idea where we are?

None whatsoever. Have the cats talked to you?

No. Have they talked to you?

No.

We'll work something out, Twofeathers.

If anyone can, you can, Captain.

I wished I shared her optimism.

'Jian?' Haruka said.

I quickly explained our situation for him. 'With the Princess out of action, we have no-one to fold for us, even if we did know where we are. We're in a warp field anyway, so there's no way out. Our only hope is that Marque finds us – but I doubt it can generate a matching warp field this big. We're hostages. I know it's obvious but – have you tried to break into the door mechanism? Is there a circuit to fry?'

'No,' he said. 'Miko has basic four-dimensional vision, and there are cables inside the door that lead elsewhere. The structure itself is solid metal. They open it manually somewhere else.'

'Not surprising. Any bugs, Miko?'

'No, Captain. The walls ... bulkheads ... are all solid metal as well. No cameras, microphones or nanos, just smooth unbroken metal and a manually-operated door.'

'Nothing for us to break into and use against them,' Haruka said.

Miko lowered her voice. 'It's strange not having Marque's reassuring presence.'

'I feel that way too.' I downed the water, handed the cup back to Miko, and slid off the bed onto my feet. I straightened my uniform and started to pace. 'They have our ship as well as all of us. And our soulstones – if they work out how to reverse-engineer the soulstone technology, it will be a catastrophe. They'll send unlimited numbers of walkers through the teleporters and we'll be attacked everywhere.' I thumped my forehead. 'What the hell did they hit us with?'

The door slid open and I turned. The cat that had killed Oliver's father was standing in the doorway. It grinned to reveal long canines. 'Good. You're awake. About time.'

My immediate reaction was to grab anything nearby that could be used as a weapon. I cast around the contents of the cabin and found nothing useful. I took a step towards him, then stopped. Attacking him while they held my soulstone would just get me killed for no benefit. He had a small laser gun in one hand and – what the hell – a writhing, suckered tentacle in the other. I wanted to kill him so much it hurt, and I shook with restraint.

'Steady, Jian,' Haruka said.

I nodded to acknowledge him. 'This is Ambassador Haruka of New Nippon. I am Captain Jian Choumali of the Imperial—'

'Dragon whatever whatever Empire, I know who you are,' the cat said. 'I am Senator Sishisti of the Cat Republic.'

'You killed my son's father.'

'You remember! Well done. That one was deeply rooted in the past. After I killed him, we made some serious changes to the way we do things.' He bowed stiffly to me. 'Many of those changes are a result of your own wise influence. The messages we received from your cat son's wife inspired us to begin a new era of freedom and equality.' His eyes gleamed with menace. 'Aishisistra no longer applies in the Cat Republic, and our women are free to pursue their own lives without being reproductive slaves – as you are to the dragons.'

'Well that's a positive sign, even though we're not reproductive slaves,' Haruka said. 'Let's try to salvage lasting peace between our people ...'

'You will remain silent,' the cat snapped at Haruka. He turned back to me and waved at the bed. 'You are famous for resisting the dragons' sexual advances, so I assume you have stronger willpower than average. Let's do this.'

I looked at the bed, then at him.

'Sit and talk,' he said, exasperated. 'Unlike you, we are selective about our mating partners. Our President is on her way, so let's start negotiations, shall we? Can Admiral Blake sign an agreement on behalf of Earth, or do we need to go higher?'

Haruka stood and straightened his kimono, then pulled his hair back and roughly braided it to reveal the green scales at his temples. 'We will never surrender.'

'You sit down and shut up,' the cat said. He turned back to me. 'Join the Republic. Free yourselves from the reproductive tyranny of the dragons. We will give you democracy, freedom, all of the things you don't have while these disgusting mind-manipulating reptiles control you. Cast them off and rule yourselves – democratically choose your leaders instead of subjecting yourselves to control by the dragons. We'll keep Haruka and Masako as honoured ambassadors and send the rest of you home to Earth with a division of cats to oversee the transition to Republic membership. If the Admiral signs the treaty, all hostilities will cease.'

'No,' I said.

Haruka glared at him. 'You entice species with these promises of democracy, but every civilisation that has joined your "republic" ends up with cats ruling them.'

'Many species need a supervised transition to full democracy,' the cat said. 'Our facilitators ensure that barbaric feudal societies like yours make the transition successfully.'

'We will not agree to be conquered by you; we will all die first,' Haruka said.

'That's the dragons controlling *you*, Prince Haruka,' the cat said. He turned to me. 'They're controlling your mind! Join us, and all humanity will be free of the dragons' domination and will rule yourselves. You won't have to be their breeding stock any more.'

'You have no idea how the Empire works,' I said. 'It *is* a democracy. The Empress only rules the dragons. Everybody else chooses their own representatives in our Parliament.'

'She has power of veto,' the cat said. 'They control your minds.'

'No, they don't!' I said, exasperated. 'We love being in the Empire, and every human, dragonscales and dragon would die before we submit to your corrupt rule.'

'It's not corrupt,' he said, protesting. 'It's just ... practical.'

'Our answer is no,' Haruka said. 'Go back to your President and pass the message on that all of us will die first.'

'I'm not asking you,' the cat said. 'I'm asking the human. You're already contaminated. You need to be purged.'

'I agree with him,' I said.

'You'll think differently after we've removed the dragons from Earth and freed you from their mind control,' the cat said.

'We will fight to the death for the Empire,' I said. 'You're wasting your time.'

'Really?' the cat said, then raised the writhing blue tentacle to his mouth, and bit down hard on it. The scream that filled my head seemed to come from inside it as much as outside, and I blacked out.

*

I fell into a chair and jerked awake. I sat up and looked around; I was in a shuttle with Senator Sishisti next to me.

'Analgesic, Captain?' he offered, gesturing towards the comms panel. 'Water? You've been out for a long time.'

I saw a soulstone that looked like my own on the panel and reached to grab it, but he took my hand first and held it away. 'Steady, now. You can have that after you've agreed to my offer.'

I took the water and had a long drink instead, then peered through the small window in front of us, searching for the cat cruiser, but I didn't see it. The *Silver Lotus* was visible in the distance, on the other side of the planetoid where we were supposed to hold the talks.

'Where are we?' I said. 'What happened? How did you *do* that?'

He raised his other hand, holding the writhing tentacle. 'Effective, eh? Does it sound like a scream when I bite down on it?'

'It's that thing? The sound ...' I shook my head.

'We thought they were just delicious food. Imagine our delight when we discovered that they did this to you. Wonderful.' He turned his seat to face me, his green eyes luminous in the reflected lights of the comms. 'We're ...' He hesitated. 'Computer. How many kilometres is three hundred eshata?'

'Two hundred and fifty thousand kilometres,' the computer said.

'That far away from the—' he growled the name of the cruiser. 'Are you outside the dragon's control? If you're still controlled by Masako, tell me and we'll move further away.'

'Princess Masako does not control me,' I said with fierce dignity. 'No dragon controls me. I serve the Empire of my own free will.'

He bared his teeth at me. 'Are you really that stupid?' He turned back to the panel. 'No, you're still controlled. Let's go another hundred thousand clicks away and see if that works.'

He didn't speak to me as he pushed the little ship into warp, and we travelled for twenty minutes. When he wound down the warp drive, we were closer to the *Silver Lotus*, the gigantic ship shining in the light of the black hole. He turned to me again. 'Now, I want to talk to you about your role after Earth is welcomed into the Republic. You are the only human, as far as we know, who has been able to resist a dragon's advances. We need someone strong-willed and intelligent like yourself to lead your people. Your adopted son is one of us, so you understand our ways. How do you feel about becoming leader of all Earth? President of humanity? If you can bring your people into the Republic, we will make it very profitable for you. And your family.'

'Profitable?' I said, feigning interest.

'You would have complete control over all Earth's finances. Humans are the most powerful chemical weapon in the civilised galaxies, and we will compensate you handsomely if you agree to join us. You, personally, will become wealthier than you can possibly imagine. All of Earth will be yours.'

'But the Dragon Empire already gives me everything I need,' I said, leading him on.

'Do you have raw, unrestrained power over any other citizen? The power of life and death? The power to break those you hate, and raise those you love? That sort of power is intoxicating.'

I opened my mouth to agree with him to keep him talking and gave up. I felt slightly nauseous. 'I have no desire to control anyone like that.'

A voice appeared from the console. 'We are ready, sir.'

'Fire,' the Senator said.

'What?' I said, and was silenced. A beam of light hit the *Silver Lotus* and it dissolved, melting into huge droplets that spun away into space and froze. Some of them hit the surface of the planetoid below it.

'My offer is vastly preferable to doing this to Earth,' he said. 'I'll take you back to our flagship and house you separately from Haruka and Miko so you can think about it. Our President will be here soon, and she can confirm this exceptional offer.'

A little version of me inside my head started screaming and running from side to side in a tiny cell. 'I'd prefer to remain with Miko and Haruka. I need Miko, she's my servant too. Putting me in solitary confinement will damage my mental health.' I tried to keep the desperation from my voice. 'Please don't put me alone. Being on that warp ship by myself for a long time was ... traumatic.'

'I see. I will put you back with them, don't worry.' I tried to control my relieved reaction but he saw it. 'Are you in a relationship with Haruka? People in the Empire seem to have no concept of chastity, modesty or virtue.'

I smiled at the irony. 'Masako and Haruka are married, in a monogamous relationship. Extremely chaste and modest.'

'Maybe there is hope for the Empire after all,' he said. 'Once we have humanity in the Republic, we will be able to negotiate from a position of extreme power and bring some temperance to the debauchery of the Empire.' He nodded. 'I'll take you back, and let you stay with Haruka and Miko. We know that the little yellow ones are worthless. The dragons are too soft, allowing these deformities to live. The President will be here soon, and you can talk to her about the opportunity we're offering you.'

'Is Masako all right?' I said as he turned the little ship and pushed it back into warp.

He glanced at me. 'As long as you and I are talking, she is. If you agree to join us and free yourself from her mind control, you can do whatever you like with her.' He smiled at the stars. 'Take revenge for years of servitude.'

I wiped my eyes. 'Just send her home, and I'll talk.'

'I think holding the Empress' favourite daughter is an advantage that we really don't want to throw away.'

*

Miko and Haruka were waiting quietly for me in the cell when I returned.

'Are you all right? You look like you were tortured,' Haruka said.

'They blew up the *Silver Lotus*.'

'Seeing the empty ship destroyed traumatised you that much?' Haruka said.

I wiped my hands over my face and my voice shook. 'He threatened to put me in solitary. I have ... issues with that.'

'I understand,' he said, sounding more compassionate than I'd ever heard him. 'Did he tell you where Masako is?'

'They're keeping her sedated as a hostage. He referred to her as "The Empress' favourite daughter".'

'That's surprisingly accurate; Masako is Mother's chosen heir. So what do they want?' Miko said, and Haruka glanced at her, obviously surprised at her forwardness. She bobbed her head. 'Sorry.'

'No. You have a brain, add it to the equation, help us out,' he said. 'I've been impressed by your analysis of the situation while Jian was gone.' He turned to me. 'She suggested that they want to bring humanity into the Republic so they can use you as a superweapon.'

'That's the gist of it.' I scowled. 'They offered to make me Queen of Earth with the power of life or death over every human, as if that is something I'd *want*.'

'They're power-hungry narcissists,' Miko said. 'They think everybody else is too.'

'We need to get out of here,' I said. 'We need to wake Masako up, and—'

Hello, are you new?

I jumped and raised my hand. The mind that contacted was deeply intelligent and full of wonder. 'Someone just contacted me telepathically. Not one of ours, and not a cat.'

'Who?' Miko said, and Haruka hushed her.

Hello, I'm a prisoner here. Are you a prisoner as well? I replied.

I suppose we are; we thought we were guests but they won't take us home. They're keeping us in a tank and taking one of our group out now and then, and not returning them. I hope they're freeing them. Some of us think they may be harming our friends and families because we're hearing them scream ... but they have no reason to harm us? We don't understand. Are they taking your friends and family as well?

The mind was childlike in its naiveté, and of a type I'd never encountered before.

What do your kind look like? I asked it.

We look like this. It sent me an image of an underwater ... it was a bright blue octopus, or as near to one as parallel evolution would generate. It appeared to have more tentacles than an Earth one, and its size was difficult to gauge.

We look like this, I said. *There are two types of us, dragons ...* I sent it an image of Masako. *And humans.* I sent it an image of myself. *We also have a dragon/human hybrid with us.*

The octopus was incredulous. *Is it possible to have children together when you are so dissimilar?*

It's something that only dragons can do, I said. *It's complicated. We can explain after we free ourselves from the cats.*

Is that the creatures that are holding us? Cats?

We call them cats. They have no name for themselves. Do you require water to live? Can you leave the tank?

Some of us left the tank to go exploring. There was no water within travel distance so they returned. We have creatures on our world who breathe air, but have never encountered this degree of intelligence in other life. We are excited to meet you! Wait until we tell the people back home!

I snapped back and turned to Haruka who was waiting impatiently.

'What did you find?'

'I found ... I found a new intelligent species. Octopuses ... Octopi? The cats are keeping them in a tank and I think they're using them as a fresh food source.' Realisation hit me. 'They're the thing that disables us. They're ripping the arms off these poor people and biting on them to make them scream.'

'They're using an intelligent species as a weapon?' Miko said, incredulous.

'They're using them as *food*,' I said.

'Can you talk to them?' Haruka said. 'How different are their minds?'

'Not that different – they communicate with ideas just as dragons do.'

Miko raised her head. 'We're dropping out of warp. Another ship has approached, and they're leaving warp together – I think they're going to dock and transfer us off.' She studied me with her huge golden eyes. 'Captain, goldenscales have the ability to build a mental image of nearby space, and when we're out of warp I can gate—'

'Gather the information, but don't even think about gating,' I said. 'Masako's still alive out there somewhere, and we will find her.'

Admiral, I said to Blake. *We're dropping out of warp. Talk to your people. Someone must have long-distance telepathic ability. We need to contact home.*

On it, Twofeathers said.

The door slid open to reveal two cats.

I sighed. 'And here's the stick.' I lowered my head and wiped my eyes. 'Either solitary and torture for me, or they'll threaten someone's life to make me comply.' I touched Miko's shoulder; she was unresponsive, her eyes blank as she gathered the information. I nodded to Haruka. 'I hope you find Masako and make it out, Haruka. If there's no other option – talk to Miko. She has skills that aren't widely known.'

'Don't give them anything,' he said, his voice fierce.

I turned to face the two cat guards who levelled weapons at me. 'Don't worry, I won't.'

They led me along a hallway with a textured carpet floor and travel platforms along the walls. They walked slowly, probably expecting me to be clumsy and slow-moving – and compared to them I was. We went along a curving corridor that had many doors leading out from it, and in a short time were at the command centre for the ship. It was massive; twenty metres to a side and soaring high above me, with platforms all the way up the wall, and the usual minimal visuals of the outside. They'd obviously put us in senior officers' quarters if we were so close to the bridge.

A female cat with a similar build and colouring to Senator Sishisti was standing next to him and waiting for me. There was a strong family resemblance between them.

He nodded to me. 'You are honoured. This is President Mesher of the Cat Republic, our first female President.' He lowered his voice. 'She isn't as patient as me, Jian. I suggest you do as she asks.'

'Look,' I said. 'You've tried to bribe me to sell out my people, and now you'll torture me into complying. Don't. Nothing you can do will push me into agreeing with you.'

'Intelligent,' the President said, pleased. 'We were planning to bring out the humans one by one and kill them. I'm still willing to give it a try. I'm sure you'll break eventually ... we have hundreds of them.'

'They're military,' I said. 'I'm military. Our lives are forfeit when we sign up. I'll salute them, they'll salute me, you kill them, end of story.'

The President turned to the Senator. 'Bring a few up and try anyway.'

He scowled, revealing sharp canines. 'Not on the bridge, we might damage something. Do it in the shooting range.'

'It will achieve nothing!' I said.

'On the contrary,' the President said. 'The crew deserve a reward for capturing all of you unharmed. It will be the most fun they've had in ages.'

They took me into an elevator that went down for a long way, then put me on a small railway with open cars. They sat on them with their knees under their chins, cat-style, and I had a moment of quiet panic as I thought of my darling Oliver refusing to ever sit like that again, even when it was more comfortable for him.

'Even if I agree to your demands, you can't just barge up to Earth and install yourselves as rulers,' I said. 'Humanity will fight back with everything they have, and the dragons—'

'Dragons don't approach planets surrounded by clouds of nanos,' the Senator said. 'That abomination of an AI is scared of them, and with good reason.'

The President was casually menacing. 'We take over planets all the time, Captain, we're very good at it. Our ways are different to the dragons', but still effective.'

'It won't work with us,' I said. 'We'll fight you.'

'The dragons meddled with your genetics to add the telepathy trait,' the President said. 'Our tentacle weapon disables anyone they did this to. Your entire species is helpless against it. They will have a brief period of unconsciousness, and when they wake up all your top leaders will have disappeared and there will be walkers on every street corner.'

'We tailor the assimilation program depending on the resistance,' the Senator said. 'With peaceful species, we only put anyone who disagrees with the new administration into re-education camps. They can be saved.' He bared his teeth. 'Your species is heavily contaminated by dragon influence. It will unfortunately mean holding public cleansings of half-dragon mongrels and human resistors so that all can see what happens to them.'

'It's unpleasant, but very effective,' the President said, and her emotions were again full of malicious pleasure. 'Instil a general terror in the population and it doesn't take long for them to capitulate. People with families, particularly, want to ensure their safety and are usually the first to turn to our side.' She turned to the Senator. 'What's the quickest we've torn through a population's resistance and welcomed them into the Republic?'

The Senator looked smug. 'Three of their days from arrival to installation.'

The President turned back to me. 'We can have your people enjoying the benefits of Republic membership in a very short time, and install you as leader of all humanity. We don't need to harm your people, dear Jian, just agree to our proposal and we'll all have a nice meal and send the dragon home.'

The little train stopped and we were in a twenty-metre-long concrete shooting range, with three shooting bays in it. Half-a-dozen humans were standing in the target zone, with a similar number of cats in the shooting bay. I buried my face in my hands as I sat on the train; I could feel the humans' fear. They knew what was about to happen, and even worse they all accepted it. My people were about to die and I had the power to stop it. Death in the heat of battle was one thing; this cold-hearted execution was unbearable. 'Please don't do this.'

'One of the males first,' the President said. 'Just to show her that we mean it.'

'I know that you mean it!' I shouted. 'We all do!'

One of the cat guards grabbed a man and pushed him from one bay to another, then stepped back. The human didn't fight him. I felt his terror and courage; he was in desperate fear for his life, but at the same time faced his death without flinching. He saluted me and said something that I couldn't hear.

'We knew this would happen,' one of the other people said. 'This isn't your fault, Captain. This is war. Hold on and don't give—'

One of the cats shot the human crew member and he fell with a smoking hole right through him. The cat continued to shoot until he was a greasy stain on the floor, and the other cats laughed.

'Next!' the Senator said, and the cats changed shooter, patting each other on the back.

One of the humans screamed and ran to the end of the bay. He hit the wall hard and fell to a crouch, screaming. The cats laughed as they followed him and dragged him back through the rest of the group, who shouted obscenities at them. They pushed him into the target zone.

'Agree and this will stop, Captain,' the President said into my ear.

His screams dissolved into loud sobbing and he knelt and begged for his life as they shot him.

'Next!' the Senator said.

One by one the humans were pushed forward and the cats took turns murdering them. I shook with rage and despair and my knees were so weak that I leaned on the wall. Everything was a blur of horror and pain and the room was full of smoke and the smell of burnt flesh.

They brought a new group of humans in and my attention snapped into focus. Merry was in this group. She smiled sadly at me and gave me a small wave.

'This one's a different colour, but has no dragon scales,' the President said from next to me. 'Is she a different species? She seems to be breathing water. Is there something wrong with her? She's awfully fat; that can't be healthy.'

'She's a civilian,' I said, my voice a moan of pain. 'There's nothing wrong with her, she's perfect the way she is. She represents one of our new colonies.' I turned to the President and tried to explain. 'The others were soldiers, but she's a *civilian*. She teaches our *children*! Send her back to the group.'

The President broadcast satisfaction. 'About time you showed some concern for your people. Agree to help us and she can go back unharmed.'

'It doesn't matter what you do. You can kill everybody and I still won't help you conquer Earth.'

'Put her in,' the President said to the other cats. 'Slowly on this one; she means something to our dear Captain.'

'Thank you for making my life brighter, Jian,' Merry said as they pushed her into the target zone. 'I wish we could have been more. I'll be dead soon anyway; this water's foul and they can't replace it.'

The cats in the shooting bay argued about who would do it. They could see she was important to me, and a higher-ranked one demanded the pleasure of killing her.

'Goodbye, dear one,' Merry said, and pulled her breathing tube out. The water gushed from the tube and she stood with her eyes closed, her gills working as they tried to get enough oxygen into her. She swayed on her feet, and fell.

I took two steps to run to her, but the President gestured for a couple of cats to hold me back. Merry lay on the floor and her limbs thrashed, then went still. One of the cats shot her anyway, burning a line across her prone body. I howled with agony and fell to my knees.

'About time,' the President said. She grabbed my arm and shook me. 'Blake is next! Then Haruka. Then Masako herself. All you have to do is *agree* and this will stop. You are killing your friends. Stop this now.' She pushed me towards the guards. 'Take her back and let her think about it for a while.'

*

They pushed me into the cell and I fell to the floor and curled up.

Miko and Haruka ran to me and knelt on either side.

'Did they torture you? What did they do to you?' he said.

'They killed a bunch of humans – including Merry – and I could have stopped it,' I said. My throat was thick. 'I didn't stop it.'

'You did the right thing,' he said.

'No, I didn't,' I said, my voice hoarse.

'We have to get out of here,' Miko said. 'My life isn't worth a thousand. I have a location we can gate to. I can do it.'

'I understand that you want to help, Miko, but you're a goldenscales,' Haruka said. 'We have to find Masako, she has the skill.'

'I have skill. I can gate,' she said.

'Not an option,' I said. 'You know the penalty!'

'Penalty for what? What is gating?' Haruka said.

'Look up,' Miko said.

Haruka yelped; he was staring at the ceiling. I looked up and saw the back of our heads through the thick glass-like wall of the gate. I looked behind me and saw Haruka's face looking up. Miko had joined the ceiling of the cell with its wall.

'You folded!' Haruka said with disbelief. 'Goldenscales can't fold. Why can you fold?' He cocked his head. 'No, this can't be you, Miko; this isn't even a fold, it's a stable wormhole. That must be exponentially harder. Is Masako doing it? I didn't know she was that skilled. Jian, can you talk to Masako?'

Miko raised her snout and the gate disappeared. 'It was me.'

'Goldenscales can't fold,' Haruka said. 'Some have a small talent, but none are good enough to be worth training.'

'Goldenscales can't fold, but they can gate – create passageways through four dimensions – wormholes,' I said, wiping my eyes. 'But the gates aren't stable, they can destroy the universe if they get it even slightly wrong. So the penalty for gating ...' I glared at Miko. 'Is death. Don't do that again.'

'I'm dead anyway,' Miko said. 'You're dead anyway. A thousand people are dead if we don't do this. They'll never let us go back home, because we'll never agree to their demands.' She raised her head to look me in the eye. 'They eat sentients!'

'You can gate us out of here?' Haruka said.

Miko nodded.

'Even if we're in warp?' I said.

'We're not in warp; the other ship is still docked.'

'Can you gate us home?' Haruka said, full of hope.

'No, sir, I don't know where we are in relation to home. But I can see the space around us and I can gate us to the planet where we were going to do the treaty.' Her voice became softer. 'There's a cavern in it that has no openings to the outside. We can travel there and take everyone with us.'

'That won't work; there'd be no atmosphere,' I said. 'You and Masako would be fine, but all the humans would die, and they took our soulstones.'

'Then the dragons should go and leave us,' Haruka said. 'Masako would be safe, and that's all that matters. As Miko said: we're dead anyway.'

'I have an idea, Captain, but I'll need help from both of you to talk to the other captives. I can fill a cavern on the asteroid with air, but you'll have to explain the gate to the rest of them.'

'I don't see how you can do that without folding,' Haruka said.

'I'll put a gate in this ship's hull, leading to the cavern, so the cats will think the hull has a leak. I'll let the ship's atmosphere leak into the cavern, then close the hole. I'll gate you to where I think the Princess is, and gate the human soldiers and Blake out during the confusion over the hole in the hull.'

'Two gates at once?' I said.

She raised her head. 'I can do it. I have to. Trust me – I won't fail.' She lowered her voice. 'You remember when I said that with training we could do it safely?'

'How long have you been training yourself to do this?' Haruka said.

'I'm nearly five hundred of your years, my Prince,' she said. 'And the universe is still here.'

'Miko ...' I hesitated. 'You saw what they did to Kana.'

'The Empress' favourite handmaid? She died, didn't she?' Haruka said. 'An accident or something.'

'As I said, Highness, the penalty for gating is death,' I said. 'She gated the black hole that was destroying Earth. She saved the planet and everybody on it. And ...' I glared at Miko. '*Her own sisters* crushed her soulstone.'

'I tried to stop them,' Miko said, her voice small.

Haruka glared at Miko, his gaze fierce. 'If you do this,' he said, 'I will personally share your skill and courage with the citizens of the Empire, and demand that you not be harmed. If they do attempt to go through with it ...' He looked to me.

'I can talk Ambassador Maxwell around,' I said, my feelings moving from despair to hope. If we did this, nobody else would die. 'The Empire is helpless against the cats without us humans.'

Haruka nodded, and turned to Miko. 'So—'

Are you still there? the octopuses said. *They took another one of us. We're beginning to think that bad things are happening. Can you help us?*

'We have to help the octupuses as well,' I said. 'The cats are *eating* them.'

'That adds another layer of complexity, if they're water breathers,' Miko said. 'I won't have anything to put them in; we'll only be able to rescue them after Masako has contacted home.'

'We must save them,' I said. 'Masako isn't responding, she might be sedated or in a coma. Blake and the other humans are in the hold. We need to find where the octopuses are. Let's organise ourselves, make a plan, and start gating.'

23

We still had our heads together when the door opened. I stood, and Miko and Haruka retreated to the back of the cell.

It was the Senator with two guards.

'Choumali, with me,' he said, and I joined him in the corridor.

'I hate doing this to you,' he said, and the lie was written all over him. 'If you agree to help us, it will stop. My mother ... the President's moved to her ship to head home; she won't torture you any more. It's just me now, and I want to work with you.'

'I've been thinking about your offer,' I said. 'Can we talk?'

He filled with glee. 'Of course. Are you hungry? Thirsty?'

'I'm starving,' I said truthfully. I was so hungry I was even willing to eat the awful kibble. 'Please feed the other humans if you feed me. It's a tradition that we eat together.'

'Agree to our terms and we'll provide them with the very best care,' he said. 'All we need is for you to sit with us and give us your guarantee.'

'I will,' I said. 'I'll do anything you ask.'

'Excellent.' He led me along the corridor and we went further than the bridge. We seemed to be going to the other side of the ship. A door opened to a medical centre.

I hesitated without going in. 'What is this?'

He gestured towards the table in the centre of the room. 'We need to ensure that you're in perfect health.'

The cat in the medical centre was next to a vat containing pale blue liquid that moved by itself.

'Nanos. You want to inject me with nanos.' I rounded on him. 'I do not agree to be mind-controlled by you! You said you'd free me from the dragons, and you want to do the same thing to me?'

'They won't control you, they'll assist you. They will monitor and preserve your health, and when you die they will move your awareness to a new body. It's our version of a soulstone – immortality. You allowed the dragons to implant a soulstone, didn't you?'

Now, Miko, he's distracted, I said. 'I have a better idea,' I said out loud. 'Do it the human way. When I die, have a trained successor ready to take over. Humans are accustomed to hereditary monarchies. Do it that way.'

'I don't think so,' he said. 'This isn't negotiable. If you're willing to work with us, then you must have them installed. They'll kill you if you attempt to betray us by returning to the Empire.' He studied me carefully. 'You did agree to work with us, didn't you?'

'Yes, I suppose I did,' I said, and went into the room. 'Let's do it.'

The cat doctor inserted a large syringe into the vat and filled it with at least a litre of the nano liquid.

'You're going to stick me with that?' I said. 'That looks awfully painful. Can't you infuse them through an IV?'

'They need to go straight into your nervous system through the base of your brain. You may feel some mild discomfort, but it's only for a short time,' the cat doctor said. 'Come and lie on the table and I'll hook you up to the monitors. Some people respond badly to the initial insertion, and this is the first time the nanos have interacted with human biology.'

I need to get out of here – they're going to inject me with nanos! I said to Miko. *I'm in the medical centre.*

Warp engines disabled, Twofeathers said. *We're moving the hostages.*

Please hurry; if they put these things into me, I'm dead.

An aide rushed into the medical centre. 'Senator, something just ... hit the middle of the warp drive. We're under attack!'

'Show me.'

A display turned on at the side of the room. It was an image of the warp drive, with Miko's gate in the middle of the nest of coils and wires. The gate was the same as the ones Kana had created on Earth: a thick-sided glass ball with a black centre. The atmosphere in the warp room was visibly blowing into the gate. She'd cleverly linked the warp drive room with the asteroid cavern to extract the atmosphere and destroy the drive with one gate.

'Is that a hull breach?' the Senator said. 'How is that even possible? Did they drill a hole through the hull?'

'New weapon. No idea what it is,' the crewman said. 'We're trying to get a team into the warp room, but the failsafe airlocks have engaged. The ship is attempting to heal the hull breach organically, but ...' It sounded desperate and confused. 'The hull breach is a sphere? And not in the hull? I don't understand.'

Senator Sishisti glared at me. 'What new weapon do the dragons have this time?'

I stared at the display, trying to broadcast disbelief. 'I have never seen anything like that before.'

'This is completely new, we have no records of a weapon like this,' the other cat said, and I did my best to hide my relief. They hadn't seen the gates that destroyed the black hole on Earth.

Have they found it yet? Twofeathers said. *She's had the gate open a long time. We're nearly at full atmosphere here, and we're moving people across.*

They're just standing around looking at it, confused, I said. *They can't even get into the warp room, and they're unaware of the gate in the hold.*

'We're ready for you,' the Senator said to me. 'This ship has multiple separate atmospheric systems in sealed sections so the chilli can't spread. We can stop you.' He turned to the medical cat. 'Inject her with nanos anyway. She's ours.'

The medical cat manhandled me onto the table, secured me with wrist straps, and began to hook monitors onto me. The Senator left the room with the others.

How many more humans to go? I asked. *They're about to inject me with nanos – I really need to get out of here!*

Fifty. Twenty. The last few stragglers ... that's all of them. She's on her way. Ready, Captain?

The cat doctor raised the syringe with the nanos active inside it like a living liquid, then grinned at me. He moved behind my head. 'This will cause some discomfort.'

Right now is good! I said direct to Miko.

A gate appeared next to me and Haruka and Miko charged out. Haruka used his momentum to tackle the medical cat to the ground while Miko undid the restraints and helped me off the table. She half-carried me into the gate, and everything went completely silent around me – my ears rang in the silence. I was stretched impossibly long and thin, and my vision filled with a pale pink fog. Noise rushed back, and I stepped into the room where they were holding Masako. She was lying prone on a cat sleeping platform, her stomach bloated with death, and from the smell coming off her she'd been dead for a while.

'There isn't a mark on her, but her brain is mush,' Miko said, as if from a million miles away. 'Whatever made you unconscious killed her.'

Haruka staggered out of the gate behind us. 'No,' he wailed. 'No.' He fell to his knees next to her. 'My love.' He looked up at us. 'Where's her stone? We need to find her stone.'

I hunted around the room. It was bare and featureless. 'No stone here.'

'We need to leave, my Prince,' Miko said. 'She wouldn't want you to die as well.'

'Go,' he said, and bowed his head. 'Go without me.'

'Nope,' I said, took three big strides to him, and grabbed his arm. I wrenched him to his feet and marched him towards Miko. 'Is the gate ready?'

'Wait,' she said, and the glass ball changed from grey to black to bright green, and then to grey again. 'Go.'

Haruka didn't fight me, he seemed dazed. I dragged him to the gate and stopped. 'Listen to me,' I said to Miko. 'Don't even think about staying here and causing a distraction. We still need your gating ability. The warp engines are disabled, so we can come and go as we please. We may need you to carry us somewhere else if we can't contact home. You're the only one not affected by the octopus weapon. You are much too valuable to sacrifice, so get your little yellow tail moving and follow me through this gate.'

Miko's eyes had gone wider and wider as I spoke to her. 'Uh,' she said. 'Yes, ma'am.'

'Come on,' I said, and dragged Haruka into the gate. I was stretched again, and stepped onto the bare stone floor of the interior of the asteroid. It was so cold that my breath caused a fog in front of me, and the only light was coming from Miko's gate. The humans were sitting on the floor and checking on each other. I turned to ensure that Miko followed me, and she didn't. Her yellow shape was moving on the other side of the gate, but she didn't come through.

'Come through right now before they work out what we're doing!' I shouted at the gate.

She said something unintelligible from the other side.

'Miko! Move!'

It seemed forever before she leaped through and the gate closed behind her, leaving us in darkness.

Blake touched my shoulder, then helped me lower Haruka. 'Thank god you made it.' Fabric rustled as he checked Haruka. 'Is he injured?'

'Grieving. Masako's dead,' I said.

'That's awful. Miko, are you here?'

'I'm here, Admiral.'

'You are remarkable. Why hasn't anyone told us about this gift before?'

'They're not allowed to do it,' I said. 'If they get it wrong, they can break reality.' I turned towards her voice and glared at the darkness. 'What took you so long?'

She touched me with her nose. 'I took some of Masako's scales. I have about a dozen of them. I hope one of these will work – not many of her scales are entangled; she doesn't have any other spouses.'

I grabbed either side of her head and kissed her hard on the snout. 'You are magnificent. Well done.'

We passed the scales around. Haruka sat to one side, sobbing without restraint and lost in his grief. Blake sat with me and Miko next to the wall and we sorted out our assets. The rest of the humans huddled together in the cold and dark, tapping Masako's scales and hoping for a response.

'Can you keep a gate open to the stars to give us some light?' Blake said.

'I'm sorry. I can't hold a gate open permanently, it's exhausting,' Miko said. 'I need to rest; if I tire too much I may make a mistake, and that would be messy.'

'I wouldn't call the end of the universe "messy",' I said.

'Pfft,' she said. 'That would only happen if I put one end of a gate inside the other and turned the universe inside out. Normally all that happens when I get a bit tired is that my accuracy fades and extra matter comes through when I don't want it. I have never overlapped each end of a gate, and none of my sisters have either.' She lowered her voice. 'Not that we'd risk doing it.'

'Wait ... a single mistake wouldn't destroy the universe? Your sisters are wrong? Marque *lied*?'

'Well, yeah,' she said. 'Marque lies all the time. It keeps telling everybody that gating is too dangerous, and they believe it. Even the other goldenscales believe it.'

'But Marque must know that you've been doing it successfully for five hundred years – why didn't it tell them?' I answered my own question. 'For the drama when they do find out.'

'All of this is beside the point if we're dead in twelve hours,' Blake said. 'We need to deal with the cold. We'll die of exposure if we can't either warm the cavern or find some blankets.'

'I can put one gate closer to the black hole and another one near the potato, and warm it with the energy flare,' Miko said. 'Can you guide me, Captain? Tell me when it's warm enough?'

'Potato. I like it,' I said. 'I can help you.'

'Are you sure you won't suck the planetoid into the black hole?' Blake said.

'Yes, of course.'

'I need a physicist!' Blake shouted.

None of the humans responded.

'You have a physics question?' Miko said.

'Yeah, about heat loss, and whether we'll lose heat from the walls once you close the warming gate. And I want someone to confirm that we can use the black hole.'

'If I warm the interior to thirty degrees Celsius your measure, it will remain above zero for ...' Miko was silent. '... Fifteen hours.'

'You just worked that out in your head?' I said.

She didn't reply, then said, 'Oh. Yes.' Her voice filled with chagrin. 'I'm nodding and you can't see me.'

'Can you see me?'

'Yes. I can see all of you, and space for about a light year around us.'

'Damn.'

'When the temperature drops too low I can just reopen another gate and warm you up again,' she said. 'Trust me, I won't go close enough to the black hole for it to hurt you.'

'How long do we have before we suffocate?' Blake said. 'It's possible the cats are using our communications scales to tell the Empire that we're fine, and it will take a while for them to realise we're in trouble.'

'I'll gate some fresh air in from the cat ship,' Miko said. 'I can see inside it; I can gate to a location on the ship with no cats nearby.'

'Good. After that our main need is water,' Blake said. 'We can only survive a maximum of three days without it.'

'All right, let me look. No, no ... here it is. I found a comet. I'll have to bring it in frozen chunks for you to drink cold, because I have nothing to hold it when it melts.'

'You have this remarkable ability,' Blake said. 'You can do major calculations in your head. You're smarter than the rest of us put together. Are all goldenscales as good as you?'

'I'm average,' she said.

'And the other dragons use you as servants,' I said.

'They're exponentially better than us. They can't destroy reality, their folds are so much more useful ...'

'I wouldn't say that,' I said. 'I wish you could have children. You at least deserve that. You're magnificent.'

She didn't reply and the space around her filled with regret.

'Oh, no way,' I said. 'You're capable of having children as well?'

'That's beside the point because it will never happen,' she said. 'My sisters would see me dead first. Now give me a few minutes to get my breath back and I'll warm your cave up and capture a comet for you.'

'That's our immediate needs taken care of,' Blake said with confidence. 'We should have contact with home through one of these scales before we need to worry about food. With their warp drive wrecked, the cats aren't going anywhere, so we can scrounge resources off them. We haven't travelled far from the treaty location, so somebody should find us soon.'

'I'll make the warming gate,' Miko said. 'Let me know when it's warm enough in here.'

'We'll check everybody over and sort ourselves out,' Blake said.

*

I woke in the darkness with Miko's smooth scales next to me. I had my arm thrown protectively over her as she lay with her four legs wrapped around me. I moved my hand over her and touched cloth – she was sandwiched between Haruka and me on the stony floor of the asteroid. The heat left the air quickly and we were staying close to keep warm. Miko was like a smooth, warm comforting blanket.

She put her head on my shoulder and whispered into my ear, the sound becoming lost into the darkness of the cavern. 'He's still unresponsive.'

'Give him time.'

She nodded into my shoulder and sighed against me. 'I've never been held like this. It feels good.' She nuzzled into me. 'I have no mistress now. Perhaps when we return – if I survive – they will permit me to break tradition and serve the Captain of the Guard instead of one of my coloured sisters.'

I ran my hand over her and she trembled. 'I will never permit you to serve me.'

She filled with disappointment and rubbed her head over my shoulder. 'I understand.'

'You will be a friend and an equal and I will give you many gentle hugs.'

She stiffened slightly, then relaxed. 'Please don't say things like that. It hurts.'

'Respect and affection hurt?'

'I have been admiring your brilliance since I first saw you,' she said. 'A life as your equal sounds glorious, but it is impossible. If I am lucky I may be permitted to serve you.'

'Some of your goldenscales sisters seem to revel in their servitude.'

'They hate themselves. They hate what we are. We can't fold, we're a second-class colour, we're not good for anything. Serving others is the only way we can atone for our failure.'

'You consider yourself a failure?' I said.

'It is difficult to see myself that way after what we just achieved,' she said. 'Forfeiting my life to have experienced such success is a small price, Captain.'

'Jian.'

'There it is again.'

'Hurting you by being kind?'

She nodded into me. She raised her head, then quickly disentangled herself and pulled herself to her feet, waking Haruka who grunted on the other side. 'The cats have launched a shuttle. It's not in warp; it has to clear their ship first. We need to hurry.'

'About time. Let's take it,' I said.

'Clear a space for the gate,' Miko said.

I woke the people nearby to move them as I shouted across the cavern. 'Blake, we have a shuttle.'

'How many can go?' he said from across the cavern. 'Who do you need?'

'It's small,' Miko said. 'Two people and me is all I can fit into it with the gate.'

'Me and Griffith,' I said.

'No,' Haruka said, and bumped into me. His voice filled with menace. 'Me. I'm bigger, stronger, and I have some real motivation here.'

'How many cats on board?' I said as the gate appeared in front of us.

'Two. Ready?'

We charged through. We used our momentum to hit the cats hard, and Haruka audibly broke the neck of the one on the right with a crunch. I wasn't as strong as Haruka, and my cat had half-fallen from his chair. He struggled to pull his legs under him and staggered to his feet, only to be punched in the face by Haruka, who then crushed his throat with the blade of his hand.

'Is that Japanese martial arts?' I said, looking with shock at the two corpses on the floor.

'Yes,' he said, and sat in one of the control chairs. 'Do you remember how the cat flew this?' He turned to Miko. 'Can you gate the whole thing?'

'No, my gates are limited to the size you've seen.' She took two-legged form and sat next to him. 'Let me see these controls.' She flicked a few switches. 'This is a basic interface; I shouldn't have any problem with it.' She shook her head. 'My gate broke the ship's warp drive, but the other engine is good. We'll have to move it to the potato with its docking jets. This will take a while.' She looked up and saw our faces. 'What?' Her hand fluttered to her mouth. 'I wasn't even thinking, I just did it. Please don't tell anyone.'

'You ...' I began, but I was lost for words.

Her two-legged – human – form was small and delicate. She would probably only reach my shoulder when she stood. Her face was ageless and ethereally beautiful, neither male nor female but a charming mixture of both. Her skin was deep gold – more golden than natural for a human – and her long, thick hair was a paler shade of yellow that frizzed around her head. Her eyes were still huge and liquid and full of intelligence. The rest of her softly curving naked body was also neither male nor female – she had minimal pert breasts and I thought I glimpsed a hairless small penis between her legs. It was difficult to allocate a specific gender to her. She smiled sadly at me, causing her cheeks to dimple. 'Please don't tell anyone I took this form. We're not supposed to have one.' Her voice was the same; high-pitched and sweet.

'You are the cutest damn thing I have ever seen in my life,' I said. 'Your coloured sisters look like huge muscular men or women. You look like a freaking *pixie*.'

'What's a pixie?' she and Haruka said in unison.

'Uh ... never mind.'

'Do you see me as male or female?' she said, her smile going coy. 'I'd love to know.'

'Neither,' I said. 'Both.'

'Definitely female,' Haruka said. 'Large breasts, long hair, uh ... yeah all the features are female.'

'I don't see that,' I said, grinning at him with mischief.

'Well, we need to move this ship and connect it to the potato,' Miko said. 'I can drive it up using the docking jets, but to create a gate between the ship and the potato I need to go outside.'

'How long will it take?' I said.

'Just a second, the main ship is pinging us. I sent a confirmation code back.' She looked over the control panel. 'There's the waste disposal control – can you put these poor cats in there while I work out the logistics of connecting the ship to the potato? I need to think about it.'

'With pleasure,' I said. Haruka and I stood and picked up one of the cat corpses with one of us at each end. The interior of the ship was five metres across and ten deep, with cat sleeping platforms bolted to the wall and a kibble and water dispenser next to them. The warp drive took up the entire back wall of the ship, and a neat line was cut in a gate-sized circle around its centre.

We carried the cat's corpse to the waste disposal chute next to the warp drive. Miko opened it, and we placed the body inside. We collected the other one, put it into the chute, and she crushed and jettisoned them. Haruka took two big strides to the water dispenser, put his hand under the tap, and took a huge drink from it. He moved back and I did the same. He pushed the lever to dispense some of the kibble, and stared glumly at it, then popped a handful into his mouth. He gagged with his hand over his mouth, chewed a few times, and swallowed.

'It tastes like *blood*.'

'Don't eat it, Jian,' Miko said without looking away from the control panel. 'See if Haruka has any adverse reactions to it first. He's tougher than you are.'

Haruka pulled himself into the other control chair. He studied the controls and shook his head. 'Completely beyond me.' He looked back at me. 'Take my place.'

'No need, I can fly it,' Miko said.

'Do you need to eat and drink, Miko?' he said.

'I will after I'm happy with our trajectory,' she said. 'Uh ... it will take nearly a day to move the ship to the potato with its docking jets.'

'I'll tell Blake,' I said, and sat on one of the sleeping platforms. 'What about the cold in the cavern?'

'I can leave the ship here and warm the cavern with a gate if needed; the shuttle will stay on course. Once I've docked this ship with the cavern and created a hole using a gate, we can use it to warm the cavern, provide you with air, light and water, and perhaps even provide you with food.'

'There are sanitary facilities back here as well,' I said. 'No more huddling in the corner.'

'Check the floor,' Miko said, still fiddling with the control panel. 'I believe there are panels in the floor and there's storage underneath them.'

'Really?' I checked the floor; it was covered in grey textured carpet tiles. I lifted the edge of one of the tiles, and it wasn't glued to the floor. She was right; there was a hatch underneath it. I lifted the hatch to find plastic and metal boxes stacked neatly inside. I reached down, pulled one out, and it sprung open when I touched the front panel. 'Bingo.'

'What is it?' Haruka said, coming to sit on the floor next to me.

I lifted the emergency pack containing the chemical lights. 'This box has at least a hundred of these.' I put them back and pulled out more boxes. 'Non-perishable food rations. Water packs. Heat packs.' The hatch under the next set of tiles was two metres long. I opened it to find a tent. 'Excellent. Batteries, lighting ...' I grunted a short laugh. 'A distress beacon. That's exactly what we need.'

'Make sure you don't activate it!' Haruka said. He lifted some more hatches. 'Clothing. Blankets.' He looked up at Miko. 'How quickly can we move these into the cavern?'

'Hold on, the ship is asking me if we've seen ... us yet,' Miko said. 'We're supposed to be in a search pattern looking for us.'

'Tell them that you saw us,' I said. 'We appear to have a new type of ship that you've never seen before. It has stealth capability and can only be seen in short bursts. It appears to be on the run, trying to get some distance from them before folding out. You're in pursuit, and request another shuttle for backup.' I looked down at the emergency rations. 'Another shuttle full of this would be very useful.'

'You think they'll believe that?' Haruka said.

'After seeing what the gates did, I think they'll believe anything,' I said.

'Good point.'

'Wow,' Miko said, staring at the console. 'They ... wow. If we don't capture ... us, we will be executed. No assistance is forthcoming. When the homeworld finds out about this disaster, all our heads are on the line.' She looked over her shoulder. 'The crew of this shuttle are being blamed for the whole thing. We're the scapegoats, and it's their ... our fault that we escaped.'

'That's technically true,' Haruka said. 'Let me know when you're free to gate, and we'll move these supplies to our people.'

'I can do it now. Captain Choumali, please ask our people to give me some space to move the equipment in.'

She stood, giving me the chance for a good look at her physique, and there was definitely maleness happening. She changed to dragon. 'Let's give these people some food, water, and warmth.'

'Do you think we can eat the food?' I said, turning one of the foil-wrapped rations over in my hands.

'Haruka should eat one of the rations, and stay with the group for observation,' Miko said. 'If you're all right in twelve hours, let the humans eat it.'

'I object to being a laboratory subject,' he said with dignity.

'Do you object to being first to eat?' she said.

'That too,' he said, the dignity becoming even more rigid. 'It's bad manners to eat when everybody else is going hungry.'

'Just eat the damn cat food and help me carry this stuff to our people,' I said, picking up a box, and shoving it at him.

24

Carrying all the supplies into the cavern took half a day with intermittent rest stops for Miko to get her breath back. At the end of it, Miko refreshed the air by gating some out of the cat ship's hold. She and I returned to the shuttle, which was now nearly halfway to the planetoid. There were a couple of messages on the comms panel, and she changed to two-legged form to deal with them.

'More threats,' she said, her hands moving over the controls. 'They've told the Dragon Empire that they're holding us hostage, and not to approach or we'll die – so they have time to recapture us. That would explain why nobody's come to rescue us. They say that we should hurry and find the humans, and if we don't return with the humans don't bother returning at all.'

'Option two, thank you,' I said.

'I said we're chasing them but they keep disappearing. They said it again: come back with the humans or not at all. The supplies are in the cavern, the cats are held off for a while, it's all done. I can stop.' She sighed and lay her head on the panel. 'That was exhausting.'

'Rest,' I said. 'You've done so much. Take a break. The shuttle is on the right track, isn't it? You don't need to supervise the panel?'

'No.' She checked the panel again, and nodded to herself. 'We'll be at the potato in twelve hours. I can rest.'

'Would you like a hug? It's just you and me in here for twelve hours; we have privacy to have all sorts of hugs.'

'I didn't deliberately give us privacy,' she said, standing and moving to one of the sleeping platforms. She curled up on it, still in human form. 'There's a couple of medical people in the cavern. They can watch Haruka for signs of toxicity from the cat food. Oh.' She raised her head slightly and smiled. 'Yes. A hug would be lovely, thank you, Captain.'

I joined her on the sleeping platform and wrapped my arms around her smooth golden skin. She buried her head in my shoulder. 'This feels so good.' She looked up at me. 'It might be better to keep your distance and not become attached to me, Captain. I won't last long once we're rescued. My fate is sealed.'

'Not if we have anything to say about it,' I said. 'Haruka, Blake and I – all the humans – we will fight for you.' I pulled her close. 'When this is all over and everybody is rescued, we could run, you know. You and me, we could find a remote planet and they wouldn't find us ...'

'Thank you, but I won't run or hide. I will stand and tell my sisters that Marque has been lying. I will tell them that gating is safe. Of course, they won't listen, but maybe next time it happens to one of my sisters they will.'

'I'll make them.' I put my hand on the back of her head and stroked her soft hair. 'I can feel your emotions, Miko, and I know that you want to make love with me because you think this is the only chance you will ever have.'

She nestled into me. 'That first day you came to Dragonhome, I was dazzled by your brilliance. Ambassador Maxwell was intelligent and driven, but your eyes ... they sang to me. I'd never seen anyone like you, and I think ... I have loved you since then? That sounds wrong; how could something like that happen the first time I see you?'

I lowered my head, full of guilt. 'And I dismissed you immediately. I believed them when they said you were inferior, and I treated you like a servant. The opposite is true. You are the match of any coloured dragon in the Empire, and your gold scales show just how superior you are.'

She sighed deeply. 'I will forgive you if you kiss me. I have seen Haruka and Masako do it, and I have wanted to try it for*ever*.'

I raised her face to mine and kissed her. Her mouth was sweet with the flavour of tea and honey and her tongue was exploring and sensitive. I ran my hands over her and her small penis grew, so I stroked it as I kissed her, enjoying the pleasure she broadcast in return. She didn't have testicles behind the penis; there were labia and full female genitalia as well. I couldn't wait to discover her most intimate parts and pleasure them.

I pulled back slightly. 'Can you gate my clothes?'

'No?'

'Then I need to take them off the old-fashioned way,' I said, and stood. 'We have twelve hours. Let's make them the best twelve hours of your life.'

Her huge eyes were full of joy ... and love. It radiated from her.

'I want you to live,' I said. 'Because when we return, I would like to hug you every day.' I stepped out of the rest of my clothes and wrinkled my nose – I hadn't bathed in days. 'When we're home we'll have a long bath so I'm clean and fresh and we'll curl up in my big bed together.'

'You smell delightful,' she said. She looked me up and down with appreciation, and I felt her need. 'I never thought I would have this chance.' She choked. 'Thank you.'

I joined her on the platform and held her again. 'Thank me when I'm finished.'

*

Her hands moved like lightning over the controls as she parked the shuttle with the airlock against the potato's skin. She rose and took dragon form.

'Ready, Captain?'

'I'm your Jian, Miko,' I said. 'You can call me that.'

'My Jian,' she said softly. 'Let's save your people. I hope Haruka's okay; it was wrong to use him as a lab rat with the food.'

'You share a special bond with him, don't you?'

She hesitated, then nodded. 'We both loved Masako dearly.'

'I hope you can continue your relationship once he's recovered. Your love would be good for him.'

'That would be ... wow,' she said, her eyes wide. 'He's so strong and protective – he looked after me.'

'I think I misjudged him,' I said. 'A lot of his attitude was because – like the goldenscales – he hates what he is.'

'That's so true,' she said. 'I would like to help him heal. I hope I have the chance.' She realised what she was saying, and panicked. 'But I am yours alone, if you would have me.'

'As I said, I think your love would be good for him,' I said. 'Give him time. I'm not possessive; jealousy wasn't a luxury we could afford with so few people left on Earth. My Earth spouses were the only people close to my age for hundreds of kilometres. I adore the idea of you receiving hugs from all sorts of people – after five hundred years without a loving touch, you definitely deserve it.'

'I don't deserve you,' she said.

'No,' I said. 'I don't deserve *you*.'

'Gate. Gate.' She turned to the airlock. 'Let's do this.' She created a gate, stepped into it, and it closed.

I couldn't see or hear what happened next, so I contacted Twofeathers. *How's it proceeding?*

Welcome back, Captain, she said. *We think the food might be edible! Haruka had no reaction and some of the humans have tried it. Apparently it tastes vile, but food is food. Oh! There's the gate, it's about two metres above the floor, in the wall of the cavern. And it's gone. Air is escaping, but not enough to suck us out of the potato. The gate appears, the air escapes for a split second, then the gate is gone and the cavern wall with it. Another gate appeared next to the hole the first one made. Holy shit this dragon is accurate: I can see the wall of the shuttle through the hole.*

Miko gated back into the shuttle. 'I need to move it closer; I hope I made the hole the right size.' She took two-legged form and sat at the controls. 'Please ask them to tell me when the atmosphere stops escaping,' she said without looking away from the controls.

She ran the docking jets, which hissed on the outside of the ship, and it lurched then bumped into the potato. Awful scraping noises came from the hull as she forced it into the hole she'd created, and there was the sound of crumpling metal. The skin around the airlock folded inwards.

Stop! The air isn't escaping, the ship's jammed in tight, and it looks good from here.

'Twofeathers said stop,' I said, and Miko shut down the jets.

'Let me check to make sure it won't float away and leave you without an atmosphere.' She took dragon form again, and gated out.

Five minutes later Twofeathers spoke to me. *She's here and says open the airlock, Captain.*

I went to the panel to use the airlock controls as Miko had shown me. Even though everything was marked in cat and I could read it, most of it was in abbreviated form that meant nothing. I tried to open the external airlock and it wouldn't go.

It's jammed, she broke it, I said.

Damn this dragon is a superhero, she replied. *She just made the side of the ship disappear, in exactly the same place as the edge of the potato, so there's an accurate join. She used multiple gates to carry the matter out without losing much air. She's masterful. She says open the interior lock.*

I opened the interior door and the rich, musty smell of many unwashed humans entered the ship. I walked to the airlock door and saw their faces below me as they stood on the cavern's floor surrounded by the blankets from the survival kits. She'd even made the angle of approach correct, and the ship's gravity was already adding to their comfort. I hopped out onto the floor and went to Blake and Haruka as the rest of the humans cheered.

Blake hugged me, and then Haruka grabbed me and embraced me as well.

'The ship is giving us food, unlimited water, an atmosphere and gravity,' Blake said. 'Let's turn on its radio to signal the Empire, and wait for rescue.'

'She saved us all,' Haruka said.

'I'm calling her inside; we want to thank her,' Twofeathers said.

Miko gated into the shuttle and the people cheered again.

'I need to make sure it doesn't float away, and I'm telling the cat cruiser that we crashed,' she shouted down to us. 'Drink the water. Eat the food. I'm sure we'll be rescued soon.'

*

Miko gated back into the dimly-lit cavern, and her face said it all.

'Is that every location for twenty light years around us?' Blake said.

'It is, sir,' she said. 'I like to think there's a place I've missed, but I've checked everywhere. The cats chose an excellent spot for the treaty: there are no stars or planets nearby because of the black hole. We won't be sucked into it, but this planetoid is the only matter for light years around us. It appears to be an orphan that was captured by the black hole.'

'Can you replenish our atmosphere?' Blake said. 'The air's thin from you coming and going.'

She lowered her head. 'The cat ship repaired its drive. It's back in warp.'

'No dragon ships?'

'No.'

'So the cats are still pretending to hold us hostage, and the negotiations are ongoing,' I said.

'The shuttle's still broadcasting the message to the Empire?' Blake said.

'Yes.'

He called Haruka over. 'How much food is left?'

'At one-eighth of a bar for each person, once every three days – we will last two more meals for everybody, and then one more meal for twelve people after that. Six days.' Haruka gestured towards the shuttle. 'I doubt its batteries will last that long, and then we'll have ... Miko, how long until we suffocate?'

She sniffed the air. 'The shuttle's battery is at three per cent. The rate of decline is ...' She thought about it. 'Ten days.'

'Until the shuttle stops or until we suffocate?' Blake said.

'I'm sorry, Admiral, until you die.'

'What about you?' I said. 'You haven't mentioned yourself at all. You can live in a vacuum. Is there any way for you to escape?'

'You are very kind, Captain, but I cannot create a gate more than twenty light years end-to-end in unfamiliar space without requiring a stop to rest and recharge in either a sun or a gravity well. The black hole is too far. This area of space is like a desert to me.'

'I guess we saw this coming,' Blake said. 'We did our best. We didn't give them the satisfaction of killing us. They don't have the Earth, and they can't approach Dragonhome without being seen. It's a shame we couldn't save the octopuses, but they aren't much good as a weapon to the cats when they can't even get within telepathy range of us.' He grunted as he pulled himself to his feet. 'Time to gather everyone together and have them record their last messages on the shuttle log, so that we have a legacy if anyone finds us.'

'This is all my fault,' Miko said as Blake called everybody to listen to him. 'If I had any telepathic ability, I could alert an energy citizen riding the black hole's flare and you would have survived.' She shook her head. 'I failed you.'

'What he said about saving Earth,' Haruka said.

'Take me,' I said. 'I'll shout into the black hole.'

'We already had this discussion, and we both know it's pointless,' she said. 'You would vaporise before you said a single word, and there's no guarantee anyone's in the flare anyway.'

I flopped to sit on the floor. 'There has to be something we haven't thought of.'

'Face it, Jian,' Haruka said, sitting next to me and putting his arm around my shoulder. I leaned into him. 'We did our best. We haven't lost. But sometimes, when you don't lose, you don't win either.'

A brilliant red flash seared through the cavern, leaving dancing after-images.

'Uh ... Did anyone else just see a light thing?' I said.

There was a chorus of affirmations.

The light flashed through again, and the people shouted with alarm and moved away from where it had gone through.

'Twofeathers!' I shouted. The light had gone through her, and she lay in two pieces. 'Oh no. I know those injuries,' I said with dismay.

'Cats?' Blake said. 'They're firing on us?'

The light flashed again. It coalesced and hovered inside the floor, moving through the stone like a red flame.

'Move back – it's melting the floor!' Blake shouted and people scrambled away from it.

The light disappeared.

'What was that?' Blake said.

'It's one of those energy beings. The red ones,' Miko said.

'The suits,' I said.

'Yes, they wear spacesuits.'

'Oh. One of those things,' Blake said with distaste.

'Come back and talk to us – we need help!' I shouted.

'They can't communicate without Marque, Captain,' Miko said. 'I may be able to talk to it the way my coloured sisters do – but I'm not sure, I've never spoken to them before. Their minds are strange.'

The energy creature reappeared, this time in its spacesuit. It stood next to the connection between the shuttle and the interior of the asteroid.

I stormed up to it. 'Get help. We're stuck here. Tell the dragons! Tell Marque! We need help!'

It walked up the wall, ignoring the asteroid's gravity, and examined the shuttle.

'We need help – tell the dragons where we are,' Miko said to it.

It still didn't respond.

'Tell Marque we're here,' I said. 'Tell Six Eighty Four. Tell the dragons. We need help.'

It sank through the wall and disappeared, leaving a puddle of molten rock behind it.

'We can only hope we got through to it,' I said.

'Why do they wear suits anyway?' Blake said. 'They obviously don't need them.'

'From what my sisters say, it's vanity,' Miko said. 'Some sort of adornment.' She shrugged. 'We don't know either.'

*

I'd died many times before, but never this slowly. The cold crept up from my extremities, and even Miko lying next to me couldn't warm me. We'd stopped eating enough to sustain life weeks ago and been slowly dying of starvation as Haruka gave everybody smaller and smaller rations of the emergency bars. The shuttle's battery had failed days ago, and now we would die of suffocation. I was desperately tired, and my eyes closed by themselves.

Haruka fell to sit next to me. 'You still there?'

'Hm.'

'We just lost another two. I'm going to be the last one alive here,' he said. 'My dragon scales mean that I'm going to die alone.'

'You've Miko,' I slurred.

'As soon as everybody but me is gone, I'll order her to leave me here and find safety. One-way trip,' he said.

'Good. She's spec ... tac ... ular.'

'You don't order me any more,' Miko said from next to me in the dark. 'I'm my own dragon and ...' Her voice filled with tears. 'I will stay here with my beloved humans for the rest of my life. I love you, Jian.'

'Love you too.' It was hard to stay conscious. 'So sleepy. Stay with me, Miko? Haruka, I'm sorry. You are a great ... man. I'm sorry we didn't get to know ...' The words were too hard. '... better.'

'Me too. I think I've been unfair to you, Jian, you're smart and capable and brave as anyone I know.'

'I think that too,' Miko said.

'Thanks, guys,' I said. 'I love you both. Blake, great friend.' I sighed a deep breath, and didn't get any air into me. 'Merry, so short a time. Aki, be happy. Miko, magnificent. Mum, Ollie, David ... sorry. Bye.'

The silence filled the cavern around me. Miko held me from behind, and Haruka lay beside me and pulled both of us close. I cuddled next to him.

'This is enough,' Miko said.

*

Things happened. There was light, and warmth, and movement. I tried to raise my head, but couldn't.

'Holy shit, Captain Jian,' someone said next to me, and the light flickered everywhere, blue-white and blinding. 'I'll get help.'

'Hurry, they're all very close to death,' Miko said.

'I can't believe the suits didn't tell us,' the voice said. 'They told us about the shuttle jammed in the wall of the planetoid as if it was a curiosity. They never mentioned people dying in it!'

'Just go!' Haruka said.

'Hang on, Jian,' the voice said. 'I need to leapfrog through a dozen stars before I'm back in the Empire and can use a scale. Don't you dare die on me!'

'Not planning to, Six,' I said. 'You in uniform?'

'Unbelievable,' Haruka said, and his butt appeared in front of my face as he sat next to me.

'How many are left?' Miko said.

'Only a couple of hundred,' Haruka said, his voice hoarse with emotion. 'And some of these are too far gone for even Marque to save.'

'Don't say that,' Miko said. 'Jian has to live!'

'Blake?' I said.

'He was one of the first to die,' Haruka said. 'He gave his food away.'

'I believe it. Always was a f...' I gasped for breath. 'Hero.'

The light reappeared. 'Here.'

'Oh, lord,' a dragon voice said. 'Let's do this.'

Someone put their hand on my shoulder and the world dissolved around me.

25

The red spawn swirled around us in a transparent haze that shifted from pale pink to deep, vivid purple. David's face was full of joy around his breather as he ran his fingers through them; they secreted mating chemicals that were similar to human endorphins, making us slightly high and full of bliss.

I let the breather push the liquid through my lungs, and floated in the transparent sea. Oliver and Aki floated next to me, and the world was full of love.

'Jian, you need to come up out of this,' David said.

'I'm glad you didn't go with Cat,' I said. 'Stay away from her, David, she's bad for you.'

'Haruka is arguing with them but they won't listen to him,' David said.

I smiled into the breather and touched the red cloud again, feeling the serenity. 'I'm glad he's a long way away; he's an asshole.' Something felt wrong. 'No, we all misjudged him. I misjudged him.'

'You have to go to him. Miko's on trial and they'll kill her.'

'Miko?'

Aki changed to Miko's human form. 'I love you, Jian.'

'I love you too, Miko. Those six weeks of cold and starvation were the best of my life – because of you.' I waved my hands through the spawn. 'Isn't this wonderful? I'm glad I could share this with you.'

Merry swam past, her oversized feet making the red spawn swirl. 'Goodbye, Jian. Keep Miko safe.'

'I will.'

Merry changed to Haruka. He stopped and floated next to me, his long green hair waving in the water.

'Jian, they're deciding Miko's fate and I can't do this alone,' Haruka said. 'I need you to come help me stop them!'

The water disappeared and I was in the hearing room where they'd killed Kana. Miko was in human form in the middle of the room, kneeling with her head bowed. Masako was in her human form, the huge man, and carried an enormous shell axe.

'Any last words?' Masako said, and didn't let Miko reply. She swung the axe and cut Miko's head off. Miko's body lay twitching on the floor, changing from human to dragon and back again, as blood spouted from her neck to form a brown puddle. Masako fell as well, took dragon form, and her stomach bloated with death.

I thrashed in the white liquid. 'Let me out!'

'Why?' Marque said.

'We have to save Miko. Tell me they haven't executed her yet!'

'About time.'

Marque lifted me out of the table and floated me into a chair. Mum was sitting next to the table and jumped up to help me. I stood and promptly fell over, and Mum caught me.

'You're weak,' she said. 'You nearly died. Oliver's on his way.'

I raised my hand and felt the new soulstone in my forehead. 'I remember. Help me up! Is Miko still alive?'

Marque entered the room in a human male android body and helped Mum guide me to my feet. I leaned heavily on it, weaker than I'd ever been. I looked down at myself; I was naked, and I'd never seen my own ribs in such relief before. My skin was sallow and pale, my breasts were gone, and my legs were like sticks.

Marque gave Mum a cotton shift, and she pulled it over my head. I winced at the scratchiness against my tender skin.

'Is Miko still alive?' I said. 'How long has it been? We have to stop them.'

'As far as we know she's still alive,' Mum said. 'They're arguing. Marque told us what happened, but they won't let anybody in. They say it's dragon-only business.'

'Let's go. Tell Maxwell to meet me there.'

'I already did.' Marque and Mum helped me to the door, and it opened by itself. 'Maxwell doesn't know what happened, the dragons won't tell her, but she says she trusts you and she's on her way.'

'Tell her everything. Is anyone else who was in the cavern lucid enough to help?' We entered the corridor, and there were five other people from the cavern there, some leaning on Marque androids, some on family members, and all emaciated.

'Let's go rescue our Princess!' Griffith wheezed from the arms of her dragonscales partner.

'What's this with the android bodies?' I said. Marque had created bodies that mimicked the body types of the humans it was assisting. 'Wouldn't energy be better?'

'I can feel if you fall. Also ...' It smiled grimly. 'Solidarity. I'm human with you and telling these dumb assholes that this is wrong and they need to stop.'

Graf was stationed at the end of the corridor. 'You shouldn't be out yet, ma'am.'

'Stand down and let me pass,' I said, clutching Marque's human body. 'I have something vitally important that I need to do – no, Graf, come with us as backup. We might need help.'

'Ma'am.'

'You should have told them,' I said as we headed towards the room with Graf bringing up the rear. Every step was more difficult. 'You knew Miko's been doing it for hundreds ...' I took a deep breath. 'Of years. Safely. You knew!'

'If I told them Miko was gating then they'd have executed her as well,' Marque said. 'Hold on, I'm adding more oxygen to the air. Is that better?'

My chest lightened and I felt more alert. 'Thank you.'

'They need more than reassurance that it's safe,' Marque said. 'They need to be forced to face their own self-loathing, and hopefully you and Haruka can do it. Here's Charlie.'

'Ambassador Maxwell to you, asshole,' she said to it. She nodded to my mother. 'Connie, good to see you.' She glared at Marque. 'I agree with Jian. You could have stopped them ages ago. You *lied*.'

'You're right, I'm wrong, I've let this go on far too long, and threatening to withdraw your services from the Empire is the only way we can stop them,' Marque said. 'Will you help?'

'Of course I will,' Maxwell said. 'This is fucking *slavery*, Marque, and knowing what I know now, I will withdraw Earth from the Empire.'

'You've been in the Empire for more than fifty years and *now* you object to them using slaves?' Marque said. 'Nobody forces the goldenscales. It's self-imposed servitude. I hope you can stop it, and you'll stay in the Empire. I like you.' Marque hefted me. 'We need to go in right now.' The door opened to reveal the Empress standing on the platform with Miko and Haruka in front of her, facing all the goldenscales.

Ambassador Maxwell stepped forward, and I lunged to stop her, dragging Marque with me. 'Charles. Let me. I love her.'

Her expression didn't shift, but she stepped back and let me go first. 'Save her, Jian, we owe her your lives.'

Mum and Maxwell waited at the bottom of the stairs as Marque helped me up to the podium to face the gathered goldenscales.

'You shouldn't be out yet,' Miko said.

'Oh yes I should,' I said.

'Thank the gods you're here,' Haruka said from her other side. 'Maybe now we can stop this stupidity.'

He was nearly as thin as I was, with his violet kimono hanging off him. He hadn't fixed his hair, and the dye had grown out so that the first ten centimetres of it was brown and the rest sickly green. His wrists poking out of the silk sleeves were bony and fragile.

'Listen to me,' I said loudly to the gathered goldenscales. 'I know you think you're inferior, but you're not. You're as good as any coloured dragon, and some of you must have worked that out. Hasn't *anybody* here plotted revolt and wanted to have freedom and independence?'

One of the goldenscales at the back called a reply. 'They murdered us! My five sisters, all dead – for asking for our freedom!' She pointed at the Empress. 'You killed them!'

'It's not what it seems,' the Empress said.

'No,' Miko said, and rounded on the Empress. 'It is *exactly* what it seems. The five of them went to you – their *mother* – and asked to be freed from servitude to live in liberty and *you said no and killed them.*'

'They couldn't fold,' the Empress said, 'but they had this gating power that should never be used. I had to make sure that one of their coloured sisters was with them all the time to make sure they were never tempted. I was protecting them!'

'You executed them to *protect* them?' I roared. I turned back to the grief-stricken gold dragon, standing in a small cleared area as the others had moved away from her. 'Why didn't you run? Find a safe place outside the Empire?' I answered my own question. 'Because you can't fold, and they told you that gating would destroy the universe.'

'That's enough for me,' Maxwell said. 'We're out. This is straight up oppression and humanity wants no part of it.'

'No, Charles, please don't leave, we need you.' The Empress lowered her head. 'It was six hundred years ago. Things were different then.'

'Things aren't that different if they're still servants, Silver,' I said.

'No goldenscales has asked for her freedom since,' she said. 'If they want their freedom, they can have it. You can have it!' She raised her head. 'I thought you were happy?'

'You made it very clear that if we attempted to free ourselves, the penalty was death,' the goldenscales said. 'You didn't give us a choice. Gating puts others at risk, and there should be consequences. But stop telling everybody that we choose to be servants. You have a hand in it too ... *Mother.*'

'Gating puts others at risk? Who told you that? The Empress?' I said.

The Empress' head went even lower.

'And Marque helped her. They had you all believing it. They've brainwashed you into thinking you're fucking inferior, when you're not.' I wheezed a few times, and Griffith cheered me quietly from the side. 'Miko has been secretly gating her whole life, and she's never made a mistake. She used gates to save a thousand humans from the cats. She created a total of sixty-seven gates—'

Some of the goldenscales recoiled with horror.

'I know that, because I counted them. Three times she did *two fucking gates at once*!'

They stared at me, stunned.

'And you know what? The universe is still here, because *it's not in any danger*!' I shook the Marque android body so hard its teeth rattled. 'This drama-baiting piece of shit *lied* to you. Tell them.'

'It's true,' Marque said. 'Gating is safe. She's been doing it her whole life and never made a mistake. She's remarkable.'

The goldenscales looked at each other.

'I love this dragon as much as I've loved anyone,' I said. 'She's magnificent. *You're* magnificent. This skill you have – gating – is magnificent.'

'Laying it on a bit thick, my love,' Miko said under her breath.

'Stick time,' I replied just as softly. I raised my voice. 'Ambassador Maxwell is horrified that smart and skilled people like you are being used as servants by your equals. She's going to withdraw all of humanity from the Empire in protest, and the Empire will be at the cats' mercy. The cats have changed their society completely – I think they had a revolution – and they don't oppress their women any more. Your enslavement gives those selfish assholes *moral superiority*, and if they hadn't tried to force us, we'd seriously be thinking about joining them!' I turned to the Empress. 'What would happen if the goldenscales stopped acting as your servants?'

'Well, I wouldn't execute them; the cats can't be trusted and we can't afford to lose their immunity to the cat weapon. We can't lose the humans either; they're needed for the chilli weapon,' she said. 'Without their service, I'd have to put my own jewels on, and keep my own journal?' She blinked a few times. 'Uh, that's all.'

'I can do that!' my Marque support said.

'This decision is yours,' the Empress said to the gathered dragons. 'You have your freedom. If you choose not to serve us, I won't stop you.' She swung her head to Miko. 'If you can gate safely, Miko, then I'll give you special permission to do it.'

'What, just me?' Miko said.

'As Marque said, you are remarkable.'

'No,' Miko said firmly. 'All of us, or none of us. I can teach my sisters to gate safely. Treat us *all* as your equals.'

I stared at her with wonder that I had earned the love of this exceptional being. She saw me looking at her and smiled her dragon smile.

'You can't gate!' someone shouted from the crowd. 'You'll kill us all. It's too dangerous. The penalty's there for a reason.'

I turned back to the goldenscales. 'You want to execute my partner here? This glowing golden piece of pure awesome?' I pushed Marque away to stand without aid and planted myself in front of Miko. I swayed as I glared with fury and jabbed my finger at them. 'Bring it. I will fucking fight you all.' I toppled and Marque caught me. 'Come on, Miko, we are going back to my place to share a bath and a bed and have an *awful lot of really good sex*.'

'Let me, Marque,' Miko said, and moved to carry me.

'No way,' I said. 'The robot carries me. You are not my servant.'

'I'll do it,' Haruka said. He picked me up, and carried me like a child. He and Miko ignored the rest of the goldenscales as he carried me down the stairs.

He stopped at the bottom of the stairs and nodded to my mother. 'Lady Choumali.'

She eyed him suspiciously. 'Prince Haruka.'

The goldenscales started to argue among themselves about what they were going to do, but none of them tried to stop us.

'Talk about your freedom!' I shouted back at them, and they went silent. 'Because you are way better than you think you are, and the Empire needs your gates!' I hesitated a moment, gasping, then hit them with the final kicker. 'I'm going to have a fucking baby with Miko as soon as I'm well enough, and there's no reason why you can't have children as well!'

The uproar started again and we went through the doors, which closed behind us. The humans celebrated, patting me, Haruka and Miko.

The Ambassador stood to one side, holding back a smile. 'Don't ever take up a career in politics, Choumali,' she said.

'I never intend to, ma'am,' I said. I looked up at Haruka. 'You can put me down now.'

'You aren't strong enough, Jian,' he said. 'I'll carry you to your quarters.'

'Can you do it?' I said. 'You're awfully thin, Haruka.'

'I'm a dragonscales. I can manage.'

'I'll take the rest of you humans to your quarters; you've had enough excitement,' Marque said. 'Some of you should go back into the table ...'

'Not me,' I said.

'Let me help you home,' Marque said, and guided the rest of the humans away.

'No movement from inside,' Maxwell said. 'I'll take that as positive. They need to work out what they'll do.' She touched Miko's shoulder. 'You're a natural leader, Miko, and I think they'll turn to you to guide them once they get over the fact that they're not worthless after all, and they're free.'

'I hope we can work towards something good,' Miko said.

Maxwell nodded to us and walked away.

'Graf, please stand guard on the door and call Six and Three to escort the Empress when she emerges,' I said.

'Ma'am.' It hesitated. 'You'll stay as Captain of the Guard? Please say yes,' it added under its breath.

'Damn straight,' I said. 'Someone needs to make sure that those assholes keep their word and the goldenscales are freed.'

Graf nearly collapsed with relief.

'Come on, Miko, we need to work out where we're going to live,' Haruka said. 'I don't want to go back to Masako's apartment.'

'You can share with me,' I said.

He smiled down at me. 'I may just take you up on that.'

'The three of you are moving in together?' Mum said.

'We've been through a lot,' I said. 'We care for each other. It makes sense.'

'Leave her with us, ma'am,' Haruka said. 'We'll look after her. Right now, all of us need to rest. Marque can bring you and Oliver to visit when she wakes up.'

'And Bartlett!' I said.

Mum kissed me on the forehead where I lay in Haruka's arms and squeezed his hand. She bent to give Miko a hug as well. 'I understand. Go rest. I'll see you later.'

Haruka hefted me and carried me down the corridor towards the Empress' tower.

'Marque, extend my quarters so that Haruka has space there,' I said.

'I'm adding to your quarters right now,' Marque said. 'I'm not sure what sleeping arrangements you want ...'

Haruka and I shared a horrified glance.

'Separate bedrooms and sitting rooms for each of us,' I said. 'We'll work it out as we go along.' I grinned at Miko from Haruka's arms. 'I hope my lovely goldenscales will spend every night in my bed.'

Miko smiled back, then glanced up at Haruka. 'What about you, my Prince?'

'I'm not your Prince, Miko,' he said. 'We've been through a lot, and the wounds are still raw. Let's recover first, and then work out where we want to be.'

She nodded, satisfied.

'Ugh, I'm sick of this body already, it's so small.' Marque's android body dissolved. 'That's better.'

'Did you mean it about the ...' She nearly whispered it. 'Baby?'

'Damn straight! I want to attune a new soulstone first – but as soon as that is done, we're starting a family.'

Haruka carried me into my quarters, which now had a large shared living room, kitchen and dining area with three doors leading from it. One of the doors lit up.

'This way,' Marque said.

Haruka took me through with Miko following, and we were in the living room of my original apartment with the windows overlooking the square. Haruka placed me to sit in the middle of the bed, then sat on the edge and put his head between his knees, gasping for air.

Miko crouched in front of him and rested her claw on his thigh. 'You haven't recovered either,' she said. She touched his cheek and they gazed into each other's eyes; she had obviously cared deeply for him for a long time, and he was clearly humbled that he'd known her for years without recognising her brilliance.

He took her claw from his face and held it. 'I'll live.'

'You need to rest,' she said.

He rose halfway, and fell to sit again. 'Oomph. Give me a moment.' He put his head between his knees again. I wanted to help him, but I could barely move myself.

'I've already transferred all your possessions into an identical room I set up here,' Marque said. 'I'll help you inside.'

Haruka looked up. 'Identical?'

'To what you had with Masako. Oh.' Marque sounded chagrined. 'Sorry. Tell me how you want it.'

Haruka fell backwards and his head was in my lap. 'Leave it for now. Why is the ceiling moving?' He focused on me. 'You're spinning.'

'Put him in the bed with me,' I said to Miko.

'But you two wanted to ... you know,' he said. He raised his head slightly. 'And I don't ... well. Not right now. Not with ...' He dropped his head. 'Everything is spinning.'

'It can wait, my Prince ... dear Haruka,' she said. 'Jian and I have our whole lives.' She lowered her voice and spoke with wonder. 'A baby ... a family.'

'Marque, help him into the bed,' I said.

Haruka's kimono lifted from him. He wore plain white cotton shorts underneath, and his once impressive physique was pale skin stretched over prominent bones. Miko lifted the covers, and Marque shifted Haruka so that he was next to me. Miko put the covers back and ran her claw over his face, then reached to do the same for mine. 'I'm so glad you're both safe.'

I waved one hand at her. 'In.'

'I don't want ...' Haruka began. 'If you're going to ...'

'Sleep,' I said. 'Rest. Nothing more.' I yawned widely and wiggled down under the covers. 'I can barely stay awake.'

'Oh.' He turned over and wrapped one arm around me, spooning into my side. 'That works.' He raised his head. 'Miko? Hugs here if you want them.'

The mattress shifted as Miko joined us on the other side of me. She wrapped her claws around me and took Haruka's hand with one of them.

Marque dimmed the lights. 'I'll put you on "do not disturb" for a few hours.'

'Monitor their life signs; they're still very weak,' Miko said.

'I am.'

'Marque, when we wake up, have some pork belly in soy, chicken katsu, toro, rice and steamed greens waiting for us,' I said.

'And a big fat steak,' Haruka said sleepily into my shoulder. 'Huge plate of assorted sushi. Did you say toro?'

'Lots of toro,' I said.

'Neither of you can handle more than rice broth right now,' Marque said.

'Then I'll have the same,' Miko said. She lowered her voice. 'I can't believe I'm doing this. Like an equal. With *both* of you.'

'Get used to it,' Haruka said. 'You remember when you said it was enough?'

'Yes?'

'It is only just beginning,' I said sleepily.

26

'Just like old times, eh, Colonel?' Leckie said as we waited on Tomoyo's ship for the cat flagship to drop out of warp.

'We must go for a beer when this is done,' I said, and grinned at Haruka's reaction.

'We're all in very different places now from where we were back then,' Leckie said, eyeing Haruka. He bowed to Miko. 'And here's the goldenscales Princess that everybody's been talking about. I can't wait to see this gating skill; it sounds really special.'

Miko's eyes were wide and she'd opened her mouth to object to being called a Princess, then closed it again and smiled. 'Thank you. Jian's told me much about her terrific team when she was in the service. I look forward to working with you.'

He nodded to her. 'Likewise.'

'Weapons check,' I said and ensured that my own laser gun was charged and ready.

'It feels good to have something lethal to fight back with,' Haruka said, checking his own. 'But only use lethal force if absolutely necessary. We still have hope that we can work out a truce with them.'

My team looked to me for confirmation.

'What he said, he's the diplomat,' I said, and they nodded.

Haruka popped his faceplate to reveal his perfectly made-up face. 'Are you sure you don't want armour like mine? Marque has some ...'

'You know what?' I said. 'On second thought, yeah. It looks badass.'

I held my arms out and Marque removed my Barracks armour and fitted me with black armour similar to Haruka's. I swung my shoulders. 'This is so light and flexible.'

Haruka holstered his gun and tightened the silk belt holding his two swords. 'When we Japanese do something, we do it right.'

I smiled sadly, thinking of Aki, then brightened because Aki was happy with a loving family. 'Yep.' I saw my breastplate; it was embossed with royal chrysanthemums and waves in gold. 'Hey, I don't get chrysanthemums.'

'You definitely do,' he said. 'The matter is not up for negotiation.' He flipped his faceplate closed, giving him an inhumanly beautiful carved black visage with what appeared to be four lit eyes, and spoke to me privately through comms. 'We regularly share a bed, madam, and that is enough to make you part of the royal family.'

'But we never—'

'We need to deal with that as well. You and Miko are planning to have a baby together, and we will have to explain to everybody how our relationship works before people start asking me difficult questions.'

'If you don't mind me asking, Prince Haruka?' MacAuley said, and both of us jumped. 'How do you manage to wear mascara inside the faceplate without it going everywhere?'

'Not mascara,' Haruka said, glancing at me and probably smiling inside the armour. 'They're lash extensions. I can show you when we're home, if you like. They're a bit fiddly, but much less irritating than tints, easily removable, and as you said – mascara just goes everywhere.'

'Thank you. I'd like to see.'

'They're out of warp, I'm leaving,' Marque said. 'I'll reconnect when you're back in Empire space and away from those damn nanos.'

'Let's do this,' Griffith said with menace.

'On your mark, Captain,' Tomoyo said.

I flipped my faceplate closed and the heads-up display appeared, similar to the one in the standard Barracks armour but with much more detail. An option appeared for basic, advanced and technical mode, and I flipped it from basic to advanced. The display swung to fill all the space around me, giving me details on everybody nearby. The cat ship was a three-dimensional wireframe outside the wall of our ship, the planet was clearly visible, and I could even see the names and locations of nearby stars.

'If I know you, you just went up to advanced mode and you're fiddling with the settings,' Haruka said, and he flashed green in time with his voice. 'People are waiting to head out, Captain.'

'Oh, yeah. Sorry. Good to fold, Tomoyo,' I said.

The heads-up display changed as we folded to give me a view of the enormous cat ship, now out of warp and in orbit around the cat colony planet. It had been in warp for nine months since leaving the treaty signing, with only a couple of short visits to normal space for staff transfers that were too quick for us to connect with. Six weeks of dilated time had passed inside the ship, and I hoped the octopuses were still alive.

I contacted the octopuses telepathically. *Hello? I'm back. I'm sorry I went away, but I'd like to take you somewhere safe.*

The telepathic response was a series of confused emotions, but no words.

Do you remember me? I said. *We talked a while ago. I've come to take you home ... if you remember where it is. If you don't, we can give you somewhere safe and comfortable to stay while we find it.*

I remember you, one of them said. *Can you take our children? The cats are eating us!*

Yes, of course. Where are you on the ship?

I received a jumbled mess of watery images combined with the feeling of hard floor beneath suckers and unpleasant gravity.

'I've found them,' Miko said. 'I can see them.'

Tomoyo took out her soulstone and placed it into its cushioned container, in case the octopus weapon was used against her and killed her. 'Gate me in, sister,' she said.

Miko created a gate and Tomoyo stepped into it.

'That is fucking incredible,' Leckie said with wonder. He nodded to Miko. 'Excuse the language, Princess.'

'I've been with Jian for a year now,' Miko said. 'I'm used to it.'

'The gating and folding dragons complement each other,' Haruka said. 'Miko can see space around us and accurately send a folding dragon to scout.'

Tomoyo returned. 'I have the location to fold to, but I think the cats have eaten nearly all of them.' She hesitated. 'The one I saw doesn't look well.'

'Let's get them out,' I said.

We put our hands on Tomoyo and she folded us onto the cat ship. We arrived in a room ten metres to a side that held a black rectangular pool for the octopuses. Pumps and filters worked on the side to keep the water clean. I climbed up the steps to where there was a net sitting on the edge, and looked in. One of the octopuses looked back at me – and it seemed to be the only one in the tank. It had only four tentacles remaining and it was pale blue with skin hanging off it in flaps that swayed in the water.

I popped the faceplate. *Hello, it's me*, I said. *I'm so sorry – are you the only one left?*

We had babies, it said, and moved back from the edge. The side of the tank was covered in white floating spheres, the size of hen eggs, on stalks. *We weren't sure if it was the right thing to do, but you said you'd come back and take us home. I am talekeeper: I refrained from having babies so I could stay and tell them who we are. Everybody else is gone.*

We can take you to a safe place away from the cats, but I need your permission.

Can you take the babies?

Yes.

Thank you! Yes! Please ... save us!

'Cats coming,' Miko said. 'Three of them. We've activated a movement sensor that tells them when the octopuses leave the tank.'

Do you know where your home planet is? I said.

What's a planet?

Can you show us what the stars look like at your home?

What are stars? You keep saying things I don't understand! Can we just go, please?

The cats opened the door and my colleagues took them down without killing them, leaving them stunned on the deck.

I stepped back from the tank. 'Tomoyo, can you put the whole thing on your ship? We'll work out where they're from later.'

'Sure thing, Captain.'

The rest of the team guarded the door while Tomoyo put her claw on the tank and folded it out. Miko created a gate, we all stepped into it, and we were back on Tomoyo's ship. She folded us back into Empire space.

I went to the edge of the tank and the remaining octopus looked up at me with its huge intelligent eyes.

We're away from them, you're safe, I said. *What do you eat? There wasn't any food near the tank.*

I am in non-food stage, it said. *I will live long enough to teach the babies, then stop living.*

'It's dying. It will teach the babies when they hatch, then die.' I looked up. 'Marque, can you nourish it and keep it alive past the eggs hatching? Extend its lifespan?'

'It's dying of old age,' Marque said. 'I can't extend its life without attuning a soulstone, and I don't think these people live long enough to do it. Perhaps I can extend the lives of future generations.'

'I see.' I turned back to the tank and leaned on it. *We will find your homeworld*, I said. *We will return these babies to their families, and make sure the cats never harm you again.*

I don't understand what families are, but it would be good to see them home. The octopus gracefully flowed over the eggs, using its tentacles to groom them clean. *They will hatch soon*, it said. *I am glad they will be safe.*

'Will you be able to provide food for the babies when they hatch?' I asked Marque.

'I shouldn't have much trouble working back from their biochemistry,' it said.

Show me a picture of what you eat, I said to the octopus.

Its reply was slow. *They will hatch soon.* It showed me four-legged crabs with green shells, and flowing sea slugs in rainbow colours. The creatures swam through shallow water with shifting sunlight rippling through it. The octopuses lived in gathered rock villages, and I saw them cultivating crabs and clams in rocky enclosures.

Your home is beautiful, I said.

The octopus didn't reply, but the air around me filled with deep, grey grief.

'Oh, I felt that,' Tomoyo said.

'I felt it too,' Griffith said. 'And I'm not an empath.'

'The water in the tank is very similar to Pacifica's; I'm telling the Pacificans about the octopuses,' Marque said. 'The people of Pacifica offer them asylum.'

A blue-skinned Aquatic man folded onto the ship with a dragon I didn't know. He had a similar curvy body shape to Merry, long purple hair, and a neat purple goatee. He wore a Pacifica swimming bodysuit with the breathing tube in his throat.

He smiled around at us. 'Hello, I'm Rin Merrysson. This is my dragonspouse, Umeko.' He nodded to me. 'Captain.' He turned to the tank. 'Marque, can you lift me in carefully so I don't disturb the eggs?'

'You're too big,' Marque said. 'You'd damage them.'

'Understood. Let me talk to them.' He leaned over the tank and his long hair slid down his shoulder to dangle in the water. A conversation happened between him and the octopus that I felt rather than heard. He reached towards the water and a pale tentacle lifted out of it and wrapped around his hand, stroking it.

'Its mind is like a wide clear sea without a single wave,' he said with wonder. 'So beautiful.'

'I know,' I said.

He nodded and the tentacle released his hand. He stepped back. 'Let's go to Pacifica. These babies really are about to hatch – in fact the octopus has asked them to refrain until we move them to cleaner water.'

*

We arrived in orbit around Pacifica and could see the planet from Tomoyo's gallery. Most of it was water, but it did have chains of islands around its equator.

'What sort of environment is ideal for them?' Rin asked Marque.

'They're copper-based, high oxygen. Temperature ...' Marque was silent, then said, 'Warm. Shallow, warm water near the equator, with a median temperature of twenty-five. I may need to boost the oxygen for them.'

'The Honour Atoll should be good,' Rin said. He concentrated on Tomoyo. 'There.'

'Got it,' she said, put one claw on the tank, and disappeared.

'I'll take the rest of you down,' Rin's dragon partner Umeko said. 'But please remove the armour before you do, it may distress our children.'

We put our arms out and Marque changed us into Pacifican bodysuits. It was good to see Haruka back to his pre-capture body size, and the bodysuit highlighted his muscular arms and tight butt.

'Thank you.' Umeko nodded to Miko. 'Will you show me a gate? I've wanted to see your special skill. I would never have believed that goldenscales were so gifted, you were always so ... reserved.'

'Charming,' I said with biting sarcasm.

'What are the co-ordinates?' Miko said, diplomatically ignoring me.

'I'm passing them now,' Marque said.

Miko created a gate.

'Let's go,' I said.

I stepped through the gate onto the pure white sand of a coral atoll under a completely cloudless blue sky in the golden light of an engineered Sol-type sun. The sandy island had some scrubby undergrowth and succulents, and a number of palm trees in groups growing over the water. The water itself was completely clear, like a sheet of glass placed over the sand, giving it a pale, turquoise hue.

'Gorgeous,' Haruka said. 'Is there surfing here?'

'Not on this atoll, but there's another one that's more exposed that has an excellent break,' Rin said, approaching us. He'd changed into a wet suit that covered him to his wrists and ankles, and was tight around his neck. 'I'd be glad to take you once we have the babies stable.'

'You feel the cold?' I said. 'It's lovely and warm here.'

Rin smiled. 'Exactly the opposite. I overheat quickly, I'm more comfortable in colder and deeper water. This suit is to keep me cool.'

'I see.'

He gestured towards the water. 'This way. We've put the whole tank into the water, and the octopus says that it's pleasant. The babies are pushing at the eggs, ready to hatch.'

'There's nothing around here that will eat them, is there?' I said.

'We've enclosed the lagoon,' Rin said. 'Marque's synthesising food for them to try.'

A brilliant crystalline squeal pinged through the air, full of joy and freedom, and Rin and I stopped dead.

Haruka turned to us. 'What happened?'

'You didn't hear that?' I said.

He shook his head.

'Telepathic,' Rin said, and we kept moving into the water. As it approached my neck, Marque enclosed my head in a bubble of air and fitted me with fins. I ducked under to swim and followed Rin out to where the sandy bottom was five metres below the mirror-like surface. The squeal sounded again, followed by a child's giggle, and a bright blue baby octopus, the size of my outstretched hand, shot past me with its tentacles trailing. It did laps around me and Haruka, broadcasting pure joy, and zoomed back again. The black tank sat on the bottom, and another baby climbed out the side and jetted in circles around us.

Marque took the form of an adult octopus and waved its tentacles. 'Hey there, kids. Come and try some of the food I've synthesised for you.'

Two of the babies ignored it, but a third went to Marque and twined its tiny tentacles around Marque's. 'Food?'

Marque passed it a piece of shell with crab meat attached to it, and the baby delicately tasted it with its tentacles. It quickly shifted the food down the suckers to its central mouth.

'Do you have more of that?' it said, then shouted telepathically. *Hey come check out this awesome, delicious food!*

The other two babies approached, their tentacles waving as they touched Marque and each other. Three more babies jetted out of the tank, and the adult's white tentacles waved above the black edge.

Rin swam next to Marque. 'Give me some so I can help. You'll be mobbed.'

The hatching was happening at full pace now, and twenty babies shot over the side of the tank, screaming with glee.

Marque handed Rin a small sack of food, and he took pieces out and gave them to the babies, who floated around him in a blue cloud, squealing at each other with delight. A couple of Pacificans who'd been watching nearby joined us to help feed the babies. I felt a touch and looked down to see that Marque was tapping me with one of its tentacles. I took the bag it offered me, removed a piece of food, and handed it to one of them.

We were in a blizzard of blue baby octopuses. When they'd had enough to eat, they started a game of tag with each other, whizzing over the sandy floor. Miko joined them, using her tail as a fin and sweeping through the water, flashing gold amongst their brilliant blues. She laughed as she played with them, a delightful sound I'd never heard before, and my heart lifted to hear her so happy.

The adult octopus climbed out of the tank and moved slowly with its limited tentacles to the middle of the sandy area. The babies stopped rushing and went quiet as they sat around the adult with their tentacles spread.

The adult went red all over, then red and white in alternating waves. It went white, then sent out a telepathic message in a single explosive burst that nearly knocked me over. I didn't receive much of the transfer; the information was too different from my own consciousness, but I saw their homeworld, their history, and their way of life. They lived peacefully in clusters that were similar to human villages, and since gaining sentience had stopped killing and eating each other. The villages worked co-operatively to gather and store food, and some of them cultivated crabs and shellfish to eat, trading between villages. Information was handed down telepathically through generations, making them more like a trans-generational single organism.

The babies went red and white, then back to blue. The adult released from the sandy floor and floated in the current, obviously dead. The babies gathered and covered it, tearing it into tiny pieces and spreading it in the water to feed the plankton and smaller creatures.

One of the babies approached me and raised one of its tentacles. *I am next talekeeper. Thank you for helping us.* It turned and joined the rest of them, scooting through the remains of their elder to spread them through the water. Fish approached to eat it, and crabs scuttled along the sand, collecting pieces in their claws. One of the babies pounced on a crab and quickly devoured it, broadcasting pleasure.

Five Pacifican children had quietly swum up with their teacher, their large feet moving slowly. They were a more slender blue body type, with their hair clipped short. Rin spoke to the octopuses, and they approached the children carefully.

The children and the octopuses touched hands to tentacles, then in a sudden and synchronised motion all of them squealed and took off together around the bay to play.

Rin came up to us. 'Thank you for saving them.'

'I hope we can find their homeworld,' Miko said. 'I'll arrange for a coloured dragon to help me scout, and I won't stop searching cat space for it.'

Rin looked out over them. 'I'm glad you goldenscales are free to use your skills to find them, because you're the only ones who can.'

27

I arrived home very late from the party where I'd been guarding the Empress, to find Bartlett lying with his nose jammed against Haruka's closed bedroom door. I went into the kitchen where a hot bowl of savoury ramen was already waiting for me, and sat at the table with it.

'They lock you out again, honey?' I said. 'Come and sit with me.'

Bartlett put his head in my lap as I ate. 'Marque, flip through the major happenings in the Empire.'

A small, three-dimensional display appeared above the table and Marque showed me the news. There was a story on the octopuses: they'd settled in to Pacifica nicely and were happy. The footage showed them giving Yuki a tour of their little stony village where they cultivated gloriously fluorescent sea slugs.

'I can show you the rest of that later,' Marque said.

'Thank you. Any news on Aki's tour of the tombs?'

The image changed to Aki in an open car, wearing the old-fashioned uniform and waving to the crowd with his wife next to him. He smiled up at his wife, who touched his hand and smiled back. I felt no pain to see him, and it was good. I glanced at Haruka's bedroom door. I was happy. I wouldn't change anything.

Aki stepped out of the car and was met by the archaeological team. They talked for a moment, he shook everybody's hands, and then they proceeded to the Yayoi Tombs excavation site. He stopped and turned to speak to the gathered vloggers.

'This tomb is my ancestors', but more importantly a part of Japan's long history. We will not disturb any of the treasured remains within: we will merely gather images of the way our ancestors – my ancestors – lived their lives. Nothing will be disturbed. This is an exceptional opportunity to add to the history of all Japans, and I'm honoured to be the archaeologist in charge of the site.'

He turned back to join the other archaeologists on a tour, and the vloggers followed.

'He still says he'd love to catch up,' Marque said. It lowered its voice. 'You've been with Miko and Haruka for more than a year now, and there's a great deal of curiosity about the three of you. Meeting the Japanese Emperor with your two spouses would be a good time to explain to the rest of the Empire how your relationship works.'

I banged the chopsticks on the bowl. 'Why do we have to explain to *anybody* how it fucking works?'

'Because we're royalty,' Haruka said from his bedroom door. He was wearing a stunning rose-coloured silk robe open to the waist, his creamy skin highlighting his strong chest and abs. Miko was next to him in human form, also wearing one of his robes, but it was way too big for her and it dragged on the floor. 'And such language from royalty is unbecoming.'

'Deal with it, I'm military,' I said. 'Did you make yourself taller, Miko?'

She looked down at herself. 'No? Am I?' She looked up at me, concerned. 'Am I too tall?'

'No of course not,' I said, and Haruka said, 'You're perfect,' at the same time.

Miko's appearance confirmed my suspicions about her human form: sex with Haruka had just boosted her self-esteem and she appeared bigger, more mature, and more confident. She was taller and more muscular and her face definitely looked older. The dragons claimed that it was our brains making the illusion, but, as usual, that wasn't the whole truth. Miko altered her human form to appear less threatening by making it small, slender and childlike, and she didn't even know she was doing it. I would talk to Haruka about it later – we could work together to make our love as brilliant as she could possibly be.

Miko shook her hands free of the robe's sleeves and joined me at the table, and Haruka sat next to me on the other side. He put his arm around my shoulders to give me a quick kiss on the cheek, and I kissed him back.

'We have to explain our relationship?' Miko said, still concerned. 'I understand that this is the first time a goldenscales has had a relationship with anybody ...'

'You two are planning to have a baby together,' Haruka said, 'and we'll need to clarify whose it is, otherwise the Royal Household will have fits.'

'Let them,' I said, drawing Miko in to kiss her as well. I returned to my food; I was starving. It had been a long day of chasing the Empress around as she did her thing. 'I can't imagine anything more satisfying than making Tokugawa suffer.'

'They won't break us up because you're a Prince, will they?' Miko said.

'They're more likely to try to force one of you – probably Jian – to leave the relationship because monogamy is the official stance,' he said. 'They're prefer I was settled down with a suitable ...' He choked on the word. '*Virginal* woman.'

'Like they can tell us how to run our lives,' I said into my ramen.

'They have in the past,' he said dryly.

'Never again.'

'That's why I'm living here and not there,' he said, and smiled at Miko. 'Among other things.'

I grinned at both of them. 'I have a brilliant idea. It will drive Tokugawa *nuts* and clarify our relationship to everybody in one go.'

'I don't want to drive anyone nuts,' Miko said.

'You're still Prince of New Nippon, right?' I asked Haruka.

'Of course.'

'So what New Nippon needs more than anything right now ...' I put my chopsticks over the top of the empty bowl and pushed it away. 'Is a *royal wedding*.'

'You and Haruka will get married?' Miko lowered her head and appeared to physically shrink. 'I suppose that works.'

'No, of course not,' Haruka said, reaching around me to touch her shoulder. 'All three of us. Royal wedding, three participants.' He grinned with mischief. 'Jian's right. That would drive Tokugawa nuts, there's no precedent and he'd have to do the organising work from scratch. The people of New Nippon would love it. Everybody adores you, Miko, it would cement your status as a full royal dragon. It would be the wedding of the century.'

'All three of us?' she said, eyes wide. Her appearance grew more confident again.

'Oliver has to be flower boy,' I said. 'Mum and Aki, Wedding Squad. No, Aki to preside and do the ceremony. Charlie and the Empress as Wedding Squad – no, Charlie as Wedding General. No, Oliver as Wedding General ... whatever. I'll work it out.'

'Western style? Even worse! Tokugawa will ...' Haruka switched from Japanese to Euro, '... have *kittens*.' He switched back to Japanese. 'I want to organise it. Green, blue, silver, gold. Hm. Outfits.' He glowed with enthusiasm. 'This will be a lot of fun. Why didn't I think of this?'

'I'm going to bed,' I said, and rose. 'Any objection to me in Miko's bed?'

'None at all,' they said in unison, Miko happy and Haruka distracted.

'I'm coming with you,' Miko said. 'It's been a long day of teaching dragons how to gate.'

'I'll join you in half an hour,' Haruka said. 'Shut the door if you want privacy.'

'You're always welcome, you know that,' I said. 'And you know how Miko feels about having both of us at the same time.'

'I don't know, Jian, our friendship is very important to me. Adding ...' he coughed, '*benefits* might change everything and ruin it.'

'We both love Miko, and we're both marrying her. It would be magnificent.' I looked down at Miko. 'I can see from here how excited she is at the concept.'

She nodded vigorously.

'Well, if it's what my Princess wants ...' Haruka's gaze went intense. 'How about saving it for the wedding night?'

Miko squeaked and jiggled with enthusiasm next to me.

'There's your answer,' I said. 'Marque, remind him to come to bed in thirty minutes, and if he's still out here drawing outfits in an hour – pick him up and physically carry him in. He has an early meeting with the delegation from New Nairobi.'

'I'll do my best,' Marque said.

'I'll only be a minute,' Haruka said, pulling up a display and a waving a stylus. 'Don't worry, I won't be long.'

I kissed Miko's cheek, and we went towards her room with Bartlett following us.

'Jian! Miko!' he called as we reached the door.

We turned back and I put my arm around Miko's shoulders, realising with delight that she appeared nearly as tall as me. 'Yes?'

'Will you marry me?'

We clutched each other and laughed, and said in unison, 'Yes!'

He raised his arms in an uncharacteristic whoop and said, 'Engagement rings all around! I need to design them too.'

'Thirty minutes, your Highness,' I said sternly.

'I'm on my way.'

SCALES OF EMPIRE

Book 1 in the Dragon Empire trilogy

Corporal Jian Choumali is on the mission of a lifetime – security officer on one of Earth's huge generation ships, fleeing the planet's failing ecosystem to colonise a nearby star.

The ship encounters a technologically and culturally advanced alien empire, led by a royal family of dragons. The empire's dragon emissary offers her aid to the people of Earth, bringing greater health, longer life, and faster-than-light travel.

But what price will the people of Earth have to pay for the generous alien assistance?

'*Scales of Empire* is not your average sci-fi adventure. This genderbending inter-stellar romp is full of delightful surprises that kept me enthralled from start to end. I am dragonstruck!' Traci Harding

'So different to her other books, but unmistakably Kylie Chan ... Imaginative, epic, and heaps of fun, while still exploring thought-provoking and important themes.'
Alan Baxter